arc Posselt 692-2320
on
692-7140
& on
692-3406

MYST: THE BOOK OF ATRUS

MYST

THE BOOK OF
ATRUS

RAND AND ROBYN MILLER
WITH DAVID WINGROVE

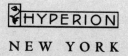

NEW YORK

Special Edition

Text and Illustrations © 1995, Cyan Inc.

Illustrations by William Cone

Cover design © 1995, The Leonhardt Group

Designed and typeset in Centaur by Beth Tondreau Design, New York, New York

Printed in the United States by Haddon Craftsmen, Inc., Scranton, Pennsylvania

*All rights reserved. No part of this book may be used or reproduced
in any manner whatsoever without the written permission of the Publisher.
Printed in the United States of America. For information address:
Hyperion, 114 Fifth Avenue, New York, New York 10011.*

ISBN 0-7868-8922-5

First Mass Market Edition

10 9 8 7 6 5 4 3 2 1

To Mom and Dad

Acknowledgments

THOUGH ONLY *OUR* NAMES ARE ON THE cover, it would be untrue to say that we wrote this story by ourselves; there were too many other people involved.

Principally, we'd like to thank Richard Vander Wende. His contributions to story development and the creative process were at least equal to our own.

Thanks to Ryan Miller for writing the first book—his contributions set a tone from which we could work.

Also, thanks to John Biggs, Chris Brandkamp, Mark DeForest, Bonnie McDowall, Beth Miller, Josh Staub, and Richard Watson for their input and output.

And finally, thanks to Brian DeFiore, our editor, and David Wingrove for accomplishing the impossible.

A special thanks to the fans of *Myst*, who've waited a long time for this history and helped it to happen. We hope it answers many questions, and raises a few more.

Prologue

GEHN'S BOOTPRINTS LAY HEAVY AROUND the tiny pool, the lush, well-tended green churned to mud. At one end of the garden, beneath a narrow outcrop, he had dug a shallow grave. Now, as the dawn's light slowly crept over the sands to touch the cleftwall twenty feet above, he covered over the young girl's body, his pale cream desert clothes smeared with her blood and with the dark earth of the cleft.

From the steps above Anna watched, exhausted after the long night. She had done what she could, but the girl had clearly been ill for some months and the exertions of childbirth had eaten up what little strength remained to her. She had died with a sigh of relief.

Even now, in the silence of the dawn, she could hear Gehn's howls of anguish, his hurt and angry ranting; could hear the words of blame which, at the time, had rashed over her. It was her fault. Everything was her fault.

So it was. So it had always been.

He turned, finished, and looked up at her, no love in that cold, penetrating gaze. Nineteen he was. Just nineteen.

"Will you stay?" she asked wearily.

His answer was a terse shake of the head. Almost

belligerently, he stomped across the surface of the garden, churning up yet more of her precious growing space, oblivious, it seemed, to the significance of what he did. She watched him crouch beside the pool, unable in her heart to be angry with him—for all he'd done and said. No, for she knew what he must be feeling. She knew herself how that felt—to lose the focus of one's life, the *meaning* . . .

She looked down at her unwashed hands and slowly shook her head. Why come when there was nothing she could do to help?

But she knew the answer. He had come only because there was no one else to turn to. He had not wanted to come, but desperation had shaped his course. Knowing his wife was ill, he had remembered his mother's healing powers. But he had come too late.

Too late for her, anyway.

Anna raised her head, hearing the baby's cries. Stretching, she stood, then went down the narrow steps, ducking beneath the stone lintel into the interior. The baby was in the small inner chamber. She crossed the room and ducked inside as its cries grew louder.

She stood over it a moment, staring down at its pale blue eyes, then picked it up, cradling it against her.

"You poor thing," she whispered, kissing its neck, feeling it relax against her. "You poor, poor thing."

She went out and stood against the rail, watching as Gehn crouched by the pool, washing. She saw how he pool was muddied, its precious liquid sullied. Again there was a carelessness about his actions that angered her. He was thoughtless. Gehn had always been thoughtless. But she held her tongue, knowing that it was not the moment to mention such things.

"You want me to dress the child for the journey?"

Gehn did not answer, and for a moment she thought that maybe he had not heard, but when she went to speak again, he turned and glared at her.

"Keep it. Bury it with its mother, if you must. But don't bother me with it. You saved it, you look after it."

She bristled, then held the child out, over the gap.

"This is your son, Gehn. Your *son!* You gave him life. You are responsible for him. That is the way of things in this world."

Gehn turned away.

She drew the child back. As she did, it began to cry again. Below her, Gehn stamped across the churned ground and quickly climbed the steps, pushing past her roughly to go inside. A moment later he was back, his glasses perched on his head. Anna stared at him, noting that he had discarded his cloak.

"Your cloak, Gehn . . . You'll need your cloak out here."

He turned from her, looking out toward the lip of the volcano, just visible from where they stood. "Keep it," he said, his eyes moving fleetingly across her face. "I'll not need it anymore!"

His words frightened her, made her fear for his

sanity after all that had happened. She stared at the child in her arms, not knowing at that moment what was best. Even so, she was determined he would hold the child once before he went.

She made to give the child to Gehn, but he brushed past her and stepped out onto the rope bridge. In a moment he was gone.

"But you didn't name him," she said quietly, holding the baby tight against her. "You didn't even name him. . . ."

Within the great volcano's shadow, the desert floor was fractured. There, in a crack some eighty feet by fifteen, the darkness was intense. The casual eye might, indeed, have passed on, thinking it no more than a natural feature, but for the strange lip—a wall of stone some five or six feet high—that surrounded it.

For a moment all was still, and then a tall, cloakless figure climbed up onto the lip of the cleftwall, stepping out into the dawn light.

All was silence; a silence as only such desert places possess. In the cool of the desert dawn, a mist rose from the warm heart of the volcano, wreathing it in a faint, mysterious veil. Anna watched as the tall cloakless figure climbed the volcano's slope, the mist swirling about him, concealing then revealing him again. The heavy lenses he wore gave his head a strange et distinctive shape. For a moment he stood there, his head turned, looking back at the dark gash of the cleft a mile below him, his tall, imperious shape backlit by the sun that bled through the shifting layers of haze. Then, with a dreamlike slowness, like a specter stepping out into nothingness, he turned and vanished.

1

THE SANDSTORM HAD SCOURED THE narrow rock ledge clean. Now, all along the sculpted, lacelike ridge, shadows made a thousand frozen forms. The rock face was decorated with eyes and mouths, with outstretched arms and tilted heads, as if a myriad of strange and beautiful creatures had strayed from the dark safety of the caldera's gaping maw, only to be crystallized by the sun's penetrating rays.

Above them, in the shadow of the volcano's rim, lay the boy, staring out across the great ocean of sand that stretched toward the mountainous plateaus that were hazed in the distance. The only thing larger than that vast landscape was the clear blue sky above it.

The boy was concealed from watchful eyes, his very existence hidden from the traders who, at that moment, had stopped their caravan a mile out on the sands to greet the old madwoman. The patched and dirty clothes he wore were the color of the desert, making him seem but a fragment of that arid landscape.

The boy lay perfectly still, watching, the heavy lenses he wore adjusted for long-sight, his sensitive eyes taking in every tiny detail of the caravan.

The storm had delayed the caravan two days, and

while two days was as nothing in this timeless place, for the boy it had seemed a small eternity. For weeks before the caravan was due he would dream of them night and day, conjuring them up in his mind; imagining himself cloaked and hooded, up on the back of one of the great beasts, leaving with them. Off into the greater world.

Of those dreams he told his grandmother nothing. No. For he knew how she fretted; worrying that one of the more unscrupulous traders might come in the night and take him, to sell him into slavery in the markets of the south. And so he hid when she said hide, and held his tongue about the dreams, lest he add to her worries.

Right now the boy's eyes were focused on the face of one of the eight men: one he often studied—a dark man with a narrow head, his features sharp and curved within the hood of his jet black cloak, his beard trimmed close to his cheeks.

Studying the halted caravan, the boy noted the changes since they had last passed by. They had nineteen camels now—two more than last time. This and other, smaller signs—new necklaces on several of the camels, small items of jewelry on the wrists and about the necks of the men, the heavier lading of the camels—revealed that trade was good right now. Not only that, but the ease of the men spoke volumes. As they haggled with his grandmother, the boy noted how they laughed, revealing small, discolored teeth. Teeth that, perhaps, evidenced an addiction to the sweet things they sold.

He watched, taking it all in, knowing that his grandmother would ask him later.

What did you see, Atrus?

I saw . . .

He saw the one with the knifelike face turn to his camel and, reaching across the ornate and bulging saddlebag, take a small cloth sack from within a strange, hemispherical wicker basket. The sack seemed to move and then settle.

Atrus adjusted his glasses, certain that he had imagined that movement, then looked again, in time to see his grandmother place the sack upon the pile of other things she'd bartered for. For a brief while longer he watched, then, when it showed no sign of moving, looked to his grandmother.

Anna stood facing the eldest of the traders, her gaunt yet handsome face several shades lighter than his, her fine gray hair tied back into a bun at the nape of her neck. The hood of her cloak was down, as was his, their heads exposed to the fierce, late afternoon heat, but she did not seem to mind. Such she did deliberately, to convince the traders of her strength and self-reliance. Yes, and suffered for it, too, for even an hour out in that burning sun was more than enough, not to speak of the long walk back, laden down with heavy sacks of salt and flour and rolls of cloth, and other items she'd purchased.

And he lay here, hidden, impotent to help.

It was easier, of course, now that he could help her tend the garden and repair the walls, yet at times like this he felt torn—torn between his longing to see the caravan and the wish that his grandmother did not have to work so hard to get the things they needed to survive.

She was almost done now. He watched her hand over the things she'd grown or made to trade—the precious herbs and rare minerals, the intricately carved stone figures, and the strange, colorful iconic paintings that kept the traders coming back for more—and felt a kind of wonder at the degree of her inventiveness. Seven years he had lived with her now; seven years in this dry and desolate place, and never once had she let them go hungry.

That in itself, he knew, was a kind of miracle. Knew, not because she had told him so, but because he had observed with his own lensed eyes the ways of this world he inhabited, had seen how unforgiving the desert was. Each night, surviving, they gave thanks.

He smiled, watching his grandmother gather up her purchases, noting how, for once, one of the younger traders made to help her, offering to lift one of the sacks up onto her shoulder. He saw Anna shake her head and smile. At once the man stepped back, returning her smile, respecting her independence.

Loaded up, she looked about her at the traders,

giving the slightest nod to each before
back and began the long walk back to th

Atrus lay there, longing to clamber do   ...ip
her but knowing he had to stay and watch the caravan
until it vanished out of sight. Adjusting the lenses, he
looked down the line of men, knowing each by the way
they stood, by their individual gestures; seeing how this
one would take a sip from his water bottle, while that
one would check his camel's harness. Then, at an unstat-
ed signal, the caravan began to move, the camels reluctant at first, several of them needing the touch of a whip
before, with a grunt and hoarse bellow, they walked on.

Atrus?

Yes, grandmother?

What did you see?

I saw great cities in the south, grandmother, and
men—so many men . . .

Then, knowing Anna would be expecting him, he
began to make his way down.

As Anna rounded the great arm of rock, coming into
sight of the cleft, Atrus walked toward her. Concealed
here from the eyes of the traders, she would normally
stop and let Atrus take a couple of the sacks from her,
but today she walked on, merely smiling at his unspoken query.

LAVA
FLOW

CLEFT

CARAVAN ROUTE

At the northern lip of the cleft she stopped and, with a strange, almost exaggerated care, lowered the load from her shoulder.

"Here," she said quietly, aware of how far voices could travel in this exposed terrain. "Take the salt and flour down to the storeroom."

Silently, Atrus did as he was told. Removing his sandals, he slipped them onto the narrow ledge beneath the cleftwall's lip. Chalk marks from their lesson earlier that day covered the surface of the outer wall, while close by a number of small earthenware pots lay partly buried in the sand from one of his experiments.

Atrus swung one of the three bone-white sacks up onto his shoulder, the rough material chafing his neck and chin, the smell of the salt strong through the cloth. Then, clambering up onto the sloping wall, he turned and, crouching, reached down with his left foot, finding the top rung of the rope ladder.

With unthinking care, Atrus climbed down into the cool shadow of the cleft, the strong scent of herbs intoxicating after the desert's parched sterility. Down here things grew on every side. Every last square inch of space was cultivated. Between the various stone and adobe structures that clung to them, the steep walls of the cleft were a patchwork of bare red-brown and vivid emerald, while the sloping floor surrounding the tiny pool was a lush green, no space wasted even for a path.

Instead, a rope bridge stretched across the cleft in a zigzag that linked the various structures not joined by the narrow steps that had been carved into the rock millennia before. Over the years, Anna had cut a number of long troughlike shelves into the solid walls of the cleft, filling them with earth and patiently irrigating them, slowly expanding their garden.

The storeroom was at the far end, near the bottom of the cleft. Traversing the final stretch of rope bridge, Atrus slowed. Here, water bubbled up from an underground spring, seeping through a tilted layer of porous rock, making the ancient steps wet and slippery. Farther down a channel had been cut into the rock, directing the meager but precious flow across the impermeable stone at the bottom of the cleft into the natural depression of the pool. Here, too, was the place where his mother was buried. At one end of it lay a small patch of delicate blue flowers, their petals like tiny stars, their stamen velvet dark.

After the searing heat of the desert sand, the coolness of the damp stone beneath his feet was delightful. Down here, almost thirty feet below the surface, the air was fresh and cool, its sweet scent refreshing after the dryness of the desert outside. There was the faintest trickling of water, the soft whine of a desert wasp. Atrus paused a moment, lifting the heavy glasses onto his brow, letting his pale eyes grow accustomed to the shadow, then went on down, ducking beneath the rock

AH KEY

S

FLOWER FOUND
NEAR STEAM VE

overhang before turning to face the storeroom door, which was recessed into the stone of the cleftwall.

The surface of that squat, heavy door was a marvel in itself, decorated as it was with a hundred delicate, intricate carvings; with fish and birds and animals, all of them linked by an interwoven pattern of leaves and flowers. This, like much else in the cleft, was his grandmother's doing, for if there was a clear surface anywhere, she would want to decorate it, as if the whole of creation was her canvas.

Raising his foot, Atrus pushed until it gave, then went inside, into the dark and narrow space. Another year and he would need to crouch beneath the low stone ceiling. Now, however, he crossed the tiny room in three steps; lowering the sack from his shoulder, he slid it onto the broad stone shelf beside two others.

For a moment he stood there, staring at the single, bloodred symbol printed on the sack. Familiar though it was, it was a remarkably elaborate thing of curves and squiggles, and whether it was a word or simply a design he wasn't sure, yet it had a beauty, an elegance, that he found entrancing. Sometimes it reminded him of the face of some strange, exotic animal, and sometimes he thought he sensed some kind of meaning in it.

Atrus turned, looking up, conscious suddenly of his grandmother waiting by the cleftwall, and chided himself for being so thoughtless. Hurrying now, stopping only to replace his glasses, he padded up the steps and across the swaying bridge, emerging in time to see her unfasten her cloak and, taking a long, pearl-handled knife from the broad leather toolbelt that encircled her waist, lean down and slit open one of the bolts of cloth she'd bought.

"That's pretty," he said, standing beside her, adjusting the lenses, then admiring the vivid vermilion and cobalt pattern, seeing how the light seemed to shimmer in the surface of the cloth, as in a pool.

"Yes," she said, turning to smile at him, returning the knife to its sheath. "It's silk."

"Silk?"

In answer she lifted it and held it out to him. "Feel."

He reached out, surprised by the cool, smooth feel of it.

She was still looking at him, an enigmatic smile on her lips now. "I thought I'd make a hanging for your room. Something to cheer it up."

He looked back at her, surprised, then bent and lifted one of the remaining sacks onto his shoulder.

As he made his way down and across to the storeroom, he saw the rich pattern of the cloth in his mind and smiled. There was a faint gold thread within the cloth, he realized, recalling how it had felt: soft and smooth, like the underside of a leaf.

Depositing the second sack, he went back. While he was gone, Anna had lifted the two bolts of cloth up into the lip of the cleftwall, beside the last of the salt

and flour sacks. There was also a small green cloth bag
of seeds, tied at the mouth with a length of bloodred
twine. Of the final sack, the one he'd thought had
moved, there was no sign.

He frowned, then looked to his grandmother, but
if she understood his look, she didn't show it.

"Put the seeds in the kitchen," she said quietly, lifting the bolt of silk onto her shoulder. "We'll plant
them tomorrow. Then come back and help me with the
rest of the cloth."

As he came back from the storeroom, he saw that
Anna was waiting for him on the broad stone ledge at
the far end of the garden. Even from where he stood
he could see how tired she was. Crossing the rope
bridge to the main house, he went quickly down the
narrow steps that hugged the wall and, keeping carefully to the smooth, protruding rocks that delineated
the pool's western edge, crouched and, taking the
metal ladle from its peg, leaned across and dipped it
into the still, mirrorlike surface.

Standing again, he went swiftly along the edge, his
toes hugging the rock, careful not to spill a drop of
precious water, stopping beside the ledge on which
Anna sat.

She looked up at him and smiled; a weary, loving
smile.

"Thank you," she said, taking the ladle and drinking from it, then offered it back.

"No," he said softly, shaking his head. "You finish it.

With a smile, she drained the ladle and handed it back.

"Well, Atrus," she said, suddenly relaxed, as if the water had washed the tiredness from her. "What did you see?"

He hesitated, then. "I saw a brown cloth sack, and the sack moved."

Her laughter was unexpected. Atrus frowned, then grinned as she produced the sack from within the folds of her cloak. It was strange, for it seemed not to hold anything. Not only that, but the cloth of the sack was odd—much coarser than those the traders normally used. It was as if it had been woven using only half the threads. If it had held salt, the salt would have spilled through the holes in the cloth, yet the sack held something.

"Well?" she said, amused by his reaction. "Are you going to take it?"

He stared at her, genuinely surprised. "For me?"

"Yes," she said. "For you."

Gingerly, he took it from her, noticing that the sack's mouth was tied with the same red twine as the seed bag.

"What is it?"

"Look and see," she said, taking her knife and handing it to him by the handle. "But be careful. It might bite."

He froze, looking to her, perplexed now.

"Oh, go on," she said, laughing softly. "I'm only teasing you, Atrus. Open it."

Slowly, reluctantly, he slipped the blade beneath the twine and pulled. The mouth of the sack sighed open.

Putting the blade down on the rock, he lifted the glasses up onto the top of his head, then grasped the sack's neck, slowly drawing it open, all the while peering into its dark interior.

There was something there. Something small and hunched and . . .

The sound made him drop the sack and jerk back the hairs at his neck standing up with shock.

"Careful . . ." Anna said, bending down to pick the sack up.

Atrus watched, astonished, as she took out something small and finely furred. For a moment he didn't understand, and then, with a shock, he saw what it was. A kitten! Anna had bought him a kitten!

He made a sound of delight, then, getting to his feet, took a step toward her, bending close to look at the tiny thing she held.

It was beautiful. Its fur was the color of the desert sand at sunset, while its eyes were great saucers of green that blinked twice then stared back at him curiously. In all it was no bigger than one of Anna's hands.

"What is it called?" he asked.

"She's called Pahket."

"Pahket?" Atrus looked up at his grandmother frowning, then reached out and gently stroked the kitten's neck.

"The name's an ancient one. The eldest of the raders said it was a lucky name."

"Maybe," Atrus said uncertainly, "but it doesn't eel right. Look at her. She's like a tiny flame." He miled as the kitten pressed against his hand and began o purr noisily.

"Then maybe you should call her that."

"Flame?"

Anna nodded. She watched her grandson a noment, then spoke again. "There's a small clay bowl n the kitchen . . ."

Atrus looked up. "The blue one?"

"Yes. Flame can use it. In fact, she could probably lo with some water now, having been in that sack."

Atrus smiled, then, as if he'd done it all his infant fe, picked the kitten up with one hand, cradling it gainst his side, and carried her across, vaulting up the teps in twos and threes before ducking inside the itchen. A moment later he reemerged, the bowl in his ther hand.

"Come on, Flame," he said, speaking softly to the itten as if it were a child, his thumb gently rubbing he top of its head, "let's get you a drink."

As darkness fell, Atrus sat on the narrow balcony that an the length of the outer sleeping chamber, the doz-ag kitten curled beside him on the cool stone ledge as he stared up at the moon. It had been a wonderful day, but like all days it had to end. Below and to his right he could see his grandmother, framed in the brightly lit window of the kitchen, a small oil lamp casting it soft yellow glow over her face and upper arms as she worked, preparing a tray of cakes. They, like the kitten, were a treat, to celebrate his seventh birthday in two day's time.

The thought of it made him smile, yet into his joy seeped an element of restlessness. Happy as he was here with his grandmother, he had recently begun to feel that there was more than this. There *had* to be.

He looked past the moon, following a line of stars until he found the belt of the hunter, tracing the shape of the hunter's bow in the night sky as his grandmother had taught him. There were so many things to know, so many things yet to learn.

And when I've learned them all, grandmother?

He remembered how she had laughed at that, then leaned toward him. *There's never an end to learning, Atrus. There are more things in this universe, yes, and more universes than we could ever hope to know.*

And though he did not quite understand what she had meant by that, simply staring at the vastness of the night sky gave him some tiny inkling of the problem. Yet he was curious to know all he could—as curious as the sleeping kitten beside him was indolent.

He looked down from that vastness. All about him

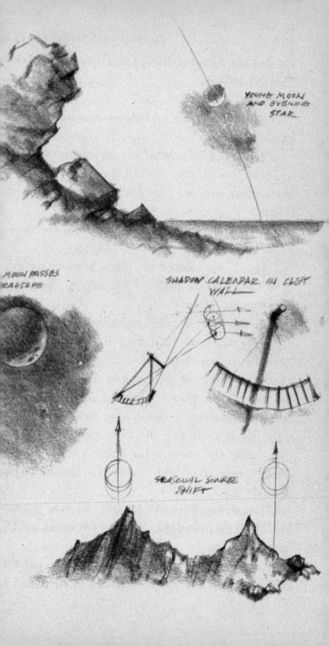

YOUNG MOON AND EVENING STAR

MOON PASSES PRAESEPE

SHADOW CALENDAR ON CLEFT WALL

SEASONAL SUNRISE SHIFT

the cleft was dotted with tiny lights that glowed warm-
ly in the darkness.

"Atrus?"

He turned, looking up as Anna came and crouched
beside him on the narrow ledge. "Yes, grandmother?"

"You have a lot to write in your journal today."

Atrus smiled, then stroked the kitten, petting it
between the ears, and feeling it push back against his
fingers.

"I wrote it earlier, while you were in the storeroom."

"Ah . . ." She reached out, gently brushing the kitten's flank with the backs of her fingers. "And how
goes your experiment?"

"Which one?" he asked, suddenly eager.

"Your measurements. I saw you out there earlier."

For nearly six months now Atrus had been studying the movement of the dunes on the far side of the
volcano. He had placed a series of long stakes deep
into the sand along the dune's edge, then had watched,
meticulously measuring the daily movement of the
dune, using the stakes as his baseline, then marking
those measurements down on a chart in the back of his
journal.

"I've almost finished," he said, his eyes shining
brightly in the moonlight. "Another few weeks and I'll
have my results."

Anna smiled at that, amused and yet proud of the
care he took. There was no doubting it, Atrus had a

fine mind—a true explorer's mind—and a curiosity to match.

"And have you a theory?" she asked, noting how he sat up straighter to answer her.

"They move," he answered.

"A little or a lot?"

He smiled. "It depends."

"Depends?"

"On what you think is a little, or what you think is a lot."

She laughed, enjoying his answer. "A little would be, oh, several inches a year, a lot would be a mile."

"Then it's neither," he answered, looking down at Flame again. The kitten was dozing now, her head tucked down, her gentle snores a soft sound in the darkness.

Anna reached out, her fingers brushing his hair back from his eyes. In some ways he was an ungainly child, yet there was something about him that was noble. The kindness, the sharp intelligence in his eyes—these things distinguished him, giving the lie to his physical awkwardness.

"It changes," he said, his eyes meeting hers again.

"Changes?"

"The rate at which the dune travels. Sometimes it barely moves, but when there's a storm . . ."

"Yes?" she asked quietly.

"It's the wind," he said. "It pushes the smaller grains up the windward side of the dune. From there they tumble over the crest, onto the leeward side That's why the dune is shaped the way it is. The larger, coarser grains don't move so much, that's why the windward slope is gradually curved. It's packed densely. You can walk on it as on a rock. But the leeward side . . ."

"Yes?" she said, encouraging him.

He frowned, wrinkling up his nose as he thought it through. "Well, the leeward side is constantly changing. The fine grains build up, forming a steep slope until . . . well, until they all tumble down. If you try to walk on it you sink down into it. It's not packed liked the windward side."

Anna smiled, her eyes never leaving his face. "You say it tumbles over. Do you know why?"

Atrus nodded enthusiastically, making Flame stir in his lap. "It has to do with how the grains balance on each other. Up to a certain angle they're fine, but beyond that . . ."

"And have you measured that angle?" she asked, pleased with him.

Again he nodded. "Thirty-five degrees. That's the steepest it gets before it begins to slip."

"Good," she said, resting her hands on her knees. "It *seems* like you've considered everything, Atrus. You've tried to see the Whole."

Atrus had looked down, gazing at the sleeping kitten. Now he looked up again. "The *Whole?*"

She laughed softly. "It's something my father used

to say to me. What *I* mean by it, is that you've looked at the problem from many angles and considered how the pieces fit together. You've asked all the questions that needed to be asked and come up with the answers. And now you have an understanding of it." She smiled and reached out again, letting her hand rest lightly on his shoulder. "It may seem a small thing, Atrus—after all, a dune is but a dune—but the principle's a sound one and will stand you in good stead whatever you do, and however complex the system is you're looking at. Always consider the Whole, Atrus. Always look at the interrelatedness of things, and remember that the 'whole' of one thing is always just a part of something else, something larger."

Atrus stared at her, slowly nodding, the seriousness of his gaze belying his seven years. Seeing it, Anna sighed inwardly. Sometimes he made her feel so proud. Such fine, clear eyes he had. Eyes that had been so encouraged to see—that yearned to observe and question the world around him.

"Grandmother?"

"Yes, Atrus?"

"Can I draw a picture of Flame?"

"No," she said, smiling down at him. "Not now. It's time for bed. You want Flame to sleep with you?"

He grinned and nodded.

"Then bring her through. She can sleep at the foot of your bed tonight. Tomorrow we'll make a basket for her."

"Grandmother?"

"Yes, Atrus?"

"Can I read for a while?"

She smiled then reached out to ruffle his hair. "No. But I'll come and tell you a story, if you like."

His eyes widened. "Please. And Nanna?"

"Yes?" she asked, surprised by his use of the familiar term.

"Thank you for Flame. She's beautiful. I'll take good care of her."

"I know you will. Now come inside. It's late."

Atrus's bed was on a shelf of rock cut into the back wall of the inner sleeping chamber like a tiny catacomb. A beautifully woven quilt was his mattress, while a large, doubled square of cloth, sewn neatly by Anna along the edges and decorated with a pattern of tiny, embroidered golden stars, served for a sheet. In a niche in the rock at the head of the shelf rested a small oil lamp, secured by narrow metal bars at top and bottom.

Anna reached in and, lifting the curiously engraved glass, lit the wick, then moved back, letting Atrus climb into the tiny space. Soon he would be too big for the sleeping shelf, but for now it sufficed.

Looking at her grandson, she felt a twinge of regret; regret for the passing of innocence, knowing that she should cherish such moments as this, for they could not last. Nothing lasted. Neither individual lives, nor empires.

"So," she said, tucking him in, then lifting the half-dozing cat onto him, so he could cuddle it a while, "what would you like me to tell you?"

He looked away from her a moment, his pale eyes seeming to read the flickering shadows within the shelf, then met her eyes again, smiling.

"How about the tale of Kerath?"

"But you've heard that several times now, Atrus."

"I know, but I'd like to hear it again. Please, grandmother."

She smiled and lay her hand on his brow, then, closing her eyes, began the ancient tale.

It was set in the land of the D'ni, dating back, so it was said, to the time, thousands of years ago, when their homeland had suffered the first of the great earthquakes that, ultimately, had caused them to flee and come here.

Kerath had been the last of the great kings; last not because he was deposed but because, when he had achieved all he had set out to achieve, he had stepped down and appointed a council of elders to run the D'ni lands. But the "tale of Kerath" was the story of the young prince's teenage years and how he had spent them in the great underground desert of Tre'Merktee, the Place of Poisoned Waters.

And when Atrus heard the tale, what did he think? Did he imagine himself a young prince, like Kerath, banished into exile by his dead father's brother? Or was it something else in the tale that attracted him, for there was no doubting that this was his favorite story.

As she came to a close, narrating the final part, of how Kerath tamed the great lizard and rode it back into the D'ni capital, she could sense how Atrus clung to her every word, following each phrase, each twist in the story.

In her mind she closed the book silently and set it aside, as she had once done for another little boy in another time, in a place very different from this. Opening her eyes, she found Atrus staring up at her.

"Are there *many* tales, grandmother?"

She laughed. "Oh, thousands . . ."

"And do you know them all?"

She shook her head. "No. Why, it would be impossible, Atrus. D'ni was a great empire, and its libraries were small cities in themselves. If I were to try to memorize all the tales of the D'ni it would take me several lifetimes, and even then I would have learned but a handful of them."

"And are the tales true?" Atrus asked, yawning and turning to face the wall.

"Do you believe them?"

He was silent, then, with a sleepy sigh. "I guess so."

Yet she sensed he was not satisfied. Reaching out,

she lifted the blanket until it covered his neck, then, leaning across, kissed his brow.

"Shall I leave Flame where she is?"

"Mmmm . . ." he answered, already half asleep.

Smiling, Anna reached across and, lifting the glass, snuffed the lamp, then stood and left the room.

The lamp was still burning in her workroom on the far side of the cleft. The half-completed sculpture lay where she'd left it on the desk, the workbox open next to it, the delicate stone-working instruments laid out in their trays. For a moment she stood there, looking down at it, considering what needed to be done, then moved past it, reaching up to take a tiny, pearl-backed case from the shelf where she kept her books.

Thumbing the clasp, she opened it and stared at her reflection, drawing a wisp of gray hair back off her brow.

"What do you see, Anna?"

The face that looked back at her was strong and firm, the bone structure delicate without being brittle; refined, rather than coarse. In her time she had been a great beauty. But time was against her now.

The thought made her smile. She had never been vain, yet she had always—always—wondered just how much of her real self showed in her face. How much the interplay of eye and mouth revealed. And yet how much those same subtle features could hide. Take Atrus, for instance. When he smiled, he smiled not simply with his lips but with the whole of his face, the whole of his being: a great, radiant smile that shone out from him. Likewise, when he was thinking, it was as if one could see right through him—like glass— and watch the thoughts fizz and sparkle in his head.

And her own face?

She tilted her head slightly to the side, examining herself again, noting this time the tiny blue beads she had tied into her braids, the colorful, finely woven band about her neck.

The face that stared back at her was pale and tautly fleshed, almost austere; the deeply green eyes were intelligent, the mouth sensitive; yet it was in those few small, surrounding touches—the beads, the band— that her true nature was revealed: that part, at least, that loved embellishment. From childhood on, she had always been the same. Give her a blank page and she would fill it with a poem or a story or a picture. Give her a blank wall and she would always—always—decorate it.

Give me a child . . .

She snapped the tiny case shut and slipped it back onto the shelf.

Give her a child and she would fill its head with marvels. With tales and thoughts and facts beyond imagining.

What do you see, Anna?

Yawning, she reached across to douse the light, then answered the silent query.

"I see a tired old woman who needs her sleep."

"Maybe," she answered after a moment, smiling, remembering the girl she'd been. Then, stepping out onto the steps that hugged the cleftwall, she quickly crossed the cleft once more, making for her bed.

2

THE FIRST SIGN WAS A DARKENING OF
the sky far to the east, high up, not where you
would expect a sandstorm. Atrus was exploring the
sun-facing slope of the volcano, searching for rare
rocks and crystals to add to his collection, when he
looked up and saw it—a tiny smudge of darkness
against the solid blue. For a moment he wasn't quite
sure what it was. He moved his head, thinking it might
be a blemish in one of the lenses, but it wasn't that.

Looking back, he found it was still there. Not only
that, but it was growing. Even as he watched it seemed
to darken.

Atrus felt a vague unease grip him.

The ten-year-old turned, making his way back
down the slope, then hurried across the open stretch
of sand between the nearest ledge and the cleft, pant-
ing from the heat. Stopping only to slip his sandals
into the gap beneath the cleftwall's lip, he clambered
down the rope ladder, making the stone rungs clatter
against the wall.

That noise alerted Anna. On the far side of the
shadowy cleft, the top half of the hinged door to her
workroom swung open. She looked out, her eyebrows
formed into a question.

"Atrus?"

"Something's coming."

"People, you mean?"

He shook his head. "No. Something big in the sky, igh up. Something black."

"A sandstorm?"

"No . . . the whole sky is turning black."

Her laugh was unexpected. "Well, well," she said, lmost as if she'd half expected whatever it was. "We'll eed to take precautions."

Atrus stared at his grandmother, perplexed. Precautions?"

"Yes," she said, almost gaily now. "If it's what think it is, we'd best take advantage of it while we can The chance is rare enough."

He stared at her as if she were speaking in riddles

"Come on," she said, "help me now. Go fetch th seeds from the store room. And bowls. Fetch as man bowls as you can from the kitchen and set them up al around the cleftwall."

Still he stared at her, openmouthed.

"Now," she said, grinning at him. "If you could se it on the horizon then it'll be upon us before long. W need to be prepared for it."

Not understanding, Atrus did as he was told crossing the rope bridge to fetch the seeds, then criss crossing it time and again, carefully ferrying every bow he could find and setting them all around th cleftwall's rim. That done, he looked to her.

Anna was standing on the cleftwall, staring ou one hand shielding her eyes against the glare. Atru went across and climbed up, standing next to her.

Whatever it was, it now filled a third of the hor zon, a great black veil that linked the heavens and th earth. From where he stood it seemed like a fragmer of the night ripped from its appointed time.

"What is it?" he asked. In all his ten years he ha not seen its like.

"It's a storm, Atrus," she said, turning to him wit a smile. "That blackness is a huge rain cloud. And we're lucky—if we're very, very lucky—then that rain will fall on us."

"Rain?"

"Water," she said, her smile broadening. "Water falling from the sky."

He looked from her to the great patch of darkness, his mouth open in astonishment. "From the sky?"

"Yes," she answered, raising her arms, as if to embrace the approaching darkness. "I've dreamed of this, Atrus. So many nights I've dreamed."

It was the first time she had said anything of her dreams, and again he stared at her as if she'd been transformed. Water from the sky. Dreams. Day turned to night. Putting his right hand against his upper arm he pinched himself hard.

"Oh, you're awake, Atrus," Anna said, amused by his reaction. "And you must stay awake and watch, for you'll see sights you may never see again." Again she laughed. "Just watch, my boy. Just watch!"

Slowly, very slowly it came closer, and as it approached the air seemed to grow cooler and cooler. There was the faintest breeze now, like an outrider moving ahead of the growing darkness.

"All right," she said, turning to him after a long silence. "Let's get to work. We need to scatter the seeds all around the cleft. Use all the bags but one. We'll not get this chance again. Not for many years."

He did as she told him, moving in a daze, conscious all the while of the blackness that now filled the whole of the horizon. From time to time he would look up fearfully, then duck his head again.

Finished, he pocketed the tiny cloth bag then clambered up onto the cleftwall.

Flame was sheltering beneath the stone ledge on the floor of the cleft. Seeing her there, Anna called to him. "Atrus! You'd better put Flame in your room. If she stays where she is she'll be in danger."

Atrus frowned, not understanding *how* she could possibly be in danger. Surely the cleft was the safest place? But he did not argue, merely went and, gathering Flame under his arm, took her into the storeroom and locked her in.

Returning to the lip of the cleftwall he saw that the storm was almost upon them. Climbing out onto the open sands, he looked to Anna, wondering what they would do, where they would hide, but his grandmother seemed unconcerned. She merely stood there watching that immense darkness approach, undaunted by it, smiling all the while. Turning, she called to him, raising her voice against the noise of the oncoming storm.

"Take your glasses off, Atrus, you'll see better!"

Again, he did as he was told, stowing the heavy lenses with their thick leather strap in the deep pocket of his cloak.

Ahead, the storm front was like a massive, shimmering wall of black and silver, a solid thing advancing on him, filling the whole of the sky ahead of him, tearing up the desert sand as it went. Strange, searingly bright flashes seemed to dance and flicker in that darkness, accompanied by a low, threatening rumble that exploded suddenly in a great crash of sound.

Trembling, he closed his eyes, his teeth clenched tight, his body crouched against the onslaught, and then the rain burst over him, soaking him in an instant, drumming against his head and shoulders and arms with such fierceness that for a moment he thought it would beat him to the ground. He gasped with shock, then staggered around, surprised to hear, over the rain's fierce thundering, Anna's laughter.

He looked down past his feet at the earth, astonished by its transformation. A moment before he had been standing on the sand. Now his feet were embedded in a sticky, swirling mess that tugged at him as he tried to free himself.

"Anna!" he called, turning to appeal to her, putting his arms out.

She came across, giggling now like a young girl. The rain had plastered her hair to her head, while her clothes seemed painted to her long, gaunt body like a second skin.

"Isn't it wonderful!" she said, putting her face up to the rain, her eyes closed in ecstasy. "Close your eyes, Atrus, and feel it on your face."

Once more he did as he was told, fighting down his instinct to run, letting the stinging rain beat down on his exposed cheeks and neck. After a moment his face felt numb. Then, with a sudden change he found hard to explain, he began to enjoy the sensation.

He ducked his head down and squinted at her. Beside him, his grandmother was hopping on one leg, and slowly turning, her hands raised above her head and spread, as if in greeting to the sky. Timidly he copied her. Then, as the mood overtook him, he began to twirl about madly, the rain falling and falling and falling, the noise like the noise at the heart of a great sandstorm, so loud there was a silence in his head.

And then, with a suddenness that made him gasp, it was gone. He turned, blinking, in time to see it drift across the cleft and climb the volcano wall, a solid curtain of falling water that left the desert floor dark and flat behind it.

Atrus looked about him, seeing how every pot was filled to the brim—a score of trembling mirrors reflecting back the sudden, startling blue of the sky. He made to speak, to say something to Anna, then turned back, startled by the sudden hissing noise that rose from the volcano's mouth.

As he watched, great billows of steam rose up out of the caldera, as if the dormant giant had returned to life.

"It's all right," Anna said, coming over and placing her hand on his shoulder. "It's only where the rain has seeped down into the deep vents."

Atrus burrowed into his grandmother's side. Yet he was no longer afraid. Now that it had passed—now that he had *survived* it—he felt elated, *exhilarated*.

"Well?" she asked quietly. "What did you think?"

"Where did it come from?" he asked, watching, fascinated, as that massive dark wall receded slowly into the distance.

"From the great ocean," she answered. "It travels hundreds of miles to get here."

He nodded, but his mind was back watching that great silver-black curtain rush toward him once again and swallow him up, feeling it drum against his flesh like a thousand blunt needles.

Atrus glanced up at his grandmother and laughed. "Why, you're steaming, grandmother!"

She grinned and poked him gently. "And so are you, Atrus. Come, let's go inside, before the sun dries us out again."

He nodded and began to climb the cleftwall, meaning to go and free Flame from the storeroom, yet as he popped his head over the rim he stopped dead, his mouth falling open in a tiny oh of surprise.

Below him the cleft was a giant blue-black mirror, the shadow of the steep walls dividing it in half, like a jagged shield.

Coming alongside him, Anna crouched and, smiling, looked into his face.

"Would you like to learn to swim, little sand worm?"

Anna woke Atrus in the dark before first light, shaking him gently then standing back, the lamp held high, its soft yellow glow filling the shelf where he lay.

"Come," she said simply, smiling at him as he knuckled his eyes. "I've something to show you."

Atrus sat up, suddenly alert. Something had happened. Something . . . He stared at her. "Was it *real*, Grandmother? Did it really happen? Or did I dream it?"

"It happened," she answered softly. Then, taking his hand, she led him out, through her own shadowed chamber and onto the narrow balcony.

The moon was two days off full, and though it was no longer at its zenith, its light still silvered the far edge of the pool.

Atrus stood there, breathing shallowly, transfixed by the sight, staring down into the perfect ebon mirror of the pool. Not the pool he'd known from infancy, but a bigger, more astonishing pool—a pool that filled the cleft from edge to edge. Staring into it he let a sigh escape him.

"The stars . . ."

Anna smiled and leaned past him, pointing out the shape of the hunter in the water. "And there," she said. "Look, Atrus, there's the marker star."

He stared at the brilliant pure blue star then looked up, seeing its twin there in the heavens.

"Is this it?" he asked, after a moment, turning to look at her. "Is this what you were going to show me?"

She shook her head. "No . . . Come. Follow me."

In the moment before he emerged from the cleft—in that instant before he saw what his grandmother had woken him to see—Atrus paused on the second top rung of the ladder and looked down.

Below him, far below, it seemed—so far that it was almost as if he had been inverted and now hung out over space—lay the star-dusted sky. For a moment the illusion was perfect, so perfect that, had he let go of the rung, he was certain that he would have fallen forever. Then, conscious that his grandmother was waiting patiently on the other side of the lip, he pulled himself up onto the top of the cleftwall.

And stopped, stone still, his jaw dropped, the sight that met his eyes incredible and dreamlike.

Between the cleft and the lip of the caldera, the whole side of the volcano was carpeted in flowers. Even in the moonlight he could distinguish those bright colors. Violets and blues, dark greens and lavender, bright reds and violent oranges.

He stared, uncomprehending. It was impossible.

"They're called ephemerals," Anna said, speaking into that perfect silence. "Their seeds—hundreds of thousands of tiny seeds—lay in the dry earth for years. And then, when finally the rains come, they blossom. For a single day—for one single night—they bloom. And then . . ."

She sighed. It was the saddest sound Atrus had ever heard. He looked to her, surprised by that sound. There had been such joy in her voice, such excitement.

"What is it, grandmother?"

She smiled wistfully then reached out, petting his head. "It's nothing, Atrus. I was thinking of your grandfather, that's all. Thinking how much he would have loved this."

Atrus jumped down, his feet welcomed by the lush, cool feel of vegetation. The earth beneath was damp and cool. He could squidge it between his toes.

Crouching, he ran his hands over the tops of the tiny blooms, feeling how soft, how delicate they were, then plucked a single, tiny flower, holding it before his face to study it.

It had five tiny pink petals and delicate stamen the color of sandstone. He let it fall.

For a moment he knelt there, his eyes taking it all in. Then, suddenly, a new thought struck him. Jerking around, he looked to Anna.

"The seeds!"

Atrus stood and, picking his way carefully about the cleftwall, stooped here and there, examining all those places where, before the storm had come, he had scattered their precious seeds.

After a while he looked to Anna and laughed. "It worked! The seeds have germinated! Look, Nanna, look!"

She stood there, grinning back at him. "Then we'd

better harvest them, Atrus. Before the sun comes up. Before the desert takes back what it's given us."

The work was done. Now there was time simply to explore. As the dawn's light began to cast its long shadows over the sands, Atrus climbed the side of the volcano, Flame in tow, the ginger cat intoxicated, it seemed, by the sudden profusion of flowers. She romped and rolled about as if the years had peeled back and she was a kitten again.

Watching her, Atrus giggled. He wore his glasses now, the sun-filter set low, the magnification high. Now was the time to indulge his curiosity, before the sun climbed too high and the heat grew too unbearable; and before, as Anna assured him they would, the blooms dried up and vanished.

For a time he wandered idly, almost as aimless as the tiny, scrawny cat that was his constant companion. Then, without knowing it, he found himself looking for something. Or rather, not so much looking as trying to pinpoint exactly what it was he'd seen but not understood.

He stood still, turning only his head, trying to locate just what it was he'd glimpsed. At first he saw nothing. Then, with a little start, he saw. *There!* Yes, there in that shallow incline that ran down to one of the volcano's small, inactive vents!

Atrus went across and stood over it, nodding to himself. There was no doubt about it, the vegetation here was more lush, the flowers bigger, their leaves thicker and broader.

And why was that?

He bent down and, reaching in among the tiny stems, pulled one of the plants up and examined its shallow roots. Earth clung to it. He lifted it and sniffed. There was something strange, something almost metallic about that smell. Minerals. Somehow the presence of minerals—specific minerals?—had helped the plants grow larger here.

He cleared a tiny space with one hand, then scooped up a handful of the earth and carefully spilled it into one of the pockets of his cloak. Straightening up, he looked back down the slope to where Flame was lying on her back in a patch of bright yellow flowers, pawing at the sky.

"Come on!" he said, excited now, wanting to test his theory.

Almost three months had passed now since the day of desert rains. Since then the ten-year-old had labored every evening, stood at his workspace, an oil lamp hung on a peg on the wall at his side, Flame sleeping on the floor nearby as he patiently tracked down which of the chemicals he had found in the sample was responsible for the enhanced growth.

His workroom was in a small, freshly cut alcove at the back of Anna's room. Working carefully, patiently, over the period of a year, he had chipped the narrow space from the rock with his own hands, using his grandmother's stoneworking tools, careful to remove the stone a little at a time as she had taught him, checking all the while for weaknesses in the rock, for flaws in its structure that might split and bring the whole wall tumbling down on them.

There was a ledge—a working surface he had smoothed and polished until the surface seemed like glass. Strange-looking technical instruments littered that surface now. Above it he had cut three narrow shelves where he stored his things: narrow cuplike pots made of stone and clay, tiny handwoven baskets filled with various powders and chemicals, the bleached bones of various desert animals, and, on the topmost shelf, his collection of rare rocks and crystals: polished agates like the pouting lips of strange creatures; a large chunk of zeolite, which reminded him of the whiskers of some exotic snow beast; nodules of blue azurite beside a cluster of bright yellow sulfur crystal; a long, beveled finger of icelike quartz, and, in a tiny transparent box, a single tiger's eye. These and many others crowded the shelf, sorted into the seven systems— cubic, tetragonal, monoclinic, orthorhombic, triclinic, hexagonal, and trigonal—he had read of in his grand-mother's books.

On the wall behind his work ledge was the hanging his grandmother had made for him from the red and blue silk she had bought from the traders that time, its fringed edge decorated with tassels of gold thread. Hand-drawn pictures and diagrams—some his, some Anna's—filled the remaining walls.

His task had not been easy, not with the basic equipment he had at his disposal. Atrus had thought, at first, that the task would prove a simple one. He had expected to find, at most, three, maybe four different chemicals in the sample, but to his surprise—and dismay—it had not proved anything as straightforward. After weeks of testing, he had identified more than thirty different elements in the sample. The vents, it seemed, were a regular cornucopia of chemical life. Nor was it easy to devise ways to test his theory. His grandmother's books, which had whole chapters on the shaping and uses of stone and metal, had few entries on agriculture. He had been forced to improvise.

When Atrus sensed the crop was ripe for harvesting, he picked a number of the bigger shoots—choosing a couple from among each different type—and, placing them in Anna's best basket, carried them up to the kitchen.

He stood there at the stone sink next to the window, staring out across the cleft as he rinsed the shoots thoroughly, taking care to remove all of the dirt from their roots. Down below, Flame had gone across to the patch and was sniffing the earth where it had been disturbed, and tentatively rooting about with her paw.

Atrus watched her a while, smiling broadly at her antics, then, giving the shoots a good shake to remove the last few drops of water, he lay them on the cutting board and went across, removing one of Anna's knives from the rack.

As he began to chop and prepare the shoots, he watched Flame stretch and settle among the remaining shoots, cleaning herself, her tiny pink tongue licking her paws before she began to groom her short orange fur.

"Hey you," he said, laughing gently. It was bad enough that she ate the spearmint grass on the far side of the pool, without her making a bed out of his special patch.

Finished, he took the chopped shoots across and scraped them into the earthenware bowl. They had a fresh, clean scent, like mint, though not as sweet. Taking a short length he put it to his nose, sniffing it, then popped it in his mouth.

It tasted good, too. Fresh and . . .

Atrus grimaced. There was a distinct aftertaste; a bitter, unpleasant tang. He ran the tip of his tongue around his gums, then shivered.

"Eeuch!"

"Atrus?"

He turned to find Anna standing there, looking at him curiously.

"What is it?"

"Nothing," he said, picking up the bowl and taking it across to the sink again. Maybe he hadn't washed them thoroughly enough. The last thing he wanted was for them to taste bad.

He felt Anna's fingers brush his back softly as she made her way past him to the scullery, then felt her breath on his neck as she leaned over him.

"They look good," she commented, smiling as he turned to look at her. "Shall I cook some rice to go with them?"

He shook his head. "No. I'll do it. And I'll make a special sauce."

She nodded, then, pressing his arm gently, moved past him and out onto the steps.

Atrus watched her go, then turned back, looking out across the cleft once more. Flame had settled now, curled up in a tiny orange ball amidst the bright green shoots. He smiled, then, pouring fresh water from the pitcher by his side, set to rinsing the shoots through once again.

Atrus was repairing the stonework at the far end of the cleftwall when the pains started. At first he thought it was just a cramp and, stretching his left arm to ease the muscles down that side, made to carry on. Yet as he reached up to take the trowel, a shooting pain went right through him, making him double up.

"*Atrus?*"

Anna was at his side in an instant.

"Atrus? What is it? What's the matter?"

He made to tell her, but the next one took his breath. He knelt, wincing with the pain.

It was like being stabbed.

"Atrus?"

He looked up at her, his vision glazed momentarily. Then, unable to help himself, he began to throw up.

After a while he lifted his head, feeling drained, exhausted, his brow beaded with sweat. Anna was kneeling next to him, her arm about his shoulders, murmuring something to him.

"What?"

"The shoots," she said, repeating what she'd been saying. "It must have been the shoots. Did you eat some?"

Atrus began to shake his head, then remembered. "I did. Just one. I . . ."

There was a tremor in his stomach, a momentary pain. He swallowed then looked back at her.

"It must have been something in them," Anna said, reaching up to wipe his brow. "What did you use."

"Use?" His thoughts were in disarray. He felt light-headed and disoriented. "I didn't . . ."

It came to him suddenly. The chemicals. It must have been something in the chemicals. And then he remembered. The aftertaste. That bitterness . . . not strong, but unpleasant enough to alert him.

He groaned. "I've let you down!"

"No," Anna said, pained by his words. "You can't get it right every time. If you did . . ."

He looked at her, angry not with her but with himself. "I could have killed you. Killed us both!"

Anna winced and made to shake her head, to deny him, but he was staring at her now, defying her to say no.

"No, Atrus," she said finally. "You haven't let me down. You'll learn from this."

But Atrus seemed unconvinced. "I nearly killed us," he repeated, shaking his head. "I nearly . . ."

She reached out and held him to her, hugging him until he grew still, relaxed. Then, helping him get up, she took him over to the pool and, kneeling him beside it, scooped up water in her hands and washed his face and neck.

"There," she said finally, smiling at him. "That's better."

Slowly, wearily, he got to his feet. "I guess I'd better dig it all up. I . . ."

He turned, staring. "Flame?"

Anna stepped past him, then crouched beside the tiny orange bundle. For a moment she was still, her ear pressed against its side, then, with a slowness that confirmed what Atrus had most feared, she straightened up.

"I'm sorry," she said. "I . . ."

Atrus stepped across and knelt beside her. For a moment he was very still, looking down at the tiny animal. Then, carefully, as if it only slept, he picked it up and, cuddling it against him, took it across to where a tiny patch of blue flowers bordered the cleft's side.

Anna turned, watching him, seeing how dignified he was at that moment; how grown up; how he kept in all he was feeling. And she knew, unmistakably, that in that instant he had shed something of his childishness and had taken a further step out into the adult world. Out, away from her.

3

IN THE BLISTERING HEAT OF THE LATE afternoon sun, faint wisps of sulfurous steam rose from tiny fumaroles in the volcano's mouth, coiling like a dancer's veils in that shadowy dark beneath the edge before they vanished in the intense glare above.

Atrus stood on the lip of the volcano, staring out across the deep bowl of the caldera, his glasses—the largest of the two pairs that had hung in his grandmother's workroom—pulled down over his face, the thick leather band hugging the back of his shaven head tightly beneath the white cloth hood he wore. Over his mouth and nose was the cloth mask Anna had made for him and insisted that he wear, while about his waist was a thick belt studded with tools—a perfect copy of the one his grandmother wore about her own.

Fourteen now, Atrus had grown fast this past year; he was almost a man's height, but he had yet to fill out. His face, too, had changed, taking on the harder, more angular shapes of manhood, both nose and chin having lost the softness they'd had in childhood. He was not a weak boy, not by any means, yet watching him from the top of the cleftwall, Anna noted how thin he was. When the desert winds blew she was afraid they would carry him away, there seemed so little of him.

For the past few weeks he had been setting up his experiment. Now he was ready to begin.

Turning, Atrus clambered down, out of the burning light, into the deep, much cooler shadow just below the lip. Here, on a narrow ledge, he had rigged up most of his equipment. Straight ahead the volcano wall fell away steeply, while to his right, just beyond a curiously rounded rock that looked as though it had been formed from melting mud, was a narrow vent. Above it he had placed a domed cap made of beaten metal. It was crudely manufactured, but effective, and he had staked it to the surrounding rock with four thick pins. On top of the dome was fixed a small metal cylinder.

Atrus reached up, his gloved hands gently turning the tiny knobs on either side of his glasses, adjusting the opacity of the lenses so that he could see better. Then, brushing a fine layer of dust from the top of the metal cap, he leaned forward and studied the finger-length silver valve, checking its welding for the dozenth time before glancing at the two crudely calibrated gauges that were set into the dome's face to either side of the valve. Just above each of the dials was a thumb-sized metal stud, a small circular hole bored through the top of each.

Atrus straightened, letting out a long breath. He had one chance at this, so it had to be right. If it went wrong, if it didn't work, then it would be a year or more before they could get all the parts they needed from the traders.

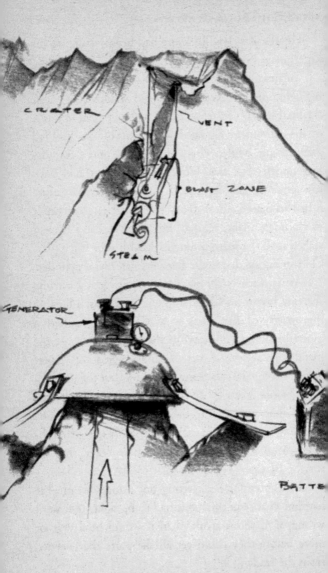

He turned, looking up to where two big, coiled wires—wires he had made himself under Anna's supervision—dangled over the edge of the crater. Just above them, jutting out over the drop, was a long arm of jet black stone. Two small wheels had been pinned into its face at the far end where it overhung the volcano. A handwoven rope ran between the wheels, forming a winch. Like the cap, it seemed crude, yet it would serve its purpose perfectly. To test it, Atrus had spent several afternoons lowering rocks into that maw, then raising them again—rocks many times the weight of the load it would have to carry now.

On the other side of the crater's lip, just next to where the rock arm was weighed down by a pile of heavy stones, sheltered by a makeshift tent, was his pride and joy—the beginning and the end of all this patient endeavor: his battery. Reaching up, he grasped one of the wires, pulling it toward him, drawing out enough of its length so that it stretched to the metal cap. Attaching it to one of the studs, he then repeated the process.

Adjusting his glasses, he clambered back up the wall and over the lip, out into the burning sunlight.

For a moment he stood there, getting his breath. Each time he emerged from the shadow, it was like stepping into a furnace. Nor did it matter how often he did it; every time, that change from the cool of the shade to the sudden, stifling heat of the open was like a physical blow.

Ducking under the thick cloth screen of the tent, Atrus smiled. This time he had tried hard to look at all the angles, to make sure he took all aspects of the Whole into account in his calculations.

The battery rested in the corner of the tent, against a ledge of rock. Looking at the massive thing, Atrus felt a justifiable pride. He had cut the block of stone himself and, using Anna's finest cutting tools, had hollowed it, following the design in the ancient D'ni book. Making the plates for the battery was comparably easy. Chemicals lay in abundance in the dry soil surrounding the volcano, and he had been fortunate to find a large deposit of galena—the ore containing a mixture of sulfur and lead—not far from the cleft. As for the sulfuric acid he had needed, the one substance that was in abundance on the volcano was sulfur. Indeed, when he finally came to make it, the only thing that had limited the size of the battery was its weight.

Adjusting his lenses once again, Atrus knelt and studied it proudly. He had spent many nights buffing and polishing the stone, then, on a whim, had carved three ancient D'ni words into its side, the complex characters tiny, elaborate works of art in themselves:

Light. Power. Force.

It looked like a tiny stone house, the metallic glint of its terminals giving it a strange, exotic look.

Beside it, altogether different, lay a second, much smaller box—the explosive device. This one was made

of an unglazed red clay, cast in his grandmother's kiln.
Undecorated, the single, rounded aperture on its top
face was plugged with a hard seal of wax, from the center of which jutted a length of thick twine which he
had treated with a solution of various highly reactive
chemicals. On its front face was a thick, clay handle.

Carefully, he picked it up and, wrapping it in his
cloak, carried it outside. Easing his way over the lip
once more, he steadied himself, one hand against the
rough, crumbling wall, as he edged down onto the
ledge.

Setting the box down, he turned and, standing on
tiptoe, reached up and caught hold of the thick, metal
hook on the end of the rope, gently tugging at it, hearing the brake mechanism click then click again on the
far side of the rim.

That, too, was his own invention.

On some of the earliest trials of the winch, he had
found that the rock dragged the rope down much too
quickly, and when he'd tried to slow it, the rope had
burned his palms. After much experimentation, he had
devised a way of stopping the supply wheel after each
rotation, so that the winch could only be operated by
a series of gentle tugs.

Bending down, he picked the box up again and
slipped the curved tip of the hook through its handle,
then turned back and, holding the rope out away from
him, slowly lowered it over the drop. As the rope went
taut, he moved back.

There was only one more thing to do now. Reaching into the inner pocket of his cloak, he removed the ancient D'ni tinderbox.

Leaning over, one hand supporting him against the rock arm, he held the flame beneath the end of the twine fuse on the dangling box, then, when it had caught, released the catch and stepped back.

For a moment he thought it had gone out, then, with a fizz, it began to burn fiercely.

Atrus turned and, half-running up the slope, scrambled over the rim, making for the winch.

This was the most crucial part. If the fuse burned too quickly, or if for some reason the winch jammed, things would go wrong.

Kneeling beside the brake wheel, he slowly began to turn it, listening to it click and click and click, all the while tensed against a sudden detonation, all the while counting in his head.

When he'd counted twenty, he threw himself down, stretched out flat behind the pile of stones, his hands over his ears.

. . . twenty-four, twenty-five, twenty-six . . .

The explosion rocked the side of the volcano. It had been four seconds early, even so that didn't matter, the box would have been in the correct place, opposite the fault.

Atrus laughed, then, dusting himself off, stood. As the echoes died, he could hear, through the ringing in his ears, the sound he'd hoped to hear—the strong hiss of steam forcing its way through the cap and an accompanying high-pitched mechanical whine.

Still laughing, he climbed up onto the lip and looked down. The winch-arm had gone, as had a large chunk of the ledge, but the vent—protected by the huge rock—was fine. Steam hissed from the cap in a steady, forceful stream.

Turning, looking down at Anna where she stood on the cleftwall, he raised his arms and waved to her eagerly, grinning with triumph.

"It works!" he yelled, pulling the mask down from his nose and mouth. "It works!"

From below Anna waved back to him, then, cupping her hands before her mouth, she shouted something, but it was difficult to make out what she was saying, his ears were ringing so much. Besides, the furious hissing of the steam, that high-pitched whine, seemed to grow by the moment. *Go back*, she'd said, or something like it. Grinning, he nodded, then, waving to her again, turned back to watch the hissing cap.

"It worked," he said quietly, noting how the cap was trembling now, rattling against the four restraining pins. "It really worked."

Climbing down, he went across and, taking care not to get *too* close, edged around until he could see the gauges.

Yes! A thrill of excitement went through him, seeing how both arrows were deep in the red. *It was passing a charge!*

He stood back, grinning, then felt himself go cold. Even as he watched, one of the metal pins began to move, easing itself slowly from its berth within the rock, as though some invisible but mighty hand were pulling it from the stone.

Slowly he began to edge away. As he did, the noise from the cap changed, rising a full octave, as if that same invisible hand had pressed down on the key of an organ.

Atrus turned and, scrambling up the slope and over the rim, began to run, ignoring the impact of the heat, fighting it . . . but it was like running through some thick, glutinous substance. He had gone barely ten paces when he tumbled forward, coming up facing the way he'd come. And as he did, the whole of the rim behind him seemed to lift into the air.

Coming to, Atrus looked up, surprised by the sight that met his eyes. On every side, the great walls of the volcano stretched up, forming a jagged circle where they met the startling blueness of the sky.

He was in the crater—the rim must have given way.

Slowly he got to his feet. Steam billowed across the rock-cluttered floor of the volcano, concealing its far edges. From time to time a figure would form from the clouds, the crystalline shapes strangely beautiful.

He saw the battery at once. Going over to it, he crouched, then shook his head, amazed by its condition. It was virtually untouched. The polished stone exterior had a few buffs and scratches, but it was still in one piece. Moreover, the dial on the top showed that it was fully charged.

Atrus laughed, delighted. Reaching out, he smoothed its upper surface almost lovingly. At least he knew now that the principle was sound. If he could only find the right vent, if he could only get the pressure right, then it would work and they would have an unlimited supply of electricity. Their lives would be transformed. The cleft would shine like a cat's eye in the desert night.

Smiling, Atrus raised his head, looking directly ahead of him. For a moment a cloud of steam obscured his view. Then, as it cleared, he found himself staring into blackness.

It was a cave. Or a tunnel of some kind.

He stood, then took a step toward it.

Strange. It seemed almost as though it had been carved from the surrounding rock.

The steam swirled back, concealing it.

"Atrus!"

He turned, looking up at Anna, high above him, silhouetted against the crater's lip.

"Come up! Come up here now!"

Atrus frowned. "But my battery . . ."

"Now!"

Walking back, she was unnaturally silent. Then, suddenly, she stopped and turned to face him.

"Atrus, what did you see?"

"I saw . . ." He hesitated, surprised by her question.

"Atrus. Answer me. What did you *see?*"

"My battery. My battery was charged."

She let out her breath. "And was that all?"

"There was steam. Lots of steam." He frowned, then. "My battery. I've got to get my battery."

He made to turn back, but she placed a hand gently on his arm. "Forget the battery. It's too dangerous. Now come, let's clean you up."

4

THE MOON WAS BARELY UP WHEN, making sure not to wake his grandmother, Atrus crept out. Taking a rope and the large piece of sack from the storeroom, he ventured out onto the volcano's slope.

Halfway up the slope he paused, feeling a renewed sense of shock at the altered shape of the caldera's rim. That physical change seemed somehow linked to another, deeper change within himself.

Atrus stood at the rim, looking down the loose path that hugged the volcano's inner slope. Staring down into that darkness he experienced a sense of threat he'd not felt before.

He climbed over the rim, moving down into the darkness, disconcerted by the unfamiliar rumbling that emanated from the depths below. A tiny shiver ran up his spine, stirring the hairs at the back of his neck.

Out on the volcano's floor it was strangely warm and humid. Atrus looked about him, then slowly made his way across, his heart pounding, his eyes searching the nearest outcrops of rock. Steam swirled and hissed, wreathing those shapes, transforming them in the moon's fine, silvered light.

The battery was where he left it. For a moment he

crouched over it, his left hand resting loosely on it familiar casing. But his eyes were drawn to the tunnel mouth. Compelled, he walked across.

Then, taking the tinderbox from his inner pocke he pressed the catch and stepped inside.

In the glowing light from the tinder he could se how the tunnel stretched away into the darkness, slop ing gradually, like a giant wormhole cutting throug the solid rock. It was cool there. Surprisingly so. As a breeze was blowing from within the tunnel.

He walked on, counting his steps. At fifty paces h stopped and turned, looking back at the way he'd com From where he stood he could not see the entrance. Th curve of the tunnel obscured it from sight.

He walked on, as if in some kind of spell, com pelled to see where this led.

The smell of sulfur was far less strong than it ha been. Other, stranger smells filled the air. Musty, unfa miliar smells.

Atrus turned and went over to the wall, placing h palm against it. It was cool and smooth and dry. H was about to move away when some irregularity farthe down the wall drew his attention. He walked over to holding up the tinder, then stopped. Facing him a si gle word had been cut into the wall—a huge thing ha his own height and twice his breadth.

D'ni! There was no mistaking it. It was a D'ni word!

Atrus stared at it, not recognizing it, but committi it to memory.

Until now, he had only half-believed the things his grandmother had told him. There were days, indeed, when he had imagined that she had made the books on her shelves herself, in the same way she seemed to conjure her paintings from the air, or turn a piece of unformed rock into an exquisitely carved figure.

Such thoughts had disturbed him, for he had never known his grandmother to lie. Yet the tales were so strange, so fantastic, that he found it hard to believe that such things had ever really happened.

Atrus began to back away, to head back for the entrance, but as he did he almost slipped on something beneath his feet. It rolled away from him, beginning to glow, softly at first, then brightly, its warm red light filling the tunnel.

He went across and crouched beside it, putting his hand out tentatively to see if it were hot. Satisfied it was cool, he picked it up, holding it between his thumb and forefinger to study it.

It was a small, perfectly rounded rock—a marble of some kind. He had collected rocks and crystals for almost ten years now, but he had never seen its like. He cupped it in his right hand, surprised by its lack of warmth.

Dousing the tinder, he slipped it into his pocket, then straightened up, holding the marble out and looking to see if there were any others, but several minutes' search revealed no more.

Then, knowing that time was pressing, he turned

and hurried out, meaning to raise the battery before Anna woke and wondered where he was.

It took almost an hour for him to drag the battery back up to the rim. Anna came and helped him the last thirty feet or so, standing on the lip above him, straining on the rope, while he knelt and pushed the battery from below.

In silence they carried it down the slope to the cleft.

Anna disappeared over the cleftwall, returning a moment later with a bowl of water. Atrus sat, staring at his hands where they lay folded in his lap, waiting for her to chastise him for disobeying her, but she was silent still.

"It was my fault," he said finally, glancing at her, wondering why she had said nothing. "I wanted to put things right."

Expressionless, she handed him the bowl. "Drink that, then come. I'll make you breakfast. I think it time I told you a story."

Atrus had been sitting on the ledge beside the kitchen window, the empty bowl beside him as he listened, fascinated, to his grandmother's tale.

He had heard all kinds of tales from her across the years, but this was different; different because, unlike the others, there were no great deeds of heroism, no man to match the hour. Yet, finishing her tale, Anna's voice shook with emotion.

" . . . and so, when Veovis finally returned, the fate of the D'ni was sealed. Within a day the great work of millennia was undone and the great caverns of the D'ni emptied of life. And all because of Ti'ana's misjudgment."

Atrus was silent a while, then he looked up at Anna. "So you blame Ti'ana, then?"

She nodded.

"But she couldn't have known, surely? Besides, she did what she thought best."

"To salve her own conscience, maybe. But was it best for the D'ni? There were others who wanted Veovis put to death after the first revolt. If their voices had been listened to . . . if only Ti'ana had not spoken so eloquently to the Great Council . . ."

Anna fell silent again, her head lowered.

Atrus frowned, then shook his head. "I didn't know . . ."

"No . . ." Anna stared a moment longer at her hands, then looked to him and smiled. "Nor does it really matter now. All that is in the past. The D'ni are no more. Only the tales remain."

He took the still-glowing marble from his pocket and held it out to her. "I found it on the floor of the volcano."

At the sight of the marble her whole countenance changed. "*Where* did you say you found it?"

"In the volcano," he said, his voice less certain than before. "Near where the battery had fallen."

She stared back at him. "In the tunnel?"

"Yes."

Slowly Anna reached out and took the fire marble from his hand, holding it up, she dropped it suddenly into the bowl of water at her side. Instantly it was extinguished.

"You must not go there again, Atrus. It's very dangerous down there."

"But grandmother . . ."

She stared at him, her normally gentle face harder than he had ever seen it. "You must not go there again, Atrus. You're not ready yet. Promise me, Atrus, please."

"I promise."

"Good," she said, more softly, reaching out to rest her hand upon his shoulder.

Each afternoon, as the sun began to descend and the shadows spread across the foot of the cleft, Anna and Atrus would sit in the cool shade on the low stone ledge beside the pool and talk.

Today, Atrus had brought his journal out and sat there, the ink pot beside him on the ledge, copying out the word Anna had drawn on a loose sheet. For a while he was silent, concentrating, his keen eyes flicking from Anna's drawing to his own, checking he had the complex figure right. Then he looked up.

"Grandmother?"

Anna, who was sitting back with her head against the cool stone wall, her eyes closed, answered him quietly. "Yes, Atrus?"

"I still don't understand. You say there's no English equivalent to this word. But I can't see why that should be. Surely they had the same things as us?"

She opened her eyes and sat forward, stretching out her bare, brown toes, then, placing her hands on her knees, she looked at him.

"Words aren't just words, Atrus. Words are . . . well, let me see if I can explain it simply. At the simplest level a word can be a label. Tree. Sand. Rock. When we use such words, we know roughly what is meant by them. We can see them in our mind's eye. Oh, what precise *kind* of tree, or sand or rock, for that we need further words—words which, in their turn, are also labels. A large tree. Or, maybe, a palm tree. Red sand. Or, maybe, fine sand. Jagged rocks. Or, maybe, limestone rocks. The first word alters our sense of that second word in a fairly precise manner. At another level, words can represent ideas. Love. Intelligence. Loyalty. These, as I'm sure you see at once, aren't quite so simple. We can't simply add an extra word to clarify what we mean, particularly when the ideas aren't simple ones. To get to the real meaning of such concepts we need to define them in several ways. Love, for instance, might be mixed with pride and hope, or, perhaps, with jealousy and fear. Intelligence, likewise, might refer to the unthinking, instinctive intelligence of an ant, or the deeper, more emotionally rooted intelligence of a man. And even within men, intelligence takes on many separate forms—it can be slow and deep, or quick and sparkling. And loyalty . . . loyalty can be the blind loyalty of a soldier to his commander, or the stubborn loyalty of a wife to a man who has wronged her. Or . . ."

She saw he was smiling. "What is it?"

He handed her the loose sheet back. "I think I see. At least, I think I know what you were going to say."

Anna found herself grinning, pleased, as ever, by his quickness, his perceptiveness. Atrus rarely needed to be told a thing twice, and often, as now, he was way ahead of her.

"Go on," she said.

Atrus hesitated, tilting his head slightly, as he always did when he was thinking. Then, choosing his words carefully, he began. "Well, just as those words that describe ideas are a level above the words that are simple descriptive labels, so there's a farther, more complex level above that. One which this D'ni word functions on."

"Yes, and?"

"I see that, but . . ." He frowned, then shook his head. "What I can't see is what could be more complex than ideas. I can't picture in my head what that higher level might be."

"And that's precisely why there is no English equivalent for this."

"Yes, but . . . what does it *mean?*"

"This word—this particular D'ni word—is to do with the circulation of the air. With wind patterns and humidity."

Atrus stared at her now, his brow knitted. "But . . . but surely such a word would be a label?"

"No. Not this word. This word does more than simply describe."

"Then . . ." But he clearly could not see what she was driving at. He looked to her, his pale eyes pleading for an explanation.

Anna laughed. "You must just accept that there is such a level, Atrus."

"But you said . . ."

"I know what I said, and I still mean it. You must question everything and find the truth in it. But this once you must simply accept what I'm telling you. There is something beyond labels and ideas. Something which is a synthesis of the two. Something the D'ni discovered many, many years ago, and learned to put into words. One day you will understand more clearly, but for now . . ."

She could see Atrus was unhappy with that. He had been taught to question everything. To look with his own eyes, and quantify, and check. He had been taught never to accept things simply because he had been told they were true. And now . . . well, now she was asking him to break the habit of his thought.

I should not have had him draw that word, she thought, wondering at the instinct which had made her do it. *He is not yet ready for the Garo-hevtee.* Yet generally she trusted her instincts. Generally they were proved right.

As he looked away, she could see how he was still struggling with the notion of how an idea could also be a label, how something so general could yet be specific and descriptive, and part of her wanted to put him out of his misery and tell him. But he wasn't ready yet.

Anna stood and stretched, then looked about her at the orderliness of the cleft. Sometimes, in her imaginings, she thought of the cleft and of her grandson's mind in much the same vein, as if the one were a metaphor for the other. Yet at that moment she understood the inadequacy of the comparison, for just as one day he would outgrow this tiny living space and venture out into the world, so his thoughts and speculations were certain one day to outgrow her careful nurturing of them.

Looking at him, she knew he was destined to be greater than herself. Wiser, more formidable of mind. Yet the thought did not scare her or make her envious. If anything, it made her sad, for she got great pleasure from teaching him, and to think of losing that . . .

Anna sighed, then, picking her way carefully across the cleft, mounted the steps. It was time to make supper.

A full month passed and as the moon came round to full once more, Atrus made his way idly up the slope, whistling to himself—one of the songs Anna had taught him as a child: a D'ni song that had the simplest of tunes. And as he whistled, he heard Anna's voice in his head, softly singing the refrain.

As he came to the end of it he looked up, and stopped dead, staring openmouthed at the sight that met his eyes.

Ahead of him, the whole of the upper slope was wreathed in a thick cloud of brilliantly white vapor, as if a thick curtain had suddenly been dropped over the volcano's edge. The mist slowly roiled, like the steam on the surface of a cooking pot, neither advancing nor retreating, yet turning in upon itself constantly.

It was so strange, so unlike anything Atrus had ever seen, that he stepped back, suddenly afraid. And as he did, a man stepped from within that glistening whiteness, seeming for a moment almost to be a part of it; a tall, unearthly figure with a large forehead and a strong, straight nose, over the bridge of which were strapped a pair of glasses identical to Atrus's own. A white cloak flapped out behind the stranger, giving him the appearance of some great mythical king.

Rooted to the spot, Atrus watched the stranger walk down the slope toward him, his fear transformed to awe by the strength and energy, the controlled power and cold assurance of the creature who approached.

Atrus staggered back, astonished. Above him, the figure stopped and, lifting the thick lenses that covered his eyes, squinted down at Atrus.

"I see you have my glasses."

Atrus stared, unable to answer. The man who stood above him was as pale as the moon, his hair as white as bleached marble, and the irises of his eyes were huge, a thin circle of pale green about them. His cheekbones were finely chiseled and yet strong, his hands both delicate and powerful. Everything about him—from the cut of his clothes to his aristocratic demeanor—spoke of an innate strength allied to an effortless elegance. He seemed old, certainly, but in a timeless way that reminded Atrus of his grandmother.

He stared back at Atrus, as an eagle stares, then spoke again. "Well, boy? Have you no greeting for your father?"

"My . . ." Recognition hit Atrus like a physical blow. He shook his head. "I . . ."

"What's your name?"

"Atrus . . ."

"Atrus . . . of course . . ." The man stretched out a hand

and placed it on Atrus's head, the contact like an electric shock. "And I am Gehn, son of Atrus."

Atrus swallowed. He was dreaming. For certain he was dreaming. Nervously he touched his tongue against his upper lip, feeling the hard, salty shape of a grit of sand.

No. Not a dream.

"Gehn," Atrus said softly, echoing the word.

The stranger nodded, then removed his hand. "Good. Now go and inform your grandmother that she has a visitor."

Atrus ran down the moonlit slope, calling to Anna loudly as he ran, the dust flying up behind him. As he came to the cleftwall, he almost vaulted it, forgetting to remove his sandals.

"Grandmother! Grandmother!"

Her head poked from the kitchen window, startled. "What's happened?"

Atrus stood on the swaying bridge, breathless, gasping his answer. "A stranger's come! He sent me on ahead!"

Anna's mouth fell open. "Gehn . . ." she said, almost whispering the word. Then, collecting herself, she ducked back inside. There was the sound of a metal bowl falling against the stone floor, and then the outside door flew open. Barefoot, she hurried down the steps that hugged the wall, her haste surprising Atrus.

"Grandmother?"

But she barely seemed to heed him as she circled the narrow rim of the inner wall and began to climb the rung ladder.

Atrus turned, watching as she clambered up onto the cleftwall, even as the stranger with the ash-white hair, the man who called himself his father, strode across and stopped, barely ten feet from the cleft.

"Mother?" he asked quietly, tilting his head slightly.

"Gehn," she said once more, hesitating. Then she stepped closer, hugging him tightly. "Where have you been, my son? Why in the Maker's name did you not come back?"

But Atrus, watching, noticed how the warmth of her embrace was not reciprocated, how lightly the stranger's hands touched her shoulders, how distant he was as he stepped back from her, like a great lord from one of the tales.

"I came to see the child," he said, as if he'd not heard her. "I came to see my son."

Atrus lay sprawled out on his belly on top of the cleftwall, staring across at the shadowed rectangle of the kitchen, and at the bright square of the window in which Anna and the newcomer were framed. Though the two had been talking for some while now, little of real importance had been said. Even so, there was a strange tension between them. Anna, particularly, seemed to be walking on eggshells, afraid to say too much, yet keen to know where Gehn had been and what he had done. By comparison, Gehn was relatively taciturn, ignoring her questions when it suited him not to answer them.

Just now, Gehn was sitting on the polished stone ledge, to the right of the tiny galley kitchen, beside the door, his booted feet spread wide, his long, delicate hands resting on his knees, as he looked up at Anna. He had removed his cloak. Beneath it he wore a close-cut suit of midnight blue, the jacket edged with scarlet and decorated with a pattern of repeated symbols in red and green and yellow. It was so rich, so marvelous, Atrus could barely keep his eyes from it. But there were other fantastic things to be seen, not least of which was the pipe that lay beside him on the ledge.

The bottom of the pipe was a hollowed wooden bowl, from which a shaped glass stock, trimmed with silver, led to a curved copper mouthpiece. A tiny domed cap was set into the bowl in front of the stock, while at the center of the bowl, feeding into the glass of the stock, was a thick silver spindle.

As Atrus watched, Gehn took a tiny glass sphere from a pouch in the thick leather belt he wore. Turning it upside down, Gehn shook it gently, revealing a clear liquid that moved slowly, glutinously, its surface reflecting the yellow lamplight like oil.

Resting the sphere on his knees, Gehn unscrewed the lid to the spindle and set it aside, then poured a tiny amount of the liquid into the stock and replaced the lid. Then, taking a small leather bag from his jacket pocket, he took something from inside.

Atrus gasped. It looked like the marble he had found earlier. Gehn placed it within the domed cap.

Anna turned from where she stood and looked at Gehn. "Will you be staying long?"

Gehn glanced at her, then replaced the lid of the cap. "No. I have to leave tomorrow," he answered, his voice heavily accented.

"Ah . . ." There was regret in Anna's voice; hurt in those dark, familiar eyes. "It's just that . . . well, I thought you might stay with Atrus a while. Get to know him, perhaps. He's a good boy. You'd be proud of him. And after all . . ."

Gehn tightened the cap and looked up at her, his face expressionless. "I intend to take him with me."

Anna turned, facing him, shock in her face. "With you?"

Atrus, watching from the darkness, felt his pulse quicken, his mouth grow dry. His heart was thudding in his chest.

Gehn lifted the pipe, staring at it, then cupped it between his hands and pressed his thumb down on the silver spindle. There was a snapping sound and the pipe seemed to come alive, burning briefly with a fierce blue light. After a moment, that same light filled the whole of the stock, making the strange, oil-like liquid gently bubble.

In that strange, unearthly light, Gehn's face seemed very different, the shadows inverted.

"Yes," he answered, meeting Anna's eyes. "Have you a problem with that?"

"But Atrus belongs *here* . . ."

"*Here?*" There was incredulity in Gehn's voice. "And where is *here?* Nowhere, that is where. A hole in the ground, that's all this is. Yes, and that's all it will *ever* be. This is no place for a son of mine. No place at all."

Anna fell silent, watching Gehn as he lifted the copper mouthpiece to his mouth and inhaled, the muscles in her cheek twitching oddly. Then she spoke again, quieter than before, yet with a firmness Atrus recognized at once. "But he's not ready yet. He's too young. There's so much he has to learn . . ."

Taking the pipe from his mouth, Gehn interrupted her. "Of course Atrus is ready. Why, he is exactly the age I was when I first left here. And as for his education, that is the very reason I returned, so that I could teach him."

"*You?*"

Anna's tone was incredulous, yet Gehn seemed indifferent to her criticism. "Who better? I am, at least, educated to the task. And I *am* his father."

Gehn set the pipe down and leaned toward Anna, frowning. "You *did* tell him about me?"

She looked away, a tightness in her face.

Gehn stood, angry now. "You mean you told him *nothing?* Kerath damn you, woman! How *could* you?"

Anna kept her voice low, conscious of Atrus outside, listening. "And what was I to say? That his father left the very hour he was born? That he didn't even care enough to *name* him?"

"I would have called him Atrus. You know that."

She turned back, glaring at him, suddenly, explosively angry. "Yes, but you didn't! *I* did. Yes, and *I* raised him. *Me*, Gehn, not you. And now you want him back, as though he were a parcel you'd left with me for safekeeping! But boys aren't parcels, Gehn! They're living, growing things. And Atrus hasn't finished his growing."

"I shall decide that," he said gruffly. "Besides, he can help me with my studies. Be my assistant."

"Your assistant?"

"In my researches. I have need of a willing helper, and the boy seems willing enough."

"Researches into what?"

"Into the D'ni culture."

"The D'ni?" Anna laughed bitterly. "All that has gone. Don't you understand that yet?"

"No," he answered, drawing himself up, a note of pride entering his voice. "You are wrong. That is where I have been these past fourteen years. In D'ni. Researching, studying, seeking out the great and mighty secrets of the D'ni culture." He gave a single, dignified nod. "I tell you, none of it was lost. It is still all there."

Atrus, watching, felt a shiver go down his spine, a tiny ripple of disbelief making him feel, for that instant, that he was in a dream.

Still there? But that was impossible, surely?

Anna shook her head dismissively. "No, Gehn. You forget. I've seen it with these eyes. It's gone. Destroyed. Can't you accept that? Can't you forget the past?"

Gehn stared back at her coldly, imperiously, accepting nothing. "Oh, I can easily believe that *you* would like to forget it!"

She stared back at him silently.

"You never valued it, did you?" he continued, not sparing her. "You never cared for it the way *I* cared. But I am not having that for my son. I want him to know about his past. I want him to be proud of it, the way *I* am proud of it." He bristled with indignation. "I shall not betray *him* the way you betrayed *me!*"

"Gehn! How can you say that? I did my best for you!"

"Your *best?* And how good *was* your best? This hole in the ground you call a home? Is *this* your best?"

Anna looked away. "Atrus should decide. You can't just take him."

Gehn leaned right in to her, his face only inches from her own. "Of course I can. I am the boy's father. It is my right."

"Then let me come with you. Let me look after the boy while you are teaching him."

Gehn shook his head. "That would not be right. It would not be the D'ni way. Or do you forget that also? Do you forget how you gave me up to the Guild when I was but four years old."

"But . . ."

His voice overrode hers harshly. "But nothing. He is coming with me and that is that. If you wish to help, you might pack a knapsack for him for the journey. Not that he'll need much."

"But Gehn . . ." She reached out to touch his arm, but he pulled away from her. Turning, Gehn reached down and picked up his pipe, then, tugging open the door, he stepped out, into the open air.

For a moment he stood there, turned away from where Atrus lay, drawing on his pipe, the light from the kitchen making a silhouette of him, then he turned back, his chest and arms and face revealed in the faint blue glow of the pipe.

"Atrus?" he said, speaking to the boy where he lay on his belly on the cleftwall. "Go to bed now and get some sleep. We shall be leaving early in the morning."

5

CROUCHING BESIDE HIS MOTHER'S grave, Atrus leaned across and, careful not to disturb the earth, plucked one of the delicate blue flowers. Placing it in the journal he had open on his knee, he closed the book gently, then slipped it into the small leather knapsack at his side.

For a moment he simply stared, taking in the sight. In the half-light he could not discern their proper color, yet he had only to close his eyes and he could see the flowers in the sunlight, like a quilt of lilac lain on that bed of rich, dark earth.

Goodbye, he said silently.

To be truthful, Atrus did not really know what to feel. Excitement? Certainly, the prospect of traveling—of seeing D'ni—thrilled him, yet the thought of leaving here, of leaving Anna, frightened him. Too much had happened far too quickly. He felt torn.

"Atrus! Come now. We must go."

He turned, looking across at the figure silhouetted against the dawn light at the far end of the cleftwall, and nodded.

Anna was waiting for him close by. Embracing her, he felt a kind of panic, a fear of not seeing her again, well up in him. She must have sensed it, for, squeezing him tightly, she then moved back, away from him, holding his upper arms and smiling at him.

"Don't worry now," she said softly. "I'll be all right. The store's full and what with all those improvements you've made for me, I'll not know what to do with myself half the time."

Her kind face lit with a smile. "Besides, your father has promised me he'll bring you back three months from now to visit."

"Three months?" the news cheered him immensely.

"Yes, so you must not worry."

She reached down, then handed him his pack. He had watched her earlier, selecting various items from their meager store and placing them into the pack for his journey, including all of the tiny cakes she had cooked only the previous day. Atrus stared at the pack, his fingers brushing lightly against its brightly embroidered cloth, moved by the simple care she took over everything, knowing he would miss that.

"Now listen to me, Atrus."

Atrus looked up, surprised by how serious her voice suddenly was. "Yes, grandmother?"

Her dark, intelligent eyes searched his. "You must remember what you have learned here, Atrus. I have tried to teach you the mechanics of the earth and stars; the ways of science and the workings of nature. I have tried to teach you what is good and what is to be valued, truths which cannot be shaken or changed. This knowledge is from the Maker. Take it with you and weigh everything your father teaches you against it."

Anna paused, then leaned in toward him slightly, lowering her voice. "I no longer know him, but I know you, Atrus. Measure your own deeds against the truths I have taught you. If you act for self-gain then no good can come of it. If you act selflessly, then you act well for all and you must not be afraid."

Anna moved back, smiling once more. "The journey down will be long and hard but I want you to be brave, Atrus. More than that, I want you to be truthful. To be a better son to your father than fate allowed him to be with his."

"I don't understand . . ." he began, but she shook her head, as if it didn't matter.

"Do what your father asks. But most of all, Atrus, do not violate what is in your nature. You understand me?"

"I think so, grandmother."

"Then I have no fears for you."

He embraced her again, gripping her tightly and kissing her neck. Then, turning from her, he climbed the steps and crossed the rope bridge.

At the cleftwall he turned, looking back at her, his eyes briefly taking in the familiar sights of the cleft, its shape like a scar in his memory. Anna had climbed the steps and now stood on the narrow balcony outside her room. Lifting an arm, she waved.

"Take care on your journey down. I'll see you in three months."

Atrus waved back, then, heaving a deep sigh, turned and jumped down from the wall, following his father up the slope of the volcano.

They were in the tunnel.

"Father?"

Gehn turned and, holding the lantern high, looked back down the tunnel at Atrus. "What is it, boy?"

Atrus lifted his own lamp and pointed at the D'ni symbol carved into the wall; the symbol he had seen that morning after the experiment. "This sign, father. What does it mean?"

Gehn motioned to him impatiently. "Come on now, Atrus. Catch up. We've wasted enough time as it is. There will be occasion for such things later."

Atrus stared at the intricate symbol a moment longer, then, hiding his disappointment, turned away, hurrying to catch up with his father.

"We need to make up time," Gehn said, as Atrus came alongside. "The journey is a long one and I have several experiments in progress. I must be back in time to see how they have developed."

"Experiments?" Atrus asked, excited by the sound of it. "What kind of experiments?"

"Important ones," Gehn answered, as if that were

sufficient to satisfy his son's curiosity. "Now hurry. There will be time to talk when we reach the first of the eder tomahn."

Atrus looked up at his father. "Eder tomahn?"

Gehn glanced at his son as he strode on. "The eder tomahn are way stations. Rest houses, you might term them. In the days of the late empire there were plans to have commerce with the world of men. Such plans, fortunately, did not come to pass, yet the paths were forged through the earth and rest houses prepared for those D'ni messengers who would venture out."

Atrus looked back at his father, astonished. "And this tunnel? Is this D'ni?"

Gehn shook his head. "No. This is simply a lava tube. Thousands of years ago, when the volcano was still active, hot lava ran through this channel, carving a passage to the surface."

Again Atrus felt a surge of disappointment. The walls of the tunnel had been so smooth, its shape so perfectly round, he had been sure it must have been the product of D'ni construction.

"Yes," Gehn continued, "but you will see things before our journey's done that will make you forget this tiny wormhole. Now, come over to the left, Atrus, and get behind me. The tunnel slopes steeply just ahead."

Atrus did as he was told, keeping close behind his father, careful not to slip, his left hand keeping his balance against the curved wall of the lava tube, his sandaled feet gripping the hard, dry floor. All went well until, by chance, he turned and looked back up the tunnel. Then, with a sudden rush of understanding, he realized where he was. The darkness behind him seemed suddenly oppressive. Who knew what waited back there beyond the lantern's glow?

He turned back, realizing just how dependent on his father he was. If he were to lose himself down here . . .

Ahead of him Gehn had stopped. "Slowly now," he said, looking back at Atrus. "It ends just here. Now we go down The Well."

Atrus blinked, seeing how the tunnel ended in a perfect circle up ahead. Beyond it was simple blackness. He went out and stood beside his father on the narrow crescent-shaped ledge, overwhelmed by the sight that met his eyes.

In front of them lay a giant oval of blackness—a chasm so huge it seemed you could drop a whole volcano into it.

The Well.

Gehn raised his lamp, letting its light glint wetly off the far wall of the great shaft, revealing the massive striations of the rock, then pointed to his left.

"Just there. See, Atrus? See the steps?"

Atrus saw them, cut like the thread of a screw into the uneven sides of the great hole, but the thought of using them, of descending that vast shaft by their means, frightened him.

Gehn looked to him. "Would you like to go first, Atrus, or shall I?"

Atrus swallowed, then spoke, keeping the fear from his voice. "You'd better. You know the way."

"Yes," Gehn said, giving his son a knowing smile. "I do, don't I?"

For the first hundred steps or so, the steps passed through a narrow tunnel cut into the edge of the chasm with only a thin gap low down by the floor to the right, but then, suddenly, the right-hand wall seemed to melt away and Atrus found himself out in the open, staring down into that massive well of darkness. Startled by the sight, he stumbled and his right sandal came away, toppling over the edge and into the darkness.

He stood there a moment, gasping, his back against the wall, trying to regain his nerve. But suddenly he found himself obsessed with the idea of falling into that darkness; and not just falling, but deliberately throwing himself. The urge was so strange and overpowering it made the hairs at the back of his neck stand on end.

Below him, almost directly opposite him across the great shaft, Gehn continued his descent, unaware, it seemed, of the immense danger, stepping lightly, almost effortlessly, down the spiral, his lamplight casting flickering shadows on the groined and striated rock, before he vanished inside another of the narrow tunnels.

I must go on, Atrus told himself, freeing his left foot from the sandal; yet the fear he felt froze his muscles. It was like a dream, an evil dream. Even so, he forced himself to move, taking first one step and then another, each step an effort of sheer will.

If I fall I die. If I fall . . .

His father's voice echoed across that vast open space. "Atrus?"

He stopped, his shoulder pressed against the wall, and closed his eyes. "Y. . .yes, father?"

"Do you want me to come back to you? Would you like me to hold your hand, perhaps?"

He wanted to say yes, but something in Gehn's voice, the faintest tone of criticism, stopped him. He opened his eyes again and, steeling himself, answered. "No . . . I'll be all right."

"Good. But not so slow, eh? We cannot spend too much time here. Not if I am to be back in time."

Controlling his fear, Atrus began to descend once more.

Imagine you're inside a tree, he told himself. *Imagine it.*

And suddenly he could see it vividly, as if it were an illustration in one of his grandmother's books. He could picture it in the brilliant sunlight, its branches stretching from horizon to horizon, a tiny crescent moon snagged among its massive leaves. Why, even the blades of grass about its trunk were several times the height of a man!

Halfway down, there was a depression in the side of the shaft—a kind of cave. Whether it was natural or D'ni-made, Atrus couldn't tell, but Gehn was waiting for him there, sitting on a carved stone ledge, calmly smoking his pipe.

"Are you all right, Atrus?" he asked casually.

"I'm fine now," Atrus answered genuinely. "There was a moment . . ."

He fell silent, seeing that his father wasn't listening. Gehn had taken out a tiny notebook with a tanned leather cover and was studying it as he smoked. Atrus glimpsed a diagram of paths and tunnels.

With a tiny grunt, Gehn closed the book and pocketed it again, then looked up at Atrus.

"You go ahead. I'll finish my pipe, then catch up with you."

It was several hours hard walking through a labyrinth of twisting tunnels before they finally came to the eder tomahn. The D'ni way station was built into a recess of a large cave, its black, perfectly finished marble in stark contrast to the cave's natural limestone. Atrus walked over to it and, holding up the lantern, ran his fingers across the satin-smooth surface, marveling at the lack of evident joints between the blocks, the way his own image was reflected back to him in the stone. It was as though the stone had been baked like melted tar, then set and polished like a mirror.

Real, Atrus thought, amazed by it.

Gehn meanwhile had walked across to face the door, which was deeply recessed into the stone. Reaching into the neck of his tunic, he drew out a magnificent golden chain which, until that moment, had been hidden from sight. On the end of it was a bevel-edged key, a thick, black thing streaked with red. Placing this to one of the matching shapes recessed into the door, Gehn pushed until it clicked. There was a moment's silence, then a strange clunk-clunk-clunk and the sound of a metal grating sliding back.

He removed the key and stepped back. As he did, the door slid into the stone, revealing a dimly lit interior.

Gehn stepped inside. Atrus, following, stopped just inside the room, surprised at how big it was. There were low, utility bunks to either side of the dormitory-sized room and a door at the end led through to what Atrus assumed was either a kitchen or a washroom of some kind. He looked to his father.

"Why are we stopping?"

To his surprise, Gehn yawned. "Because the hour is late," he answered. "And because I am tired."

"But I thought . . ."

Gehn raised his hand, as if to stop any further argument. Then, turning, he gestured toward a large knapsack that rested on the bunk in the right-hand corner.

"That is yours," Gehn said unceremoniously. "You can change now or later, it is entirely up to you."

Atrus went across and, unfastening the leather buckle, looked inside. Frowning, he tipped the bag up, spilling its contents onto the mattress.

Standing back, he gave a little laugh, surprised, then turned, looking to Gehn, who was sitting on the edge of one of the facing bunks, pulling off his boots.

"Thank you," he said. "I'll change later, if that's all right."

Gehn grunted. "Do as you will, lad. But I would not sleep in the boots if I were you. I don't know if they fit. I had to guess at the size."

Atrus turned back, gently brushing one of the boots with his fingertips, then lifted it, cradling it, sniffing in its rich, deep smell. It was strangely beautiful. Studying it, he could see that it had never been worn before.

Beside the knee-length boots, there was a cloak—a smaller version of his father's, a black shirt with a strange book symbol on it, a skull-shaped hat made of some kind of metal that seemed soft unless you really pressed it hard, and a small leather-and-metal pouch.

Atrus squatted on the edge of the bed to examine this last, untying the drawstring and peering inside. For a moment he didn't understand, then with a gasp of delight, he poured a number of the tiny objects out into his palm.

Fire-marbles! It was a whole pouch of fire-marbles! Why, there must have been fifty, sixty of them!

He looked to his father, meaning to thank him again, but Gehn was sprawled out on his back, fast asleep.

Going across, Atrus stood there a moment, staring down at his father. In sleep he could see the similarities to Anna, in the shape of Gehn's chin and mouth particularly. Both had striking, noble faces. Both had that same mixture of strength and delicacy in their features. Yes, now that he had the chance to really look he could see that it was only the pallor of Gehn's skin, the ash whiteness of his hair that made him seem so different. That and the dignified austerity of his manner.

Noticing that Gehn had removed only one of his boots, Atrus gently eased the other boot off and set the two side by side at the head of the bunk. Then, taking the cover from the adjacent bunk, he spread it out over his father.

He was about to move away, when something drew his attention. Reaching down, he picked up the pipe from where it had fallen. For a moment he held it up, studying the engravings that covered the silver bands about the stock, astonished by the detail of the work. Curious, he placed the spout beneath his nose and sniffed. It had a strange, sweet scent; the same as that he had noticed on his father's breath.

With a sigh, Atrus placed the pipe beside the boots, then went back across, sitting there a while, his fingers idly sorting the fire-marbles, noting the variations of color and size. Then, putting them away, he set the pouch down on the floor beside the bunk and stretched out, his hands behind his head. He was asleep in an instant.

He woke to find Gehn shaking him.

"Come on, lad. We have a long journey ahead of us today. Get changed and we shall be off."

Atrus sat up slowly, wondering where he was, surprised not to find himself on the ledge in his own room, his mattress beneath him, the smell of his grandmother's cooking in the air.

Knuckling his eyes, he put his feet round onto the floor, struck at once by how cold it was, how damp the air.

Feeling sluggish and despondent Atrus stood, beginning to dress, the texture and smell of the new clothes—their smooth softness after the roughness of his own garments—making him feel strange. Pulling on the boots, he felt extremely odd, transformed almost, as if the change went deeper than the surface of appearance.

Atrus looked about him, as if at any moment he

might wake, but he could not delude himself: he w
awake, and he was traveling with his father, down int
the depths of the earth.

That thought now thrilled him. He looked t
Gehn. "Will we reach D'ni today, father?"

"No. Not today."

Disappointed, Atrus turned back, beginning t
pack away his surface clothes, but Gehn, seeing what h
was doing, came across and pulled them from the pacl
throwing them to the floor. "You will not need tho
rags now, Atrus. You are D'ni now. You shall wear on
D'ni clothes henceforth."

Atrus stared at the discarded clothes, reluctant t
part with them. They were a link to the past, to Ann
and the cleft. To leave them here seemed . . . impossibl

"Well, boy? What are you waiting for?"

Atrus looked up, stung by the sharpness in h
father's voice, then, remembering his promise to Ann
bowed his head obediently. Slipping his own bag in
the knapsack, he packed the pouch of fire-marbles a
the strange protective hat.

"Good," Gehn said, nodding decisively as l
heaved his knapsack up onto his shoulders. "We sh
eat as we go along."

Atrus blinked, wondering just what his father h
in mind, but it was clear Gehn was in no mood f
explanations. Buckling his own knapsack, Atrus thre
it over his shoulder, then followed his father out.

They went down through an ant's nest of damp, narrow tunnels that, from time to time, would open out into small caverns before running on into the rock.

At the bottom of a particularly steep and narrow tunnel, they emerged into the largest cavern they had yet encountered. The ceiling was forty, maybe fifty feet above them, while the light from their lanterns revealed only the nearer end of the tunnel, the far end being obscured in darkness. Ahead and to their left a long pool hugged the rock, while to the right the way was made difficult by a jumbled slope of small boulders.

Stopping, Gehn removed his pack and took out what looked to Atrus like some sort of pot or caddy. Setting it down, he then took out his hat and, turning to Atrus, gestured that he should do the same.

"The way gets difficult from here," he said. "You'll be grateful for those boots before long."

But Atrus wasn't so sure. The boots might look beautiful and smell wonderful, but already both of his heels and the outside of the big toe on his right foot were beginning to rub uncomfortably.

Taking his knapsack off, he found the D'ni helmet and strapped it on, then looked to his father. Gehn shrugged on his pack, then, reaching down, picked up the "pot."

"Come on," he said, turning to smile at Atrus. "I think you might like this next part."

Atrus nodded, then reached down to retrieve his pack. As he did, the whole of the cave in front of him lit up as if a breach had suddenly been made in the roof and the sunlight had rushed in. He looked up, startled, seeing at once that the brilliant light emanated from the "pot," a broad and powerful beam spreading to fill the far end of the cavern, revealing a sight so amazing that Atrus blinked and rubbed the backs of his hands over his eyes.

It was like a waterfall of crystal, cascading from the ceiling to the floor, its melted, flowing forms unlike anything Atrus had ever seen.

"What is it?" Atrus asked, a note of pure awe in his voice as he followed his father up onto that great pile of rocks, his eyes drawn constantly to the glistening, crystalline curtain.

"It's called dripstone," Gehn answered matter-of-factly, moving the beam of the torch across the frozen face of it. "It's formed by mineral deposits in the water leaking through the roof of the cavern, building up over thousands upon thousands of years. Such deposits take many forms—flowstone and dripstone, stalactites and stalagmites, shelfstone and helictites. Some are as delicate as lace, others as brutal as the rock itself." Gehn laughed. "Never fear, Atrus. You will see many such wonders in the next few hours."

As they came close, Atrus stopped, staring open

mouthed at the sight. He would never have guessed, ever in a thousand years—but Gehn was already moving on, down the slope toward the entrance to another tunnel. Taking one last look, Atrus turned, then clambered down the rock, hurrying to catch up.

Gehn had not been wrong. In the hours that followed Atrus saw a dozen such splendors—caves filled with long, delicate columns no thicker than his arm, jutting like an inverted crystal forest from the ceiling, or huge but delicately ridged candles, endless fringes of tiny, frozen fingers dripping from them, melting into the liquid rock. At the same time, however, his boots began to chafe him badly. Discomfort became soreness, which in turn became pain, such that, after a while, Atrus could not take a single step without wincing.

When, finally, they stopped, in a long, low cave that was edged with shallow pools, the first thing he did was to remove one of his boots.

Gehn came across and knelt beside him. "Show me."

Gingerly, he let Gehn take his foot by the ankle and study it. The skin had rubbed away in three separate places. Blood streaked his heel and between his toes.

Gehn looked up at him soberly, as if to judge his reaction. "I have some ointment in my pack. It ought to alleviate your discomfort."

Atrus quickly applied the cream and bandaged his feet, then pulled on his boots again.

"Good," Gehn said, pleased with him. "Then let us proceed. The path begins just ahead of us."

Atrus stood slowly, flexing his toes within the bandages. "The path?"

"Into D'ni," Gehn said, slipping his pack back on.

The words raised Atrus's spirits, making him momentarily forget his injuries.

D'ni! he thought, his mind filled with a dozen colorful images from the tales his grandmother had told him over the years. *D'ni!*

Atrus stared up at the elaborately decorated stone and metal arch that framed the entrance to the tunnel, then turned, looking to his father.

"Are we there?"

"No," Gehn answered, "but this is where the path begins."

Immediately beneath the great arch, the tunnel floor was smoothly paved, the floor covered in an intricate, abstract swirl of variously colored stones and metals that seemed to merge and melt and never repeat itself. The path ran arrow-straight into the tunnel, neither rising nor falling, in a manner that suggested it had been cut by the D'ni, not bored by natural forces.

Following Gehn, Atrus stepped beneath the arch

their booted feet clicking on the marbled floor, the sound echoed back and forth along the tunnel. He was limping now, trying not to put too much weight on his right foot, but he was determined not to complain.

When will we be there? he wanted to ask, bursting with the excitement he felt at the thought of finally seeing D'ni, but he could see how Gehn was lost in his thoughts and was loath to disturb him.

Partway down the tunnel the air seemed to change, to grow warmer, stuffier, and suddenly there was an old, familiar smell in his nostrils. Sulfur! It was the sharp, eye-stinging tang of sulfur.

Gehn turned and gestured to him. "You had best put your lenses on, lad."

Atrus did as he was told; then, feeling in his tunic pocket, he pulled out the one item of his clothing he had managed to save, the mask Anna had made for him, and tied it about his nose and mouth. Then, wincing, he hobbled after his father.

Slowly the tunnel grew brighter, warmer, the air stuffier. The tunnel ended abruptly in a sheer drop. Ahead the D'ni path ran on, smoothly, uninterrupted it seemed, on giant pillars of stone. Below it, no more than eighty feet beneath where Atrus stood, was a bubbling lake of lava, black at the edges, a fiery golden yellow at the center.

The heat was intense, the fumes almost suffocating. Gehn, he noted, now wore a mask about his mouth and nose, and for a moment he wondered what his father had meant to do, whether he'd meant him to venture out across that lake without any form of protection.

The thought disturbed him.

Gehn turned, beckoning him on. "Walk quickly," he said, "and don't pause for a moment. Things are much cooler on the other side."

Atrus hesitated, then followed his father out onto the bridge, the heat from the path immediately evident, even through the thick soles of his boots. Ten paces on and he was half-running, trying to keep his feet off the stingingly hot paving.

Ahead, he now realized, the bridge, which he'd thought continuous, was breached. A single span had collapsed, leaving a jagged gap, over which a narrow beam of D'ni stone had been laid.

He watched his father cross this narrow causeway effortlessly, without breaking stride, yet when he came to it Atrus found himself unable to go on.

Just below him the red hot surface seemed to slowly undulate, like some living thing, a great bubble of superheated air emerging every now and then to break the surface with a giant "glop," the air filled suddenly with steam and the stinging scent of sulfur.

Atrus was coughing now. His feet seemed to be burning and his chest felt fit to burst. If he did not cross the beam soon he would collapse.

"Come on!" Gehn urged from the other side. "Don't stop, boy! Get going again. You're almost there!"

His head was swimming now and he felt that any moment he would fall. And if he fell . . .

He took three paces out onto the beam, feeling its intense heat through the thick leather of his boots.

"Come on!" his father urged, but he could not move. It was as if he, too, had been turned to stone.

"*Come on!*"

The beam lurched under him and for a moment he thought he was going to fall, but some instinct took hold of him. As the narrow beam tilted, he jumped, his feet thudding against the stone on the other side.

His vision blurred. He couldn't breathe. Staggering, he took a step backward . . .

6

ATRUS WOKE IN A COOL, BRIGHTLY-
lit cavern, the air of which was fresh and sweet
after the air in the lava cavern. There was a blanket over
him and from close by he could hear the echoing drip
drip drip of water. Shivering, he sat up, wondering
where he was, and immediately saw his father, less than
thirty feet away, standing beside a pool, the surface of
which seemed to glow as if illuminated from below.

His feet and legs ached and his head still felt
strangely heavy, but otherwise he felt all right. Piecing
things together, he began to understand. He had
almost fallen from the bridge. His father must have
rescued him.

Thinking of it, he looked down, smiling. It was the
kind of thing Anna would have done. The same thing
he himself would have done had their positions been
reversed.

Atrus looked across again, trying to get the measure of this man—this stranger—who had come into
his life so suddenly and changed it. He was strange,
there was no doubting it, and his manner was abrupt
almost to the point of rudeness, but maybe there was
a reason for that. Maybe he was simply not used to
dealing with people: as unused to the idea of a "son"

as he, Atrus, was unused to the idea of a "father." If so, he should make allowances. Until they knew each other better. Until that tie of blood was also one of friendship.

This line of reasoning cheered him. Throwing off the blanket he got up and hobbled over to where his father stood, standing beside him silently, looking out across the strangely lit pool.

"What does that?" he asked, pointing to the water's surface.

Gehn turned. He had clearly been preoccupied with some matter. "Ah, Atrus . . . you're up."

"I . . . I guess I have to thank you."

Gehn shrugged, then looked back across the pond. "It's good to talk again," he said, pushing out his chin in a strange gesture. "It's been very isolated down here on my own. I've longed for a companion for a long time now. An intellectual companion, that is. When I knew you were alive . . . well," he turned. "To be honest with you, Atrus, I was surprised. I did not expect you to survive. But I was pleased. I thought we might get on. Eventually."

Atrus smiled shyly. "I hope so. I want to learn."

"Good. That is a healthy attitude to have." Then, "Are you up to traveling on? I have been pushing you, I realize, but there is good reason."

"I'll be okay," Atrus said, feeling a sudden warmth toward his father. "It's just so . . . strange."

Gehn stared at him thoughtfully. "Yes. I suppose it

must be, after the cleft. But the best of it lies ahead, Atrus. And I mean the best. D'ni. Tonight we shall reach D'ni."

Atrus's face lit. "Tonight?" Then an expression of confusion crossed his features. "But what time is it now? Morning, afternoon? I can't follow it any longer. Down here time seems to have no meaning."

Gehn took out his D'ni timer and handed it to Atrus.

"See there," he said, indicating the five differently shaded sectors—three light, two dark—that were marked on the circular face. A thin trail of silver spiraled from the center of the circle, stopping just inside the second of the lightly shaded sectors. "Right now it is the D'ni midday. We D'ni measure time differently from those who dwell on the surface. They set their clocks to the passage of the sun. We, however, set our clocks to the biological rhythms of our environment. Each of those sectors represents just over six hours in surface time."

"So the D'ni day is longer?"

"Very good, Atrus. You learn quickly."

Gehn took the timer back and, shaking it, held it to his ear, almost as if to check it was still working. Then, satisfied, he slipped it back into his pocket and looked to Atrus.

"If you're ready?"

Despite Atrus's expectations, the way grew harder. Fallen rock blocked the way in several places and they had to climb over piles of jagged stone or squeeze through narrow gaps. The tunnels, too, seemed to grow smaller and darker, and though he could not be sure of it, Atrus sensed that they had long strayed from the straight path that led direct to D'ni. Certainly there was no sign of that wonderful stone-and-metal path beneath their feet. Despite everything, however, his spirits were high, his whole being filled with an excited anticipation that coursed like a drug in his veins.

D'ni! He would soon be in D'ni! Why, even the dull pain in his feet seemed insignificant beside that fact.

They had traveled only an hour or so when Gehn called back to him and told him to get over to the right. Just ahead, part of the tunnel floor had fallen away to form a kind of pit. As he edged around it he could see, far below, a valley, with what looked like a broad, dark river flowing through it. He strained his ears, thinking he could faintly hear the sound of it—a roaring, rushing noise—but could not be sure.

Farther on, that noise, which he had begun to think was merely in his head, began to grow, until, coming out of the tunnel into a massive opening, the far walls of which could not be glimpsed in the darkness, that same sound filled the air, seeming to shake the walls on every side. The air was damp and cold, tiny particles of glittering mist dancing in the light from their lanterns.

Atrus backed against the wall. Then, as Gehn switched on the big lamp, he saw what it was.

Water fell in a solid sheet from a ledge two hundred feet above them, plunging a thousand feet into a massive pool below. In the torch's beam the water was like solid crystal.

Atrus turned, in time to glimpse Gehn returning the notebook to his inner pocket. He gestured past Atrus, indicating the way with his torch, the beam illuminating a broad ledge that circled the massive cavern.

Coming out into the smaller cavern at the back of the falls, Gehn stopped and called him over, holding his lantern out over a shelf of rock that was filled with crystal-clear water.

Atrus leaned close to look, then gave a little gasp of surprise. In the water were a number of long, colorless fish that looked like worms. They had frilled transparent gills and fins. As he looked, they scurried across and, slipping through a tiny rent in the lip of the rock, seemed to jump into the pool below with a plip-plop-plip that echoed throughout that tiny space.

"What were they?" Atrus asked, looking up into his father's eyes.

"Salamanders," Gehn answered. "They live down here, along with crickets, spiders, millipedes, and fish.

They're troglodytic, Atrus. They never leave these caves. And they're blind, too. Did you notice that?"

Gehn turned away and walked on, his boots crunching across the littered floor of the cavern.

For a long time they had been descending; now they began to climb, the way getting easier, until the tunnel they were following suddenly swung round to the right and met a second, larger tunnel.

Stepping out into it, Atrus gave a little gasp of surprise. It was the D'ni path! Both ahead and behind it stretched away, straight and perfectly cylindrical, into the darkness of the rock.

Staring back at the way they'd come, he understood what they must have done. For some reason—a cave-in, possibly—the straight path had been blocked, and they had taken an alternate route.

For a moment he recollected his father studying the diagrams in his notebook and the faint anxiety that had been in his eyes, and wondered how he had come upon those paths; whether it had been a question of stumbling aimlessly in the darkness, constantly tracing and retracing his path until he'd found a way through.

"Atrus?"

He turned. Gehn was already fifty feet up the tunnel.

"I'm coming!" he called, hobbling to catch up. But in his mind he was imagining his father, all those years ago, when he had first returned to D'ni, struggling in the darkness here beneath the earth—alone, completely and utterly alone—and felt a deep admiration for the courage that had driven him.

"Are we close?"

"Not far," Gehn answered. "The Gate is just ahead."

The news thrilled Atrus. Not far! There had been times when he'd thought they would walk forever and never arrive; but now they were almost there. The land he'd dreamed about all his life lay just ahead. A land of wonder and mystery.

Atrus hurried on, catching up with his father, keeping abreast with him as they neared the tunnel's end. He could see it now, directly ahead, and beyond it, on the far side of a massive marble plaza . . .

"Is *that* the Gate?" he asked, awed, his voice a whisper.

"That's it," Gehn said, grinning proudly. "It marks the southern boundary of the D'ni kingdom. Beyond it, everything for a hundred miles belongs to the D'ni."

Atrus looked to his father, surprised that he talked of the D'ni as if they still existed, then he looked back, taking in the sheer size of the great stone gate that was revealed beyond the tunnel's exit.

As they came out, he looked up and up and up, his mouth open in wonder. Though the surface was

cracked in places and fragments had fallen away, littering the great expanse of marbled floor that lay before
him, it was still magnificent. Filling the whole of one
end of what was clearly a vast cavern, the huge stone
barrier plugged that space from wall to wall, its surface
filled with what seemed like an infinity of intertwining
shapes—of men, machines, and beasts; of flowers and
shields and faces; and D'ni words, some of which he
recognized—all of it cut from a jet black granite that
seemed to sparkle in the light from Gehn's lantern.

The Gate dwarfed them, like nothing they had so
far seen. As he walked toward it Atrus felt the hairs on

his neck rise. Whatever he had pictured in his head, whatever he'd imagined while listening to Anna's tales, the reality exceeded it by far.

Stepping beneath that arch, he looked up; its massive thickness impressing him. How had the D'ni fashioned such a vast artifact? How had they cut the blocks, how fashioned them? From his own limited experience, he knew the difficulties of working stone, but the D'ni had thought nothing of throwing up such a huge mass of it.

Ahead of him the marble floor ended abruptly. Beyond it a cavern stretched away, its walls pocked with tunnel entrances. Hundreds of them. Thousands maybe.

It was suddenly very warm, the air much closer than it had been. Gehn glanced at his notebook again, then began to make his way across the floor of the cavern.

Selecting one of the larger tunnels, he gestured to Atrus to catch up with him, then turned and disappeared inside. The tunnel was much larger than any they had been in, with countless tunnels and small caverns—clearly artificially excavated—branching off.

Atrus followed his father, his eyes constantly surveying what lay to either side, noticing new things every second: great wheels and gantries; factories and warehouses; great mounds of loose rock and equally huge pits over which massive abandoned cranes stood like sentinels—all these and many other things, most of which he could not recognize at first sight.

Great machines stood idle everywhere he looked, as though abandoned only hours before, their oil-like, lacquered surfaces gleaming darkly in their passing light. Huge mining rigs rested on great pneumatic platforms beside the gaping holes of shafts bored into the foot of the cavern's walls, like massive insects feeding, their squat dark shapes still and silent.

Steam rose unchanneled from great fissures on every side: steam that had once powered the industrial might of D'ni. Elsewhere simple stone houses stood empty, roofless in the D'ni style, the thin cloth screens that had once maintained their privacy shredded by the same force that had toppled the stone towers of the factories.

Seeing it all, Atrus wondered just how it could have come to an end. It was so vast, so extraordinary.

From time to time other paths crossed their own, making him realize that there was not one D'ni path but an endless labyrinth of them, threading their way through the dark earth.

Suddenly, without warning, Gehn began to climb the wall of the tunnel, ducking into a much smaller shaft. Atrus, catching up, looked across to his right and saw that the tunnel was blocked some twenty yards ahead, collapsed in upon itself. Fearful of losing Gehn, he climbed the tunnel wall, following him inside.

They had been walking for hours and all the way their path had got slowly narrower, hotter, stuffier. Gehn now walked with the notebook open in one hand, consulting it almost constantly. The path had taken so many twists and turns that Atrus felt numbed by it, but still Gehn went on, confident, it seemed, that it led somewhere.

Then, suddenly, the quality of the light changed. Atrus blinked, his senses sparked to life by that sudden change. There was a faint breeze, a slight cooling of the air. As they turned the next corner there was a marked increase in the intensity of the light, a definite orange glow up ahead. The air was cool and clear, heavy suddenly with the scent of vegetation. The path climbed.

Ahead there was an opening. A circle of brilliant orange light.

As Atrus stepped out, it was to be met by the most astonishing sight he had yet encountered.

Facing him was an enormous valley, six miles across and ten broad, its steeply sloping shores descending to a glowing orange lake that filled at least half the valley's floor. At the center of that lake was a huge island, a mile or more in width, two twisted columns of rock pushing up from that great tumulus to soar more than a mile into the air. Beyond that, to its right, the great rock walls were curiously striped

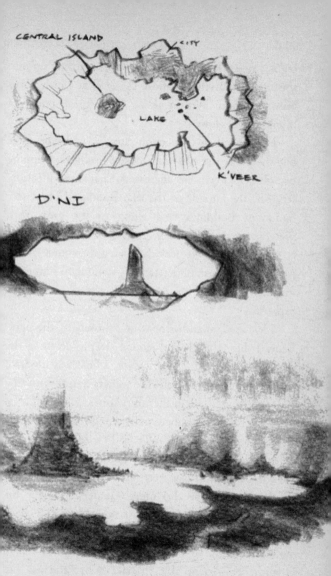

CENTRAL ISLAND

CITY

LAKE

K'VEER

D'NI

regular tiered levels of colored stone reaching up into the shadows overhead, above the level at which Atrus himself stood. Within those levels great pools of orange water glowed.

He looked up, expecting clouds, or maybe stars, but the blackness was immaculate overhead. Slipping his glasses down, he increased their magnification, studying the far side of the lake. Buildings! They were buildings! Buildings that clung to the great rock precipice, seeming to defy gravity!

Atrus craned his neck, following the course of the rock walls upward, understanding coming to him in an instant. He was inside! Inside a vast, cavernous expanse.

He stared, awed by the strange beauty of the sight. Beneath him the ground sloped steeply down to the sea's edge where, in a tiny harbor, a boat was moored. To the right, just offshore, the sea was dotted with tiny islands, like dark blemishes in that orange mirror.

"There," Gehn said, coming alongside. "Now, perhaps, you might understand why I could not leave you in that ridiculous crack in the ground. Is that not the grandest sight you have ever seen, Atrus?"

It was, and he did indeed understand why his father had brought him, yet the reminder cast a shadow over what he was feeling at that moment. Suddenly he wanted Anna to be there with him, wanted to share it with her—to be able to talk to her and ask her questions.

"Come," Gehn said from just below him as he began to make his way down the steep slope. "Another hour and we're home."

Atrus stood on the foredeck, his right hand gripping the rail as Gehn maneuvered the strange craft out onto the mirror-smooth waters, digging the pole deep, his muscles straining.

Atrus looked about him excitedly, conscious of the absence of echoes in that vast space, of the sound Gehn's pole made as it dipped into the water. The cavern was so vast, it felt almost as if they were back outside, on the surface, sailing on a moonless night, but for that orange glow that underlit everything.

As the blunt, wedge-shaped prow of the boat came around, Atrus saw the city in the distance once again. From here it seemed immaculate and beautiful, a vast bowl of towers and spires, as if it alone had not been touched by the destruction he had seen elsewhere. But they were not going to the city. Not yet, anyway. "Home," it seemed, was on one of the cluster of islands that skirted the right-hand wall of the cavern.

Atrus let out a little sigh. Now that he had stopped walking, his muscles had finally begun to seize up. His body ached and his eyelids felt like lead weights. The gentle movement of the boat didn't help either. It lulled him, like a voice singing in his head. He blinked, trying to keep his eyes open, trying to stay awake a while longer, but it was hard. It felt like he had walked a thousand miles.

For a moment Atrus dozed where he stood, then he jerked awake again, looking up, expecting to see stars littering the desert sky.

"Where . . . ?"

He turned, looking back to where his father sat in the center of the boat, slowly rowing them toward the island, and shook his head to clear it, convinced he was in the grip of some strangely vivid dream.

Facing front again, he saw the island looming from the shadows up ahead, its twisted, conical outline silhouetted black against the surrounding sea. Briefly, he noticed how the water about the far end of the island was dark and wondered why.

Home, he thought, noting the fallen walls, the toppled tower of the great mansion that sat upon the summit of the island like a huge slab of volcanic rock. *Home . . .*

Yet even as he saw it, sleep overcame him. Unable to prevent himself, he fell to his knees, then slumped onto the deck, unconscious, so that he did not see the boat pass beneath the island, into a brightly lit cavern. Nor did he see the waiting figure standing on the flight of winding steps that led up into the rock above.

"Atrus? Are you awake?"

Atrus lay there, his eyes closed, remembering the dream.

The voice came closer. "Atrus?"

He turned onto his back and stretched. The room was warm, the mattress strangely soft beneath him.

"What is it?" he asked lazily, uncertain yet whether he was awake.

"It is evening now," the voice, his father's voice, said. "You have slept a whole day, Atrus. Supper is ready, if you want some."

Atrus opened his eyes, focusing. Gehn stood there two paces from the bed, a lantern in one hand. In its flickering light the room seemed vast and shadowy.

"Where are we?" he asked, the details of the dream receding as he began to recall the long trek through the caverns.

"We are on K'veer," Gehn said, stepping closer, his pale, handsome face looming from the shadow. "This will be your room, Atrus. There are clothes in the wardrobes over there if you want to change, but there is no real need. When you are ready, you should turn left outside the door and head toward the light."

Atrus nodded, then, with a shock, realized that his feet no longer hurt. Nor were they bandaged. "My feet . . ."

Gehn looked down at him. "I treated them while

you were asleep. They will be sore for several days, but you can rest now."

"And your experiments? Were we in time?"

Gehn turned away, as if he hadn't heard, then walked across the room, drawing back the heavy curtains to reveal, through a massive, latticed window, the orange glow of the cavern beyond. There was a broad stone balcony and a view of the distant city.

"I shall leave you now," Gehn said, setting the lantern down on the table beside the bed. "But try not to be too long, Atrus. There are things we need to talk about."

Atrus waited for his father to leave the room, then sat up, sliding his legs around and examining his feet in the lamp's light. Where the sores were worst, on his heels and ankles and on the balls of his feet, Gehn had smeared them with an ointment that left a dark stain on the skin. Atrus touched one of the patches gingerly, then sniffed his fingers. It was the same as the ointment his grandmother had always used whenever he'd grazed his knees or shins or elbows on the rock.

Atrus?

Yes, Grandmother?

What do you see, Atrus?

I see the D'ni city, grandmother. I see . . .

Atrus stepped out onto the balcony, looking at it, trying to fix it in his memory so that he could tell her when he saw her again.

Far out there was a moving shadow on the water.

He narrowed his eyes, watching it a while, then shrugged and looked beyond it at the city once again. *Yes*, he thought. *I see the most incredible sight I've ever seen.*

"Ah, Atrus . . . come and sit with me."

Atrus hesitated in the doorway, then stepped inside, into the clear blue light of the kitchen. His father sat at a table to his left, a plate of food set before him.

It was a big V-shaped room with two large windows overlooking a stone-paved terrace garden that jutted out over the orange sea. The light outside seemed much darker now, and to compensate, Gehn had placed several lanterns in niches about the room.

Looking about him, Atrus noticed that the kitchen was solid stone. The cupboards, the table, the benches, even the sink and oven, were made of a strange, smooth banded gneiss that, like the path they had followed into D'ni, seemed to have been softened and then molded like clay. Tiny strips of metal, intricately fashioned, were threaded into the black-and-white-striped stone in a manner Atrus found hard to fathom. Though it was stone, it had a light warm feel that was unexpected. How they had managed it was a mystery to him, yet it was clear that the D'ni had developed processes well advanced of the ways of men.

"How do you feel now?" Gehn asked, gesturing for him to take a seat across from him.

How *did* he feel? Homesick, but also, now that his waking mood had passed, immensely curious. What did his father want of him? Gehn had said something to Anna about teaching him. But teaching him what?

"Hungry," he answered finally, finding it safest.

"Good," Gehn said. Turning, he picked up a small handbell from the table beside him and rang it.

At once a figure filled the far doorway, looming briefly in the shadows before it entered the room.

"Atrus, this is Rijus, my serving man."

The man who stood there, holding a large, shallow basket piled high with fruit, was tall, taller even than Gehn, and had a great domed head that seemed to be made of polished ivory. He wore a baggy dark blue one-piece, tied at the waist with a length of similarly colored cord, but the most remarkable thing about him were his eyes; lidless eyes that were like blemished eggs in his otherwise undistinguished face.

Atrus looked to his father, uncertain how to behave, then, when Gehn gave him no clue, he turned back and, bowing his head slightly, said, "I'm pleased to meet you, Rijus."

"It is no use trying to engage Rijus in conversation, Atrus. Rijus is a mute. He was born that way and he will die that way. But he understands commands well enough. If you need something, you should simply ask Rijus."

Atrus hesitated, then gave a little nod.

"Well, boy? What are you waiting for? Are you hungry or not?"

Atrus stood and, conscious of the servant's unnaturally staring eyes upon him, went over to him. A dozen different kinds of fruit were spread out in the basket—only a few of which he recognized, and then only from the traders' packs. Tiny beads of moisture speckled their brightly colored surfaces, enhancing their strange but perfect forms.

He looked back at Gehn. "Did you grow these, father?"

"In a manner of speaking."

Atrus turned back, wondering what to choose, almost afraid to touch them, they seemed so perfect. Then, reaching out, he picked one of the long, yellow, oval-shaped fruit, attracted by its strange, five-ribbed form.

It was rotten. It fell apart as he lifted it, revealing its dark brown innards. He looked to his father, surprised.

Gehn gestured to Rijus impatiently. "Take them away." Then, turning to Atrus, he fixed him with his stare.

"Come, Atrus. I think it is time we began our task. Time you found out why I brought you here to D'ni."

A twist of steps led up to a broad, high-ceilinged corridor, the end of which opened out onto a balcony directly above the terrace. On the far side of the balcony, set into the rock face, was a massive metal door, the jet black face of which was decorated with the same elaborate patterns Atrus had glimpsed on the Inner Gate. Pausing before it, Gehn reached inside his cloak and took out a large key, fitting it into the lock and turning it twice before removing it.

He stepped back. There was a faint shudder and then the door began to rise, sliding into the rock smoothly and silently, to reveal a dark, wedge-shaped opening. Six steps led down into a spacious room, lit from above by a massive star-shaped lamp. At the very center of the room was a raised dais, surrounded by three steplike ledges. On top of that dais were five large granite pedestals. Atrus turned, looking about him, impressed by what he saw. The walls were covered with massive shelves made of thick slabs of stone, and on those shelves were hundreds, possibly thousands of leather-bound books, similar to those his grandmother had kept back on her shelf in the cleft.

Gehn turned, looking to his son. "This, as you see, is the library. This is where you will come for your lessons every day." He gestured toward a low stone table in one corner. "That will be your desk. But before we commence, I want to show you why I brought you here, and why it is so important that you learn the ways of D'ni."

Raising his right hand, he beckoned Atrus to him, then, as the young man came alongside him, took his elbow and lead him up the steps and onto the dais.

At the center of the dais, recessed into its bone-white marble floor, was a circular pool surrounded by five marble pedestals.

Gehn stood before him. "Choose a book. Any book on the shelves."

"What?"

"Choose a book."

Atrus went across to the shelves, letting his eyes travel across their richly bound spines. There was no writing on any of them. A few had symbols, but none made any sense.

He turned, looking to his father.

"*Choose* a book."

Atrus took one down, the smell of its light green cover strangely intoxicating, exciting.

Gehn reached out, taking it from him. Opening it, he scanned it quickly, then nodded. Turning the book about, Gehn placed it reverently on the pedestal, watching Atrus all the while.

Atrus stepped closer, looking down at the open pages. The left-hand page was blank, but on the right . . .

He gasped, amazed by the clarity of the picture in

that small, rectangular box. Why, it was like staring through a window!

A strange, rust red conical mound filled the foreground, reminding Atrus of a giant termite's nest. Behind it was a lush backdrop of vivid, almost emerald green, with a glimpse of a cloudless sky above.

As Atrus watched, the image on the page slowly changed, seeming to tilt to the right, like an eye attempting to follow something just out of vision. The mound slowly disappeared, to be replaced in the foreground by a fast-flowing stream that tumbled between the rocks, then fell spectacularly into a crystal pool. But no sooner had it focused on that, than it lifted again, swinging out and over the surrounding gully, to reveal, beyond it, a valley filled with low, almost bush-like trees, on which could be seen a host of vividly colored fruit. There was a glimpse of a long, clear pool surrounded by grassy slopes and of distant, snow-capped mountains, and then the image returned to the rust red mound.

Gehn stepped across. "Give me your hand. You'll live as the D'ni now. This is what you were born for."

Atrus felt the skin on his palm tingle as though a faint electrical current had passed through it. His hand seemed drawn to the image on the page, *attracted* to it. For a moment that was all. Then, with a sudden, sick-

ening lurch, he felt himself sucked into the page. Or
rather, it was as if the page grew suddenly huge,
enveloping him in the weave of its fibers. At that same
instant he felt a curious shifting sensation. It felt as
though he were melting, the fragile shell of him
imploding, collapsing back in upon himself, and then
the blackness seeped through.

And as he finally surrendered to that blackness, so
he found himself back in his body, standing on the
grass just in front of the mound, a fresh breeze blowing into his face, the stream below him, the waterfall
and the valley just beyond.

Gone were the marble pedestals, the book-lined
walls, the solid rock ceiling overhead! Atrus reached
out, as if to touch them, but there was nothing.

Atrus looked up, startled by the transition. Huge
white clouds drifted in a sky so blue it looked like a
child's painting. The air hummed with tiny insects,
while all around him the heady scents of fruits and
flowers swamped his senses.

He fell to his knees, astonished. This was magic,
surely! Behind him Gehn shimmered into being.

"Get up onto your feet, boy," Gehn said, quietly
but firmly.

Atrus struggled to his feet, then turned to face his
father. He was unable to believe what had just happened to him.

"Where . . . where *are* we?"

Gehn stepped past him, standing beside the

stream, his booted feet on the edge of a steep incline, looking down at the waterfall.

As Atrus came alongside, Gehn looked to his son, his chest swelling with pride. "Once the D'ni ruled a million worlds, using what was grown in them to clothe and feed and provision themselves. So it was in the time of their greatness." He shook his head. "But all that is passed. Now there's only you and I, Atrus. We two, and the worlds we shall make."

"*Make*, father?"

Gehn looked out across the land that lay beneath them and nodded, a fierce pride in his face as he spoke. "Yes, Atrus. I made this world. I made the rock on which we stand, and the very air we are breathing. I made the grass and the trees, the insects and the birds. I fashioned the flowers and the earth in which they grow. I made the mountains and the streams. All that you see, I made."

Turning to face Atrus, Gehn placed his hands on his son's shoulders, his eyes burning with excitement now.

"I plan to make you my apprentice, Atrus, and teach you about the books. Would you like that?"

Looking up at his father, Atrus remembered suddenly how Gehn had stepped from that great veil of whiteness at the volcano's edge, awed by the power in the figure that stood facing him.

"Yes, father," he answered clearly, "I'd like that very much."

7

"THAT PHRASE . . . NOW WHERE DID I see that phrase?" Gehn placed the quill pen back in the marble ink pot, then, sitting forward, reached across his desk, taking the second of the big, leather-bound books from the stack. Edging aside the book he had been writing in, he drew the ancient volume toward him, then opened it and quickly flicked through until he came to the passage he had marked with a thin blue strip of paper.

"Ah . . . that's it. That should do it."

He looked up, his eyes focused inward briefly, as he considered what else he might need. It was barely midday, but here in Gehn's study it was permanently night, the shadows of that cavernous room kept at bay by a small stone lamp perched on the corner of his massive wooden desk.

Gehn read the line again, tracing it with his index finger, then squinted at the page.

"Perhaps a little overelaborate . . . remove those two descriptive words. . . . embellishment, that's all they are."

He nodded, pleased with himself, then, moving the book he had been working on until it rested beside the ancient text, he began to copy out the D'ni phrase, taking care to leave out the two words he considered served no purpose.

"There," he said softly, looking up again, aware of his surroundings for the first time in over three hours.

Every surface in that huge, cavelike room was filled with books. Shelves lined the walls from floor to ceiling, leaving space for little else. Just across from Gehn was an ancient hearth. And then there was the door, of course. Otherwise there was nothing but shelves—not even any windows. Even the floor was covered in stacks of books—some new, some old—some piles of which had tumbled over, remaining where they fell, thick layers of dust covering their musty leather bindings, like ash on a volcano's slope.

Across from Gehn, between two standing shelves containing Gehn's own journals, was a smaller desk, laid out with pens and ink and a pile of copying books, like those his son wrote in.

Focusing on them, Gehn seemed to wake with a start and glanced at the timer that lay to his left on the desk.

"Kerath preserve me!" he muttered, getting up and pocketing the timer, realizing he was late.

He hurried across the room, then, taking the long silver key from the bunch attached to his waist, he unlocked the door and went outside, taking care to lock the door again before he turned and hurried down the narrow stone steps.

At the bottom of the steps lay the library. As Gehn stepped out, he saw that Atrus was seated at his desk in the far corner, his arms folded before him, his copy-book open, ready.

"Father?"

Making no apology for his tardiness, Gehn strode across and, taking a long white chalk from the pot, turned to the great slate board and began to sketch out a D'ni word, taking great care as he did to demonstrate the flow of each stroke.

Turning back, he noted how attentively his son was watching him. Seeing him like that, Gehn felt a momentary frustration at the boy's innate placidity. Oh, it was a fine quality in a servant or in a subject species, but in a D'ni they were absurd. For a second or two, Gehn felt something akin to futility at the task he'd set himself.

Unaware, Atrus labored on, slowly copying down the figure from the board, his tongue poking between his lips as he painstakingly mimicked the shapes his father's hand had made to form the strokes and curls of the D'ni word.

"*Atrus!*"

The boy looked up. "Yes, father?"

"You must learn to concentrate. It is not easy, I know. It has taken me close to thirty years to master the art. But you must try hard, Atrus. You will achieve nothing unless you are willing to harness yourself to the yoke of learning."

Atrus, his head down, his eyes staring at his desk, nodded. "Yes, father."

"Good," Gehn said, placated by the boy's humility, by his willingness to listen to his father's instruction; by his innate quickness of mind. Then, seeing a way he might improve matters, he went across and took a large, extremely thick volume from one of the shelves and carried it across.

"Here," he said, setting it down on the desk beside Atrus's open workbook. "As it is clear that you need extra tuition, and as my own time is presently tied up in a number of experiments, I think we must try an experiment of a different kind."

Atrus looked up at him, his eyes eager suddenly.

"Yes, Atrus. This book is a very special book. It is called the *Rehevkor*. Once every school in D'ni had several copies of this book. From it pupils would learn how to write those fundamental D'ni words that formed the basic vocabulary of our race. I suppose the nearest comparison you would have for it is a lexicon but this is far more complex."

Gehn took the edge of the massive cover and pulled the book open, then pointed down at the detailed diagrams that filled both pages.

"As you can see, each double-page spread concerns a single D'ni word, and shows clearly what pen strokes must be used and in what precise order. What I want you to do, Atrus, is to work through the *Rehevkor* from the first page to the last, concentrating on twenty words a night to begin with. I will provide you with a supply of copying books to work in, but you must promise me to practice these figures until they are second nature to you. Until you could sketch them in your sleep. You understand me, Atrus?"

"I understand."

"Good." Gehn reached out, closing the book, then made to turn away.

"Father?"

"Yes, Atrus?"

"How old is the text?"

"The *Rehevkor?*" Gehn turned back. "Ten thousand years old. Maybe older."

He saw the awe in his son's eyes at that and smiled inwardly. Atrus's eagerness, his clear appreciation of the greatness of the D'ni, was something that he, Gehn, could work upon.

"Father?"

Gehn sighed, for the briefest moment tempted to yell at the boy and tell him to stop this endless questioning. Then, realizing that he must be patient if he was to undo all the harm Anna had done to the child, he answered him.

"Yes, Atrus?"

"I just wondered why the sea is less bright now than it was earlier, that's all."

Gehn leaned back, relaxing. "That is easy to explain. The plankton has a thirty-hour cycle that corresponds with that of the D'ni. It sleeps when we sleep, and is most active when we are most active. Thus we have night and day down here. Of a distinctly black and orange kind."

If it was a joke, it was either a very bad one, or touched on something Atrus did not understand, yet Gehn seemed to find it funny, for his laughter went on for some while, and Atrus, pleased to discover that his father did, after all, possess a sense of humor, laughed with him.

Later, after Atrus had returned to his room, Gehn walked over to the central dais and, climbing up onto the marbled floor, looked about him at the great books where they rested on their pedestals.

Talking to Atrus about various matters, he had realized suddenly just how much he had missed the chance simply to talk these past fourteen years.

Alone. He had been so alone. Not emotionally, for he considered himself as emotionally self-sufficient as any man could be, but intellectually. He had missed the chance to stretch himself in debate, yes, and to demonstrate the vastness of his knowledge. And though the boy, as yet, was little more than a sounding board for his ideas, yet there was immense potential in him.

Yes, but then how could he have been certain that the boy even existed? The chances were that he had perished. After all, it was hard to imagine anyone surviving in that desolate little crack in the ground!

"Patience. I must have patience with the boy, and then, in time . . .

But right now time was the one thing he found himself severely lacking. Over these past few weeks not one but several of his experiments had suddenly gone badly wrong, and he had been forced to spend more and more time attempting to deal with the problems that had arisen. To try to give Atrus as much attention as he needed was . . . well, impossible.

Still, Atrus was an obedient child. He could see that the boy tried his best. And maybe a few sessions with the *Rehevkor* would bring him up to scratch. Time would tell.

Right now, however, other matters needed his attention. Crossing the dais, Gehn stood over one of the open books, staring down at the descriptive box. Then he placed his hand upon it. A moment later he was gone.

8

IN THE WEEKS THAT FOLLOWED, ATRUS fell heavily beneath his father's spell. Mornings he would work hard, repairing the walls and paths of the many-leveled island. Then, in the afternoons, after he had bathed and eaten, he would sit at his desk in the great library, while Gehn taught him the rudiments of D'ni culture.

Much of what Gehn taught him was familiar from his own reading and from things Anna had told him over the years, but there was also a great deal he had never heard before, and so he kept silent. Besides, now that he knew it was real, even those things he knew seemed somehow transformed: different simply because they *were* real.

For several days he had been working on the question of why the water at the north end of the island was clear of the light-giving plankton, and had traced the problem to the spillage from an old pipe that led down from his father's workroom. He had taken samples of that spillage and found traces of lead and cadmium in it—elements that were clearly poisoning the plankton. Not having the equipment to make a proper filter, he decided that, as the spillage was only a trickle, it would probably be best to block the pipe off altogether. He was busy doing this one morning, standing on the steps below the seawall, leaning across to fit the tiny stone cap he'd fashioned to block the end of the pipe, when Gehn came out to see him.

"Atrus?"

He turned and looked. His father stood at the head of the steps, cloaked and booted as if for a journey, looking out across the sea toward the great rock and the city beyond.

"Yes, father?"

"I have a new task for you."

Atrus straightened up, then threw the steel facing-tool he had been using down onto the sack beside him, waiting for his father to say more.

Gehn turned, combing his fingers through his ash-white hair, then looked to him. "I want you to come into the city with me, Atrus. I want you to help me find some books."

"The city? We're going to the city?"

Gehn nodded. "Yes, so you had better go and change. You will need your boots. And bring your knapsack, too."

Atrus hesitated a moment, then, with a curt nod to his father, gathered up his tools and hurried up the steps.

"I shall go down to the dock and prepare the boat," Gehn said, stepping back to let his son pass. "Meet me down there. And hurry now. I want to be back before nightfall."

K'VEER

Gehn was standing at the stern of the boat, his hand on the tethering rope, ready to cast off, as Atrus came down the twist of stone steps and out into the low-ceilinged cave that housed the jetty.

Since that evening when he had first arrived on K'veer, Atrus had never been off the island. Nor had a day passed in all that time when he had not looked to the distant D'ni city and dreamed of going there.

Climbing aboard, he looked to his father for instructions.

"Sit there," Gehn said, pointing to a low bench that dissected the shallow craft. "And try not to lean over too far. I don't want to have to pull you out."

He nodded, chastened by his father's words.

As his father cast off, then swung the boat around, poling it out through the narrow entrance, Atrus turned in his seat, staring out across that vast expanse of orange sea, past the scattering of intervening islets, toward the D'ni capital, seeing yet again how its crowded levels climbed the cavern wall into the darkness.

Ancient, it was. Ancient beyond all imagining.

As they came out into the open water, Atrus turned, looking back as Gehn's island emerged into view. The day he'd arrived, he had been too exhausted to take in all its details, but now he stared, fascinated, seeing K'veer properly for the first time.

By now he knew every room and corridor, every stairway and terrace of the sprawling, many-leveled mansion, yet seeing it now from that slight distance he pieced it all together for the first time, making sense of it; seeing how its spiral shape had been determined by the rock on which it had been built.

From a quarter mile away its dark stone walls—fallen in places, shored up in others—gleamed almost metallically in the light from below.

It was a strange, unearthly vision, but no more so than any of the sights that met the eyes down here. Besides, the sensitivity of his eyes, which had meant he'd had to shield his eyes from the brightness of the desert sun, here was a positive advantage. He found this light soothing to his eyes ... almost *natural*. Maybe the fact that he was part D'ni made his eyes weak. All he knew for certain was that he had not needed to wear his glasses down here, except for magnification.

Atrus looked to his father, conscious for the first time of just how distracted he was. In his own excitement he had missed his father's mood. As he watched, Gehn grimaced, as if some hideous thought had crossed his mind, then pulled hard on the oars, moving them along through the water.

Atrus turned, staring across at the city once again. Tiny islands littered the surrounding waters, each straddled by its own dark and sprawling mansion, each of those ancient buildings uniquely and distinctly shaped, and every last one of them in ruins.

On one of the larger islands, a strange, angular fortress had been built high up into the face of a massive cliff, embedded, it seemed, into the rock—a thing of spikes and towers and heavily buttressed walls. Beneath it the cliff dropped five hundred feet, sheer into the motionless sea.

Atrus let out a long breath, conscious more than ever of the desolate magnificence of this place.

As they steered through the last narrow channel, out into the open sea, he looked to his right, his eyes drawn by a disturbance on the water a quarter of a mile away. There was a kind of haze over the water, like windblown sand, that cast an erratic shadow on the orange surface. As he watched, it came nearer, attracted, perhaps, by the boat's slow passage through the plankton-rich water.

When it got to within fifty yards, he stood, open-mouthed, staring at it, then looked to Gehn, but his father seemed not to have noticed.

"What's that?" he asked, intrigued, seeing tiny glittering shapes within the cloud.

Gehn glanced across. "Ah, those . . . They are a kind of damselfly. They feed on tiny insects that live within the plankton."

Atrus nodded, then turned back, watching in wonder as the cloud of insects drifted just aft of their boat's trail, unable to keep up with their progress. He was about to look away when suddenly the water beneath the cloud rippled violently and a long, thin snout poked out, stabbing the air. A moment later and the water beneath the damselflies began to thrash and boil as a host of brilliantly colored fish went into a feeding frenzy.

In less than thirty seconds the cloud was gone, the water calm again.

"And those?" Atrus asked, his voice almost a whisper.

"Fish," Gehn answered, with what seemed like aversion. "The water's much deeper out here beyond the islands. Usually they live deep down, but they surface now and then to feed."

"I see," Atrus said quietly, suddenly wary of the placid waters that surrounded them, noting, through the clear yet glowing water, the presence of much larger, fleeting shadows in the depths.

Disturbed, he looked away, trying to focus his mind on something else.

Books . . . His father had said they were going to find some books. But Gehn had plenty of books. So what did he want with more of them?

"How long will it take us to get there?" he asked.

"Not long," Gehn answered patiently, pulling on the oars regularly, inexhaustibly, it seemed.

Atrus nodded. For a while he fiddled with his knapsack, then he looked back at his father.

Gehn was watching him, his large eyes half hooded. "What is it now, Atrus?"

Atrus swallowed, then asked what he'd been thinking. "The books . . . What's so special about the books? You said they can't make them anymore. I don't understand."

Gehn's face was blank, expressionless. "All in good time. Right now, all you have to do is find them for me."

Atrus dozed for a while, then woke with a start, surprised to find himself still on the boat, still traveling. Yawning, he stretched his neck, then looked up at his father.

Gehn smiled tightly. "So you're awake at last. Look. Just behind you. You almost missed it."

Atrus stood and turned . . . to find the city looming over him, seeming to fill the whole of the skyline, its ancient buildings rising level after level into the great ceiling of the cavern.

And, directly in front of him, an arch—bigger than any of those he had seen on his journey down. By comparison to the other D'ni architecture Atrus had seen, it seemed crude, made as it was of undecorated blocks, yet each block was the size of a great mansion, the whole thing ten blocks tall, its entrance so big that you could quite easily have passed even the largest of the islands through that gap.

"Kerath's arch," Gehn said proudly, staring ahead at it.

"Kerath . . ." Atrus whispered, the merest mention of his hero's name enough to send a thrill through him.

"All of the D'ni kings sailed through this arch," Gehn said. "They would be sent to the southlands to be tutored in the arts of kingship, then, after a year, they would come here to be crowned, on the harbor front, before the Steward's House. A million citizens would watch the ceremony, and after there would be a whole month of feasting."

And yet it was named after Kerath, Atrus thought. *Because he was the greatest of them.*

As they slowly sailed beneath it, Atrus could see how the stone was blotched and pitted, *aged*, not as the rocks of the desert were aged, by sand and wind, but like a skin that has grown tight and dry.

For countless thousands of years this arch has stood, he told himself, remembering, even as he did, the story of Kerath returning to D'ni on the back on the great lizard. Now, of course, he was forced to change the picture in his head—to imagine Kerath returning not across a desert, but across this vast open sea, the lizard, perhaps, resting peacefully beneath him on the boat.

The thought made him frown and wonder how much else he had imagined wrongly. Tre'Merktee, for instance, the Place of Poisoned Waters, did that still exist? He turned, looking to his father, but before he could ask the question, Gehn spoke to him again.

"You must stay close to me this first time, Atrus, and not wander off. Today we must confine our explorations to a single sector of the city."

Gehn pointed past Atrus and to the right, indicating a part of the city not far from the main harbor.

"That is where we shall make our search, in the J'Taeri district. With luck we shall find what we are looking for in the Common Library there."

Atrus nodded, then stepped up onto the prow, watching the city slowly appear from beneath the arch. Directly ahead of them massive walls of cracked white marble were arranged in three tiers, like giant steps, about the harbor.

At intervals along the front, a number of massive statues—each one several times the size of a man—had once stood, facing the arch, but only two were standing now, and even they were cracked and damaged. The rest had been toppled from their pedestals and now lay, either in pieces on the marbled flagstones or on the floor of the harbor itself, broken limbs the size of pillars protruding from the glowing surface.

Beyond the statues, on the far side of an impressively huge square, was what looked like a huge, porticoed temple, fifteen white stone pillars holding up what remained of a massive dome. Beyond that, the city climbed, tier after tier of streets and buildings, covered walkways and delicate arches, no single level the same as another.

From afar the city had seemed an amorphous mass of stone. From close up, however, it revealed an intricacy and variety that was astonishing. Even the color of the stone changed as the eye traveled up that vast bowl of jumbled architecture, the lowest levels slate gray or a dull red-brown, the higher levels the same black streaked with red that was used for the island mansions and the Inner Gate.

What could also be seen from close up was the sheer extent of the devastation the D'ni capital had suffered. Wherever Atrus looked, he saw evidence of ruin and collapse. Indeed, there was barely a structure that was not damaged in some way or another.

He lowered his eyes, staring down through the pellucid water. Far down, so deep they seemed more shadows than actualities, he could see the remains of the great fleet of merchants' barges that had once anchored here.

"Was it the quake that killed the people?" Atrus asked, looking back at his father.

Gehn ignored him, concentrating on the task of bringing the boat alongside one of the great stone pillars that supported the jetty. He brought the small craft to a halt alongside the pillar. A rope ladder dangled from the jetty above, trailing against the side of the cracked stone.

He glanced at Atrus, then signaled that he should climb the ladder, holding it taut from below while Atrus climbed the rungs. Then, as Atrus neared the top, he tied the mooring rope to the bottom of the ladder and began his own ascent.

Atrus stepped up onto the jetty, more awed by his

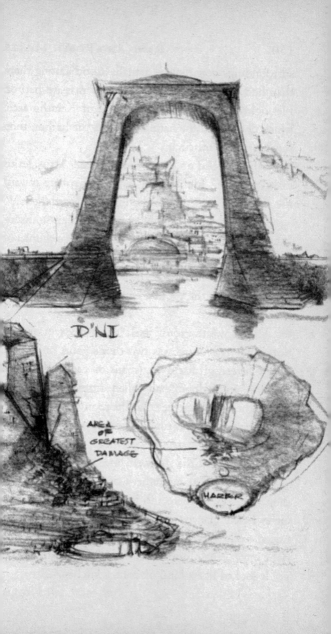

D'NI

AREA
OF
GREATEST
DAMAGE

HARBOR

surroundings now that he actually stood among them than he'd been while sailing into that massive harbor. He looked back at the brutal shape of Kerath's arch, which dominated the natural bowl of the harbor, then slowly turned full circle.

Gehn climbed up beside him. "Come, Atrus, let us make up time." He pointed across the square toward the shattered dome. "Our destination is over there."

The great square might once have been immaculately kept, but now it was littered with huge chunks of stone that had fallen from the city above. In places huge cracks ran in zigzags through the marble paving, while in others the ground simply vanished into tiny craters.

The Steward's House itself was a study in desolation. The great dome was two-thirds gone, only three of the fifteen great curving spans of roof still intact, and the great doors had fallen from their hinges. Inside, there was evidence that the rooms and corridors had been put to the torch, possibly long before the final tragedy had struck. Overhead, charred beams stood out against the stony skyline.

Atrus stared at his father's back, wondering what they were doing there inside that ruined place, but Gehn barely glanced at his surroundings, making his way directly down the main corridor before turning right into a small room at the back of the building.

It looked like a kind of pantry kitchen.

Atrus watched as Gehn walked over to one of the shelves and, reaching to the back of it, seem to pull something toward him. There was a low clunking sound, as if something were sliding back beneath their feet.

Gehn turned, a brief smile flickering across his features, then crossed the room and, edging behind a long stone workbench, placed his hands flat against the wall, moving them back and forth as if searching for something.

With a little grunt of satisfaction, he flexed his shoulders and pushed. At once a whole section of the wall swung back and tilted to the side, sliding into a niche in the rock behind.

An unlit passage was revealed, leading up into the rock.

It was all done so effortlessly, so quietly, that Atrus stood there a moment, staring in disbelief.

Gehn turned, beckoning to him. "Come on then, boy! What are you waiting for?"

Atrus went across and ducked inside, then stopped, unable to see more than a few feet in front of him.

"Here," Gehn said, pressing a lantern into one hand and a fire-marble into the other.

Atrus crouched, balancing the lantern on his knee, while he fitted the fire-marble, then, as it began to glow, he straightened up. Turning, he saw his father light his own lantern, then look to him.

In that fierce blue glow Gehn's eyes seemed huge

and unnatural. Looking into them, Atrus realized how much a stranger his father remained, even after all these weeks. He still knew so little about him.

"I shall go ahead," Gehn said, unaware, it seemed, of his son's close scrutiny. "But keep up with me, Atrus. These tunnels are like a maze. If you fall behind and lose sight of me, you are likely never to find your way out."

Atrus nodded nervously, then, as his father squeezed past him and began to make his way down the sloping curve of the tunnel, hurried to keep up.

Behind Atrus there was the grating of the stone as the wall slid back into place. A dull, resounding thud echoed up the tunnel after him.

Passages led off to either side, some leading up, others down into the earth, but Gehn kept striding straight ahead. It was a good ten minutes before he stopped and, turning, making sure Atrus was still with him, pointed up a narrow flight of steps.

"It's a long climb," he said, "but quicker than trying to get there by the lanes."

Up and up the steps went, twisting first to the right and then back to the left, as if following some natural fault in the rock. Briefly it opened out into a narrow chamber with a balcony overhead and stone benches cut into the rock, then it went on again, climbing more steeply.

"Not far now," Gehn said finally, as the steps ended and they came out into a relatively flat piece of tunnel.

"Who made these paths?" Atrus asked, noting the words and patterns carved into this final stretch of wall.

"That," Gehn answered, "is a mystery. For when people have been in a location as long as the D'ni have been here, then many things are done the reasons for which are either unknown or lost in the haze of time. That said, I should imagine there have been tunnels here since the very beginning. Some scholars—the great Jevasi among them—claim that the wall of the cavern is so riddled with them, that were any more to be cut then the whole great edifice would cave in upon itself!"

Atrus narrowed his eyes, imagining it.

Just ahead there was a glimpse of orange light. It grew, until he could see the tunnel's exit outlined up ahead.

They came out into a narrow, unfurnished room. Above them the ceiling gaped. One could look straight up at the roof of the great cavern. This, Atrus knew, was the D'ni style. Only a very few of their buildings—official residences, like the Steward's House—had roofs, the rest were open to the air. After all, what need was there for roofing when the rain never fell and there was never any variation in the temperature? At most a typical D'ni dwelling would have a thick awning of some kind stretched over its topmost story, and some of the two- and three-story buildings didn't even bother with that, their occupants sleeping and bathing in the lower floors.

The room led out onto a small balcony. To the right a set of steps led down into a narrow lane. Atrus went to the rail, looking down the empty thoroughfare, fascinated by the jumble of gray stone buildings that met his gaze, the labyrinth of walkways and stairways and covered paths.

They went on, their heels clicking on the worn stone. The narrow lane curved to the left, climbing slowly between high walls that, in places, were cracked and fallen. Behind those walls lay a number of imposing-looking mansions, surprisingly few of which had collapsed, leading Atrus to think that they had been built to survive such shocks.

It was a strange and fascinating place to be, and as he walked, a familiar voice sounded in his head, asking the question it always asked.

Atrus? What do you see?

He hesitated, then:

I see faded paint on the walls. I see boards at windows and piles of rubbish, untended thirty years. I see . . . disrepair and dereliction. Signs of shared habitation. Abandoned sedans and ragged washing hung on threadbare lines.

Good. And what do you make of it?

He looked about him once more, then answered Anna in his head:

The mansions are old and grand, from a time when

this was, perhaps, a respectable, even fashionable place to live, yet in more recent times this must have been a poor district: a place of considerable squalor, even before the great quake did its worst.

Good. Then why has your father come here? What could he possibly want in a place like this?

Books, he answered silently, yet it hardly seemed a good enough reason. Why should his father want more books?

9

AT THE END OF A BROAD, ONCE TREE-lined avenue bordered by massive houses, stood the D'ni gatehouse. It was a huge, squat, square thing with twin turrets and a pair of massive studded doors that were closed against them. On the great slab of a lintel above the doors, two D'ni words had been cut deep into the ancient stone. Looking up at it, Atrus translated it in his head.

District of J'Taeri.

Stepping up to the left-hand door, Gehn braced himself, then leaned against it, straining against it, but despite his efforts it did not move even the tiniest amount. Gehn turned, looking about him, then walked across, venturing into the garden of one of the nearby houses, to emerge a moment later with a heavy-looking piece of metal, clearly the ornamental spout of a fountain.

Standing before the doors again, Gehn lifted the thick rod of metal high then swung it against the wood, aiming for the lock. There was a cracking sound and splinters flew, but the door held firm. Grunting loudly, Gehn raised the spout time and again, smashing it against the door, the wood splintering more and more each time. Finally, on the seventh or eighth blow, the lock fell away.

Gehn threw the spout down, then, leaning against the door, he heaved, his whole body straining, his neck muscles taut. Slowly but surely the massive door eased back.

They went through, into J'Taeri.

The buildings here were smaller but much better maintained than in the district they had left, yet both had that same feeling of immense age, of ancient histories piled up layer upon layer like geological strata. In places, where it had not been replaced, the stone floor of the lanes was so worn by the passage of millions of feet over the millennia that it dipped markedly in the center, its appearance fluid, like wax that had melted and re-formed, that likeness reinforced by the dark red of the stone.

Coming to a massive crossroads—a place where covered walkways crisscrossed overhead, and tunnels dipped darkly into the earth—Gehn stopped and took the small tanned leather notebook from his pocket, studying it closely.

Atrus had often noticed Gehn consulting the book, which seemed to contain information on all manner of things, yet strangely he had never seen him write in it.

Maybe he does it at night, when I'm not there, Atrus thought, thinking of his own journal. *Or maybe he doesn't need to. Maybe he's already mapped out where everything is in this city.*

To be honest, he was in awe of his father's knowledge of the capital. Gehn seemed to know every street, every important building in D'ni. And even when he didn't, he was sure to have it in his book.

Closing the notebook, Gehn pointed up the avenue to his left.

"We need to go this way. The main square is ten minute's walk from here."

Atrus waited as Gehn tucked the book away, then set off again, silently following his father, staring about him as he walked.

The houses in J'Taeri were richly furnished; not only that, but there were huge pentagonal stone shields on many of the houses, decorated with symbols identical to those on Gehn's tunic, the night he'd come to the cleft to claim Atrus.

Curious, Atrus had asked Gehn what they were and had discovered that they were Guild badges, and that those who lived in the houses that displayed them were senior Guild members.

J'Taeri, it transpired, had been a Guild district, and thus something of an anomaly in that the families who had once stayed there were not from the locality, but were drafted in to oversee Guild activities in the lower districts.

The houses were very different in J'Taeri; more elaborate in their design. Some of them reminded

Atrus of the forms he had glimpsed in the caverns traveling to D'ni—seeming to mimic the form of dripstone and flowstone, narrow towers pushing up from their walls like great stalagmites, while large draperies of lacelike stone decorated their front arches. Others, much more prevalent, were constructed to resemble great slabs of rock, three or four stories resting one atop another like layers of smoothed slate, no sign of any doors or windows evident to the casual eye.

Two of the bigger houses stood out, not just because of their imposing design but also because they were made of the jet black, red-streaked stone he had noticed was used mainly in the uppermost levels of the city, and again he asked Gehn what, if anything, this signified.

"Those were the houses of important men," Gehn had answered distractedly. "Only the very rich could afford to build with such materials."

The avenue opened out onto a massive square enclosed by high stone walls, on the far side of which was a building that resembled the Steward's House. Six broad white marble steps led up into the shadowed portico. Remarkably, its facade had survived the quake almost intact.

On the top step Atrus turned, looking out across the labyrinth of walls and rooftops toward the harbor far below, the great arch dominating the skyline, its top almost level with them. Then, turning back, he stepped up into the shadows of the Common Library.

Inside, beyond a row of five cracked pillars, was a small entrance hall, its floor covered in a mosaic. A dark, jagged crack ran through the center of it, but the picture was still clear. It showed a man standing beside a lectern, on which lay an open book, exactly like the books which stood on the pedestals in his father's library back on K'veer. The man's hand hovered just above the image on the page.

On the far side of the hall were two doorways, one to the left, one on the right. Cut into the plinth over the left-hand door was the D'ni symbol for "Enter," while on the plinth to the right the same symbol had a circle about it, from which jutted seven short, wedge-shaped rays, like a star. From Anna's lessons he recognized it as the D'ni negative. That sign read "Do Not Enter."

He went to the left-hand door. It opened onto a long, caged passageway with ornately latticed sides of interwoven bronze and iron that went directly down the middle of a much bigger sloping corridor, the cracked walls of which were covered in carvings of open fields and blazing suns, and of men and women standing in those fields wearing strange glasses—*his* glasses, Atrus realized with a start of surprise!—as they looked up into those limitless, unfamiliar heavens.

At the end of the caged walk was a barrier. Gehn vaulted it effortlessly and walked on, into a big, high-ceilinged gallery, on the far side of which was a massive stone screen. Behind that could be seen three tall, black-painted doors.

Atrus clambered over the barrier, then went across, joining his father.

"Over there, through those doors, is the Book Room," Gehn said. "From there the common people of D'ni would have the opportunity of traveling to an Age."

He looked to Atrus, clearly proud of his race's achievements.

"Did *everybody* use these places?"

Gehn shook his head. "No. That is why they are called the Common Libraries. These places were for the common, workingmen and -women of D'ni. The great families had their own books, their own Ages. They were rigidly administered by the Guilds, just as these Ages were, yet they were exclusive. Only those permitted by the families could enter them."

Atrus frowned. "And the harvest worlds?"

"Those were Guild worlds. The books they used were specialized books, much less restrictive than the ordinary books. They had to be to take the great loads that were regularly brought back from those Ages."

Gehn gestured toward the doors. "Anyway, let us go inside."

Following his father, Atrus went around the screen and through the central doorway, into a big, long chamber filled with pedestals, divided in two by a central walkway, the whole thing mounted on a huge, white marble dais. Barely half the pedestals now stood, and the great dais itself was riven with cracks. There was no ceiling to the chamber, but overlooking it was a railed balcony, parts of which had fallen away. Even so, looking up at it, Atrus could imagine the cloaked Guild members standing there like gods, calmly supervising the comings and goings down below.

Atrus stepped up beside his father. On the nearest pedestal lay an open book, its thick leather cover secured to the lectern by a heavy gold chain.

"Here they are," Atrus said.

Gehn looked to him. "No. Those are of no use to us."

Atrus frowned, not understanding, but Gehn had crouched and was examining the top of one of the elaborately decorated pedestals, his fingers feeling beneath the beveled edge. With a huff of disappointment he straightened up, moving quickly on to the next, examining that, again with the same response.

While he was doing so, Atrus stepped up to the pedestal and looked down at the image on the right-hand page.

He frowned. It was dark, only the vaguest outline visible. Then he understood. There was thick layer of dust over the "window," suspended there just a fraction above the page.

He went to touch it, to brush it aside, but Gehn,

who had seen what he was about to do, grabbed his hand and pulled it away, gripping it tightly and shaking it as he spoke.

"You must *never* do that, Atrus! *Never!* You understand? For all you knew, that Age might be dead, destroyed by some calamity. You would be drawn into an airless void."

"I'm sorry," Atrus said, his voice very small.

Gehn sighed, then released his hand.

"The Art can be a dangerous thing, Atrus. That is why the D'ni took great precautions to protect these books and ensure they were not misused."

"Misused?"

But Gehn had already moved away, searching again. He was crouched down, studying the edge of one of the pedestals in the second row.

"Atrus. Come over here."

Atrus frowned, but did as he was told, stepping up beside his father.

"I want you to search all of these pedestals for a catch or switch of some kind."

"Father?"

Gehn pointed to the door at the far end of the chamber. "We need to go inside. Somewhere here there is a switch or lever that will let us in."

Atrus set to work, examining the pedestals, one after another, until, with a little cry of excitement, he found a tiny brass hemisphere set into the back of one of the great stone lecterns.

He pressed it. At once the door on the far side of the room slid open.

"Good," Gehn said, straightening, then making his way across.

"Is this it?" Atrus said, standing in the doorway, staring with disappointment into what seemed like an unfurnished corridor from which no doors led out.

"No," Gehn said, turning to look back into the main gallery. "The Book Room is below. I hoped the trapdoor would be open, but it looks like we shall have to force our way in."

As his father stepped out again, Atrus moved past him, noticing for the first time the big square slab of stone that hung like a painting against the left-hand wall.

Standing before it, Atrus frowned. From its smooth surface protruded a number of geometric symbols—stars and semicircles, triangles and squares, and several others—arranged in what appeared to be a haphazard fashion.

Atrus squinted at it, trying to make out what it was he had noticed. There was a pattern. No . . . not a pattern, a progression. Each symbol had a mathematical value, and if you took those values . . .

A map. It was a map!

Gehn came back into the room, carrying one of the fallen pedestals, his muscles straining as he kept the massive piece of marble balanced against his chest and shoulder.

"Out of the way!" he gasped, then, lifting the huge stone with both hands, heaved it right through the middle of the slab, embedding it in the wall.

"But father . . ."

"Mind back, boy," Gehn said, ignoring him, grasping the pedestal once again, and beginning to extricate it from the wall, heaving at it and rocking it back and forth until it came free.

But I could have solved the puzzle, Atrus said silently, as his father threw the pedestal aside, revealing, behind the slab, a matrix of metal pullies and wires.

He watched as his father pulled and pushed at the wires, trying to work the mechanism that activated the trapdoor. For a moment there was nothing, and then there was a resounding click as something slotted into place.

"Stand over by the door, Atrus," Gehn said, gesturing to him with one hand, the other buried deep inside the workings of the mechanism.

Atrus did as he was told, then watched as his father made a small little movement of his shoulder.

There was the hiss of hydraulics and then a low grating sound. A moment later a two-by-three rectangle of the floor beside them began to sink into the earth with a loud hissing noise, revealing a stairway.

Atrus followed his father down, into a large, well-lit space, filled with long workbenches piled high with all manner of clutter. Shelves crowded the walls. Eight cloaked skeletons sat in their chairs, slumped forward over their work. Another—their supervisor?—lay where he had fallen against the far wall.

"What *is* this place?" Atrus asked, sniffing the musty air, noting that the seated skeletons were chained to their desks.

"This is the main Book Room," Gehn answered. But there was no sign of any books in that chamber. The shelves were crowded with all manner of things— boxes and bottles, papers and files, tools for writing and carving—but no books. Of *books*, at least of the kind that Gehn seemed to want, there was no sign. There were only those upstairs, and it was clear that Gehn did not want *them*.

Atrus stared at his father, confused. But Gehn was looking about purposefully, searching the nearest shelves as if he might unearth real treasures here.

"What should I look for?" he asked, after a moment.

Gehn turned, staring at him, as if he had forgotten he was there, then gestured to a door at the back of the room, behind the stairway they'd come down.

"Have a look in there, Atrus. There should be a narrow passageway with four or five rooms off it. One of them will be the bookstore. If it is locked, call me. But it should be open. They would not have had time to lock it."

No, Atrus thought, beginning to understand how quickly catastrophe had fallen upon D'ni. At night, so his father had said, while most decent folk were in their beds.

Gehn turned away, rummaging among the shelves, stopping to take out a strange-looking glass vial and shake it, then throwing it aside.

Atrus watched him a moment longer then went through, finding it exactly as Gehn had described. The passageway was eight paces long. Two doors led off to the left, two to the right; one lay directly ahead. He tried that first, noting the D'ni "Book" symbol cut into the center of the elaborate carved pattern on its polished wooden surface.

The door swung back silently on its hinges at his touch. Inside was the tiniest of rooms—almost a cupboard it was so small—with broad shelves on all three sides, reaching up into the ceiling space well above his head.

Most of those were empty, but on one of the higher shelves there were seven, no eight, of the big, leather-bound books.

Atrus reached up and pulled one down, a red-covered book, surprised by how heavy it was, as if it were made of something more than paper. Then, kneeling, he placed it on the floor in front of him and opened it.

Nothing! The pages were blank. Disappointed, he closed the book and slipped it back into its place, then took another, this time with a pale green leather cover. That, too, proved blank. One by one he took the books down, certain that he would find at least one that had something written in it, but they were all, as far as he could see, the same.

Defeated, he placed one of the books beneath his arm and went outside, walking back down the passageway despondently.

Gehn had cleared a space on one of the workbenches and was bent over what looked like a wooden tray filled with a dozen or so large amber-colored inkpots. After a moment, he straightened, holding up one of the big, five-sided crystals to examine it, its rich amber color reflected in Gehn's pallid face. Then, noticing Atrus standing there, he looked across.

"Well? Did you find any?"

"It's no good," Atrus said, steeling himself against his father's anger. "There's nothing in them."

Putting the inkpot back in the case, Gehn came and took the book from Atrus. "Here, let me see that."

He opened it and flicked through a number of pages, then looked up again. "This is fine. This is just what I was looking for. Are there others?"

Atrus went to shake his head, then nodded, utterly confused now. "But I thought . . . I thought you wanted ones with Ages in them. These . . . these are just books."

Gehn laughed. "No, Atrus. These are not just books, these are *Kortee'nea*. Blank books, waiting to be written."

Written . . . Atrus stared at his father.

Gehn unslung his knapsack and slid the book

inside it, then looked to Atrus again. "How many books are there in the store?"

"Eight."

"Good. Then bring them back in here. There is ink here," he said, gesturing toward the case of amber-colored pots, "and pens, too, so we have everything we need. Come then. Quick now, boy. We can be home by supper!"

10

"Atrus?"

Atrus looked up from his desk to where Gehn stood on the far side of the library.

"Yes, father?" he said, setting his pen aside, careful not to drip any ink across the copy paper.

"Come with me."

Atrus stood uncertainly, then, skirting the dais at the center of the room, joined his father at the foot of the steps.

Two weeks had passed since the expedition into the city, and Atrus had begun to think that his father had forgotten his promise, but Gehn was smiling now.

"Are you ready, Atrus?"

"Ready, father?"

"To begin your work. It is time you learned how to Write."

He followed Gehn up into a large, yet strangely claustrophobic room. At first he didn't understand why, then he realized that it had been cut directly from the surrounding rock, which was why, perhaps, the ceiling was so low—a cave within a cave.

Books crowded the undecorated stone walls and were heaped up on the floor on all sides, while in the center of the room was a large desk, lit by a curiously shaped lamp—the only source of illumination in that dim and musty place. Facing that massive desk was another smaller one that had been cleared.

Gehn led him across, standing Atrus to one side while he sat in his chair and, reaching into one of the drawers, drew out a shallow metal tray on which was a large quill pen and a number of the amber-colored ink pots they had found on their first book hunt.

Setting the tray to one side, Gehn leaned across and pulled one of the big, leather-bound books toward him—its brown cover flecked with white—opening it to the first page.

It was blank.

He looked up at Atrus, his pale eyes fixing his son. "You have spent six weeks now, learning how to copy a number of basic D'ni words and have discovered just how complex and beautiful a script it is. But those characters also *mean* something, Atrus. Something much more than you've previously understood. And not just in this world. They were developed over tens of thousands of years for a specific task—that of describing Ages . . . of *creating* other worlds. They are not like the words you and I speak casually, nor can they be used so in the books. Writing—D'ni Writing—is not merely an Art, it is a science. The science of precise description."

He turned, looking to the blank page. "When we

begin, there is nothing. It is . . . *uncreated*. But as soon as the first word is written—just as soon as that first character is completed, the last stroke set down upon the page—then a link is set up to that newly created world, a bridge established."

Atrus frowned. "But where does it lead, this bridge?"

"Anywhere," Gehn answered, glancing at him as he removed the lid of the amber-colored crystal ink pot. "The D'ni called it Terokh Jeruth, the great tree of possibility."

Atrus laughed. "It sounds like magic!"

"And so it is. But you and I are D'ni, and so I shall share a secret with you. We are not ordinary men, Atrus, we are *gods!*"

"Gods?" Atrus stared back at his father, bewildered.

"Yes," Gehn went on fervently, his eyes lit with a passion Atrus had never seen in him before. "Common men but dream and wake. We, however, can live our dreams. Within limits—limits that the finest D'ni minds took great care to define over the millennia—we can create whatever we can visualize. We use words to conjure worlds."

Atrus's mouth had fallen open.

"Why, I could show you worlds so rich, so vivid in their detail, that they would make you want to burst with admiration for their makers. Worlds of such splendor and magnificence that they make this marvelous world of ours seem ordinary!"

Gehn laughed, then held the ink pot up for Atrus to see. Within the thick, yellow, glasslike walls of the container, was a fine black liquid.

"What do you see, Atrus?"

Atrus looked up, meeting his father's eyes, momentarily startled by that echo of Anna's customary words.

"Ink?"

"Yes . . . but not just any ink. It has special powers that ordinary ink does not possess. So, too, with the pages of the book. They are made of a special paper, the formula for which was kept secret by the Guild."

"And the pen?" Atrus asked, pointing to it. "Is that special, too?"

Gehn smiled. "No. The pen is but a pen. However, if anyone else tried to do what we are about to do—anyone, that is, without D'ni blood—then they would fail. It would be impossible."

Turning to face the page, Gehn set the ink pot down, then, dipping the metallic tip of the quill into it, lifted the pen above the page and began to write.

Slowly a D'ni character—the word "island," Atrus noted—began to form, its intense blackness *burned* almost into the pure white surface by the pen.

Gehn wrote another dozen characters onto the page, then lifted the pen and looked to Atrus.

"Is it done?" Atrus asked, surprised that there had

not been more. He had expected fireworks or the heavens to open. "Have you made a new Age?"

Gehn laughed. "It exists, yes . . . but as yet it is very crude. It takes a great deal of work to create an Age. There are special formulas you have to follow, precise laws to obey. As I said, it is not simply an Art, it is a science—the science of precise description."

He gestured toward the open book. "As yet, I have merely sketched out the most basic elements of my new world. Ahead lies an immense amount of hard work. Every aspect of the Age must be described, each new element fitted in. But that is not all."

Reaching across, Gehn took another, much smaller book from a pile at the side and held it out to Atrus. "Once the Age is complete, one must always—*always*—make a Linking Book."

Atrus took the small book and opened it, noting at once how few pages were in it. All of them were blank.

"Yes," Gehn continued. "Whenever you travel to a newly written Age you must always carry a Linking Book with you. If you did not, you would be trapped there, without any way of traveling back."

Atrus looked back at his father, wide-eyed. "But what's actually in one of these Linking Books?"

Gehn took the book back. "Each Linking Book refers to one of the larger descriptive books—to one specific book. You might say that it contains the essence of the larger book—certain phrases and words that fuses it to that book and no other. But that is not all. For a Linking Book to work, it must also include an accurate description of the place one wishes to link to on that particular Age, which is recorded by writing a special D'ni symbol, a Garo-hertee. Yes, and a Linking Book must be written in the Age and location it is meant to link to. And so a Linking Book is, in a sense, a working substitute for a descriptive book."

Atrus thought a moment, then. "And can there be only one Linking Book for each descriptive book?"

"Not at all," Gehn answered, delighted by his son's understanding. Then, setting the slender book back on the pile, he added. "You can make as many Linking Books as you want. But you must always make at least one. That is the first rule. One you must not forget."

Atrus nodded, then, "But what if you change the Age? What if you decide to write more in the descriptive book? Would the Linking Book cease to work?"

"No. If the descriptive book is changed, then all Linking Books associated with it will link to the changed world."

Atrus's eyes lit, imagining it, only now realizing just how complex and powerful this Writing was. "It sounds . . . *astonishing!*"

"Yes," Gehn said, his eyes looking back at Atrus, godlike and wise beyond all human years. "Oh, it *is*, Atrus. It is."

That night, Atrus decided he would speak to his father, to remind him that it was almost time for them to go back and visit Anna.

Encouraged by Gehn's high spirits over supper, Atrus waited until he had lit his pipe and settled back in his chair in the corner of the kitchen before he broached the subject.

"Father?"

Gehn stretched his legs and stared at his boots, the gently-glowing pipe cradled in his lap. "Yes?"

"When are we going back?"

Gehn looked to him languidly. "Back? Back where?"

"To the cleft."

Surprisingly, Gehn laughed. "*There?* You want to go back there?"

"Yes," Atrus said quietly. "You said . . ."

"I said I would try. I said . . ."

Gehn sat up and, setting the pipe aside, leaned toward Atrus. "I said that to keep your grandmother quiet. I never meant . . ." He shrugged, then started again. "Look, Atrus, it would take us the best part of four or five days to get there and another three or four to return here. And for what?"

"Well, couldn't you write a book to the cleft and bring her here?"

"And how would you set about writing such a book? This world has already been created."

"Then can't you write a Linking Book?"

Atrus stopped, realizing that, of course, he couldn't. He would have to be at the cleft in order to write that Linking Book.

Gehn watched him, seeing that he understood, then spoke softly. "I should, perhaps, have said you cannot link to another location in the Age you are in. It is impossible."

Atrus was silent a moment, then. "But you told me you would take me back."

"Oh, Atrus, grow up! There's nothing there."

Atrus looked down. "But you *promised*. You said . . ."

Gehn stood. "I simply do not have the time, and even if I did, I would scarcely waste it going there. The place is a pit, Atrus. Literally so. Besides, that woman is poisonous. Don't you understand that yet? I *had* to take you away from there."

"You're wrong," Atrus said quietly.

But Gehn simply shook his head and pointed at the chair. "Sit down. I shall tell you a story. Then you can tell me if I am wrong or not."

Atrus sat, angry still and resentful, refusing to meet his father's eyes.

"Close to thirty years ago, when I was but a child of four, there was a war. A young man named Veovis started it. He was the son of a nobleman, and the sole heir to a powerful estate. In time he would have become one of the ruling Council, a lawmaker. But he was not content with what he had, nor with the promise of what would be. Veovis broke D'ni law. He abused his privileged position."

"In what way?"

"His crimes were heinous, unmentionable. He was a cancer that needed to be cut from the D'ni culture. Eventually he was caught and, despite his father's intercession, he was tried before the Five Lords. For more than twenty days witnesses gave evidence. Finally, the Five gave their decision. Veovis was to be imprisoned. To be kept in a place from which he would never escape. But before the decision of the Five could be implemented, several of Veovis's young friends helped him to flee D'ni.

"For six months, nothing was heard of Veovis, and it was assumed that the problem had taken care of itself. But then rumors began to circulate. Rumors that Veovis had taken a new name and was to be found in the drinking houses of the lower city, stirring up discontent against the ruling faction.

"At first, nothing was done. Rumors were only rumors, it was argued. But then a number of incidents occurred. A stabbing of a senior official in one of the guilds. A bomb in one of the main ink works. The desecration of a book."

Atrus frowned, not understanding, but his father was staring off into the distance, caught up in his recollections.

"After this last incident, a Council meeting was

called. At last, they decided to take action. But already it was too late. Veovis had indeed been staying in the lower city. Furthermore, he had been fermenting trouble among the lower classes. What none of the ruling Council could have known, however, was just how deep that discontent ran, nor how raw a nerve Veovis had touched. Only two days after the Council met, serious rioting broke out in one of the lower city districts. Before curfew that evening, the whole of the lower city was in chaos as the mob roamed the streets, maiming or killing whoever dared to stand against them."

Gehn stopped, turning to face Atrus.

"As I said, I was but a child at the time. I was staying in one of the great Guild houses in the upper precincts. My home was several miles away, on a great bluff of rock that I could see from one of the windows in the refectory. I remember standing there all that afternoon, as the roar of the mob and the awful cries of the dying came up to us from below, and wondering if it was the end. It was a terrible time, made worse by my fears for my own family. We were safe in the Guild houses, of course. At the first sign of trouble, the Council had barred the gates to the upper city and trebled the guard. But many on the outlying estates died that day, victims of their own servants—men and women they had trusted all their lives.

"It was fully six weeks before the last of the rebels

was subdued and Veovis himself captured, trying to make his escape through the lower tunnels."

"This time, when the Five met, their decision was unanimous. Veovis was to die. He was to be executed, there on the steps of the Great Library."

Gehn looked away, clearly pained by what came next, then spoke again. "It was a wise decision. Yet before it could be sealed and passed as law, one final witness stepped forward, begging their leave to speak out on the young man's behalf."

Ti'ana, Atrus thought, recalling what Anna had told him.

Gehn slowed once more, staring out past Atrus. "That witness was a woman, Ti'ana."

Atrus opened his mouth, aching to finish the tale—to show his father what he knew—but Gehn seemed not to be aware of him. He spoke on, in the grip of the tale; a sudden bitterness in his voice.

"Ti'ana was much respected by the Five and so they let her speak. In her view, the danger had passed. Veovis had done his worst and D'ni had survived. Furthermore, she argued, if it had not been Veovis, some other rabble-rouser would have stirred the mob to action, for the discontent had not been that of a single man, but of a whole class. In the circumstances, she said, her eloquence swaying those venerable lords, should not the Council's original decision be carried out."

Coming to the bottom of the steps, Gehn stepped

out onto the second ledge and, looking to his son, sighed deeply. "And so it was done, Atrus. Veovis was placed inside his prison. The prison from which he could not escape."

Gehn paused, his eyes on Atrus. "It was three days later when it happened. They had checked on him, of course, morning and evening, but on the evening of that third day, the guard who was sent did not return. Two more were sent, and when they returned, it was with the news that the prison was empty. There was no sign of either Veovis or the guard.

"They should have known that something was seriously wrong, but they had not learned their lessons. And when Veovis did not reappear, they assumed that all was well, that he had fled—who knew where?—and would not be seen again. But Veovis was a vengeful young man who had seen his hopes dashed twice in the space of a year. Only a fool would think he'd simply go away and lick his wounds. Only a fool . . ."

Atrus blinked, surprised by the sudden anger in his father's voice.

"And so it was that Veovis *did* return. And this time it was not in the company of an unwashed and uncontrollable rabble, but at the head of a small but well-trained force of fanatics who had but one thing in their minds: to destroy D'ni. Ti'ana was wrong, you see. The danger had not passed, nor had Veovis done his worst."

"But she was not to know, surely?"

"No?" Gehn shook his head, a profound disappointment in his face. "The woman was a foolish meddler. And my father no less a fool for listening to her."

"Your father?"

"Yes," Gehn said, walking across to the edge and standing there, looking out across the ruined landscape. "Or is that something else she hasn't told you?"

"She?"

"Anna. Your grandmother."

"I . . . I don't understand. What has she got to do with it?"

Gehn laughed bleakly. "You still do not know?"

"Know what?"

And now Gehn turned and looked at him again, his face hard. "That she *was* Ti'ana. Anna, I mean. That was her D'ni name, given to her by my father—your grandfather—when he married her."

Atrus stared, shock in his face. "No. *No.* It isn't possible. She would have said."

"It's true," Gehn said bitterly. "Her words destroyed it . . . her *meddling*. It would all have been over, finished with. Veovis would have been dead, the threat dealt with, but no . . . she had to interfere. She could not help herself. As if she knew *best* all the while! She would never listen. *Never!*"

Atrus shook his head, unable to believe it.

"Did she ever tell you about *me*, Atrus? *Did* she?

No! Of course not! So ask yourself, what else did she fail to tell you?"

"But she couldn't have!" he blurted, unable to help himself. "She *couldn't!*"

"*No?*" For a moment Gehn stared at him, as if studying an exhibit beneath a microscope. "You should not let sentiment blind you, Atrus. The world we inhabit is a harsh one, and sentiment can kill just as surely as a falling rock. It was a lesson your grand-mother never learned. And that is why I cannot let you go back to her. For your own good."

Atrus was silent a moment, staring down at his hands where they were clasped in his lap. Then he spoke again, his voice quiet now, lacking the defiant conviction it had had only minutes before.

"Anna was good to me. She looked after me, made sure I never starved. Yes, and she taught me, too."

"*Taught* you?" Gehn's laughter was scathing. "Taught you what? How to survive in a crack? How to eat dust and dream of rain, I bet!"

"*No!*" Atrus yelled, hurt now and confused and angry—angrier than he'd ever been—though at who it was hard to tell. "She taught me more than *you've* ever taught me!"

Gehn's laughter died. He stepped across and stood over Atrus, looking down at him coldly, threateningly. "What did you say?"

Atrus lowered his eyes, intimidated by his father's

physical presence. "I said she taught me more than you."

Gehn reached down with his right hand, gripped Atrus's chin, and forced him to look at him. "Tell me, boy. What did that woman ever teach you that was any use at all?"

He shrugged off Gehn's hand and moved his head back. "She taught me D'ni, that's what!"

Gehn laughed and shook his head. "Taught you to lie, more like!"

Atrus met his father's eyes squarely, then spoke slowly, calmly, in fluent D'ni.

"She taught me what is good and what is to be valued, those truths which cannot be shaken or changed."

Slowly, like the sunlight bleeding from the horizon at the day's end, the mocking smile faded from Gehn's lips.

"You mean, you *knew?*" Gehn said coldly. "All this while?" His face was hard now, his eyes cold. Once again there seemed something dangerous—something frightening—about him. "You sat there all that time, pretending not to know? *Mocking* me?"

"No," Atrus began, wanting to explain, but Gehn was not listening. Grasping Atrus with both hands he pulled him up out of his chair and shook him.

"Why, you deceitful, ungrateful little boy! It would serve you right if I took you back and let you rot there in that pathetic little hole! Ah, but she would like that, wouldn't she? And that is why we are *not* going back. Not now, not ever!"

"But you must!" Atrus cried out, appalled at the thought. "She'll be worried! When she doesn't hear . . ."

Taking Atrus by the scruff of the neck, Gehn half marched, half dragged him to his room and threw him inside, then slammed the door and locked it.

"Wait!" Atrus cried, picking himself up and throwing himself at the door. "Father! *Please* . . . you've got to listen!"

For three whole days, Gehn did not return. When he finally did, he announced himself by rapping loudly on the door to Atrus's room.

"Atrus?"

Atrus was in his sleeping niche in the big wardrobe, a spot that felt more like his bed at home, reading a D'ni book, a half-eaten apple in one hand. The sudden knocking made him jump. Hiding the apple and the book, he quickly closed the wardrobe door and hurried across to the bed, slipping beneath the silken sheets.

"Atrus?" Gehn's voice came again. Significantly, he spoke D'ni now. "Are you awake? I need to talk with you."

He ought to have told him to go away, but the

anger he'd first felt had now evaporated. Besides, he wanted to know just what his father had to say for himself.

"All right . . ." he called back, feigning indifference.

He heard the key turn in the lock. A moment later Gehn stepped into the room. He looked immensely weary, his pale eyes ringed from lack of sleep, his clothes unwashed—the same clothes he had been wearing the evening he had argued with Atrus.

Atrus sat up, his back against the massive, carved headboard, looking across at Gehn, who was outlined in the half-light by the door.

"I've been thinking," Atrus began.

Gehn raised a hand. "We speak only D'ni henceforth."

Atrus started again, this time in D'ni. "I've been thinking. Trying to see it from your point of view. And I think I understand."

Gehn came closer, intrigued. "And what conclusion did you come to?"

Atrus hesitated, then. "I think I understand why you feel what you feel about Anna. Why you hate her so much."

Gehn laughed, surprised, yet his face was strangely pained. "No, Atrus. I do not *hate* her. It would be easy if it were that simple. But I do *blame* her. I blame her for what she did to D'ni. And for leaving my father here, knowing he would die."

"I don't see the difference."

"No?" Gehn came closer, standing over him. "It is hard to explain just what I feel sometimes. She is my mother and so she *has* to love me. It is her duty. Why, I even saw it in her eyes that last time. But she does not like me. To be honest, she never has." He shook his head, then continued. "It was the same with Veovis. She never liked *him*. She thought him odious; ill-mannered and foul-tempered. Yet when it came down to it, she felt that her duty was to love him—to save him from himself.

Gehn sighed heavily. "She was a hypocrite. She did not act on what she knew to be the truth. It was a weakness that destroyed a race of gods!"

"And yet you two survived," Atrus said quietly. "She saved you. Brought you out of D'ni."

"Yes," Gehn said, staring away into the shadows on the far side of the room. "Some days I wonder why. Some days I ask myself whether that, too, was not weakness of a kind. Whether it would not have been better for us both to have died back there and end it all cleanly. As it is . . ."

Atrus stared at his father in the long silence that followed, seeing him clearly for the first time. There was something quite admirable about the spirit within him; about the determination to try to restore and recreate the D'ni culture single-handedly. Admirable but futile.

"So can I go and see Anna?"

Gehn did not even look at him. "No, Atrus. My mind is made up. It would be too disruptive, and I cannot afford disruption."

"But she'll worry if I don't go back . . ."

"Be quiet, boy! I said no, and I mean no! Now let that be the last word on the matter! I shall send Rijus with a note, informing your grandmother that you are well and explaining why she cannot see you again. But beyond that, I can permit no further contact between you."

Atrus looked down. It was as if his father had physically struck him. Not see her again? The thought appalled him.

"As for the matter of your deception," Gehn went on; unaware, it seemed, of the great shadow that had fallen on the young man's spirit, "I have to tell you that I was gravely disappointed in you, Atrus. That said, I shall overlook it this once. Indeed, it may prove a great benefit in the long term. It will certainly save me a great deal of time and hard work, and it will also mean that I can press on more rapidly than I had anticipated. It is possible you might even start a book of your own."

Atrus looked up. "A *book?*"

"Yes. But you must promise me something."

Gehn loomed over him, his manner fierce, uncompromising. "You must promise me never—and I mean *never*—to question my word again or to scheme behind

my back. You must be absolutely clear on this, Atrus. I
am Master here and my word is law."

Atrus stared at his father, knowing him at that
moment better than he had ever known him; then, realizing he had no other choice, he bowed his head.

"I promise."

"Good. Then come and get something to eat. You
must be starving."

11

"WHERE ARE WE?" ATRUS ASKED, looking about him at the cave into which they had "linked," his eyes taking a moment to adjust to the darkness.

Gehn edged past him. Standing on tiptoe, he reached into a narrow recess high up at the back of the cave. "This is one of my more recent worlds," he answered, removing a slender box. Within was the Linking Book that would get them back to D'ni. Quickly checking that it had not been tampered with, he slid it back into the hole in the rock, then turned, looking to Atrus. "This is my Thirty-seventh Age."

"Ah . . ." Atrus said, if only because he could think of nothing else. Personally, he would have spent a little time and effort thinking of a name for the Age—something mystical and romantic, perhaps—but Gehn was pragmatic when it came to his creations.

For three years now he had been accompanying his father to these Ages, and never once had Gehn thought to give an Age a name. Numbers. It was always numbers with his father.

At the front of the cave, a narrow tunnel curved away to the left, sloping steadily upward. Fastening his

LINK TO CAVE

LAGOON

LOWLANDS

VILLAGE IN ESTUARY

OCEAN

GE 37

HIGH TID

cloak at the neck, Atrus followed Gehn out, wondering what kind of world this was.

Up above it was night. They emerged into a rough circle of open grass surrounded on three sides by the bare rock of the hillside. Below them, under a dark, blue-black sky in which sat two small moons—one white, one red—lay an island. At the center of the island was an oval lake.

Atrus stood there, taking in the sight, impressed by the circle of low hills that formed a natural bowl about the lake. The lake itself was dark and still, reflecting the twin moons, the surrounding sea shimmeringly bright.

Looking at it, Atrus began to question it, as he always did, wondering what words, what phrases his father had used to get that soft, sculpted shape to the hills? Or was that a product of the underlying rock? Was it limestone? Or clay, perhaps? And those trees, over to the right—were they a natural variant, or had Gehn written them in specifically?

The air was sweet and cool, rich with the varied scents of living things.

"It's very beautiful," he said finally, looking to his father, but Gehn merely grunted, surveying his work with what seemed a haughty disregard.

"I have done much better work than this," he answered, climbing up onto one of the rocks, then stepping down the other side. "In some ways this is my least successful experiment. I tried to keep it simple. Too simple, possibly."

Atrus climbed up onto the rock, hurrying to catch up. He had seen quite a few of his father's Ages these past three years—he hasn't begun to try making ages yet—but it had never ceased to astonish him that mere words could create such vivid and tangible realities.

There was a path leading down between the scattered rocks. After a dozen paces it opened out onto a bare slope covered in thigh-high grass. Below them, maybe a mile or so distant, huddled around the left-hand side of the lake, was a scatter of low, rectangular buildings, oddly shaped, as if half made of stone; maybe forty in all, lit by the lamps which hung over doorways and on poles along the harbor's edge. Suspended walkways linked the huts. Beneath the eaves of the nearest huts a number of dark, upright figures could be glimpsed.

Atrus turned to stare at Gehn, surprised. "It's *inhabited?*"

"Yes, but don't expect too much, Atrus. The people of this Age are an immensely simple folk. Crude, one might almost say. They manage to eke out a meager existence by way of fishing and basic agriculture, but as for culture, well . . ."

Gehn's laugh was dismissive. Even so, Atrus felt a strange excitement at the thought of meeting them. Though Gehn had occasionally brought in working parties from one or other of his Ages, he had never taken Atrus to an inhabited Age. Not before today.

They walked on, descending the thickly grassed slope. At first Atrus thought they would come upon the islanders unobserved, but then, a hundred yards or so from the edge of the village, a shout went up. Someone had spotted them. At once there was a buzz of voices down below and signs of sudden, frantic activity.

Gehn touched his arm, motioning that he should stop.

Atrus glanced at his father, alarmed. "Are we in danger?"

Gehn shook his head. "Be patient, Atrus. You are here to observe, so observe."

Atrus fell silent, watching as a dozen or so of the tall, manlike figures came up the slope toward them, carrying flaming torches.

Ten paces from them, the party stopped, dropping to their knees and bowing their heads, abasing themselves before Gehn. One of their number—the tallest of them—stood, then, coming forward, his head bowed, held out a garland of yellow flowers, offering at the same time a few words of broken D'ni.

"You are welcome, Great Master. Your dwelling is prepared."

In the flickering light of the torches, Atrus saw what he was wearing. It was a crude, handwoven copy of a Guild cloak!

"Good," Gehn said, lowering his head so that the man could place the garland over it. Then, straightening up, he gestured to the man, "Gather the villagers. I shall speak to them at once."

"Master!" the acolyte answered, glancing at Atrus, his dark eyes curious.

"Now lead on!" Gehn said, his voice stern, commanding.

They went down, through a narrow lane flanked by low but spacious huts with steeply sloping roofs of thatch, their wooden walls rising out of a bed of large, shaped boulders. Suspended, slatted wooden walkways swayed gently overhead as they walked through, and as they came out beside the lake, Atrus saw how the earth there had been covered with boards; how steps had been cut into the face of the rock, leading down. Below was a kind of harbor, one wall of which had been created by sinking hundreds of long poles into the bottom of the lake to form a sunken barrier. In the harbor were a dozen or so small but sturdy-looking fishing boats, their masts laid flat, their cloth sails furled.

People were gathering from all over now—men, women, and children. They were pale-skinned, stocky, clearly human in their dark-brown smocks. Their hair was uniformly light in color and spiky, reminding Atrus of straw.

Farther along, a channel had been cut through the rock, linking the lake to the open sea. It was not very broad—barely wide enough for a single boat to navigate—but a strong wooden bridge had been thrown across it.

On the other side, the land began to climb again, and on the top of a narrow ridge, behind which was the more massive slope of the hill, was what looked like a meeting hut of some kind, much larger than the huts that faced the harbor. As they crossed the bridge and began to climb the slope, Atrus saw lights being hastily lit up ahead, garlands hung between the wooden posts at the front of the building.

Behind them, the people of the village gathered, following silently, their torches burning brightly in the moonlit darkness.

Coming to the front of the building, Gehn turned, facing the crowd, whose number had grown to several hundred.

"People of the Thirty-seventh Age," he began, speaking loudly, the circle of hills making his words echo back to him across the lake. "This is my son, Atrus. I have decided that we shall stay with you for a time. While he is here you will treat him with the same respect you accord me."

Atrus stared at his father, surprised. This was the first he had heard of any of this. But Gehn spoke on, his voice booming now.

"Whatever he wants, you will give to him. Whatever he asks, you will do. Is it understood?"

"It is understood," two hundred voices answered as one.

"Good!" Gehn said, then raised his left hand imperiously, dismissing them. He turned to Atrus.

"Come, Atrus. Inside."

Atrus hesitated, looking back down the slope at the dispersing villagers, then, pulling his cloak about him, followed his father into the great hut.

The interior of the hut was shockingly familiar. It was just like the Worship Rooms he had seen in several of the great houses back in D'ni. Symbolic tapestries hung on three of the walls: elaborate and colorful silks which, Atrus guessed, had been taken from D'ni and brought here. There were rugs and screens and, on a low table to the right, a number of golden goblets and bowls—big, jewel-encrusted things that, once again, looked to have been taken from D'ni. Dominating the room, however, was a huge, wooden desk, like the desk in Gehn's study.

He looked to his father. Gehn was watching him, amused.

"You want to know why I brought you here?"

Atrus hesitated, then nodded.

Gehn walked over to the desk and took his seat, then leaned across, taking a long, thin book from a pile to the side.

"The truth is, Atrus, I brought you here for a number of reasons, but mainly so that I might answer a few of those questions you are forever asking me concerning the making of an Age. I wanted to flesh out your theoretical knowledge. To that end, you will keep a notebook while you are here; in it you will write down all your observations about this Age."

He held the book out, letting Atrus take it.

"I also wanted you to experience things for yourself, without preconceptions. I wanted you to see, with your own eyes, the awe in which we are held in the Ages."

"Awe, father?"

"Yes, Atrus, awe. And so they should, for are we not gods? Do they not owe their lives, their very breath, to us? Would they be *here* had I not written on the whiteness of the page?"

Gehn paused, then. "I want you to stay here a while and observe this Age, to see just what is possible. It will help you with your own writing. You will stay with one of the locals—an old woman whose husband died some years back. You will be courteous to her but aloof, you understand?"

"I understand."

Gehn sat back. "Good. Then go now. My acolyte is just outside. He will take you to where you will be staying."

The acolyte walked silently before Atrus, his ceremonial torch, its shaft, carved with tiny D'ni symbols, held up before him. Curious villagers knelt and bowed their heads as they passed, a low whisper going from one to another in their wake.

When they came to the path through the village, however, the man did not go straight on toward the cave, but turned to the left, climbing a narrow set of steps between two huts that climbed up past their steeply sloping roofs. Atrus followed, coming out above the village on a path that seemed to lead nowhere. Ahead of them was only the dark, moonlit slope of the hill.

The man led on, walking slowly, solemnly, as if at the head of a great procession.

Atrus looked back toward the harbor, his eyes finding the bridge and, beyond it in the darkness, the meeting hut. Beyond that, visible only now that the lanterns had been lit inside, was a long, low tent. As Atrus watched, he saw his father walk across and duck beneath the canvas flap.

He turned back. Ahead of him, to his left, just over the hump of the hill, there was a hint of light. As they climbed, it grew, revealing the outline of a hut just over the brow of the slope. The light was from its open doorway.

As they drew nearer, a figure stepped into the light—outlined for one brief moment before it merged with the darkness.

The old woman.

As the light from the acolyte's torch fell over the

front of the hut, she was revealed. Like most of her people, she wore a simple, dark-brown smock of coarsely woven cloth. Her hair, likewise, was unsophisticated, its thick gray strands framing her deeply lined face in an unkempt halo. She was the oldest person Atrus had ever seen.

She looked away, bowing awkwardly, then stepped back, allowing him to enter the hut.

Atrus hesitated, then ducked under the low lintel, into a clean, warm space that was filled with the strong, fresh scent of herbs. Looking about him, he saw them at once, all along the right-hand wall, above two narrow shelves of pots and pans: sprig after sprig of herbs, hung on tiny wooden hooks.

The floor was covered in planed wooden boards, the low roof made of rafter and thatch. Halfway down its length, a plain blue curtain cut off his view of the rest of the hut.

"You want to eat?" the old woman asked, uncomfortable in his presence, her D'ni even more rudimentary than the acolyte's.

Atrus shook his head. "Thank you, I'm not really hungry."

"Ah . . ." Her nod seemed more from nervousness than agreement. She looked at him anxiously, her brown eyes never leaving his face. "You want to sleep?"

"I . . ." The truth was, he wasn't really tired. After all, back in D'ni it was barely suppertime. Yet he could sense how awkward he was making her feel and felt awkward himself for doing so. "Yes," he said, after a moment. "If you would show me my bed."

There was a slight movement in her face which he didn't understand. She seemed . . . *regretful?* Then, with a tiny shrug, she went across and, pulling the curtain aside a little way, looked back at him, pointing to what seemed a kind of stall.

He went across and looked, then laughed; a pleasant laugh of surprise, for there, between the thin wooden walls of his sleeping stall lay a simple, straw-stuffed mattress.

"Like home," he said quietly.

The old woman was staring at him, curious now. "Beg pardon, Master?"

He looked to her, realizing his eyes were moist. "When I was a child, with my grandmother, I had a mattress similar to this."

"Is it no good?" she asked, as if he had been speaking a foreign language.

"No, no . . . it's . . . wonderful." He looked to her and smiled, strangely grateful to her. Then, on impulse, remembering the pleasure his grandmother had always got from feeding him, he said, "Can I change my mind? I mean, about the food?"

"Of course!" the old woman said, a smile lighting her face for the first time. "I bring you soup and bread, yes?"

He grinned. "It sounds marvelous!"

"Then you wait, Master. I bring you some."

Atrus watched her go, then looked about him, suddenly at ease, breathing in the pleasant scent of the herbs.

He knelt, setting his knapsack and the notebook down in a corner of the stall, then removed his cloak and stowed it in the sack. As he straightened up again, the old woman returned, carrying a wooden tray. On it was an earthenware bowl of soup, a wooden spoon, and half a small loaf of brown bread. Atrus accepted it gratefully, then sat, the tray in his lap. Smiling at her, he broke off a hunk of the bread and dipped it into the bowl.

For a while he ate in silence, enjoying that simple meal. Finished, he looked up at the old woman.

"Was it okay?" she asked, a look of deep concern on her heavily lined face.

Atrus grinned. "It was *wonderful!* The best I've *ever* tasted!"

The truth was, he had no idea what it had been, but what he'd said wasn't a lie. It had been wonderful. The best soup he had *ever* tasted, Anna's notwithstanding.

His words brought a ray of spring sunlight to the old woman's face. "You want more?"

"*Can* I?"

It was as if, with those two little words, he had offered her all the riches of D'ni. She beamed, then hurried away, returning in a moment with a second bowl and the other half of the loaf.

"There," she said, standing over him as he ate, grinning broadly. "You growing boy! You need your food, eh?"

Atrus woke in the darkness before dawn, wondering for an instant where he was, the scent of herbs in that tiny, enclosed space oddly disturbing.

He sat up, listening to the silence, then stood, making his way quickly, quietly outside.

Both moons had set and the land was dark now, intensely dark, the sky almost bright by comparison, like the desert sky at night. Yet looking up he knew he was not on earth. Where was the Hunter now? Where the Dipper? Were they elsewhere in that vast, star-dusted sky, or was he somewhere else entirely? In another universe, perhaps?

The thought was one he had had more and more often these past few months. A dangerous, unspoken thought.

And yet the more I discover about Writing, the more I challenge my father's view that we are creating the worlds we travel in.

What if they weren't so much *making* those worlds as linking to pre-existing possibilities?

At first he had dismissed the notion as a foolish one. Of course they created these worlds. They had to be! How else would they come into being in such precise and predictable forms? Besides, it was simply not possible that an infinite supply of different worlds existed out there, waiting to be tapped. Yet the more he'd thought about it, the more he had come to question his father's simpler explanation.

He walked down the slope until he came to a slab of rock overlooking the lake. There he bent down, squatting on his haunches, looking out across the dark bowl of the lake.

Now that the moons had almost set, it was close to impossible to distinguish where the lake ended and the land began. It was like peering into the volcano on a moonless night. You could see nothing, but you might imagine everything. That was the thing about darkness—the way it refused to remain a simple *absence*. Unlike snow, which he had seen on one of Gehn's other Ages, the darkness took on forms—thousands of forms—for the dark was both fluid and potent.

Behind him, over the crest of the hill, the day was making an appearance. Slowly, very slowly, light bled into the bowl, etching sharp-edged shadows on the hillside facing him. Atrus watched it, fascinated, then turned, squinting against the bright arc that peeped above the curve of the hill.

Turning back, he noticed something just below him on the edge of the lake.

At first he thought it was some kind of sea creature—a seal, perhaps—but then, as it straightened up, he saw it clearly, silhouetted in the half light.

A girl. It was a girl.

As he watched, she bent down again, making a series of little bobbing motions. He frowned, puzzled. What in Kerath's name was she doing? Then, with a little jolt, he understood. Washing! She was washing! That little mound beside her was a basket full of sodden clothes!

He laughed, and as he did, he saw her tense and look around, like a startled animal.

Gathering up her basket she scurried up the hillside, disappearing over the dark hump of the hill, her tiny figure briefly outlined against the arc of the sun. Atrus watched, astonished by her reaction, then stood. The sun was half risen now. In its light he could see the thatched roof of the hut, its long, dark shape embedded in the deeper darkness of the slope.

Atrus turned, making a slow circle, his arms outstretched as he breathed in the rich, clear air. Then, determined to make an early start, he hurried up the slope, making for the hut.

12

"YOUNG MASTER?"

Atrus turned onto his side, wondering for an instant where he was. Herbs. The smell of herbs. Ah, yes. The old woman's hut. He was on the Thirty-seventh Age of Gehn, and it was morning.

He sat up, rubbing his eyes, then looked to the old woman, who stood with her back half bent in the opening to the stall.

"Forgive me, young Master," she said breathlessly, "but the Lord Gehn wants to see you at once."

Nodding his thanks, he stood and stretched. What time was it? And how long had he slept? He seemed to sleep longer, deeper, while he was here. Maybe it had something to do with the air.

He yawned, then, knowing how his father hated to be kept waiting, went outside.

Pulling on his glasses, he studied the scene that met his eyes.

Beneath him the slope was a tawny brown, furred like an animal's back. Beyond it the folds of land that surrounded the lake were revealed in browns and greens—so many different shades that he caught his breath to think of such subtle variation. And the textures! He walked out slowly, onto the ridge. Tall, dark

trees, their crowns explosions of jet black leaves, covered the left flank of the nearest hill, ending abruptly
in a smooth covering of bright green grass. Atrus
laughed.

"Why do you laugh, Master?"

Atrus turned, facing the acolyte, the smile gone
from his face. He had not seen him when he'd stepped
out.

"I laughed because of that hill there. It reminded
me . . . well, of a half-shaven head. The way those trees
end in a straight line . . ."

The priest stepped up and looked, then nodded;
but there was not the slightest trace of amusement in
his expression. He looked back at Atrus, then, with a
bow, said, "Your father awaits you, Master."

Atrus sighed inwardly. It was his fourth day on the
island and still the man retained his distance.

He walked slowly down the slope, silent now and
thoughtful, looking about him at the swell and fold of
hills surrounding the lake. As the village came into
sight, he stared at it a while, then looked to
the acolyte.

"What is your name?"

"My *name?*" The man seemed strangely intimidated
by the query.

"Yes, your name. What is it?"

"My name is . . . One."

"One?" Atrus gave a small laugh. "You mean, the
number one?"

The man nodded, unable to meet Atrus's eyes.

"And was that always your name?"

He hesitated, then shook his head. "My birth name was Koena."

"Koena," Atrus said, walking on, his eyes taking in the pleasant shapes of the thatched roofs just below him now, the covered walkways, the delightful contrast of the lake's vivid blue against the bright greens and russets of the land sloping down to it. "But One is the name my father gave you?"

Koena nodded.

A faint smile appeared at the corners of Atrus's mouth. Of course. He should have known. He turned his head, studying the man a moment, not disliking his long, rather severe features, noting in the unforgiving daylight just how coarse the cloth of his cloak actually was, how crudely fashioned the symbols on it.

"Have you been my father's helper long?"

"A thousand days."

Then this Age was indeed "recent." Gehn had created it only a matter of three years ago at most. But what about before that? Had it existed in any form at all? Did these people have any memories of a time before the Lord Gehn had come among them? And if they did, were those memories true memories, or were they also *written in?*

He knew from his studies that you could not actually *write* such things: not directly, anyway. Yet when you created an Age, with all of its complexities, then a great shadow of cause and effect was thrown back, such that the Age, though new created, still had a "history" of a kind. Not a real history, of course. How could it have a real history, after all? But in the minds and memories of its inhabitants it would seem as if it had. To them, the past would seem as real as it did to him or Gehn.

Or so Gehn argued. For himself he was no longer quite so sure.

A strange, high-pitched cry from somewhere to his left made Atrus start, then turn to look for its source. There was a strange flapping noise in the air, then a shadow whisked past his feet. He looked up in time to see a strange, plump-bodied animal shoot past, swimming, it seemed, through the air.

Koena was staring at him, astonished. "Master?" he asked. "Are you all right?"

"That!" Atrus said, pointing after it. "That . . . *animal* . . . what is it?"

"*That?* That is a bird, Master."

Atrus stared openmouthed, watching the "bird" circle over the lake, the flapping noise coming from the long arms it used to pull itself through the air. He watched it swoop, then dive.

"Amazing!" Atrus said. "I've never seen its like!"

Koena was staring at him now.

Atrus shook his head. In the other Ages there had been many birds, but never anything like this. This was simply bizarre. It was more like a small rodent than a bird and seemed far too heavy to fly, and those strange, furred wings.

What did he write? he wondered. *Why would Gehn create such a creature? Or had he? What if this wasn't deliberate? What if it was an accident?*

Atrus turned, looking to Koena.

"Come," he said, intrigued by the thought that his father might purposefully have created such a creature. "Let's go down. My father will be angry if he is kept waiting."

Gehn, who was finishing his breakfast, sat at a table covered in a thick red cloth edged with golden tassels. He was eating from a golden bowl, a golden goblet at his side. Behind him, on a stand, was a silk pennant, the D'ni symbol of the book emblazoned in black on its pure white background. Atrus stepped into the tent, looking about him, noting the luxuries that were on display on every side. In the far corner of the tent was a massive wooden bed, the headboard clearly of local design. Beside it was a D'ni dressing screen, painted gold and blue and carmine.

He stepped forward. "You sent for me, father?"

"Ah, Atrus . . ." Gehn said, wiping his mouth with a silken cloth, then threw it aside. "I thought we should continue with your lessons, Atrus."

"Father?"

Gehn nodded, then took his arm and led him across to a low table in the corner on which a large-scale map of the island had been spread out.

Atrus stretched out a hand and touched the bottom left-hand corner with his index finger. "Where's that?"

"Gone," Gehn said, looking at him strangely.

"And that?" he said, noting another, smaller island just beyond the sea passage.

"Gone."

Atrus looked to his father and frowned. "How?"

Gehn shrugged.

"I . . ." Atrus shook his head. "Is this what you want me to look for? Things disappearing?"

"No, Atrus. I want you simply to observe."

Atrus stared at his father a moment, then looked back at the map. As far as he could see everything else was precisely as he recalled it from his preliminary journeys around the island, down to the smallest detail.

Gehn went across to his desk and, opening the leather case he had brought with him from D'ni this time, took a slender notebook from inside and handed it to Atrus. "Here."

Atrus opened it and scanned a few lines, then looked back at his father. "What are these?"

"What you have there are a number of random phrases from the Age Thirty-seven book. What I want you to do, Atrus, is to try to ascertain what aspects of this Age they relate to, and how and why they create the effects they do."

"You want me to analyze them?"

"No, Atrus. But I do want you to begin to grip the relationship between the words that are written on the page and the complex entity—the physical, living Age—that results. You see, while our Art *is* a precise one, its effects are often quite surprising, owing to the complexity of the web of relationships that are created between things. The meaning of an individual phrase can be altered by the addition of other phrases, often to the extent that the original description bears no relation whatsoever to the resultant reality. That is why the D'ni were so adamant about contradictions. Contradictions can destroy an Age. Too often they simply make it break apart under the strain of trying to resolve the conflicting instructions."

Atrus nodded. "Yet if what you say is true, how can I tell if what I am observing relates directly to the phrases in this book? What if other phrases have distorted the end result?"

"That is for you to discover."

"But if I have only these few phrases . . ."

Gehn stared at him, then raised an eyebrow, as if to indicate that he ought to be able to work that one out for himself.

"You mean, you want me to guess?"

"Not guess, Atrus. Speculate. I want you to try to unravel the puzzle of this world. To look back from the world to the words and attempt to understand exactly why certain things resulted. It is, you will come to see, every bit as important as learning the D'ni words and phrases that purport to describe these things. Indeed, much of my experimenting over the years has been along these very lines. I have learned a great deal from my observations, Atrus, and so will you."

"Father."

"Then go now. And take the map, if you wish. I have no further need of it."

Atrus sat in the long meadow above the lake, the folded map in his lap, his father's notebook open at his side. Surrounded by the thigh-high grass he could not be seen, unless by someone working on the slopes on the far side of the lake, but right now it was midday and the villagers were in their huts, eating.

He had begun with the simplest of the twenty phrases his father had copied out for him—one which related to the composition of the soil here. From his own studies he knew how important the underlying rock and soil was to the kind of Age that resulted, especially the soil. A good rich soil, full of nutrients and minerals, would produce good harvests, which in turn would allow the people of that Age to spend less time carrying out the backbreaking task of cultivation. That was crucially important, for a people who did not have to spend every daylight hour providing food for their tables was a people that would quickly develop a culture. For culture, Atrus understood, was a product of excess.

Yes, he thought, recalling his days in the cleft. He understood it now. Had Anna been born and raised in the cleft, they would not have survived. Had she been simply a cultivator and no more, they would never have had enough, for there had never been enough growing space, enough seeds, enough water—enough of *anything*—to allow them to survive. What there *had* been was Anna's talent as a painter and a sculptor. It was that, ironically, which had kept them alive: that had provided them with the salt they needed, the seeds and flour and fuel, yes, and all of those tiny luxuries that had made life there bearable. Without them they would have died.

As it was, he had grown beyond the expectations of such a dry, uninhabitable place. The rich soil of Anna's mind had nurtured him, bringing him to ripeness.

Only now did he understand that. After years of blaming her, he saw it clearly once again.

The soil. It was all down to the soil. Growth began not in the sunlight but in the darkness, in tiny cracks, deep down in the earth.

Atrus smiled, then looked to the side, reading the D'ni phrase again. By rights, the soil here ought to have been rich and fertile, yet from his own observations he saw that other factors had affected it somehow. There was a slight acidity to it that was unhealthy.

He frowned, wishing that his father had given him the whole book to read and not just random phrases. Yet he knew how protective his father was of his books.

He was about to lay back and think the problem through, when he heard a tiny cry from somewhere just behind him. Setting the map aside, Atrus stood, looking about him at the meadow.

Nothing. At least nothing he could see. He took a few paces, then frowned. He couldn't have imagined it, surely?

It came again, this time a clear cry for help.

He ran toward the sound, then stopped, astonished. Just ahead of him the thick grass ended in a narrow chasm about six feet across and twelve or fifteen long—a chasm that had not been there the last time he had looked.

He stepped up to its edge, careful not to fall, and peered down into its darkness. It was the girl—the one he'd seen that first morning. She had fallen in and now seemed stuck up to her knees in the dark earth at the bottom of the crack some eight or ten feet down.

"It's okay," he said. "Don't worry. I'll get you out."

He turned, looking about him. He needed a rope or a branch or something. Anything he could throw down to her, then haul her up. Yet even as he stood there, thinking about it, he heard the soft fall of earth and, looking back, saw how it had fallen over her, making her position worse.

The edge of the nearest copse was fifty yards away. By the time he got there, broke off a branch and came back, she might quite easily be buried under it.

There was only one way.

He sat down on the edge, then, testing that it would take his weight, turned, and began to lower himself down into the crack, searching the face of it for footholds as he went.

"Reach up!" he called to her. "Reach up and take hold of my right foot."

He felt something brush the tip of his boot. Too high. He was still too high. The earth he was clinging to didn't feel all that secure, but he could not abandon her. He moved down a fraction more and felt, as he did, her hand close about his ankle.

"Good!" he said, thankful that she was only a waif of a girl. "Now get a grip with your other hand."

Two seconds passed, and then he felt her other hand grip his ankle.

"Okay. Now hold on tight. And don't struggle. If you struggle, we'll both fall in again!"

Slowly, painfully slowly, he hauled himself up and over the edge, turning at the end, to reach down and grab her wrists, pulling her up the last few feet.

She sat there, beside him on the grass, trembling, her chest rising and falling as she tried to get her breath, her frightened eyes staring at the black wound in the earth that had almost claimed her.

"Are you okay?" he asked, after a moment.

She went to nod, then shook her head.

He stared at her a moment, then, standing, went back across to where he'd left the map and notebook, and, picking up his cloak, took it back and wrapped it about her shoulders.

She looked to him, grateful, then stared back at the crack. "What is it?" she asked, her voice a whisper.

"I don't know," he answered, troubled suddenly, remembering the missing islands on the map. *But perhaps my father does.*

Gehn reached across the desk and drew the case toward him, then, taking the tiny key from the chain about his neck, unlocked the clasps.

"I shall be gone only a few hours," he said, glancing up at Atrus, who stood on the other side of the desk, the girl beside him. "She will remain here with the acolyte until I return. And you shall say nothing. You understand, Atrus? I do not want the islanders panicked by this. There is a simple explanation and I shall find it."

Atrus bowed his head.

"Good." Gehn nodded decisively, then began to pack away all of his books and papers.

"Father?"

"Yes, Atrus?"

"I had planned to go out to the fishing grounds this afternoon. I'd made arrangements with one of the fishermen. Should I cancel that now?"

Gehn paused, considering, then. "No. You had best carry on as though nothing has happened. But try not to be out too long. I shall have need of you when I return."

"Of course, father."

"Good. Now go and fetch the acolyte." He looked to the girl. "You . . . take a seat in the corner there. And take that cloak off. Only those of D'ni blood should wear such a cloak!"

Once his father had gone, Atrus went directly to the harbor. The boat he was to go out on was owned by an old fisherman named Tarkuk, a wizened little man with strangely long fingers. His son, Birili, was a short heavily muscled young man of few words. He gave Atrus a single glance as he stepped on board; thereafter he barely acknowledged him.

They sailed out through the sea channel into the open sea.

Out there, unprotected by the bowl of hills, a breeze blew across the water's surface, making the boat rise and fall on the choppy surface. As Tarkuk watched from the stern, one long, sun-browned hand on the tiller, a small clay pipe clenched between his small yellow teeth, Birili raised the mast and unfurled the sail.

Atrus watched, fascinated as the square of cloth caught the wind and seemed to swell, tugging against the restraining rope in Birili's hand. As the boat swung around it slowly gathered speed, gently rising and falling as they made their way around the curve of the island.

He leaned out, looking down through the clear, almost translucent water. The seabed was still visible this close to the island, flat and cluttered, the odd tangle of weeds giving it the appearance of scrubland.

Somewhere around here there had been a second tiny island. Nothing large, but significant enough to have been marked on Gehn's original map. Now there was nothing.

So what did that mean? What was happening here on the Thirty-seventh Age?

He sniffed the air, conscious of its strong salinity. The lake, too, he'd been told, was salty. The villagers got their water from springs in the surrounding hills and from a single well just behind Gehn's tent.

Or did, when he wasn't in residence.

Behind him the island, which still dominated the skyline, was slowly receding. He turned, looking out past Birili and the billowing sail. The sea stretched out into the distance. There, where the horizon ought to be, it seemed hazed.

"What's that?" he asked, pointing toward it.

"What's what?" Tarkuk asked, leaning forward, trying to see past the sail, as if something was actually on the water itself.

"That mist . . ."

The old man stared a moment, then turned his head and spat over the edge of the boat.

"It is the mist. It is where the sea ends."

Atrus frowned. "But surely there's something out there, beyond the mist?"

But Tarkuk merely looked away.

Atrus looked back. Now that they were closer, he could see that the mist was like a solid barrier, forming a curving wall about the island.

Strange, he thought. *It's as if it all really does ends there.*

As they came farther around the curve of the island, other boats came into sight, anchored a mile or so out from the land—seven of them in all, forming a huge elliptic on the open water, gently rocking in the warm, pleasant breeze.

They joined the others, lowering the sail, anchoring at what was clearly Tarkuk's position in that flattened circle.

Each in his place, Atrus thought, conscious of how docile, how amenable these people were.

The old man turned back, a coil of fine-meshed net between his hands. "Would you like to fish, Master?"

"No. I'll watch, thanks."

With a nod to his son, Tarkuk turned and, with a strange, looping motion, cast his net out onto the surface of the sea, keeping only the knotted end of a guide string in his hand. Slowly the net drifted to the right, forming a great figure eight in the water. As the string grew taut, he began to haul it in. As he did, Birili cast his own net from the other side of the boat, his stance, his movements so like his father's that Atrus gave a little laugh of recognition.

The old man had hauled the net over to the side of the boat. Now he leaned over and, with a quick little movement of the wrist, began to loop the net up out of the water and onto the deck.

Atrus sat forward, his eyes wide. The dull brown mesh of the net glistened now with shimmering, wriggling silver. Hundreds and hundreds of tiny silver fish, none longer than his hand, now filled the net. As Tarkuk threw the last coil of the net onto the deck, so Birili, on the other side of the boat, began to draw his in.

So simple, Atrus thought, watching Tarkuk take one of the big rectangular woven baskets from near the bow and, crouching, begin to pluck fish from the net and throw them into it.

Careful not to get in his way and mindful of the gentle sway of the boat, Atrus stepped across and, kneeling, looked into the basket. It was like looking into a chest of silver—only this silver was alive.

Reaching out, he closed his hand about one of the

wriggling shapes and tried to pick it up, and found he was holding nothing. The fish had slipped from his grasp.

Atrus raised his fingers to his nose and sniffed, frowning at the unfamiliar smell, then rubbed his thumb across his fingertips. He had not known they would be so slippery, so slick with oil.

Tarkuk had stopped and was watching him, a deep curiosity in his eyes. Atrus met those eyes and smiled, but the old man was not to be reached so easily. He made a small motion at the corner of his mouth, then looked down, getting on with his work again.

He looked to Tarkuk. "It looks like there are enough fish here in this boat to feed the whole village!"

"You think so?" The old man shrugged. "Once you've lopped off the head and taken the bones and skin into consideration, there's not much meat on a single fish. It would take several dozen of them to make a half-decent meal. Besides, we use them for other things, too. For their fat, mainly. We make oil from it, for our lamps."

Atrus nodded. "And your clothes?"

"Those are made of linen."

"Linen?"

"There is a plant. It grows on the island. We harvest it and dry it and then weave it into cloth."

He had seen it but not known what it was. And in his head, Atrus put another piece of the puzzle into place. Fish that had an oily fat for fuel. A plant that could be woven into clothes. Such things, when written in, would allow human life to thrive in a place like this.

He felt a tinge of admiration for Gehn. It was simple, certainly, but clever. Very clever.

"Can we go out farther?"

"Farther?" The old man seemed puzzled by the question.

"Yes . . . out there, where the mist is."

Tarkuk stared at him, his face hard, his whole manner suddenly very different. "Why?"

"Because I'd like to see it," Atrus said, for the first time slightly irritated by the old man's response.

Birili, he noted, had stopped hauling in his net and had turned to stare at him.

"The currents are too strong out there," Tarkuk said, as if that settled the matter.

"Nonsense," Atrus said, knowing suddenly what it was. They were afraid of the mist. They had a superstitious fear of it.

He watched as Tarkuk and his son tersely finished gathering in their nets. Then, when the baskets were fastened and the nets furled beneath the bow seat, a stony-faced Birili hauled up the anchor, then, hoisting the sail again, held the rope taut as the canvas filled.

As they moved out between the boats, Atrus noted the startled looks on the faces of the other fishermen.

Ignoring Tarkuk's piercing look, he went to the side and trailed his hand briefly in the water, noting how warm it was. The breeze had dropped, but the water was still choppy. Indeed, it seemed to get choppier the farther they sailed from the island.

Ahead, the wall of mist came closer and closer.

Again he let his hand trail lightly in the water, then jerked it back, surprised.

Cold . . . the water was freezing cold!

Atrus stared down into the water. Out here the water was dark. One could not see where it ended—*if* it ended—beneath them. He had the sudden, gut-wrenching feeling that they had sailed out over some kind of shelf and that beneath them was a mile or more of water.

Ridiculous, he thought, then turned, looking to where Birili stood, the rope slack in his hand.

He looked to the sail, then frowned. The wind had dropped completely. By rights they ought to be slowing, but the boat was traveling faster than ever.

The currents, he thought, beginning to understand. He turned, looking to the old man. Both he and his son had their eyes closed now, and were kneeling in the bottom of the boat, as if in prayer. As for the boat, that was sailing itself now, in the grip of something that was drawing it along at a clipping pace.

Slowly the wall of mist approached, filling the sky in front of them. It was cold now, bitterly cold, and as they raced along, the water beneath them seemed to boil and bubble. Then, suddenly, they were alongside

that great wall of whiteness, flying along on the surface
parallel to it.

Atrus reached across and took the old man's arm.
"Tarkuk! Listen to me! We have to do something!"

Tarkuk opened his eyes and stared at Atrus as if he
didn't recognize him. "*Do* something?"

"Yes!" Atrus yelled. He looked around, then spied
the oars that lay in the bottom of the boat. "Come on!
If we all row then we might pull free!"

Tarkuk shook his head slowly, but Atrus would not
let him lapse back into his fear. Gripping his shoulders
now, he shook him hard.

"Come on! I command you! Now row!"

Coming to himself, Tarkuk met Atrus's eyes and
bowed his head. "As my Master commands."

Tarkuk stood unsteadily, then, raising his voice,
barked orders at his son. At first Birili seemed reluctant, as if he had already consigned himself, body and
soul, to the deep. Then, like a sleepwalker waking, he
took up his oar and sat.

"Here," Atrus said, sitting beside him. "Let me
help."

He had sculled his father's boat often enough in
the past to know how to row, and he knew they would
get nowhere unless they all pulled together.

"Come on!" he called, encouraging them now.
"Row if you want to live!"

They heaved and heaved, fighting the current,

struggling to turn the boat back toward the island. For a while it seemed that the current was too strong and that all their efforts were about to end in vain, but then, suddenly, they began to pull away.

Sinews straining, they hauled their way, inch by inch across the dark surface of the water, that massive wall of whiteness receding slowly at their back, until, breathless from the effort, they relaxed, staring back the way they had come.

Atrus stretched his neck and looked up, straight into the sky. He ached. Every muscle in his body ached, yet he felt a great surge of triumph.

"Well done!" he said, looking about him and laughing. But Tarkuk and his son were looking down, silent—strangely, eerily silent.

"What is it?" he asked after a moment, touching the old man's arm. At the touch, Tarkuk jerked away.

Atrus blinked. What was going on here? What had he missed? He had made a mistake, true, but they had survived, hadn't they? Why, he had forced them to survive! He had made them row when they had given up.

He reached out, shaking the old man by the arm. "What is it? Answer me! I have to know!"

Tarkuk glanced at him, then dropped his eyes again. "We have cheated the Whiteness."

"*Cheated . . .?*" Atrus laughed, astonished. "What do you mean?"

But the old man would say no more. Slowly Birili

got to his feet and, adjusting the sail, turned the boat back toward the island.

In silence they sailed back.

As they climbed from the boat and mounted the steps, Atrus made to speak to Tarkuk again, but the old man seemed reluctant even to acknowledge him now.

Atrus shook his head, perplexed. What had happened out there? Just what exactly had he missed?

He didn't know. But he would. He would make it his business to find out, before his father returned.

Atrus hurried across the bridge, conscious of the gathering clouds overhead, then ran up the slope toward his father's tent.

Surprised by his sudden entrance, Koena got up hurriedly, making a little bowing motion, still uncertain quite how to behave toward Gehn's son. "Young Master? Is everything all right?"

The girl was sitting on the ground nearby, staring up at Atrus.

"No," Atrus answered, walking past Koena and sitting in his father's chair.

"Master?" Koena came across and stood before him. "Are there more cracks?"

"No. But there is something I want an explanation for."

"Master?"

Atrus hesitated, then. "Something happened."

"Something?"

"Yes, when I was out on the boat. The old man said something about cheating the Whiteness."

Koena gasped. "You have been out there."

"Out *where?*" Atrus said, knowing where he meant, but wanting to hear it from his lips.

"To the Mist Wall."

Atrus nodded. "We sailed the dark current. And then we rowed back."

Koena's mouth had fallen open. "No," he said quietly.

"What is it?" Atrus asked. "What am I missing? What don't I understand?"

Koena hesitated, his eyes pleading with Atrus now.

"Tell me," Atrus insisted, "or I shall have my father wring it from you!"

The man sighed, then answered him, speaking reluctantly. "The Whiteness . . . it was our Master. Before your father came."

He fell silent. There was the rumble of distant thunder.

Atrus, too, was silent for a time, taking in this new piece of information, then he looked to Koena again. "And my father knows nothing of this?"

"Nothing."

"The old man and his son . . . what will happen to them?"

Koena looked down. It was clear he did not want to say another word, but Atrus needed to know.

"Please. You have to tell me. It's very important."

The man shrugged, then: "They will die. Just as surely as if you had left them out there."

Atrus shook his head. Now that he understood it he felt a kind of dull anger at the superstitious nonsense that could dream up such a thing. He stood, his anger giving him strength, making him see clearly what he had to do.

"Listen," he said, assuming the manner of his father. "Go and fetch the villagers. Tell them to gather outside my father's hut. It is time I talked to them."

The sky was darkening as Atrus mounted the steps of the meeting hut and turned to face the waiting crowd. A light rain fell. Everyone was there; every last man, woman, and child on the island, Tarkuk and Birili excepted. Atrus swallowed nervously, then, raising his hands the way he'd seen his father do, began to speak, trying to make his voice—not so powerful or deep as his father's—boom in the same sonorous way.

"This afternoon we went out to the Mist Wall. We sailed the dark current and came back . . ."

There was a strong murmur of discontent at that. People looked to each other, deeply troubled.

"I have heard talk that we have somehow *cheated* the Whiteness, and it is for that reason that I have summoned you here."

He paused, looking about him, hoping that what he was about to say next would not prove too difficult for his father.

"I understand your fears," he went on, "but I am proof that the Power of the Whiteness is waning. For did I not sail to the Mist Wall and return? Did the Whiteness take me? No. Nor shall it. In fact, when my father, the Lord Gehn, returns, he and I shall go out beyond the Mist Wall."

There was a gasp at that—a great gasp of disbelief and shock.

"It cannot be done," Koena said, speaking for all gathered there.

"You disbelieve?" Atrus asked, stepping down and confronting his father's man.

Koena fell silent, his head bowed. Overhead there was the faintest rumble of thunder. Great clouds had gathered, throwing the bowl of hills into an intense shadow.

Atrus glanced up at the ominous sky, then spoke again. "All will be well," he said.

There was a great thunderclap. Lightning leapt between the clouds overhead, discharging itself in a vivid blue-white bolt on the crest of the hill facing them. Atrus stared at its afterimage in wonder, then looked about him, seeing how everyone else had fallen to the ground in terror.

"It's nothing," Atrus said, lifting his voice above the now-persistent grumble. "Only a thunderstorm!!"

There was a second, blinding flash and one of the trees on the far side of the lake was struck, blossoming in a great sheet of sudden flame.

"The Whiteness is angry," someone cried from just below him. "See how it searches for you!"

Atrus turned, angry now, knowing he must squash this at once. "Nonsense!" he cried. "It's only the storm!"

But no one was listening. The islanders were pulling at their hair and wailing, as if something horrible was about to descend among them.

Then, as a third lightning bolt ionized the air, sending its tendrils of static hissing through the rain-filled darkness as it sought the earth, Atrus saw, in the brilliant flash, the figure of his father, striding down the path between the huts, heading for the bridge.

13

ATRUS STOOD, HEAD BOWED BEFORE his father in his tent as the rain hammered down on the canvas overhead. The terrified islanders had fled back to their huts while the storm raged, but Gehn was in no mood to placate or reassure them. Right now he was sitting forward in his chair, glaring at his son, his hands gripping the edge of his desk tightly.

"There was trouble, you say. What brought that on?"

"I wanted to see the Mist Wall. I sailed out to it."

"And you found the dark current?"

Atrus looked up, surprised that his father knew of that. He nodded, then proceeded to tell his father all that had transpired in his absence. When he'd finished, Gehn stared at him thoughtfully, then, loosening his grip, sat back.

"It is unfortunate, but it seems that the experiment here has failed. This world is unstable."

"In what way?"

"The island is on a kind of pedestal. A massive pedestal of rock reaching up from the ocean floor. Surrounding it there is an ocean—a deep, intensely cold ocean."

Atrus frowned. "But the water here is warm. And there's fresh water in the lake."

"That comes up from the crust, far below the surface. There is geothermal warming. That same warming creates the Mist Wall. It is where the hot water from below meets and reacts with the cold oceanic currents." Gehn nodded thoughtfully. "As you can imagine, this really is an island, in every possible sense. It is as cut off as a community can be and yet survive."

"But now it's going wrong."

"Precisely. Slowly but surely, this Age is deteriorating. I cannot make out why, but it is. I have tried my utmost to find solutions, yet without a radical rewriting of this Age, I fear it is fated to deteriorate still further."

"And the cracks, father? What causes those?"

Gehn shook his head.

"It must be some fault in the underlying structure. Perhaps the same fault that made the two tiny islands subside."

"Can you fix it?"

Gehn looked to him. "No doubt I could, but I am inclined to leave it. After all, it is only a tiny crack. If it gets any worse, I shall reconsider. Right now, however, we have other problems, like this business with the so-called Whiteness. Let us deal with that first, and then consider other matters."

Gehn crouched beside the crack in the meadow as the rain fell, his eyes narrowed.

He had spent hours back in D'ni, finding the right words in the ancient book, but for some quite incomprehensible reason they had made no difference.

Gehn stood, combing his fingers back through his rain-slicked hair, then kicked a lump of earth into the crack, the frustration he felt at that moment making him want to hit out at something. The problem was a simple one—he knew that instinctively. It had something to do with the underlying structures, but precisely what it was he didn't know. Yes, and that was the worst of it, for whenever he thought, finally, that he understood it, something would come along to prove him wrong—to show him that, far from having grasped the solid principles beneath it all, he was as far from understanding it as he had ever been.

If it had only been written down somewhere. Yes, but the Guild Masters had been too clever for that. Such secrets had been passed down by word of mouth from generation to generation. The book did not exist wherein those formulas were written. That was why he had always to search old books, looking for clues, looking to unearth those wonderful, delicate phrases that would best describe this effect or that. But nothing ever said just *why* this phrase worked and that one did not.

Gehn huffed, exasperated with it all, then turned,

realizing only then that his acolyte was standing there, ten paces off, his cloak drenched, the dyes run, his dark hair plastered to his head.

"What is it, man?"

"I . . . I wondered if you wanted anything to eat, Master."

Eat? He waved the man away impatiently. How could the fellow think of food at a time like this?

Gehn turned, staring out toward the gap in the hills. If only he could remove the Mist Wall . . .

He laughed quietly. Of course! It had been staring him in the face all the time! The ocean. He had only to make the ocean warm.

"One!"

The man turned, looking back up the slope at him. "Yes, Master?"

"Tell Atrus I shall return in an hour. In the meantime, have the villagers prepare a feast on the harbor front. A feast such as they have never had before!"

Atrus stood beside the bridge, watching the islanders go sullenly about their business, while he went over in his head what his father had said to him.

Gehn's decision not to stabilize this Age played heavily on Atrus's mind. He felt somehow *responsible* for these people. It was not their fault there were flaws in the underlying fabric of their Age. And if there really *was* a steady deterioration, surely it was their duty, as the Masters of this Age, to set things right.

Atrus sighed, then walked across, conscious of how, in these last few hours, so much had changed among the islanders. Before now they had been nothing but pleasant to him, but now, as they set up the trestle tables and prepared the food, there was an air of resentment, even of hostility, about them which made him feel uncomfortable.

If only he could do something . . .

He stopped dead, then turned, staring up the slope toward the old woman's hut. An idea had suddenly come to him: a way both of salving his conscience about these people and of furthering his own first attempts at D'ni Writing.

What if he were to settle here, rather than K'veer? What if he were to persuade his father to let him continue to observe this world, not simply for a few more days but over a period of months, maybe even years? Why, he could have them build an extra room onto the hut for him to use as a laboratory.

Yes, but would Gehn agree?

Atrus took out the map and studied it, tracing the circle of the lake with his fingertips. There was a way of persuading his father that it was a good idea, but it would mean taking a risk. It would mean showing Gehn what he had been working on these past few months.

He let out a long, shivering breath. *Yes, but what if my*

father doesn't like what I've been doing? What if it only goes to prove to him that I'm not ready yet?

In truth, Atrus had wanted to wait a lot longer before he showed Gehn the Age he had been writing in his practice book. He had wanted to make sure he'd got things absolutely right before he attempted a proper book, but if doing so meant abandoning this Age, abandoning Koena and the girl and the old woman who looked after him, then surely it wasn't worth it?

He slipped the map away again, then stood there, touching the tip of his tongue to his upper lip.

What would Anna have done?

He knew the answer without thinking. She would have stayed and tried to help, even if it meant sacrificing her own plans.

So be it, then. He had only to persuade his father.

Gehn returned that evening, just as he had promised, appearing on the crest of the hill just as the sun was setting at his back. Silhouetted against that bloodred orb, he raised his arm and called to the islanders gathered below, his voice booming out across the silent lake.

"Look!" he said, pointing out beyond the gap in the hills. "The Mist Wall is down! The Whiteness is no more!"

The islanders crowded across to gape, witnessing

for themselves the absence of the Mist Wall. In the blazing orange light of sunset they had a vista of endless ocean. They turned, a great murmur of awe running through them, then, almost as one, fell to their knees, staring back up the slope as Gehn strode down toward them.

Watching from the steps of the temple, Atrus frowned. When his father had not returned within the first few hours he had begun to worry, but now he understood. Gehn had written a new entry in the Book of Age Thirty-seven—something unseen, unobserved, that had got rid of the Mist Wall.

Going down to join his father on the harbor front, where the feast had been set up, Atrus felt a tenseness in his stomach. He was determined to ask him tonight whether he could stay here, to get the matter settled and done with at the earliest opportunity, but he remembered the last time he had asked his father for something—that time when he had wanted to go back to the cleft and visit Anna—and was afraid lest Gehn said no again.

And if he does?

Atrus sighed, then made his way across the bridge. If Gehn refused, that would be it. There was no way he could defy his father over such an important matter. Besides, all Gehn had to do was refuse him access to the book.

No one noticed him come out onto the harbor front. All eyes were focused up the hill, watching as

Gehn came down among them, magnificently attired in velvet and leather.

As Gehn stepped out into the open space, his acolyte, Koena stepped forward to greet him. He bowed low, then scattered a handful of tiny yellow petals at Gehn's feet.

Gehn looked about him, coldly imperious at that moment, then, spying Atrus between the tables, gestured for him to come across.

"Father?" he asked quietly, noting the strange look in Gehn's eyes, but Gehn was not to be interrupted. Turning to face the crowd, he raised his arm again.

"From henceforth, there will be no mention of Mist or Whiteness. From this hour the very words are forbidden! But now let us eat. Let us celebrate this new beginning!"

Atrus stared at his father's back, wondering what he meant by that—whether it was, truly, a "new beginning."

Yet as the islanders filed past to take their seats at the long tables and begin the evening's feasting, Atrus saw how their eyes stared at Gehn in awe, scarce able to credit that such a wonder had come to pass.

It was late—very late—when they finally retired. Making his bed up in the corner of the tent, Atrus was conscious of his father pacing up and down behind his screen, the glowing pipe visible through the thick silk panels. They had barely spoken since Gehn's announcement, and Atrus had a good dozen questions he wanted to ask his father, but he sensed that now was not the time. Besides, he was tired, and if there were things to discuss, nothing was that urgent that it could not wait until the morning. Not even his idea of staying here.

He was just settling, turning on his side to face the tent wall, when he grew aware of the scent of Gehn's pipe close by. He turned, to find Gehn standing over him.

"We must be gone from here tomorrow."

"Gone?"

"I have things to do elsewhere. Important things."

Atrus hesitated, then sat up, staring at his father in the half dark. "I was going to ask you something."

"Then ask."

"I thought I might be able to help you . . . you know, if I made some long-term observations of the island. I thought maybe we could have the islanders build a hut for me. I could move my things here from K'veer and maybe have them make me an extra room for my experiments."

"No."

"No? But . . ."

Gehn turned away. "No buts, Atrus. The notion of you being here on your own, unsupervised, is completely out of the question. It does not fit with my plans."

"But if we could understand why things are going wrong . . ."

"You will not persist with this, Atrus. I have more important concerns than this trifling Age."

"Then why did you give me the phrases to study? Why did you remove the Mist Wall if you were thinking simply of abandoning this Age?"

"You presume to know my reasons, Atrus?"

"No, it's just that I feel your original instinct was right. If we can understand what is going wrong here, we can prevent such things from happening elsewhere."

He heard his father's sharply indrawn breath, but instead of the expected explosion of anger, Gehn was silent.

Atrus sat forward. He could barely see his father in the darkness. The white moon was still up, but its light barely penetrated the thick canvas. The only real illumination in the tent was the gentle glow of Gehn's pipe, which cast its faint blue light over his chin and mouth and nose.

"Father?"

Gehn turned his head slightly, but still there was no answer.

Atrus fell silent, waiting. After a moment, his father turned and came across again.

"What you say has some merit, Atrus, and, as you say, accords with my original intentions. And even should this Age deteriorate further, it might prove useful to investigate the manner of that deterioration.

Likewise, the building of a special hut here—for experimental use—is a good one, provided, that is, no books or journals are left here which might fall into the wrong hands. That said, I still cannot permit you to stay here alone, Atrus. It is too dangerous. Besides, we must keep up with your lessons, and as I have other Ages to attend to, I cannot be forever coming here. No. You shall remain on K'veer, but we shall continue to visit this Age from time to time, and while we are here you will continue with your detailed observations."

It was far less than Atrus had hoped for, yet it was something. He knew now that his guess had been right. Gehn had been willing to abandon this Age and leave it to its fate. Now, at least, he had the chance to do some good here. And if he *could* discover what was going wrong, then perhaps his father would begin to trust him and allow him greater liberty.

But that was for the future. As he lay down, the scent of Gehn's pipe lulling him in the darkness, he recalled the look of astonishment and awe on the islanders faces as they stared out at the endless ocean. And as he drifted into sleep one final insight came to him from the darkness.

He made the ocean warm . . .

14

GEHN STOOD SEVERAL PACES OFF, watching as Atrus dug the spade deep into the grassy surface of the meadow, using his booted heel, then pushed down on the handle, turning back the turf, exposing the dark richness of the earth beneath.

Throwing the spade aside, Atrus knelt beside the hole. Taking a dark blue cloth from inside his pocket, he lay it beside him, then began to lay out the instruments he needed—spatulas and droppers, scoops and pipettes, and four small capped jars containing variously colored chemicals—removing them one by one from the broad leather belt he wore about his waist.

Finally, he took a slender black case from the inside pocket of his tunic and, opening it, took out four long glass tubes and lay them next to the shining silver instruments. That accomplished, he looked up at Gehn, his glasses glinting in the afternoon sun.

"I'm ready, father."

Gehn lifted his chin slightly, his own glasses opaqued against the brightness. "Then let us see what has resulted, eh?"

Atrus set to work, using one of the scoops to place a small amount of earth into each of the tubes. That done, he picked up the first of the jars, uncapped it, then set it down again.

Using one of the droppers, he drew up a measure of the clear amber liquid and, taking the first of the tubes, added it to the earth, swilling the mixture around at the bottom of the tube.

Lifting it up into the light, he studied it a while, then, nodding to himself, threw the dropper aside and, taking a cork, sealed the tube.

He went through the motions again, this time taking a heaped spatula of light blue powder to add to the earth in the second tube, mixing the two together thoroughly.

Twice more he carried out the procedure, until all four tubes lay stoppered on the cloth. Pleased with himself, Atrus looked to Gehn once more.

"I think it's worked."

"You *think?*"

Atrus looked down. "I'm pretty sure it has. The reactions certainly correlate with what I expected, but I'd like to make absolutely sure. I'd like to test them again, back at the hut."

Gehn nodded, then turned away, drawing his cloak about him as he went. "I shall see you there then, in a while."

Atrus watched his father a moment, then set about packing away his equipment. He had expected more from Gehn, a smile, perhaps, or some small indication, by word or gesture, that he was pleased with what he had achieved, but as ever there was nothing.

Glancing up, he noticed that the young girl, Salar, was watching from the far side of the meadow, and smiled to himself. He was rather fond of her, in a big brotherly kind of way, but she was not the best of company. It was not as if he could really talk to her; at least not the way he had talked to Anna.

He pushed the thought away, determined not to be morose. Not today, anyway. For today, if his further tests did prove him right, he had achieved a great thing.

As he fastened the sample case, then slipped the instruments back into his belt, he allowed himself a smile.

By rights Gehn should have been inordinately proud of him for finding such an elegant solution; but Gehn was Gehn, his distance part of his intelligence. It had been a full week before Gehn had even read the brief phrase he had written for the Age Thirty-seven book. With a shrug, Atrus stood, looking about him a moment, checking he had not left anything. Then, with a brief wave and a smile to Salar, he started back.

They had built a new hut close to the old woman's, extending it, as he'd suggested, to include a separate room where they could carry out experiments. Gehn was waiting for him there, his own equipment already set up.

"Here," he said, gesturing to Atrus. "Give me the samples. I shall carry out my own tests."

"Father . . ." He bowed, hiding his disappointment, then handed over the slender case.

But at least Gehn was taking him seriously. When he had first proposed this, Gehn had ridiculed the idea:

"Why, I have been searching for close to twenty years for such a phrase! And you say you have found one that will solve the problem?"

It was not strictly true. He had not found it in a book, he had worked it out for himself from first principles, after studying the matter for nearly eight months. But Gehn had not wanted to hear his explanation. Gehn was interested only in whether it worked or not.

And now it was his turn to watch as Gehn took a little of each sample and, placing each on a separate slide, began to examine the first of them under the big, gold-cased instrument he had brought with him from D'ni.

For a tense few minutes Gehn barely moved, only the faintest movement of his fingers on the calibrated knobs, then he removed his eye from the long tube and looked across at Atrus.

"The bacteria are different."

"Not all of them."

Gehn stared at him silently, as if expecting him to say something more; when he didn't, he looked away, taking the second of the slides and fitting it into the viewing slot.

Atrus watched him, smiling now. Adding to the mix of different bacteria had been the final touch—the thing that had finally made it work. Years ago, in the cleft, he had tried a much simpler, purely chemical solution to the same kind of problem, and had failed. Here he had tried to look at the whole picture—chemical and bacteriological—and it had worked.

It wasn't the solution to everything that was wrong—and he had been careful, when he'd first presented it to his father, not to offer any form of criticism of the Age—but it was a start. And maybe, if his father trusted him more after this, he could make further changes.

He longed to see the Age Thirty-seven book to confirm his hypotheses and discuss it with his father, but he knew how sensitive Gehn was.

He let out a long breath, remembering the long hours he had spent researching the subject. Until he had begun to study the composition of soil, he had not understood the full complexity of it. But now he saw it clearly. One had to build worlds from the bottom up, beginning with what was below the soil.

Gehn grunted, then looked across again, giving a terse nod.

"This is good. You must show me the book where you found this. It may have other things we can use."

Atrus looked down. Maybe Gehn would forget. Maybe he'd be distracted by something else. Or, if the worst came to the worst and he insisted, the "book" could have an accident somehow.

"All right," Gehn said, taking the slide from the viewer, then beginning to pack away the microscope, "let us clear up and get back to D'ni. I think our work is done here for a time."

"Done?"

Gehn nodded, then clicked the lid shut on the box that held the microscope. "I think we should leave this Age alone for a week or two and see how things develop. If there are any side effects, they should show up in that time."

"Side effects?"

But Gehn was impatient to return. "Come, Atrus. Pack your things. I want to be back within the hour."

Two days had passed now since their return from the Thirty-seventh Age, and in all that time Atrus had not seen hide nor hair of his father.

He knew where Gehn was, of course, for the very moment they had linked back, Gehn had rushed up the stairs to his study and locked himself in.

Atrus had thought his father might reappear at mealtimes, but he had not come down even then.

And now the darkness was falling on another day, and still he had no idea of what his father was up to.

Walking over to the desk in the corner of his room, Atrus picked up his journal and, stepping out onto the balcony, opened it at one of the earliest entries; one written when he was barely nine years old:

Anna says that the cleft is an "environment" and that an "environment" is composed of many different elements, all of which have an effect upon each other. She says that though some of those things—the sun, for instance—are not actually in the cleft itself, they must still be taken into account when we look at how the cleft works. Too much sun and plants die, too little and they never grow. I asked her—how do we manage to live here at all?

He sat upon the balustrade, looking out toward the great rock and the city beyond, and sighed. Looking back across the years, it was indeed a wonder that they had survived. How much of a wonder, he had not fully realized until now.

I have come a long way, he thought, *but I have still not half the understanding that she had.*

Atrus turned, meaning to go back inside and write a line or two, and saw that Rijus was standing in the middle of the room, looking across at him.

He had long ago got used to the man's silence and

to his sudden appearances in rooms, yet he found himself still curious about what the man knew, what secrets he had. Yes, and what it was like to inhabit a world of words one could not penetrate.

Walking through, he set his journal down, then looked across at the man.

"You have a message for me, Rijus?"

Rijus bowed his head, then held out the note.

At last, he thought, knowing it was a summons. *What has the man been up to?*

He unfolded it and cast his eyes quickly over the elaborate handwriting. It was terse and to the point.

"My study. Now."

He nodded to Rijus, dismissing him, then went across and slipped the journal into the case he kept it in, locking the clasp with the key. Then, satisfied that all was secure, he hurried out.

Gehn was waiting in his study, ensconced behind his desk. There was a pile of copy books at his elbow, another five spread out along the front of his desk.

With a jolt of surprise, Atrus recognized them. They were his!

"Ah, Atrus," Gehn said, glancing up, then continuing to write in the open book in front of him, "come and sit down across from me."

Atrus took the seat, facing his father, watching as Gehn finished the sentence he was writing, then put the pen back into the ink pot.

Gehn looked up at him, then nodded toward the books. "As you see, I have been reading your practice books, and I have selected five which, I feel, have some small merit."

He waited, tensed now.

"I want you to choose one."

"Father?"

Gehn passed his hand over the five books. "At present these are but words on paper. But now I am giving you the chance to make one of these books real."

Atrus blinked.

"Yes. I am giving you a blank book, a *Kortee'nea*. You will choose one of these five books and write it out properly into the *Kortee'nea*."

Here it was, the moment he had dreamed of, and he was unprepared for it.

"Well?" Gehn said, frowning at him. "Which one is it to be?"

Atrus leaned forward, looking to see which books his father had selected, surprised by the choice of two of them. But his main book was there. He reached out and tapped it. "This one."

Gehn nodded. "A good choice." Turning in his seat, he reached down, then lifted a big, leather-bound book from the pile beside him, then held it out to Atrus.

Atrus took it, his mouth suddenly dry, his heart pounding. A book! His father had given him a book!

"You must be very careful, Atrus. Any mistakes you make in copying will be set into the Age. You must check every word, every phrase after you have copied it. Yes, and recheck it. And if you *do* make a mistake, then be sure to bring the book to me."

He bowed his head. "Father."

"Good. Now take your copybook and go. And Atrus?"

"Yes, father?"

"You might add that phrase you recently discovered. The phrase about the soil. It will do your Age no harm, after all."

Gehn lay the book flat on the desk before Atrus, then opened it to reveal the empty descriptive box on the right-hand page. Until he linked, it would be blank— or almost so, for there was a chaotic swirl of particles, like a snowstorm—yet as soon as he emerged into the new Age, the image would appear, as if by magic, on the page.

"Shall I go first?" Gehn asked, looking to him, "or would you like that honor?"

Though he had linked many times now—so often that it had almost become a thing of routine—this once he was afraid: afraid because *he* had made this Age.

"Well?" Gehn insisted when he did not answer.

"I'll go," he said, then, taking a long, calming breath, he placed his right hand on the empty page.

There was a crackle of static, as though a faint electrical current had passed through his hand. It seemed drawn into the very fabric of the page, then, with a sudden, sickening lurch, Atrus felt himself sucked into the rapidly expanding whiteness of the page.

In that instant he felt the familiar "shifting" sensation of the link. For that brief moment it felt as though he were melting. And then, with a shocking suddenness that never diminished, the blackness seeped through until there was nothing *but* the blackness.

And as he finally surrendered to that blackness, so he found himself back in his body, standing on the cold damp earth inside a low-ceilinged cavern.

Relieved, Atrus shook himself, then stepped aside, conscious that his father was linking after him.

He waited, expecting Gehn to appear at any moment, for the air to take on that strangely fluid quality it had when someone was linking through—a quality that, looking at it, was like a flaw, an *occlusion*, in the eye itself.

Strange. Atrus frowned and made to step toward the space he'd just left, even as the air changed and, like a bubble squeezed out of the nothingness, his father appeared.

Gehn looked about him, eyeing the walls critically. "Good," he said quietly, taking in a deep breath. "The air smells very fresh."

Atrus watched his father, conscious that he was being judged, that this was a test of sorts.

"You have the Linking Book on you, I assume?"

Slowly, Atrus's mouth fell open. The Linking Book! In his excitement he had completely forgotten about the Linking Book! He was so used to traveling in Ages where the Linking Books were already in place, that he had overlooked it!

He groaned, the blood draining from his face.

Gehn held out a Linking Book before his eyes. "You forgot. But fortunately *I* did not."

Atrus closed his eyes, the thought that he might have trapped them there forever making him tremble.

"I'm sorry . . ." he began, but Gehn cut him short with a terse little gesture of his hand. His father's eyes were livid with rage.

"Do *not* tell me how sorry you are, Atrus. Sorry is utterly inadequate. Sorry is for fools and idiots who cannot think straight. I considered you better than that, but your gross carelessness in this instance is a sign of your immaturity. There was but one single, crucial thing you had to remember, and you forgot!" Gehn huffed out a great sigh of exasperation, then smacked the book against the top of Atrus's head, his voice rising with controlled anger. "What if I had not thought to bring your Linking Book? What then? Where would we be?"

Here, Atrus thought. *Forever here.*

Gehn thrust the book into his hands, then turned away, making for the entrance.

Atrus stood uncertainly, then followed his father across.

"Well," Gehn said, slowing down to let Atrus catch up, but refusing to look at him. "I suppose you had better show me what you have written."

He led his father out, through a narrow stone passage that was very different from how he'd imagined it—how he *thought* he'd written it—and into a cavelike depression that was open to the sky, bright sunlight pouring down into it from the clear blue heavens. There was a pool to one side, surrounded by lush vegetation and a few light-colored rocks, while on the far side a flight of tiered rocks climbed the rock face.

Gehn pulled his glasses down over his eyes then stepped out into the sunlight. For a long while he was silent, almost as if he disapproved of what he saw, but when he spoke, it was with an air of surprise.

"This is good, Atrus. You appear to have chosen the different elements well. They complement each other perfectly." He turned, looking directly at Atrus, who still stood in the shadow. "Which books did you use?"

As ever, Gehn thought that he had derived the different elements of his Age from various ancient books, the way Gehn himself did. But Atrus hadn't done that here. This was all his, uniquely his. The greatest trouble he'd had was in finding the right D'ni words to express what he wanted.

That was why it had taken him so long. Why he had had to be so patient.

"I . . . I can't remember," he said finally. "There were so many."

"No matter," Gehn said. He glanced at Atrus briefly, then walked on.

Skirting the pool, Gehn paused to look about him, then began to climb the steps. Pulling down his glasses, Atrus hurried after, surprised that Gehn had made no other comment. Didn't all this remind him of something? Couldn't Gehn see what he'd tried to do here?

It was the cleft. Simplified, admittedly, and without the buildings that had been in the original, but the shape of it, the physical materials were, as far as he could make it, precisely as he remembered them.

Halfway up the steps he stopped and turned, scanning the floor of the cleft to see whether the one specific he had written in had taken as he'd hoped. His eyes searched a moment, seeing nothing, then, with a jolt of pure delight, he saw them, just there in the deep shadow on the far side. Flowers. Tiny, delicate blue flowers.

He grinned, then began to climb again. It had

taken him a lot of time and effort choosing the precise soil type and the balance of minerals in the soil, but it had worked!

Gehn was waiting for him up above, one hand stroking his chin as he surveyed the view.

Joining him, Atrus looked out, seeing, for the first time, the Age he had created.

It was a rolling landscape of hills and valleys, with lush pasture and thick, dark green forests. Rivers threaded their silver way through that verdant paradise, winking now and then into the blue of lakes. To the far left, in the distance, there were mountains—snow-capped and majestic, and beneath them a blue-green stretch of sea.

And over all a rich blue cloudless sky, dominated by a large yellow sun, like the sun of Earth. Atrus stood there, entranced, listening to the peaceful sound of birdsong. For a moment he didn't even notice, then he half-turned, his eyes widening.

Birds? I didn't write birds!

His father stepped up beside him. "You should have experimented more."

Atrus looked to his father, surprised by his comment, which seemed a complete contradiction of his own style of writing.

"You might have tried a different sun, for instance," Gehn said, pointing to it, "or chosen a different kind of rock to make those mountains."

"But . . ."

"Next time you should use a few less conventional touches, Atrus. It would not do to make your worlds too staid."

Atrus looked down, dismayed by his father's words. But what about that view? Wasn't that spectacular? And the air and the soil here—wasn't it good that they were so healthy? Oh, he knew this Age was simple, but he had planned to take one step at a time. *And this world wouldn't fall apart . . .*

"Still," Gehn added, "you need not keep this Age. Now that I know you can write, I shall give you other books. You can experiment in them. Then, once you have finally made an Age that I am happy with, you can call that your First Age."

"But I've *named* this world."

"Named it?" Gehn laughed dismissively. "That was a trifle premature. I could understand, perhaps, if there were people here, but . . ."

"I called it Inception."

Gehn stared at him a moment, then turned away. Walking across, he pulled a leaf from a bush, rolling it between his gloved fingers, then lifted it to his nose to sniff it before he threw it away.

"All right. I think we had better go back now."

Atrus, who had been about to walk on down the slope, turned to face his father again. "Go back?"

Gehn barely glanced at him. "Yes."

"But I thought . . ." Atrus swallowed. "I thought we

could see more of this Age. I wanted to take samples
of the soil, and catch one of the creatures for study. I
wanted . . ."

"You heard me, Atrus. Now *come!* If you must, you
can come back another time, but right now I must get
back. I have a great deal to arrange before the Korfah
V'ja."

Atrus had never heard the term before. "Korfah
V'ja?"

Gehn looked to him. "Tomorrow, at noon on the
Thirty-seventh Age." And with that he walked on.

Back in the library on D'ni, Gehn closed Atrus's book
and, slipping it beneath his arm, headed for the steps
that led up to his study.

"Quickly now," he said, gesturing for Atrus to follow. "We need to prepare you."

The room seemed unaltered since Atrus had last
seen it. If anything, it was even more untidy than
before, with even more books piled about the walls.
Gehn's cloak lay, carelessly discarded, over the back of
the chair beside the fireplace, the grate filled with the
ashes of a recent fire.

Atrus blinked, imagining his father working here
late into the night, the flickering firelight making the
shadows in the room dance.

"Sit down," Gehn said, pointing to the chair across the desk from him. "We have much to do before the morning."

Atrus sat, watching as Gehn put his book down on the pile at the side of his desk, then peeled the glasses from the top of his head and stuffed them into the draw beside him.

"Father?"

"Yes, Atrus?"

"What is the Korfah V'ja?"

Gehn barely glanced at him. He took a book from the side, then set out a Writing pen and an ink pot on the desk beside it. "It is a ceremony for a new god," he answered, sitting down and opening the book.

The book was not blank. It was already written in. From where he sat, Atrus could see that the last two entries had been added to the page only recently.

"I don't know . . ."

Gehn looked at him. "Of course you know."

He took the ink pot and unscrewed the top, then looked across at his son. "You are a true D'ni now, Atrus. A Writer. You have made an Age. That fact ought to be recognized. Besides, it does not do to become too familiar with the peoples of our worlds. They must be reminded of our godhood now and then, and what better way than a ceremony?"

"Yes, but . . ."

"I am arranging something special for the occasion."

Gehn hesitated a moment, his eyes half-closed, thinking, then dipped the pen into the pot.

"What are you doing, father?"

"Making changes."

"Changes?"

Gehn nodded. "Small ones. Things you cannot see."

"Then that . . ." Atrus pointed, "is the Age Thirty-seven book?"

"Yes."

Atrus felt himself go cold. He thought Gehn had finished with making changes. He thought that Age was "fixed."

"Father?"

Gehn glanced at him distractedly. "What is it, Atrus?"

"What you said, about me being less conventional in my writing. What did you mean exactly? Did you mean I ought to take more risks?"

Gehn looked up, then set his pen aside. "Not risks, so much, as . . . Well, let me be blunt with you, Atrus: you take too long about things. Far, far too long. These copybooks," he gestured toward the stack beside him, "there's barely a thing in most of them! When I gave you the choice of five, I knew which one you would pick, because it was the only one that was even vaguely like a proper Age!"

Gehn stood, leaning over his desk. "Dammit, boy, you should have made a dozen, twenty Ages by now!

You should have experimented a little, tried out a few things to see what worked and what didn't. Sticking to the tried-and-tested, that is all well and good for scribes, but not for us, Atrus! Not for us!"

Atrus stared at Gehn, bewildered by the patent contradiction in his father's words. Did his father want quick worlds or stable worlds? Or something else entirely?

Gehn huffed, exasperated. "You are no good to me if you work at this pace all the time. I need Ages. Dozens of them. *Hundreds* of them! That is our task, Atrus, don't you see? Our sacred task. To make Ages and populate them. To fill up the nothingness with worlds. Worlds we can own and govern, so that the D'ni will be great again. So that my grandsons will be lords of a million worlds!"

Gehn stood there a moment longer, his eyes piercing Atrus, then he sat, shaking his head slowly, as if disappointed.

"You had best go to your room now. I shall send Rijus down to see you. He will bring you the special clothes you are to wear for the ceremony."

Something was wrong. They knew it even as they stepped out beneath the dark, cloud-dominated sky of the Thirty-seventh Age. As they stood there, a warm, unsavory wind blew into their faces, gusting as if from a vent, its normal strong salinity tainted by other, more bitter presences.

Atrus looked to his father and saw how Gehn grimaced then touched his tongue against his upper palate, as if to get a better taste of that unwholesome air.

"What is it?"

Gehn concentrated a moment longer, then, ignoring Atrus's question, strode on. But he had not gone more than a dozen paces before he stopped dead, his whole face drained of expression, his lips parting the merest fraction.

Atrus walked across and stood beside his father on the ridge, looking out over the village and the lake, shocked by what he saw.

The lake was dry, its exposed surface filled with dark cracks. Two dozen fishing boats lay on their sides in the bone-dry mud.

Atrus turned, looking toward the sea. There, through the gap in the hills, where the channel ended and the sea had once begun, was a ledge of solid rock. Dry rock, crusted with dried up seaweed and barnacled rocks.

Like a desert scrubland, he thought, recalling the first time he had had the thought, in the boat with Tarkuk and his son.

And beyond that ledge . . . nothing. Only air.

A great sound of wailing and groaning came up to them on the wind. Atrus looked, trying to locate its source in the village, but the village was deserted. Then, suddenly, he saw them, on the other side of the bridge, in front of the meeting hut. They were all there, huddled together in fear, staring out across the gouged eye of the lake or looking woefully up at the black and hostile sky. Only Koena stood, moving among them, bending down to talk to this one or lay his hand upon that one's arm.

"What's happened here?" he asked, turning to Gehn once more.

Gehn slowly shook his head. There was a look of disbelief in his face. "It was all right," he said quietly. "We fixed it. Those phrases . . . there was nothing wrong with them."

And yet something was wrong. Something had drained the lake and left the island stranded above the level of the surrounding ocean. *Something* had caused that. It must have. Because things like this did not happen on their own.

A phrase swam into Atrus's mind. *He made the ocean warm . . .*

Was that it? Had that seemingly small alteration set up a contradiction? Or, to achieve it, had Gehn tampered with some other crucial element in this Age? Had he tilted the axis of the planet, perhaps, to bring it closer to the sun so that the water was warmer? Or was it something else? What if he'd tampered with the plates beneath the ocean? What if Gehn had set up a weakness in the ocean floor that had finally succumbed to the great pressures down there, causing this lowering of the ocean's level? Or what if he had simply picked a phrase from a D'ni book that referred to a warm ocean without understanding where it came from or what its context was?

He would never know. Not without consulting the Age Thirty-seven book, and Gehn was quite adamant that he was not to read his books.

Great black-fisted thunderclouds were gathering overhead now. There was the low grumble of thunder.

Looking about him, his face much harder than it had been only moments before, Gehn began to walk slowly down the hill toward the village.

"But Great Master, you *have* to help us. You *must!*"

"*Must?*" Gehn turned his head and stared at the kneeling man disdainfully. "Who *says* I must?"

An hour had passed since they had come and Gehn sat in his chair, at his desk in the great tent, the glowing pipe cradled in his hands.

The first thing Gehn had done was to send the islanders back to their huts, forbidding them to set a foot outside, then he had come here and lit his pipe. Since then he had not moved, but had sat there, silently brooding, his brows heavily knitted.

And now Koena had come to petition his Master; afraid to defy his command, yet equally afraid to leave things be. His world was dying and there was only one person who could save it—the Lord Gehn.

Atrus, standing just behind Koena, felt a great wave of respect and admiration for the man swell up in him.

"Forgive me, Master," Koena began again, his eyes not daring to meet Gehn's, "but have we angered you somehow? Is this our punishment? If so, tell us how we might make amends. But please, I beg you, save us. Bring back the sea and fill the lake for us, Master, I implore you!"

Gehn slammed the pipe down on the desk and stood. "Enough!"

He seemed to take a long, indrawn breath, then slowly stepped around the table until he stood over the cowering Koena.

"You are right," Gehn said, his voice cold and imperious. "This *is* a punishment. A demonstration of my awesome powers."

Gehn paused, then, turning his back on the man, began to pace the floor. "I thought it necessary to show you what would happen should you ever think to defy me. I felt it . . . appropriate."

Atrus stared at his father, openmouthed, in the silence that followed.

Gehn made a slow circuit of the tent, moving behind Atrus as if he wasn't there. Then, as if the thought followed on from the last, he threw a question at Koena. "Are the preparations complete?"

"Master?" The kneeling man dared the smallest glance.

"The preparations," Gehn repeated, as if speaking to a child, "for the ceremony."

Koena blinked, then nodded; then, realizing what he had done, he hastily dropped his head again and said, "Yes, Master. Everything is ready."

"Then we shall hold the ceremony in an hour. You will gather the islanders on the slope in front of the temple."

"The temple?" Then Koena understood. Gehn meant the meeting hut. Even so, he seemed rooted to the spot.

"Well?" Gehn said, turning around so that he faced his servant again. "Had you not better go and arrange things?"

"Master?" Koena's face was suddenly a blank. He seemed bemused, in shock.

"I said go. Gather the villagers and prepare for the ceremony. I do not wish to be kept waiting."

Koena backed away a little. "But Master . . . aren't you going to help us? The lake . . ."

"Go!" Gehn yelled, his face dark with fury. His hand had gone down to his waist and produced a long dagger from beneath his cloak. "Now! Before I slit you open like a fish!"

Koena's head jerked up, his eyes staring fearfully at the razor-sharp blade; then, with a tiny bow, he turned and almost ran from the tent.

Atrus took a step toward him. "Father?"

But Gehn wasn't listening. He stared blackly at the tent flap where Koena had just departed, then made a sour movement of his mouth. He glanced at Atrus, as if looking at a book or some other object he had forgotten he had placed there, then, sheathing the knife, turned and went back to his desk.

Picking up his pipe, he drew deeply on it, then sat back, resting his neck against the back of the chair and closing his eyes.

"Father?"

But Gehn was impervious to words. Pursing his lips, he blew a long stream of smoke into the air.

An hour. The Korfah V'ja—the god-crowning ceremony—was in an hour.

Koena had gathered the islanders, all two hundred of them, and made them kneel, heads bowed, on the slope before the meeting hut. Five great torches burned on the top of tall poles that were set into the ground between the people and the hut, their flames gusting and flickering in the wind. Deep shadows danced in that mesmeric light, like an evil spirit searching among that gathered mass for one specific soul to torment.

They were mainly silent, cowering beneath the mass of dark and threatening clouds, yet each growl or rumble of that heavenly chorus provoked a corresponding moan from those frightened souls.

At the prearranged signal, Koena turned and raised his arms, calling upon the god to come down. At once, Gehn stepped from the darkness between the wooden pillars, resplendent in a long, flowing cloak of pure gold thread lined with black silk, his white hair framed by a strange, pentagonal halo of gold that flashed in the flickering torchlight.

"People of the Thirty-seventh Age," he commanded, his voice booming over the noises of the storm, "prostrate yourselves before your new Master, the Great Lord Atrus."

Reluctantly, Atrus came down the steps until he stood beside his father. He was wearing a cloak and halo much like Gehn's, only his were a brilliant red, the material shining transparently, as though it were made of a million tiny rubies.

In genuine awe, the people pressed their foreheads to the earth, murmuring the words the acolyte had had them prepare.

"The Lord Atrus is our Master. He blesses us with his presence."

Gehn beamed, then called to the two men still inside the temple. "Attendants! Come!"

Slowly, with great ceremony, the two attendants—recruited from among the fishermen—came from within the temple, carrying between them on a velvet cushion an astonishing pendant of precious metals and bloodred jewels and delicate porcelain.

Stepping forward, Koena stood before the two men, passing his hands over the great pendant in blessing in the way Gehn had shown him. Then, moving back, he looked to Atrus, who had turned to face him.

"And now," Gehn said, his voice echoing across the black and empty lake, "behold the Great Lord Atrus!"

And as Koena lifted the pendant and placed it around Atrus's neck, careful not to knock the halo, so Gehn pointed up toward the sky.

There was a great clash of thunder and a flash. For the briefest moment Atrus saw the surprise in his father's face and knew the moment was sheer coincidence. Yet in an instant Gehn's face changed, swelling with pride, his eyes blazing with a fierce intelligence.

"Behold, the rain!"

And then, as if he really had commanded it, the heavens opened, the torrent so heavy that each drop seemed to rebound from the earth, drenching things in an instant.

The earth trembled like a beaten drum.

Atrus stared, astonished. Before him on the slope, two hundred faces were turned up in awe as the precious water fell on them like a solid weight.

Koena looked to his Master, as if to ask whether or not he should continue, but Gehn seemed undaunted by the downpour. It was almost as if he *had* planned it.

"The handmaiden . . . where is the handmaiden?"

Koena turned, then gestured toward the girl Salar, who was clutching a garland of woven flowers, like the one they had presented to Gehn when Atrus had first come to the Age. But Salar could not move. Salar was petrified. She stared up at the sky, her eyes like tiny, startled beads.

Seeing how it was, Gehn strode down and grasped her by the arm, then began to drag her across the muddy slope toward the hissing torches and the temple beyond.

Appalled by his father's treatment of the girl, Atrus started forward. "Father! Let her go!"

Coming closer, Gehn glared at him, the fierceness in that look enough to make Atrus lower his gaze.

Gehn threw the girl down at Atrus's feet. "The garland!" he growled. "Present the Lord Atrus with the garland!"

Atrus wanted to reach down and pick the girl up, but his father's eyes were on him, defying him to help her.

And still the rain beat down relentlessly.

Slowly Salar got up onto her knees. The garland, which she still held loosely in one hand, was ruined now—mud-spattered and ripped in several places. She glanced up at him, frightened now and tearful.

"Lord Atrus . . ." she began, her voice almost inaudible beneath the noise of the storm.

"Speak up, girl!" Gehn bellowed. "Let's hear you now!"

"Lord Atrus . . ." she began again, her voice struggling to keep an even tone.

There was a great flash, a huge thunderclap. The young girl shrieked and dropped the garland.

"Kerath help us!" Gehn said impatiently, then, placing the heel of his boot against her shoulder, pushed her roughly aside and bent down to pick up the ruined garland. He studied it a moment, then, with a grimace of disgust, discarded it.

Gehn turned, looking to Koena. "Dismiss them," he said. "The ceremony is over!"

But Koena wasn't listening. Koena was staring at the lake, watching the precious water drain away into the cracks. The rain fell and fell, but it did no good. It would have to rain for a thousand years to fill that lake, for the lake drained into the sea and the sea into the ocean, and the ocean . . . the ocean now lay a hundred yards or more below that great ledge of rock that once had been a seabed.

Koena turned, looking to Gehn. "Master, you have to save us! Please, Master, I beg you!"

But Gehn, who had seen what Koena had seen, simply turned away. Throwing off his crown, he unfastened his cloak at the neck and let it fall, then, going over to the tent, ducked inside, emerging a moment later with his knapsack, into which he quickly stowed his pipe.

"Come," he said, gesturing to Atrus. "The ceremony's over."

Atrus stared a moment, then, casting aside the pendant, ran after Gehn, catching up with him and grasping his arm, turned him so that he faced him, shouting into his face over the sound of the storm.

"We must get back and change things! Now, before it's too late!"

"Too late? It is already too late! Look at it! I said it was unstable!"

"No!" Atrus yelled, desperate now. "You can change it. You can erase the changes you made and put things right. You *can*. You told me you can! After all, you are a god, aren't you?"

That last seemed to hit home. Gehn gave the briefest nod, then, pushing past his son, hurried across the bridge, making his way back up the rain-churned slope toward the cave, leaving Atrus to run after him.

15

FOR AN HOUR NOW GEHN HAD SAT AT his desk in silence, deaf to Atrus's pleas, staring into the air blankly as he sucked on his pipe.

"You have to do something," Atrus said, taking up the cause again. "You *have* to! They're dying back there!"

Nothing. Not even the flicker of an eyebrow.

Atrus grimaced, trying not to imagine their suffering back there on the Thirty-seventh Age, trying not to think of the old woman and the girl, but it was impossible.

He stared at Gehn. It was the first time he had seen this side of his father; this *indecisiveness*. This hideous indifference.

"Won't you help them, father? Won't you?"

Nothing.

Something snapped in him. Stepping up to the desk, Atrus leaned across, meaning to take the book.

"If you won't, then let me . . ."

Gehn's hand gripped his like a vice. He looked up into Atrus's face, his eyes hard. "*You?*"

It was the first thing Gehn had said for ages.

Atrus pulled his hand free. "They're dying," he said for what seemed like the thousandth time. "We *have* to help them. We could make changes."

Gehn laughed bleakly. "Changes?"

"To fix things."

Gehn's eyes held his a moment, then looked away.

In his mind Atrus saw it again, the water pouring from the edge of the great rock table as it rose and rose on a cushion of red hot lava.

"So that's it, is it?" he said, glaring at his father. "You *can't* fix it?"

Gehn straightened up, looking at Atrus, something of the old arrogance in his eyes. "Did I *say* that?"

For a moment longer Gehn glared back at his son, then, opening the Book of the Thirty-seventh Age, he reached across and, dipping the pen into the ink pot, proceeded to cross out the last few entries in the book, using the D'ni negating symbol.

"There," he said, handing the book to Atrus. "I have fixed it."

Atrus stared at it, stunned.

Gehn nodded at the book. "Well? You want to check for yourself?"

He had been almost too afraid to ask. "Can I?"

"That *is* what you wanted, no?"

Atrus nodded.

"Then go. But try not to be too long. I have wasted enough time already on those ingrates!"

The air in the cave was musty, but no more so than on the other occasions he had gone there. It was—and this was the important point—free of the hideous stench of sulfur. The very normality of it raised his spirits.

There, he heard his father say, handing him the book, *I've fixed it.*

Well, now he'd know.

Atrus climbed up out of the cave, then stood on the boulder, overlooking the slope, breathing in the clear, sweet air.

It was true! Gehn had fixed it! There was water in the lake and rich grass on the slopes. He could hear birdsong and the sound of the wind rustling through the nearby trees. Down below the village seemed peaceful, the islanders going about their lives quite normally.

He laughed, then jumped down, hurrying now, keen to ask Salar just what exactly had happened in his absence, what changes she had witnessed—but coming around the hump, he stopped dead, perturbed by the sight that met his eyes.

He ran to the ridge, then stood there, breathing shallowly as he looked out across the harbor. The boats were there, moored in a tight semicircle, just as before, and there was the bridge . . . but beyond?

He gasped, his theory confirmed in a moment. The meeting hut was gone, and the tent. In their place was a cluster of huts, like those on this side of the bridge.

Hearing a noise behind him he turned, facing Koena, surprised to see that the man was in ordinary village clothes.

"Koena?"

The man tensed at the word, the thick wooden club he held gripped tightly. There was fear in his face.

What is it?" Atrus asked, surprised

"*Usshua umma immuni?*" Koena asked, his hostility unmistakable now.

Atrus blinked. What was that language? Then, realizing he was in danger, he put his hands up, signaling that he meant no harm. "It's me, Koena. Atrus. Don't you recognize me?"

"*Usshua illila umawa?*" the frightened native demanded, waving his club.

Atrus shook his head, as if to clear it. What was wrong here? Why was everything so different? Out of instinct he turned back toward the cave, then stopped, realizing that there would be no Linking Book there. He felt in his pocket anxiously, then relaxed. His copy Linking Book was there.

Koena was still watching him, his eyes narrowed. But, of course, he wasn't Koena, or not the Koena he knew anyway, for his father had never been here to make him his acolyte. *No*, Atrus thought, *and nor have I.* For this was not the Thirty-seventh Age—or, at least, not that same Age his father had "created" and he,

Atrus, had lived in; this was another world entirely, like it—so like it as to be frighteningly familiar—and yet somewhere else.

His head swam, as if the solid ground had fallen away from him. *I am in another universe entirely, in another Age; one that my father tampered into existence.*

No, he told himself, thinking it through; *that's wrong. My father didn't create this—this was here all along, merely waiting for us to link to it.*

An Age where he knew everyone and was not known. He nodded to himself, understanding what had happened. His father's erasures in the Book had taken them back down the central trunk of the great tree of possibility and along another branch entirely.

Atrus took one last long look at the Age, then, knowing he was not wanted, turned and fled toward the cave, where, after he was gone, his Linking Book would never be found.

In Atrus's absence Gehn had lit the fire and had sunk into the chair beside it. That was where Atrus found him, slumped back, his pipe discarded on the floor beside him, his mouth open in a stupor.

Gehn was not sleeping, or if he was, it was a fitful kind of sleep, for his eyelids fluttered and from time to time he would mutter then give a tiny groan.

Looking at him, Atrus felt angry and betrayed.

Gehn had said that he was going to fix it, but he hadn't. That other world, the *real* Thirty-seventh Age, had been destroyed, or, at least, his link to it. And that was all Gehn's fault, because he hadn't understood what he was doing. Atrus stood over his father, feeling a profound contempt for him.

"Wake up!" he shouted, leaning over Gehn and giving him a shake. "I need to talk to you!"

For a moment he thought he hadn't managed to wake Gehn. Yet as he went to shake him again, Gehn reached up and pushed his hand aside.

"Leave me be!" he grumbled. "Go on . . . go to your room, boy, and leave me in peace!"

"No!" Atrus said defiantly. "I won't! Not until this is settled."

Gehn's left eye pried open. A kind of snarling smile appeared at one corner of his mouth. "*Settled?*"

"We need to talk," Atrus said, keeping firm to his purpose, determined not to let his father browbeat or belittle him this time.

"*Talk?*" Gehn's slow laughter had an edge of mockery to it now. "What could we possibly have to talk about, you and I?"

"I want to talk about the Art. About what it is. What it *really* is."

Gehn stared at him disdainfully, then, sitting up, reached beside his chair for his pipe.

"Go and get some sleep, boy, and stop talking such nonsense. What do *you* know about the Art?"

"Enough to know that you're wrong, father. That your Ages are unstable because you don't understand what you've been doing all this while!"

Atrus had only guessed about most of Gehn's worlds being unstable, but it seemed he'd hit the bull's-eye with that comment, for Gehn sat forward, his pallid face suddenly ash white.

"You're wrong!" Gehn hissed. "You're just a boy. What do *you* know?"

"I know that you don't understand the Whole!"

Gehn roared with amusement. "And you think *you* have all the answers, eh, boy?"

Atrus leaned over the table, determined to outface his father. "Some of them. But they're not ones *you* want to hear. You'd rather carry on as you are, stumbling blindly through the Ages, copying this phrase out of that book and that one out of another, as if you could somehow chance upon it that way."

Gehn's hands had slowly tightened their grip on the arms of the chair; now, pulling himself up out of the chair, his anger exploded. As Atrus reeled back, Gehn shouted into his face, spitting with fury.

"How *dare* you think to criticize me! Me, who taught you all you know! Who brought you here out of that godforsaken crack and educated you! How dare you even *begin* to think you have the answers!"

He poked Atrus hard in the chest. "How long have you been doing this now, eh, boy? Three years? Three and a half? And how long have I been studying the Art? Thirty years now! Thirty years! Since I was four."

Gehn made a small noise of disgust. "You think because you managed to make one measly Age that you know it all, but you don't, boy! You do not even know the start of it. Here . . ."

Gehn turned and went over to the desk. To Atrus's dismay he picked up Atrus's book and leafed it open. For a moment or two he read in silence.

"This phrase here . . . look how unnecessarily ornate it is . . . that's how a novice writes, boy. It lacks strength. It lacks economy of expression." And, reaching across, he took the pen and dipped it in the ink pot.

Atrus watched, horrified, knowing what was to come, yet still unable to believe that his father would actually dare to tamper with *his* Age.

But Gehn seemed oblivious of him now. Sitting at his desk, he drew the book toward him, then began to delete symbols here and there, using the D'ni negative, simplifying the phrases Atrus had spent so long perfecting—phrases which Atrus knew, from long reading in the ancient D'ni texts, were the perfect way of describing the things he wanted in his world.

"Please . . ." Atrus pleaded. "There is a reason for all those words. They *have* to be there!"

"In what book did you find this?" Gehn asked, tapping another of his phrases. "This nonsense about the blue flowers?"

"It wasn't in a book . . ."

"Ridiculous!" Gehn said, barely masking his contempt. "Frivolous nonsense, that's all it is! This is overwritten, that's all! There is far too much unnecessary detail!"

And, without another word, Gehn proceeded to score out the section about the flowers.

"*No!*" Atrus cried out, taking a step toward the desk.

Gehn glared at him, his voice stern. "Be quiet, boy, and let me concentrate!"

Atrus dropped his head and groaned, but Gehn seemed not to notice the pain his son was in. He turned the page and gave a tiny laugh, as if he'd found something so silly, so ludicrous, that it was worthy only of contempt.

"And this . . ." he said, dipping the pen into the ink pot once again, then scoring out one after another of the carefully-written symbols. "It's no good, boy. This description . . . it's superfluous!"

"*Please* . . ." Atrus said, taking a step toward him. "Leave it be now. Please, father. I beg you . . ."

But Gehn was unstoppable. "Oh no, and this won't do, either. This will have to go. I mean . . ."

Gehn looked up suddenly, the laughter fading from his face. "You understand me clearly now?"

Atrus swallowed. "Father?"

Gehn's eyes were cold now; colder than Atrus had ever seen them. "You must understand one thing, Atrus, and that is that you *do not* understand. Not yet, anyway. And you don't have the answers. You might *think* you have, but you're mistaken. You can't learn the D'ni secrets overnight. It's simply not possible."

Atrus fell silent under his father's stern gaze.

Gehn sighed, then spoke again. "I misjudged you, Atrus, didn't I? There is something of your grandmother in you . . . something *headstrong* . . . something that likes to meddle."

Atrus opened his mouth to speak, but Gehn raised his hand. "Let me *finish!*"

Atrus swallowed deeply, then said what he'd been meaning to say all along, whether it angered Gehn or not; because he had to say it now or burst.

"You said that you had fixed the Thirty-seventh Age."

Gehn smiled. "I did."

Atrus shook his head.

Gehn met his eyes calmly. "Yes . . .?"

"I mean, it's not the same. Oh, the lake's the same and the village, even the appearance of the people. But it's not the same. They didn't know me."

Gehn shook his head. "It's *fixed.*"

"But my friends. Salar, Koena . . ."

Gehn stared at the cover of the book a while, then picked it up and turned toward the fire.

Atrus took a step toward him. "Let *me* fix it. Let me help them."

Gehn glanced at him contemptuously, then took another step toward the flickering grate.

"Father?

The muscle beneath Gehn's right eye twitched. "The book is defective."

"*No!*" Atrus made to cross the room and stop him, to wrestle the book from him if necessary, but the desk was between them. Besides, it was already too late. With a tiny little movement, Gehn cast the book into the flames, then stood there, watching, as its pages slowly crackled and curled at the edges, turning black, the symbols burning up one by one, dissolving slowly into ash and nothingness.

Atrus stood there looking on, horrified. But it was too late. The bridge between the Ages was destroyed.

In the blue light of the lantern each object in that quiet chamber seemed glazed in ice—each chair and cupboard, the massive wooden bed, the desk. In contrast, the shadows in the room were black, but not just any black, these were intensely black—the empty blackness of nonexistence.

To a casual eye it might have seemed that nothing there was real; that every object trapped within that cold, unfeeling glare was insubstantial—the projection of some dark, malicious deity who, on a moment's whim, might tear the pages from the book in which all this was written and, with a god's indifference, banish this all into the shadow.

All, that is, but for the young man seated on a chair at the center of it all, the light reflected in his sad, pale eyes.

Slowly Atrus returned to himself, then looked about him. The last few hours were a blank; where he'd been and what he'd done were a complete mystery. All he knew was that he was sitting in his room once more, the lantern lit, his journal open on the desk beside him. He looked, then read what he had written on the left-hand page.

My father is mad.

Remembering, he shuddered, unable to believe what his father had done. And yet the memory was burned into the whiteness of his mind. If he closed his eyes, he could see the pages slowly charring, each one lifted delicately by the flame, as if the fire had read each phrase before consuming it.

Unless, of course, that memory is false, and I, too, am one of my father's "creations" . . .

But he knew beyond question that that wasn't so. The experience on the Thirty-seventh Age had proved that to him beyond all doubt. Gehn was no god. No. He was simply a man—a weak and foolish man, irresponsible and vain. Yes, and for all his bluster about making D'ni great again, he had forgotten precisely what it was that had made the D'ni extraordinary. The reason why their empire had lasted for so long. It was not their power, nor the fact that they had once ruled a million worlds, it was their restraint, their astonishing humility.

Gehn claimed that he, Atrus, knew nothing, but it wasn't so. He had read the histories of D'ni, and had seen, in those pages, the long struggle of the D'ni elders to suppress the baser side of their nature; to instill in their people the virtues of patience, service, and humility. Yes, and for the best part of sixty thousand years they had succeeded. Until Veovis.

So where did he go from here? What were his options? Should he try to get back to Anna and the cleft? Or should he, perhaps, find a hiding place in the city?

Whatever, he had to go and see Gehn one last time, to say goodbye. And to tell him, face-to-face, just why he had to leave.

The thought of it disturbed him. He had grown a great deal this last year and was almost the physical equal of his father, yet Gehn still intimidated him.

Even so, it had to be done. He could not simply run away, with his tail between his legs. For if he did, he would be forever in his father's shadow.

He went out, climbing the levels of that dark and twisting house, until he stood there in the library, at the foot of the steps that led up to his father's study. Up there, on the landing, the lantern was still lit, the door still open, as he'd left them.

He went up, steeling himself against his father's anger, against that mocking laugh that made him feel a little boy again.

But he was no "boy" anymore. He had grown

beyond mere boyishness. And now Gehn must be made to recognize that fact—must be forced to acknowledge it once at least before he left his house.

Atrus paused in the doorway, surprised to find the room so dimly lit. The fire had gone out, the lantern on the table faded to the faintest glimmer. As for Gehn, there was no sign.

He turned, taking the landing lantern from its hook, then stepped inside.

Books had been scattered here, there, and everywhere, as if in some fearful rage. And the desk . . .

Atrus hurried across, setting the lantern down beside the other, then searched among the books stacked on the desk, but there was no sign of his own book. He turned, looking to the fire anxiously, fearing the worst, and almost tripped over his father.

Gehn lay on the floor just behind the desk, sprawled out before the guttered fire.

For a moment Atrus thought his father dead, he was so still. Then he noted a slight movement of Gehn's right hand and knew that this wasn't death, only its counterfeit—a kind of stupor brought on by overindulgence with his pipe.

The pipe itself lay to one side, the fire-marble glowing dimly in its chamber. Atrus crouched and picked it up, sniffing the spout then wrinkling up his nose in disgust.

He was about to leave, to turn away and go, when he noticed, just beyond his father's outstretched hand, the notebook with the tanned leather cover he was always consulting.

For a second or two, he held back, the feeling of *wrongness* strong in him; but then the compulsion to know what was inside the book overcame him and, reaching out, he grasped the notebook then moved back into the lantern's light.

Taking a long, calming breath, he opened it to the first page, reading what was written there:

The Book of Atrus . . .

He frowned. Surely that was wrong? Surely it meant . . .? And then he understood. It didn't mean him. The handwriting wasn't his, nor was it Gehn's. No, this was his grandfather's book. Not Atrus, *son* of Gehn, but Atrus, *father* of Gehn.

He read on, then stopped, the last thread that had connected him to his father broken in that instant. Slowly he sat down in Gehn's chair, nodding to himself, a bitter laughter escaping him.

There he'd been, admiring his father, exalting him almost, for his courage, his patience in finding a path through the darkness of the tunnels back to D'ni. And all the while the path had been clearly marked, here in his grandfather's notebook. It wasn't Gehn who had taken the risks, but Gehn's father.

Atrus closed the book and pushed it away from him, then turned, staring at the shadowy figure stretched out on the floor beside his feet.

"Why weren't you what I wanted you to be?" he

asked quietly, pained by the great weight of disillusion he was feeling at that moment. "Why did you have to be so . . . so *small* a man?"

Gehn groaned and stirred slightly, but did not wake.

Atrus sat back, a long, shivering breath escaping him. For a moment longer he stared at Gehn's prone figure, then, his eyes drawn to the lantern, he reached across and picked the notebook up again.

16

GEHN WOKE WITH A POUNDING HEAD
and so many aches that he wondered briefly if he had
not perhaps blacked out and fallen. It would not be the
first time. Yet it was the first time he had allowed himself such license while Atrus was on K'veer, and he
cursed himself for not locking the door before suc-
cumbing to that second pipe.

He got up, groaning softly. Aches, yes, but nothing
broken.

"No damage done," he said, walking slowly to the
door. Then, steadying himself against the landing wall,
he looked down the steps, squinting now, his pupils
tight, painful.

"Atrus? Atrus, where are you?"

But the library was empty. He went down, then out
through the empty chamber, feeling a vague misgiving.

Something had happened. Something . . .

He stopped, remembering. The boy. He had
argued with the boy.

Crossing the open space between the library and
the upper cabin, he threw open the door and hurried
across the unlit chamber, until he stood in the shadowy
opening on the far side.

"*Atrus?*" He waited a moment, then called again. "*A-trus!*"

Nothing. The great mansion was empty.

Unless the boy's asleep . . .

He hurried down, bursting into Atrus's room without knocking.

"Atrus?"

The bed was empty. He turned, looking to the great carved wardrobe in the corner, then strode across and pulled it open. No. Atrus was not there, and none of his things were there either.

The thought made Gehn blink.

He hurried back to his study and searched the cluttered desk, but the notebook was not there. Reaching down to his right, he pulled out the second drawer and took out the metal box he kept there, placing it on the desk. Then, taking the key from the tiny bunch about his neck, he unlocked it.

He took the single page from the box and, folding it in half, slipped it into his pocket.

Leaving the box where it was, he went over to the door and shouted down the unlit steps. "Rijus! Rijus! Where are you, man?"

Not waiting for the mute, Gehn hurried down through the house. On the final twist of steps, he slowed, then stopped, his suspicions confirmed. The jetty was empty, the boat gone from its mooring.

Gehn slumped down onto the bare stone wall, letting his head fall forward.

"Curse the boy! Curse his ingratitude!"

Gehn lifted his head, the pounding at his temples momentarily making his vision swim. As it cleared, he saw that Rijus was standing on the turn of the steps just above him.

"The boy has gone," Gehn said. "He took the boat. We need to follow him."

The big mute hesitated a moment, taking in what his master had said, then came down the steps and, moving past Gehn, went over to the far side of the cavern. There, in the shadows, a number of boxes were stacked against a wall. Removing them, Rijus exposed an old, unpainted doorway. He looked about him, then stepped over and took down an old boat hook from the wall. Placing the tip of the hook under the bottom edge of the door, he heaved. The door splintered and fell away.

Gehn stood, then went across.

Inside, in the musty darkness, Rijus was removing an old canvas cover from over something. Gehn blinked, then discerned what it was. It was a boat. An old D'ni craft.

How did you know? he wondered, looking to the mute.

Ignoring the stabbing pains in his head, Gehn stepped inside and helped Rijus haul the ancient boat out onto the jetty.

It was a strangely long and elegant craft, more a canoe than a raft, and, handling it, he realized that it was made of a durable but curiously lightweight stone.

Gehn shook his head, marveling that he had never suspected its existence. It made him wonder what else there was about the mansion that he did not know about.

He looked to Rijus, watching as he attached the ropes, then winched the ancient boat out over the water.

Atrus held the lantern up, studying the page a moment longer, then closed the notebook and slipped it back into his tunic pocket.

Left. He had to turn left at the next fork. From there a narrow tunnel led through to a small diamond-shaped cavern with a low shelf of rock to the right, at the far side of which was a series of limestone ledges, leading to a flight of steps.

He walked on, the lantern raised, following the slightly curving tunnel, conscious of the sound of his own footsteps in that confined space.

How many times now had he stopped and listened, thinking he was being followed? And how many times had he heard nothing but the silence of the rock surrounding him?

Ahead now, the tunnel widened, then spilled out into a kind of groin in the rock. There the tunnel split in two. That much, at least, accorded with the diagram in the notebook. Atrus took the left-hand fork, walking on quickly now, his heart pounding again.

If it *was* the diamond-shaped cavern he would rest there a while and get his breath.

And if it wasn't?

Twice already he had had to retrace his steps, but this time it would mean a long trek back through the tunnels, and he did not relish that at all.

The trouble was that you had too much time down here to think. If he could have walked on thoughtlessly, like a machine, it might have been okay, but as it was he could not help himself imagining all kinds of things.

And the worst of his imaginings was a vivid picture of the cleft, abandoned, choked with sand.

It had been almost four years since he had last seen it. Four years since he had last heard Anna's voice.

He heard her now.

What do you see, Atrus?

I see rock, grandmother. And tunnels. And darkness. Everywhere I look, darkness.

But her voice did not return. There was only the sound of his own footsteps, going on ahead of him and behind, filling the darkness beyond the lantern's reach.

Atrus looked at the notebook again, turning the page, then turned it back again and frowned. Then, with a tiny start, he felt *between* the pages, locating the torn edge of the missing page, and groaned.

He looked about him, trying to remember—to retrieve from memory the path he'd taken all those years ago. Had he descended into the cavern or had he come up into it?

If he chose wrongly he would be lost.

And if he chose correctly?

Then, judging by the other pages, he would face the same kind of choice another five, maybe six times before he could be sure he was back on course. Before he reached the safety of the next page.

He swallowed bitterly, wondering just when his father had torn the page from the book, then looked up.

"So you thought you would make a journey, did you?"

Atrus froze, then slowly turned, facing his father, noting at once the cloth wrapped about his boots.

"I thought it time I kept my promise to my grand-mother."

"Your promise?" Gehn laughed humorlessly. "What of your promise to me? Besides, I think you have something that belongs to me and I mean to have it back."

"Then you'll have to take it from me."

"I see." Gehn half turned, gesturing to Rijus, who stepped from the shadows just behind him.

At the sight of the mute, Atrus realized that he stood no chance. If it had just been his father, he might—just might—have got the better of him, but he knew the mute's strength of old. Why, he'd seen the man lift heavy rocks—rocks he himself could barely budge—and throw them out of the way.

Atrus moved quickly. Taking the notebook from his pocket, he threw it high into the air, then, casting his lantern away, turned and ran, climbing the rock face like an ape before vanishing into the tunnel.

He heard his father's cry—of anger and frustration—and knew that Gehn had not expected that. Gehn had thought he would come quietly, just as he'd always done in the past. But the past was the past. He knew now that he could not stay with the man, even if it meant losing himself here in the depths of the earth.

He went quickly, his right hand keeping contact with the tunnel wall. Then, unexpectedly, the tunnel dipped and, with a cry, he found himself tumbling head over heels, coming to a jolting halt against a wall.

He lay there a moment, stunned, listening to his father's shouts.

"Atrus! *Atrus!* Come back here, boy!"

Atrus groaned and sat up. For a moment he

blinked at the darkness, wondering which way he was facing now, then saw, distant yet unmistakable, the glow of a lantern above him and to his right, at the head of the tunnel.

He had to go on. On into the darkness.

Pulling himself up, he stumbled on, making his way down as quickly as he dared, away from the approaching light.

And now, strangely, it came to him. He remembered where he was. If he closed his eyes he could see it vividly. Just ahead the path branched to the right, then climbed. Where it opened out there was a broad ledge of rock and, beyond that, a gap—a narrow chasm—straddled by a tiny rope bridge. If he could get to that, then maybe he had a chance. Maybe he could hold them off somehow, or find a way of destroying the bridge so that they could not pursue him.

Feeling a faint breeze coming from his right, Atrus stopped and turned, searching with both hands until he found the entrance. As he'd thought, the tunnel went sharply upward, forcing him to scramble up on his hands and knees, his head bent forward. There was a faint light up ahead, and as he came out of the narrow tunnel, he saw that he was precisely where he'd thought he'd be.

Only the ledge was brightly lit, a lantern standing off to one side, while ahead . . .

Atrus groaned. Once more his father had anticipated him. Once more, Gehn had had the final laugh.

The rope bridge was gone, the four metal pins jutting up nakedly from the rock.

He went across and stood there, looking down into the chasm. It was too deep, the jump too great. Or was it?

Atrus turned, hearing noises in the tunnel behind him. There was a flicker of light, growing stronger by the second. In a moment they would be upon him.

He turned back, staring at the chasm. It was now or never. Stepping back, he took a deep breath, then ran at it, hurling himself across the gap.

"*Atrus!*"

His chest slammed against the edge of the rock, winding him. Yet even as he began to slide, his right hand reached out and grasped one of the metal pins.

He spun about, his shoulder thudding against the rock, his right arm almost pulled from its socket as he held on for dear life. Yet he could feel the strength draining from his fingers; could feel them slowly slipping, the sweat from his palms sliding on the metal.

And then a shadow passed over the top of him. There was a deep grunt and then something gripped his upper arm and began to lift him slowly up.

Surprised by the strength of that grip, Atrus turned his head, expecting to see Rijus, but it was

Gehn who stared back at him, a sullen anger in those pale eyes.

"Acch, boy!" he said, his fingers pinching mercilessly into Atrus's flesh as they hauled him inch by inch to safety. "Did you really think you could outjump me?"

17

ATRUS STOOD THERE A LONG TIME after his father had gone, staring at the shadowed door in shock.

He turned, looking across that huge, high-ceilinged space toward the desk. There lay the Age Five book.

A trap, he thought. *Another door he'll hope I'll walk through. And when I do . . .*

Atrus heard again the slam of the door as his father closed it on him.

He stepped out from beneath the great curved arch, the pinkish light of the lamp above giving his features a false glow of health. Beneath his feet alternating black and white tiles—circles on squares—stretched away to every corner of that great space, while a large mosaic at the center portrayed Ri'Neref, the most famous of all the Grand Masters of the Guild, his graybearded features somber, almost melancholic as he stared back across the ages.

The stone, once polished and beautiful, was webbed with tiny cracks, worn with age.

A prison, Atrus thought, recognizing it for what it really was.

The stone here was not the lavatic black used elsewhere in the house, but a dull metallic gray carved with intricate patterns, like lacework, great bulbous pillars holding up the massive arch of the roof. He had seen that same stone in some of the most ancient structures in the city and realized that this was probably the oldest part of the house.

How old? he wondered. *Ten? Twenty thousand years? Or older yet?* It was hard to tell. The D'ni had built for eternity, not knowing that their days were numbered.

Finally, in the northern corner of the chamber, beneath a massive arch, stood the locked doorway that led out of his prison, bloodred stone pillars standing like sentries to either side.

Remembering what his father had said about the D'ni love of secret passages, of doors in solid walls and tunnels through the rock, he began a search.

Slowly, patiently, he went from arch to arch, searching each of the massive alcoves carefully, his fingers covering every inch of stone, as high as he could reach right down to the floor.

It took the best part of two hours, and though he found no secret doors or passages, it was still well worth the effort. In the floor of one of the more shadowy recesses, half embedded in the unfinished stone, he found a D'ni stonecutter. It was a big old machine, like a massive crouching spider, and its power source was long exhausted, yet one of the cutting blades was as good as new.

At first Atrus thought he might have to leave it

there, it was so firmly wedged into the rock, but after half an hour rocking it back and forth, he freed it from the stone.

He lifted the heavy cutter, feeling its weight, then nodded to himself. The door was solid metal and he would get nowhere trying to break through it, not even with this, but if he could chip away at the rock to either side, then maybe he wouldn't need to.

Knowing there was no sense in delaying, he set to work at once. Taking off his top, he wrapped the cloth about the main body of the cutter, then went across and, kneeling in the deep shadow beside the door, began to attack the stone, low down and to his left.

He could not properly see what he was doing, but after ten minutes he stopped and, setting the cutter aside, checked with his fingers.

It wasn't much of a notch, considering—in fact, he had barely chipped away more than a few flakes of the iron-tough stone—but at the top of that tiny, uneven depression the stone had split.

He traced the crack with his forefinger, then grinned. It was more than a foot long.

Atrus turned, looking toward the desk. There was a lamp there and fire-marbles. Hurrying across, he brought them back and, placing the lamp to one side so that it threw its light over the door, set to work again, aiming each blow at that split, aiming to widen it and crack the stone.

The first few blows did nothing. Then, with a sharp cracking noise, the split widened dramatically.

Atrus smiled and lifted the cutter again, meaning to extend the fissure, but even as he did, he heard the rock above him creak and groan.

He looked up. In the light from the lantern he could see that the roof directly above him was badly cracked. Even as he looked, tiny splinters of rock began to fall, as those cracks widened.

Snatching up the lantern, Atrus scampered backward. And not a second too soon. With a great sigh, the two pillars collapsed inwardly and a huge section of the roof caved in with a great crash.

Atrus lay on his back, some dozen paces off, staring back at the great pile of rock that had fallen, the dust in the air making him cough violently. As the dust slowly settled, he saw that the door was totally blocked. He edged back, then got to his feet, sneezing and rubbing at his eyes. Now he'd done it! Now he was trapped here for sure!

He coughed again, trying to clear his throat, then moved farther away, his eyes watering now.

Trapped, yes, but at least there was one advantage to it. If he could not get out, then Gehn could not get in.

Atrus turned, looking to the Age Five book, and blinked, reassessing the situation.

So just what did Gehn want? And why, if this *was*

a prison, had he provided him with the means to escape—the book? Why give him pen and ink? And why provide him with a Linking Book from the Fifth Age back to this chamber?

A trap, he thought again. But now he wasn't quite so sure. Maybe his father had given him the book simply so he wouldn't starve.

That thought intrigued him. He went over to the desk and stood there, staring down at the Age Five book. At the very center of its cover was a circular metal medallion, fixed to the leather by five tiny tacks. The D'ni number five—a square halved by a narrow bar—was raised in metal above the porcelain base, on which was engraved an intricate floral pattern.

Atrus opened the book and looked at the descriptive panel.

From the distant image it seemed a pleasant, peaceful place, the island heavily wooded.

Yes. But what's the catch?

For there had to be a catch. He knew that now. If he had learned one single thing today it was that Gehn never—never—did anything without some self-serving reason.

It was many hours before he finally decided to venture into Gehn's Fifth Age, deciding, before he did, that he would read it first, for if it really was a prison, he should at least know beforehand what kind of Age he was to end his days in.

For several hours he sat there, slowly leafing through the pages, noting all the flaws, all the possible contradictions that Gehn's particular writing style threw up. More than ever, he could see his father's limited vision on every page, like a hideous tapestry quilted together from exquisite patches of silk. The entire work was shortsighted and disjointed and yet it was also, paradoxically, quite clever. Surprisingly so.

Even so, it was one single thing which, in the end, caught Atrus's imagination; one element which made him catch his breath and make him want to go and *see*.

The tree.

Atrus sat back, amazed by the elegance, the sheer economy, of the D'ni phrases that had described it, then leaned forward again, tracing each symbol with his finger, a thrill of pure aesthetic delight passing through him.

A tree. A giant tree, whose topmost branches speared the sky!

Atrus smiled at the thought, then read on, memorizing the details of the world, fixing them in his mind like the symbols on a map.

And if it *was* a trap?

He looked about him at the huge and gloomy chamber. Even if it was a trap, at least he would get to see the sun again. At least he would feel the wind upon his skin, the rain falling on his arms and upturned face, the sweet and gentle pleasure of birdsong.

For a moment he looked down, his face creased with pain at the memory of Salar and the old woman, recalling what had happened to their world.

Never again, he swore, picking up the Linking Book, then opening the Age Five book to its descriptive page.

Hesitating no longer, Atrus placed his hand against the image on the page. At once he felt the page expand . . .

He had linked into a dense copse of tall, bearded grass which grew beside a circular pool that bulged strangely. He had stared at it, fascinated by the apparent motion of its convex surface, then, hearing voices, had hurried from the spot quickly, making his way over a lightly wooded hill, then along a narrow dirt path that led steeply down a sheer cliff wall, dropping beneath an overhang of rock and down onto a rocky beach. An azure ocean lapped gently against the shore, washing over a line of smooth tapered rocks that edged the beach like the teeth of some great submerged creature.

There he paused, getting his breath, listening to the gentle slush and hiss of the sea.

Turning, he looked about him, searching for somewhere safe to hide the Linking Book he'd brought.

Almost at once his gaze fell on the sandstone cliff beneath the overhang, the face of which was pocked with hundreds of tiny holes.

Atrus walked across and, choosing from among a number of likely candidates, picked one of the larger ones, some way up, well above what he saw was the normal tidal level. He glanced about him, then, convinced no one was watching, climbed up, using the lips of other holes as footholds. Squeezing his whole body into that narrow space, he crawled a little way along then set the Linking Book down on the dry ledge— wedging it with a loose rock so that it wouldn't slide.

Satisfied, he backed out, then jumped down onto the sand again, wiping his hands against his sides.

He had noticed a sloping path around the edge of the enclosed bay, over to his left, and headed there now, picking his way slowly up the jumble of rock. For a moment he was in shadow, the rock ledge blocking his view of the sky, then, as the path turned slightly, there was a break in the rock and he came out into a sloping meadow.

It was surprisingly windy. A strong, gusting breeze bent the heads of the long grass stalks and tugged at his cloak. Pulling it tight about him, Atrus walked on, head down, then, noticing how the shadow ended in a jagged line just ahead of him, he looked up.

Slowly, very slowly, he turned to his right, until he was facing it, his mouth fallen open in astonishment, his head going back to try to take it all in.

The tree.

It seemed to rest on a peninsula of rock, its roots like the pillars of some huge stone temple, reaching down the cliff face to pierce the rocky beach, great humps of root, like the slick backs of a dozen massive sea serpents, stretching out into the ocean.

Its trunk, likewise, was monumental. It was not by any means as tall as Atrus had imagined, yet the sheer breadth of it was enough to make him feel not simply small in its presence but insignificant.

Like Time itself, Atrus thought, letting his eyes slowly climb its branches. Then, realizing how exposed he was to watchful eyes, he hurried on, making for the rock face just ahead.

A set of steps were cut into rock, leading up through the trees. And there, in a clearing, the sunlight filtering down upon it through the treetops, was a large wooden hut.

Atrus walked up to it, his heart hammering in his chest, recognizing it at once. It was like the meeting hut—Gehn's temple—on the Thirty-seventh Age. Almost identical, in fact.

Seeing it, Atrus knew suddenly exactly where he was on the island, picturing it in his mind as on a map.

He stepped up, into the cool interior, passing between the painted wooden poles and into a space that was furnished in the most luxurious manner imaginable, with marvelous tapestries and statuary and silver-poled banners lining the walls.

At the far side of that shadowed space was a throne—a massive thing that looked as though it had been cast from a single piece of glowing gold. Coming closer, however, Atrus saw that it wasn't gold but a beautiful, tawny stone, the like of which he'd never seen, even in D'ni. Atrus stopped briefly to examine it, brushing his fingertips over the smooth, cool surface of the arm, wondering in which ancient book Gehn had found the formula or phrase to produce such a wonderous material.

Behind the throne was a large free-standing screen, on the pale lemon silk of which was embroidered the silhouette of a man. That silhouette, with its high, domed head and its familiar lenses, was unmistakable. It was Gehn.

Atrus nodded to himself at this evidence of Gehn's presence. On how many other worlds had his father built such temples? In how many Ages was that man a "god?"

Knowing now what he would find—recalling all of this vividly from the Age Five book—he went over to the screen and looked around it. There was a shadowy space beyond, a narrow set of steps leading down.

He went down, into the darkness.

A low door, cut crudely from the rock, led to a long but narrow cave. From what he'd read, he knew that farther back, the walls that were pocked with thousands upon thousands of tiny holes in much the same manner as the cliff face.

It's there! he realized, peering through the half light. *Gehn's Linking Book is there!*

He was about to turn away, to go back through the temple and explore the wood surrounding it, when he remembered that the cave actually led somewhere. He couldn't recall exactly what it led to—there had been several areas in the Age Five book where Gehn's phrasing was unclear, and this was one of them—but he had a definite recollection that it was important somehow.

He walked on. The warm stuffiness of the cave was making him sweat, yet the cave was definitely leading somewhere. He might be imagining it, but just as the air grew constantly warmer, so there seemed to be a faint, shimmering blue light in the tunnel now, enough to allow him to see a couple of feet in front of him. As he went on, the light grew, until he found himself in a second, smaller cave, filled with that same shimmering blue light.

It was hot in the second cave, unbearably hot, steam rising from a great vent in the floor, but Atrus's eyes were drawn upward, into the roof of the cave. There, the most astonishing sight met his gaze. The flat gray rock of the ceiling was pierced at its center by a large, roughly circular hole, perhaps eight or ten feet in diameter. Within that hole, suspended *above* the cave, was a pool of water, its gently shimmering surface flush with the rock surrounding it. Beside it stood a metal ladder, leading up into the pool.

Atrus stared, openmouthed. It was an illusion. It

had to be. Yet if that were so, what power sustained i
He frowned, willing himself to understand. He walke
across and stared. The massive, natural vent glowe
redly far below.

He looked up into the pool. Sunlight was filterin
down through the water, the curved walls of whic
seemed to form a kind of well. He narrowed his eye
trying to estimate its length, but it was difficult to te
He knew, from his reading, that the refractive quali
of water could distort such things. Besides, who kne
even if this *was* water, for when had he ever seen wat
behave in such a fashion? Up there, on the far side
that unnatural barrier, however, there was somethin
There had to be. Or why the ladder?

Atrus stepped over to the ladder, taking hold of
determinedly.

How far is it? he wondered, pausing, his head or
inches beneath that strangely quivering surface. *Twer
feet? Thirty?*

Raising his right hand, he tentatively immersed
in the pool.

It was extremely warm and felt like water, exce
that, when he withdrew his hand, the drips fle
upward, merging with the pellucid surface of the po

Atrus closed his eyes, then pushed up, immersi
his head and shoulders. For five full seconds he he
himself there, then ducked down again, sputtering.

There, he told himself, opening his eyes wide a

drawing a hand back through his sodden hair, grinning to himself.

He closed his eyes again and counted, taking slow, calming breaths. At twenty he thrust upward, dragging himself up the last few feet of the ladder with his hands. And then, suddenly, he was fully immersed!

Opening his eyes, he let go of the ladder and kicked, reaching up instinctively, trying to claw his way to the surface.

Slowly, very slowly it came toward him, the walls sliding past. His lungs were aching now, but he was very nearly there.

And then, suddenly, there was a shadow on the sunlit surface just above him, the outline of a human figure. He tried to hold back, putting out his arms, trying to slow his upward drift, fighting to stay where he was, but it was impossible, and in the struggle something gave.

The sudden choking pain was awful. It was like swallowing hot tar. His lungs were suddenly on fire, his mind flaring like a bonfire with the pain. He spasmed and threw his arms out, trying to grasp the edges of that strange, unnatural well, yet even as he did, the blackness leaked in again, robbing him of consciousness.

Slowly, arms out, he floated to the surface of the circular pool he had seen when he first arrived.

The hut was dark after the bright sunlight of the bay, and as Katran sat herself in the corner, out of the way of her two cousins who were tending to the stranger, it took a while for her eyes to adjust to the shadows.

At first they had thought he was dead. It was the strangest thing they had ever seen. They were reluctant to take him from the water. His flesh was pale and corpselike and there had been no pulse at his neck. The old man, Hrea, had advocated throwing him back into the water, but her eldest cousin, Carel had persevered, pushing the water from out of the stranger's chest and breathing his own air into the youth's blue mouth until, with a choking sound and the expulsion of a plentiful amount of water, the corpse had begun to breath again.

They had wrapped the stranger in a blanket then carried him back to the hut.

That had been this morning. In the hours between the stranger had slept, at first lightly, feverishly, but then peacefully. For the last few hours Carel and his younger brother, Erlar, waited for the stranger to wake.

"How long?" she asked impatiently, the D'ni she spoke clearer, less accented than theirs.

Carel, who was standing beside the bed, looked to her across the full length of the room and shrugged, but Erlar, who was at the stove, preparing a pot of soup, smiled and said gently, "Not long now, Katran. Let him sleep a little longer. If he doesn't come around soon, we'll wake him."

"Is there any . . . *damage?*"

At that Erlar looked to Carel.

"It's hard to say," Carel answered.

"Who is he?" she asked, posing the question that all of them had asked in their minds. "Do you think he belongs to Gehn?"

"One of his servants, you mean?" Carel sighed, then shrugged. "I don't know. He has a pair of eye instruments like Gehn's."

"*Eye instruments?*" She sat forward slightly. "I didn't see them."

"No . . . they were in the pocket of his cloak." Carel reached across and took them from a table beside the bed. "Here."

She took them and studied them, remembering what she'd been told by Erlar about the stranger's first appearance among them—unearthly white, his arms spread as if to embrace them as they knelt there looking down.

Katran studied the lenses a moment longer, then handed them back. "Is he marked?"

Carel shook his head. "There's nothing on his neck."

Unconscious of the gesture, she put her hand to her own neck, her fingers tracing the boxlike symbol imprinted in the flesh.

"Then maybe . . ."

Both cousins looked to her, waiting for her to go on, but she merely shook her head.

Erlar smiled, then looked back at the pot he was stirring. "He was talking in his sleep earlier . . ."

"Talking?" Katran stared at her cousin, her deeply green eyes intent.

"He was murmuring something about flowers."

Her narrow mouth opened, the lips barely parting, then she turned her head, anxiously looking across to where the stranger lay on his back on the wooden bed.

There was a faint groan, a movement of the body. Katran half stood, then sat again. Carel, beside the body, reached down and, dipping the flannel in the bucket by his side, wrung it out, then began to wipe the stranger's brow, as he'd done now many times. Yet even as he did, the youth's hand came up and firmly held his wrist.

Carel swallowed nervously as the young man opened his eyes.

There was surprise in those pale yet clearly human eyes; fear and curiosity.

"Where am I?"

Carel made no attempt to free his hand. "You are on Riven. In the village."

"Riven?"

"Yes, Riven," Carel repeated, that one word sounding strange among the heavily accented D'ni words. "We found you in the pool. You were in a bad way. The water had got inside you."

The young man's eyes opened wide, suddenly remembering. "The pool . . ."

"Are you hungry?"

"Hungry?" The stranger nodded. "Famished!"

"Good . . ." Carel looked to his younger brother and gave a nod. At the signal, Erlar poured soup into a large wooden vessel and, after sprinkling a measure of dark powder into it, carried it across.

"Here," Erlar said, holding it out, as Carel helped the young man sit up, placing two pillows behind his back, between him and the wooden headboard.

"Thank you," the stranger said, taking the bowl. After sniffing it, he began to spoon it into his mouth, slowly at first, then with an appetite that made the brothers look to each other and smile.

"Would you like some more?" Erlar asked, taking the empty bowl back from him.

"Please."

They watched, astonished, as he ate a second bowl and then a third. Then, drowsy once more, the effort, it seemed, too much for him, he slept again.

And all the while Katran sat there in the corner, her green eyes watching.

Atrus woke with a start, as if he'd fallen in his sleep, conscious of the unfamiliar yet not unpleasant smell of the shadowed place in which he found himself.

Turning onto his side, he stretched, then lay still, hearing voices from outside. He remembered now: the two young men who'd sat there while he ate, smiling kindly at him. He smiled himself at the thought. What had they called this place? Riven, that was it. Gehn's Fifth Age.

He yawned, then lay still again, staring at the far wall. It was a simple mud and daub hut, not so dissimilar from those on the Thirty-seventh Age, but bigger, and with a finish to the walls that spoke of a high level of technical skill. And they had stoves, too—cast metal stoves on which they cooked. That spoke of complexities to this Age that Age Thirty-seven did not have. They would have to have a supply of metal, yes, and the skills to use it.

His eyes went to the stove, noting its simple, unadorned shape, so unlike all of the D'ni artifacts he was used to. Such simplicity appealed to him.

Idly, his eyes traveled upward, searching the shadows of the ceiling, curious to see what kind of structure this was, what materials they used here. So much of this, as ever, had not been in the descriptive book. Only the building blocks were there in Gehn's Age Five book: the basic elements from which the complexities of such cultures developed. That thought fascinated him. It made him think of subtle ways he himself might have influenced the mix, what factors he personally would have built into the equation of this Age.

His eyes traveled down from the shadows, noting the simple square-cut window, the undecorated plainness of the whitewashed wall, then stopped, surprised to find the eyes of a young woman staring back at him.

Green eyes. Startlingly green eyes.

For a moment he simply stared, his lips slightly parted, taking in the strange, almost delicate beauty of her face; then, realizing what he was doing, he averted his eyes, suddenly, acutely embarrassed.

How long has she been there? he wondered. *How long has she been watching me?*

He heard her soft footsteps on the bare earth floor.

"You almost died," she said. "What were you doing in the pool?"

Atrus turned to find her kneeling beside the bed, her face almost on a level with his own. He found that strangely disconcerting, as if she were some kind of threat to him. Unlike the young men who had nursed him, her face was tense, almost ill-humored.

"I don't know," he answered.

She blinked, then looked away, allowing Atrus the chance to study her. The others had been tanned, and so was she, but he noticed that the skin of her lower arms was strangely "banded"—pale and tanned—as if she had at some point placed strips of cloth about them to create that pattern. She was wearing a simple dark green dress. There were tiny white feathers braided into her hair and about her neck was a wide, embroidered choker, but his gaze kept returning to her eyes, which were deep and mysterious, so deep and dark . . .

"Where did you come from?" she asked, her face still turned from his.

"Another place," he said, thinking that it could do no harm, but he could see that his answer didn't satisfy her. There was a flash of irritation in her eyes.

Atrus sensed as much, as she stood and turned away from him. He risked a tiny glance. There was something tense about the way she stood there, her head slightly tilted forward, her hands up to her mouth.

She turned back, focusing those dark eyes on him once again. "What's your name?"

"Atrus. What's yours?"

"Katran."

He nodded. "Catherine. That's . . ."

"Ka-*tran*," she said again, placing the emphasis on the final syllable. "I dreamed of you."

"You *dreamed* . . .?"

Then, without another word, she turned and quickly left the hut, leaving the door wide open, the sunlight spilling in in a wide bar of gold that climbed the far wall.

Atrus lifted his head, staring at the doorway, wondering what all that had been about, then, swallowing, his throat strangely dry, he let his head fall back.

18

A TRUS SAT CROSS-LEGGED BESIDE THE shallow bowl, his eyes closed, his fist clenched tightly, counting.

"Atrus?"

He turned, looking up at her. "Yes, Catherine?"

There was a slight flicker of annoyance in her face at the mispronunciation of her name, but she had given up trying to correct him. "What are you doing?"

At the count of sixty he relaxed his hand, letting the fingers unfold. As he did, a small bubble of water, its surface fluid and reflective like a drop of mercury, floated up out of his palm.

Atrus looked to her. She had a slightly quizzical look on her face.

"Water shouldn't do that when it gets warm."

"No? Then what should water do?""

Atrus shrugged. "Well, it shouldn't *float* and it shouldn't give me a *stomache ache*."

She laughed, then quickly grew serious again.

Atrus stared at her, surprised. It was the first time she had laughed since he had met her, and the change it made to her face was quite remarkable.

"I'll get you some of the powder."

"Powder?"

Catherine gave a single nod. For a moment she simply stared, as if trying to fathom something about him, then, without even the slightest movement, she seemed to shrug and look away.

Her eyes were still on him, but she was no longer there. Not looking out at him, anyway. It was as if, briefly, she had gone into a trance.

Atrus reached out and picked up the brass cooking pot he had been examining earlier, pleased by its symmetry, by the way the double pans—top and bottom linked by four strong brass spindles—like all the cooking implements in Age Five, were designed to cope with water which, when heated, rose into the air. Everything here had special "catchment lids" and spouts with tiny valves which did not open unless you tilted the thing a certain way.

He looked to Catherine again, and saw she was still distracted.

"What are you thinking?"

She turned to face him. "I'll tell you what I'm thinking. You have those pale eyes and wear those strange eye instruments. What have you to do with Lord Gehn?"

"I am Atrus, his son."

There was a brief look of triumph in her eyes. Then, as if she suddenly saw what it meant, she took a step backward. "So what do you want?"

He paused as he considered the question—sweeping away the cloud of Gehn and all he'd witnessed over the last few years.

What do I want?

"I want to go home," he said softly.

"Home?"

"To the cleft."

"The cleft?"

"It's where I was born," he said. "Where I grew up. It was just a crack, a hole in the earth surrounded by desert," he added, thinking of what Gehn had said of it, "yet it was like . . . well, like *paradise*."

"And your father lived there with you?"

Atrus shook his head, looking away as he answered her. "No. I didn't know my father. Not until I was fourteen. I grew up with my grandmother, Anna. She fed me, clothed me, taught me. She gave me everything."

Catherine stared at him intensely.

"And then your father came?"

Atrus nodded. Standing, he brushed himself down, then looked past her down the grassy slope. The village was in the crater behind him, just the other side of the slope—literally *in* the crater, the mud and daub huts fixed into the crater wall using great wooden stakes, like the rooms in the cleft had been.

He smiled, remembering. The first time he had seen it had almost been his last. Feigning sleep, he had let the elder of the two brothers, Carel, leave the hut, then had slipped out of bed, intending to go outside and look around. It had only been his natural caution that had stopped him falling into the bay fifty feet below.

It also explained why the sounds changed in the evening. He had thought that the sea came in to a beach close by the hut; he had not understood that it actually came in *beneath* the hut, let in through a tunnel inlet to the left of the cliffside village.

He turned, looking about him. To the left, no more than half a mile distant, lay the forest, its strange, golden-leaved trees dominating the view there, their massive branches flattened, as if under enormous pressure from the sky.

Directly south, on a raised promontory, was the copse in which the temple stood, while over to the right, clearly visible from wherever one stood on the island, was the tree.

Catherine stepped up beside him, her eyes on him all the while, almost as if she knew him. Her tone was different now . . . Steady.

"I had a dream of you."

He turned to face her, recalling the first time she had said it to him, in the hut. "A dream?"

"Yes," she said, slowly walking down the slope away from him, her green dress flowing about her, her bare feet seeming almost to float upon the grass. "I dreamed of a dead man floating in the pool, and now you're here!"

"Well?" Gehn asked, sitting down in front of the young woman. "Has anything . . . *unusual* been happening?"

Katran looked up from the copybook and met her Master's gaze, her own eyes innocent. "Nothing unusual."

"Good," he said, turning away, sucking deeply on his pipe. "Shall we pick up where we left off?"

The lesson went well, but then they always did. Katran was a good student—his best—and he never had to tell her anything more than once. Some of the other Guild members were good at copying, but none of them, with the exception of Katran, had begun to grasp the true meaning of the symbols they were copying. She, by contrast, had understood at once. And now, after only two years' tuition, she was almost fluent. *Almost*, he thought, thinking of all the key words he had kept from her; certain garo-hertee words, without which it would be impossible to write. But soon he would begin to give her those keys. One by one. If she was good.

He had formulated his plan long before he had imprisoned Atrus. Furious with his son, but determined to fulfill his dream of a great D'ni resurgence, he had found himself wondering if it were not possible to go about things in a different manner. He still needed Atrus—there was no doubt of that, for such talent should not be squandered—yet it seemed impossible to work with him.

But did it have to be Atrus at his side? Wouldn't another do just as well? Someone not quite as talented, perhaps—yet certainly more docile than his son? Someone he could control much easier than Atrus?

At once he had thought of Katran.

Gehn smiled and turned to face her, setting his pipe down on the desk. "There's something I have to tell you, Katran. Something important."

"Master?" She stared back at him, intent yet obedient, her eyes the eyes of the perfect acolyte, the perfect servant.

"I want you to prepare yourself. There is to be a wedding, you understand? Thirty days from now. I will give instructions to the other Guild members as to the ceremony, but you must make special preparations."

"You are to take a bride, Master?"

"Yes, Katran," he said, looking at her fondly now. "You are to be my wife. You will sit at my right hand and rule a thousand worlds with me."

"But Master," she said, bowing her head, "I am not deserving of this honor."

Gehn laughed softly, pleased by her humility. "Maybe not. But I have chosen you, Katran, and you will prepare yourself. Thirty days, you have. Thirty days . . . and then the ceremony will take place."

Atrus had been looking for Catherine all over the main island, surprised that no one knew where she had gone. Then, suddenly, she was there again, standing among the trees at the edge of the forest.

He almost called to her, almost shouted out her name, yet something about the way she was standing there—distracted—made him stop and then double back into the wood, coming out behind her, one of the massive spongy boles hiding him from her sight.

In the mottled shade of the massive branches, her slender figure seemed unreal—a thing of earth and grass, the green of her cloak, the raven black of her hair blending with the surrounding shadows.

Even from where he was standing, Atrus could see that something had disturbed her. Her eyes, which were normally so bright and inquisitive, were now deep in thought, while her hands were clasped tightly in front of her.

What is it? he asked silently, feeling a natural sympathy for her.

Slowly, his feet carefully finding their way over the thick leaf cover between the trees, he moved toward her, until he stood less than a dozen feet away.

"Catherine?"

She did not turn, merely looked up

"Catherine . . . are you all right?"

She nodded.

"Shall I walk you back to the village?"

"All right," she said quietly, turning and walking beside him as they moved out from beneath the great overhang of branches into the sloping meadow.

Atrus found his Linking Book where he'd left it in the cliff face and linked back.

The chamber was as he'd left it, the Age Five book open on the desk, the ink pots and pen undisturbed.

Returning to the desk, Atrus settled in the chair, then drew the book toward him and began to read it, more carefully this time, seeing how each phrase, each small description, contributed to the totality of what he'd seen.

Now that he had been there, he understood just how good it really was. The Fifth Age of Gehn was quite remarkable. Yet there were clear flaws in the way the book had been put together, particularly in the structure of the writing. Elegant passages lay side by side on the page, each uniquely beautiful, yet disturbingly unrelated to each other. It was the trademark of his father's style. The boldness of Gehn's eclecticism—his drawing from such disparate sources—was indeed astonishing, close to brilliant.

Had Gehn built his Ages from structural principles, they might have been different, for it was possible that in so doing he might have reconciled the gaps. As it was, his method was piecemeal and the flaws that resulted quickly compounded into a complex network of interrelated faults—faults that could not be tackled by simple solutions.

Atrus turned the final page, nodding to himself as he read the last few entries—seeing there his father's crude attempts to make small changes to the Age Five world, to stabilize its inherent faults.

"All wrong," he said quietly, wishing he could just score out those final entries, but, remembering what had happened on the Thirty-seventh Age, fearing to do so. No, if he was to make changes, he would do so only with great care and after long and patient deliberation. One could not meddle with an Age. At least, not with an Age as complex as Gehn's Fifth Age.

Riven, he thought. *She called it Riven.* And as he looked up, it was to find Catherine standing there, looking down at him, a large blue book clutched to her chest.

19

ATRUS STOOD THERE, STARING AT Catherine, stunned by her sudden appearance.

She quickly looked around her, then set the book down on the table. "I followed you," she said, before he could speak. "Saw where you hid your Linking Book."

He glanced at the big, blue-covered book where it lay on the table between them, then pointed to it.

"I got it," she said, "from your father."

"Got it? How? He doesn't allow books out of his library."

She looked directly at him. "I stole it from his study, while he was asleep."

He stared at her openmouthed. "But why?"

Things were moving far too fast for him. He stood, putting his hands out, as if to fend her off. "Slow down. What were you doing in my father's study."

"He takes us there."

"Who?"

"The Guild. He has us copy things from books. He says it saves him time."

"The Guild?" He laughed. In his mind he saw again how mad his father was, trying to re-create the D'ni Guilds.

She stepped around the desk and, reaching out, pulled down the edge of the choker she was wearing. Beneath it, burned into the flesh, was his father's sign.

He met her eyes. "How long ago was this?"

She made a face, as if she hated to recall it. "He placed the mark on me four years ago. I was the fourth to have it. Since then he's increased our number to ten. We are an elite. The other islanders have to do as we say. Your father insists on it."

"So why bring me the book?" he asked, laying his hand on the flecked blue cover.

"You can write. I want you to fix our world."

Atrus stared back at her a moment, then went around the desk and sat, opening the book. It was blank. She had stolen a blank book. He looked up at her. "Why should I do that?"

"Because you must."

"*Must?* Who says I must?"

"Don't you understand? It's falling apart. I'm asking for your help."

Atrus sat back. "Go on."

"It's been happening for a while now. There have been small tremors in the earth, and cracks, and schools of dead fish have been floating into the bay. And then the tree . . ."

He waited, his stomach muscles tensed, remembering what had happened on the Thirty-seventh Age. There, too, it had begun with little things. Instability: there was a fatal instability in all his father's worlds.

"The great tree is dying," she said.

"Why didn't you say this to me earlier?"

"Because I wasn't sure of you at first."

"Why?" he laughed.

"Because of your power. The power that your father has. The power to create and destroy worlds."

"You think I have that power?"

"Haven't you?"

He hesitated, then nodded. "I can write."

"Then help us, Atrus."

He let out a long, sighing breath. What if this were another trap? After all, how likely was it that she had managed to steal books from his father's study? Then again, he remembered the voice he'd heard that time, when he'd been standing at the bottom of the steps that led up to Gehn's study. He should have known, even then, that Gehn was bringing people back from his Ages?

"Okay," he said. "I'll help you." He paused. "But I need more books. More blank books."

"Why?"

He studied her momentarily. "There are things I have to try out. Experiments."

"I have more books on Riven. You'll need to help me carry them."

"You've . . ." He laughed. "You mean, you stole more than one?"

"Yes. Your father trusts me. He . . ."

"What is it?" he asked.

"Nothing. Just that we'd better be getting back, to pick up the books. The quicker you get to work . . ."

He shook his head. "Why are you in such a hurry? It can't be rushed. To fix an Age . . ."

She leaned closer. "There're only thirty days."

Atrus sat back. "I don't understand. What's happening in thirty days?"

But Catherine did not answer him. Instead she reached across and, placing her hand over the Age Five image on the page, linked back, leaving Atrus staring at the empty air, openmouthed, his heart pounding in his chest.

He linked back to the grassy plateau beside the pool.

Catherine was waiting for him. Taking his hand, she hurried him through the trees and along the edge of the cliff top opposite the tree. Water lapped softly at the rocks a hundred feet below. Looking at the tree across that narrow gap, Atrus could see little wrong with it. From this distance it seemed the epitome of rude health, a vast symbol of natural fecundity, yet he had no reason to doubt Catherine.

"It would be best if we were not seen," she said, hurrying him down a narrow path that hugged the cliff, then up a curving twist of wooden steps set into the earth between steep slopes of grass.

He shrugged, then went on with her, up the final

few feet of the path and onto a lush stretch of grass that nestled between two spurs of the great tree's massive trunk.

"Here," Catherine said, beckoning him across.

He went over to where she stood, then frowned deeply, seeing at once what she meant. Just beside her the bark was deeply split, a huge crack reaching in to breach the medullary ray that carried the tree's necessary nutrients, and on, deep into the sapwood. The split was large enough for him to walk into.

"You see?" she said softly, her green eyes troubled. "This was his punishment."

"His *punishment?* For what?"

She walked past him, then sat, looking out across the water toward the copse, the white stone of the temple barely visible among that rich dark green.

"One of the Guild spoke out of turn. He questioned something the Lord Gehn said to him. Your father was angry. I've never seen him so angry. He had us . . . *sacrifice* the man."

Atrus went across and crouched, facing her. "What do you mean?"

"We fed him to the sea."

"I still . . ."

She put her hand out to stop him. "It doesn't matter. What does matter is that he threatened us. All of us. Gave us a warning. 'Question me again,' he said, 'and I shall destroy your world. For just as I made it, I can unmake it! Look to the great tree,' he said. 'I shall leave my sign upon it.'"

Another fissure, Atrus thought, remembering once more what had happened on the Thirty-seventh Age. *Yes, everywhere he goes he leaves his mark, like a signature of his incompetence. And is that why I'm here? Is that the reason why he imprisoned me with the Age Five book? To clear up after him? To put right what he has so abjectly failed to make good?*

He looked back at Catherine. "And the other Guild members . . . do they know what you plan to do?"

She shook her head. "They would kill me if they did. They are in fear of your father, Atrus. They tremble before his every word."

"And yet one of them gainsayed him."

Catherine looked down, as if ashamed.

"That was *your* fault?" he said, after a moment. "You . . . *influenced* him?"

She looked up, her eyes beseeching him now. "I didn't mean to. I only thought . . ." She took a long shuddering breath, then, much quieter. "I thought Lord Gehn might listen to him. I thought your father was a reasonable man."

"My father? No," Atrus said matter-of-factly, "my father's mad."

He turned and looked, seeing, in the distance beyond the temple mound, another promontory.

"What's there?" he asked, trying to remember what Gehn had written in the book.

"That's where the Guild members live. That's where we have our enclave."

For some reason the thought of her living alone with nine men disturbed him. "Are they . . . like you?"

She laughed, then patted the grass beside her. "What do you mean, *like* me? Young?"

He went to shrug, then nodded.

"No," she said. "Most of them are old . . . even older than my father. Gehn seems to like them that way. More docile, I guess. Apart from Eavan."

"Eavan?"

She nodded, sucking in her lips a moment. "My friend. He was the one Gehn sacrificed."

Atrus looked past her a moment, his eyes drawn to the dark shape of the split in that massive trunk. "Did you love him?"

"*Love?*" The word came out surprised, but after a moment she nodded. "He was like a brother to me. As dear to me as Carel and Erlar. When the other Guild members took him . . ."

"I'm sorry," he said when she didn't go on. "I feel . . . responsible somehow."

"You shouldn't," she said, looking sharply at him. "After all, he's not been particularly kind to you, has he? What kind of father imprisons his son?"

He stared at her. "How is it you know so much?"

She looked away, then: "Because your father tells me. Oh . . . some things he doesn't even realize he's telling me. He likes to talk to himself, and sometimes he forgets. Sometimes I'm in his study, copying, and . . ."

"Hold a moment," Atrus said. "Tell me . . . why does he do that?"

She blinked again. "It's as I said. It speeds up his work."

"Yes, but . . . what does he *want?*"

His eyes held hers a moment, begging an answer, his head following hers when she tried to avoid his gaze. She smiled.

"I guess," she began, sitting up a little and turning herself to face him square-on, "I guess he wants to teach us how to write."

"Is that what he told you?"

She nodded.

"But that's impossible. No one but D'ni can write. It simply doesn't work for anyone else."

She was staring at him curiously now. "You're sure of that?"

He nodded. "It was the first thing he ever taught me about the Art. And the books—the *Histories*—confirm it. Time and again they stress the fact."

Strangely, Catherine seemed relieved.

"What is it now?" he asked, puzzled by her reaction.

"I just thought . . . well, in my book . . ."

"Your *book?*"

She stared at him a long moment, then nodded. "Would you like to see it?"

He shrugged. "Okay . . ."

"Then come," she said, taking his hand and pulling him up after her. "I'll show you."

Katran had always been somewhat uncomfortable with the idea that she could make a book. Somehow the whole notion, which at first had fascinated and intrigued her, now horrified her, for if she could conjure up her dreams from ink and paper, what did that make *her*? A mere figment. Just another conjuration of the Lord Gehn's fitful imagination!

She turned, looking across the shadowed hut to where Gehn's son, Atrus, sat cross-legged on the narrow bed, reading her book.

So different from his father, so . . .

So *true*.

Her eyes went to the young man again, finding it strange the way his presence so disturbed her. It was just . . .

Atrus looked up from the book and met her eyes, and she instantly knew what it was. It was his kindness. His simple, natural kindness.

"This is quite beautiful," he said. "I've never read anything like it. It's like . . . well, it's like nightfall over the desert or . . . like the cleft when it was filled with stars."

She went across and sat beside him.

"The writing . . . well, as I said, the writing's wonderful. It's poetic. But in practical terms . . . it's riddled with contradictions, I'm afraid. It breaks almost every single law of D'ni writing. It has no structure, no *architecture*. And some of these symbols . . . I've never seen them before. I'm not even sure they mean anything. Where did you learn them? Gehn never taught these to me."

Catherine shrugged.

"For such a place to exist . . ." Atrus sighed, then, closing the book, handed it back to her. "I'm afraid it wouldn't work, but it does paint wonderful pictures in my mind."

She smoothed her fingers over the pale lemon cover. The green and light blue flecks in it had always reminded her of grass and water, the predominant yellow of the sun. Fecund, it was, like the world surrounding her, but inside . . .

"That's good," she said. "It must be like a dream."

He stared at her, not understanding.

"When I go there . . ."

He shook his head. "But you can't . . ."

"It was just like my dreams," she said, turning to face him again.

"No," he said forcefully, taking the book back from her. "It simply wouldn't work. Writing isn't like that. It's a science. A precisely structured equation of words."

She leaned across him, then opened the book,

pointing to the descriptive image on the right-hand page. It was dark, so intensely dark that he had thought it blank. But there was something there.

He looked to her.

"I want you to see it."

"It's . . ." he said, softer now, the word almost a whisper. Yet even as he said it, she leaned across him and placed his hand upon the image, smiling at him, her smile dissolving in the air as he linked.

20

" . . . Impossible."

Atrus stepped out of the air into a huge, conical bowl of darkness. And in the middle of that bowl, at the precise center of the massive, mile-wide hole that pierced it, a powerful column of water—as broad as a river—thundered straight up into the darkness until it was lost from sight, a great spike of brilliant, crystalline light glowing like a fierce flame at its center where it emerged from the glowing depths.

Atrus stared, dumbstruck.

A group of large, fireflylike insects glided past, their translucent bodies glowing gold and red, their movements more like the movements of fish than the darting flight of insects. Atrus looked down, meaning to brush one away and was shocked to see it pass right through his legs, re-forming like a soap bubble on the other side. Other creatures, their forms no less fantastic—sporting long sparkling quills and fans, extravagant crests or tails like golden chains—fluttered and weaved across that midnight landscape, their forms merging and re-forming, constantly in movement, constantly, it seemed, in transformation.

"It must be a dream, don't you think?" Catherine said, stepping up alongside him.

There was the scent of lemon in the air, the faintest trace of pine and cinnamon.

Atrus nodded absently, his eyes following the course of one of the fireflies, drawn to it, seeing how it seemed to merge and then detach itself from a rocky crag nearby, traces of its bright color left behind in the sparkling black surface of the rock, which pulsed momentarily then was still again.

Not that the rock was like real rock. It had a glassy look to it, as if it were made of gelatin, yet it had the warm, textured feel of wood. Most surprising of all, it smelled . . . Atrus sniffed, then shook his head, amazed . . . of roses and camphor.

Everywhere he looked, forms met and merged, the barriers that normally existed between things dissolved away here, as in a dream.

He shivered then looked up, pointing out toward the great chute of water that cascaded endlessly into the night sky.

"Where does it go?"

She laughed; the softest, gentlest laugh he'd ever heard. "Did you ever wonder what it would be like to go swimming out among the stars?"

"Swimming?" For a moment he thought of Anna and the cleft, that evening after the desert rain.

"Yes," she said wistfully. "If it is my dream, we could fall into the night and be cradled by stars and still return to the place where we began."

Atrus stared at her, wondering what she meant. Sometimes she was like her book—beautiful and poetic, yes, and incomprehensible, too.

"I'm not very lucky with water," he said, making her laugh. "But this . . ." He turned, raising his arms to indicate the Age she'd made. "I can't understand it." He looked to her, shaking his head in amazement. "I just can't see how it works."

He looked about him, disconcerted by the way a bright blue snakelike creature split in two as it brushed against his arm, then split again and again, until there was a whole school of tiny snakes, swimming with identical motions in a tight formation.

"Did you *imagine* all of this?"

"Most of it," she answered, walking past him, then stooping to pluck something from the ground close by. "Some of it I can't remember writing. It's almost like I stop thinking and just . . . *write*."

She turned back, offering something to him. It was a flower. But not just a flower. As he went to take it from her, it seemed to flow toward his hand and rub against him, like a kitten brushing against its owner's legs.

Atrus moved back.

"What is it?" she asked.

"I don't know." He smiled. "It's just strange, that's all."

Catherine bent down and put the flower down carefully, then looked at him and smiled. "There's nothing here that's harmful. You're safe here, Atrus. I promise you."

Maybe so. But he still felt ill at ease. Nothing here behaved as it ought to behave. Wherever he looked the rules of normality were broken. This was an Age where the laws had been stood on their head. By rights it ought not to exist, and yet it did. So what did that mean? Was it as Catherine had said? Did some other set of laws—laws not discovered by the D'ni—prevail here? Or was this simply an anomaly?

Catherine straightened up, then put out her hand to him. "Come. Let me show you something."

He walked down the slope with her until he stood only a few yards from the edge. Beyond it there was nothing. Nothing but the glow far below them, and the water, spewing up out of the center of that brightness.

"Here," she said, handing him something small, smooth, and flat.

Atrus looked at it. It was a polished piece of stone, small enough to fit into his hand.

"Well?" she said. "Have you never skimmed a stone before?"

He looked to her, then swung his arm back and cast the stone across the darkness, imagining he was skimming it across the surface of a pond.

The stone skimmed rapidly across the vacant air, and then, as if it had suddenly hit a rock, soared in a steep curve upward, finally disappearing into that mighty rush of water.

Atrus stared, openmouthed, as he lost it in that mighty torrent, then turned, to find that Catherine was laughing softly.

"Your face!"

Atrus snapped his mouth shut, then looked back. He found that he wanted to do it again—to see the stone skim across the emptiness then soar.

"Where does it go?"

"Come," she said, taking his hand again. "I'll show you."

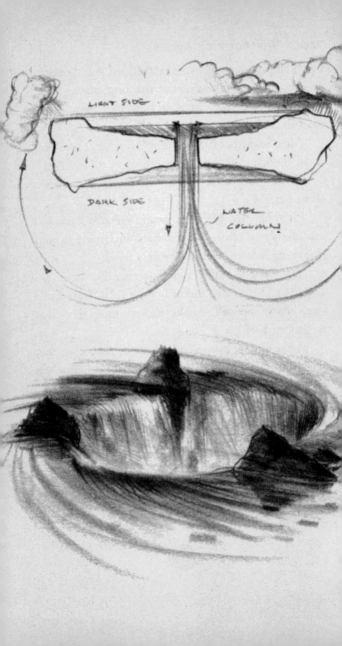

The tunnel through which they walked was small—just big enough for them to walk upright—and perfectly round, like a wormhole through a giant apple, the passage unevenly lit by some property within the rock itself. It led down, continually curving, until it seemed as though they must be walking on the ceiling. And then they came out. Out into brilliant daylight. Out into a landscape as amazing as the one they had left at the far end of the tunnel.

Atrus winced, his eyes pained by the sudden light, and pulled his glasses on, then straightened, looking out.

Just as the dark side had been strange, so this—the bright side of Catherine's nature, as he saw it—was wonderful. They stood at the top of a great slope—a large rocky hill in the midst of an ocean, one of several set in a rough circle—each hill carpeted with bright, gorgeously scented flowers over which a million butterflies danced and fluttered.

And at the very center of that circle of rocklike hills, a great ring-shaped waterfall rushed inward at an angle, toward a single central point far below. Directly over that huge vortex, flickering in and out of visibility, were twisting, vertical ribbons of fast-moving cloud that appeared high up in the air then vanished quickly into the mouth of that great circular falls.

With a shock of recognition, Atrus understood. "We're on the other side! It's the source of the great torrent . . . it falls *through* . . ."

And even as he said it, his mouth fell open with wonder.

But how? What physical mechanism was involved? For he knew—*knew*, with a sudden, absolute certainty—that if this existed, then there was a physical reason why it existed. This did not break the D'ni laws, it merely twisted them; pushed them to their limits.

He looked to Catherine, a sudden admiration in his eyes.

"This is beautiful. I never guessed . . ."

She took his hand. "There's more. Would you like to see?"

"Yes."

"Out there," she said, pointing, directing his eyes toward the horizon.

Atrus stared. Huge thunderclouds massed at the horizon, rising up into the sky like steam from a boiling pot. Incredible thunderstorms, their noise muted by distance, filled the air out there, the whole of the horizon, as far as he could see to left and right, filled with flickering lightning.

It completely surrounds the torus, he realized, turning, looking back at the great hole in the ocean, remembering the great jet of water on the far side of that massive hole. There seemed to two separate forces at work here—one a jet stream force and the other a ring force to which the water was attracted.

Atrus blinked, then looked to Catherine. "You put

most of the mass of the torus at its outer edge, didn't you?"

She simply smiled at him.

"So the gravity . . ." Atrus paused, his right fist clenched intently, frown lines etched deep in his brow. "That circle of gravity . . . *forces* the water through the central hole . . . then some other force sucks it up into the sky, where it fans out . . . still captured by the gravitational field of the torus, and falls down the outer edges of that field . . . *right?*"

She simply smiled at him.

"And as it slowly falls, it forms clouds and the clouds cause the storms and . . ."

It was impressive. In fact, now that he partly understood it, it was even more impressive than he'd first thought.

He turned, standing, looking about him, then stopped dead. Just across from him was a patch of flowers, nestled in among the lush grass. He walked across, climbing the slope until he stood among them.

Flowers. Blue flowers. Thousands of tiny, delicate blue flowers with tiny, starlike petals and velvet dark stamen.

Moved by the sight, he stooped and plucked one, holding it to his nose, then looked to her.

"How did you know?"

"Know?" Catherine's brow wrinkled in puzzlement. "Know what?"

"I thought . . . No, it doesn't matter." Then, changing the subject. "What are you to my father?"

She looked down. "I am his servant. One of his Guild members . . ."

He looked at her, knowing there was more, but afraid to ask.

After a moment, she spoke again. "I am to be married to him."

"*Married*?"

She nodded, unable to look at him.

Atrus sat heavily, the flowers all around him. He closed his fingers, squeezing the tiny, delicate bloom, then let it fall.

His head hung now and his eyes seemed desolate.

"He has commanded me," she said, stepping closer. "Thirty days, Gehn said. There is to be a great ceremony on Riven . . . Age Five."

He looked up, a bitter disappointment in his eyes.

She met his eyes clearly. "I'd rather die."

Slowly, very slowly, understanding of what she'd said came to his face. "Then . . ."

"Then you must help me, Atrus. We have thirty days. Thirty days to change things."

"And if we can't?"

Catherine turned her head, looking about her at the Age she had written, then looked back at Atrus, her green eyes burning. Burning with such an intensity that he felt transfixed, frozen, utterly overwhelmed by this strange woman and the odd powers she possessed. And as she held his gaze, she reached out for his hand, clenching it tightly in her own, and spoke; her voice filling him with a sudden, almost impulsive confidence. "We can do wonders, you and I. Wonders."

21

As the sun slowly set, Atrus stood on the top of the tiny plateau, his glasses pulled down tightly over his eyes, his journal open in his hand, looking out across the Age he had written. Below him lay a cold, dark sea, its surface smooth like oil, or like a mirror blackened by age, its sterile waters filling the great bowl that lay between the bloodred sandstone cliffs.

On the shores of that great sea, the land was bare and empty; more desolate even than the desert he had known as a child. Titanic sandstone escarpments, carved by the action of wind and sun, stretched to the horizon on every side, their stark, bloodred shapes interspersed with jagged, night-black chasms.

He had written in the bare minimum this time. Enough to conduct his experiment and no more. Enough to see whether his theories about the flaws in the Age Five book were true or not.

He had built ten such Ages in the past few weeks. Two for each experiment. In this and one other he was testing whether the changes he sought to make in the orbital system of Age Five would have the desired effects, while in others he was experimenting with the structure of the tectonic plates beneath the planet's crust, the type and strength of the oceanic currents, fluctuations in gravitational fields, and the composition of the crust itself.

What he had done, here and elsewhere, was to re-create the same underlying structures that he had found in the Age Five book, only incorporating specific minor alterations—additions mainly—to the way the thing was phrased. If that new phrasing was correct, then this Age was now stable. And if this was stable, then so would Age Five be once he had written the changes into the book.

Looking about him, he jotted down his observations, then, closing the journal, slipped it into his knapsack.

Thus far his tests had proved one thing conclusively. Age Five was doomed. It would degenerate and be destroyed within a generation, unless he made these vital, telling changes to the book.

Lifting his glasses, he blinked, then rubbed at his eyes. He was tired, more tired than he'd been in years, yet he could not let up now. It was only ten days until the ceremony, and everything—everything—had to be ready for that time.

Pulling his glasses back down, Atrus waited. The moon would be rising soon, and then he'd know.

If he was right, Gehn had placed Age Five's single moon well inside the synchronous orbital distance from the planet. This had the effect of increasing the planet's tides dramatically, and, ultimately, would result in the moon being dragged into ever-lower orbits until it would finally smash into the planet's surface. That final catastrophe would take many lifetimes, but long before that happened, the great tides generated by the moon's ever closer orbit would destroy the island, smashing it into the surrounding sea.

He needed to push Age Five's moon back into a stable, synchronous orbit: one where its rotation rate would be equivalent to the planet's. What complicated the task was that he would have to achieve this in a matter that could not be directly observed.

As the light dimmed, Atrus pulled his cloak tighter about him. The air here was thin and cold, and it would be good to get back to D'ni, if only for some sleep.

He waited, watching as the sun winked then vanished beneath the edge of the horizon. Atrus turned and, pulling up his glasses, looked for the moon. He saw it at once, directly behind him in the sky, low down, the silver-blue orb huge and ominous.

Wrong, he thought, chilled by the sight. *It's much too close.*

The tremors began at once, the tiny plateau gently vibrating, as if some machine had started up in the rock beneath his feet.

The sea was stippled now, like a sheet of black, beaten metal.

Atrus stared up at the moon. What had gone wrong? Had he written in a contradiction of some kind? Or were the changes he'd made simply the wrong ones?

Or, in his tiredness, had he mixed up the two books? Was he in the wrong Age—the Age where he had exaggerated the moon's deteriorating orbit?

The trembling grew, became a steady shaking. There was groaning now from deep within the earth, sharp cracks, the sound of rocks falling, splashing into the sea below, while the sea itself seemed to be boiling, as if in a great cauldron.

In the distance, the land was glowing, not with the silver-blue of moonlight but a fiery orange-red.

A cold wind gusted across the plateau.

Frowning, Atrus stepped over to the edge and, lowering his glasses, increased their magnification.

That distant glow was the molten glow of magma, spewing out from deep within the fiery mantle. Out there, beneath that low and massive moon, the planet's crust was tearing itself apart.

The noise all about him was deafening now, and the shaking was so bad that he found it hard even to stand without bracing himself. It was time to link back.

Atrus half-turned, lowering his right shoulder, meaning to slip the knapsack from his back and take the Linking Book from inside, but as he did the ground lurched violently.

Knocked from his feet, Atrus reached out blindly, grabbing a nearby outcrop, but though it stopped him sliding, it was no good, for the whole plateau was slowly tipping over, sliding inch by inch toward the sea below.

What's more, the knapsack was trapped beneath him and when he tried to lift himself to free it, he lost his grip and began to tumble down the tilted face of the plateau.

For a moment his fingers scrabbled at the surface of the rock, and then, abruptly, he was falling through the air.

"*No . . .!*"

His cry was cut short as he hit the cold, dark surface of the sea.

For a moment he panicked, not knowing which way he faced, the water in turmoil all about him, and then his head breached the surface and he gasped for air.

Water splashed his face constantly now, filling his mouth and nose. He struggled not to swallow any, struggled to bring his knapsack around so he could get the book.

And then he saw it.

Directly ahead of him, its thundering crest lit almost demonically by the obscenely huge moon that seemed to ride on its back, was the wave. A huge, black wave that towered over the surrounding pinnacles of rock, smashing and splintering them as if they were nothing.

And as it came on the water all about Atrus grew

still and smooth, an eery silence falling. A silence that contrasted with the great roar of the oncoming mountain of water.

For a moment Atrus forgot. For a moment he simply stared at the sight.

Then, abruptly, he snapped into action, and, scrabbling at the sack, his fingers numb from the coldness of the water, he took the Linking Book out and flicked it open.

Home . . .

And even as Atrus placed his hand upon the page, the moon blinked out and the whole of the sea in which he rested seemed to lift up to join that great black wall of water, the noise so loud it made his whole skull tremble, as if at any moment it would shatter.

Coming to his senses, Atrus found himself lying in an exhausted heap on the cold floor of the chamber, back on D'ni, a puddle of water from his drenched clothes forming beneath his body.

The air was cool, and the silence, after that hideous destructive roar, was the most welcome sound he'd ever heard.

He let out a long breath, remembering that final moment as the wave towered over him, lifting him up into its sightless maw as if to devour him, then sat up.

Tearing off his glasses, he turned toward his desk.

Catherine was sitting there in his chair, unaware of his return, her whole attention focused on the book she was reading.

"Catherine?"

She looked up, closing the book and setting it aside. Then, taking in the state of him, she quickly stood and came around the desk. "Atrus? Are you all right?"

He stood, fending her off. "I'm okay. Just a little trouble with the moon."

"The moon?"

He waved her query aside, then, softly. "Why are you here? I thought we said it would be best if you stayed on Riven."

"I know but . . ." She stopped, then went over to the desk and turned the book around to face her. "I don't want to go back."

"But you must. You can't stay here."

"I've been working on something," she said, as if she hadn't heard him. "I wanted to surprise you."

Catherine turned and handed him the book.

Atrus stared at her, then, when she said no more, took the book over to the desk, sat and opened it. For a while he was silent, the sound of a turning page the only noise in that great chamber. Then, with a little shake of his head, he looked up.

"What is this?"

She stepped up next to him, looking down at the

open pages. "I've written us an Age. Somewhere we can go. I've named it Myst."

"But this is so different from your other Age."

"You don't like it?"

"No . . . it's what I would have done, had I time. You . . ." He laughed, and covered her hand with his own. "I think you are astonishing."

"I've been studying."

Atrus looked at it again, astounded by the sudden restraint in the writing, the deep understanding of D'ni principles that surpassed even his own. He was silent for a long time.

"There are one or two final touches," she said, breaking that silence. "But when they're done . . ."

"You'll take me there?"

Catherine smiled. "Of course. Now out of my way, I've work to do."

Atrus sat back after Catherine had gone.

Whatever he felt for Catherine, whatever she might feel for him, this was far more important. If his father was allowed to triumph on Age Five, then he would triumph everywhere, for there was no end to Gehn's ambitions. Having seen what Catherine had—through chance or design—created in her two Ages, he knew now it was possible that Gehn might yet achieve his dream of resurrecting the D'ni empire, or at least a shadow of it; of creating countless slave worlds, with himself as lord, the fate of millions subject to his will.

There was but one solution: to trap Gehn on Age Five and destroy all of the Linking Books that led out of that Age. But to do so he would have to take the risk that he, too, might be trapped there. And now that Catherine had created Myst island for them—as a sanctuary, away from Gehn—the thought of failure seemed suddenly quite hideous.

Of course, they would have to write another, separate Age—a simple, uninhabited world they might reach from Myst, one where fruit and herbs were plentiful, so they would be provided for, for her new Age was curiously lacking in such things.

Thinking of what he had read of Catherine's latest book, he wondered briefly if she really had written it, or whether, like his father, she had copied elements of it. It was so different, after all, from her other world.

Or was that fair? After all, if she had been studying . . .

He shook his head, trying to clear it, to keep focused on what he had to do.

His main priority was still to stabilize the island. Once that was done, he would need to find where Gehn kept his Linking Book, for unless he knew that he could not trap him. He would have to go there and look—to search all the likely places until he found it.

And the most likely place was the cave behind the temple.

Right now, however, there were other things to do. Yawning, Atrus took the Age Five notebook from his pocket, then, pulling his journal toward him, turned it to the page on which he had written out the changes he was to make to the Age Five book, and began to write.

"Atrus! Atrus!"

He woke, wondering what on earth was happening. Catherine was standing over him, shaking him by the shoulders, calling his name time and time again.

"Atrus! Come on, wake up! You have to listen to me!"

He sat up, groggy, barely able to open his eyes. "What?"

"It's Gehn . . . he's moved the date forward!"

"The date?" Atrus was suddenly wide awake. "Moved it to when?"

"Three days. We've got three days."

He groaned. Then it was impossible! There were still more tests to be made before the Fifth Age could be put right. And then there was the matter of Gehn's Linking Book. Unless he could get hold of that . . .

"Catherine . . . you know where Gehn keeps his Linking Book."

She nodded.

"Could you take me back to Riven and show me where?"

Again she hesitated, then, "What are you going to do?"

"Does my father expect to see you again before the wedding ceremony?"

Catherine shook her head.

"Good." He looked about him at the cluttered desk. "Then we'll take all of this to Myst. All but the Myst and Age Five books. Then I want you to stay there, Catherine. I want you to keep away from both D'ni and Riven."

"But you'll need help . . ."

Atrus looked at her sternly. "The biggest help to me will be to know that you're safe."

"But what are you going to do?"

He stood up then came around the desk, taking her arms gently in his hands. "Do you trust me, Catherine?"

She smiled, then nodded.

"Then wait for me. As soon as I've dealt with my father, I'll come and join you on Myst island."

There was a slight flicker in her expression, as if, for a moment, she was going to disagree, then she nodded.

"Good. Then let's get back to Riven. It's time you showed me where my father keeps his Linking Book."

22

CAREFUL NOT TO BE SEEN, THEY walked quickly up the temple's steps and into the shadowy interior. Since Atrus had last been here, the place had been decked out with great gold and red banners, ready for the wedding ceremony.

My father, with Catherine . . . no, it will never happen.

He followed Catherine through, behind the great golden silk screen that had Gehn's silhouette embroidered at its center, and down the narrow flight of steps, into the cave. It was just as he'd thought.

"He used to bring us here," she said quietly, almost whispering. "There would be a linking ceremony. He'd make the chosen one drink something from one of the golden chalices. It had the faintest taste of aniseed. And afterward . . . well, afterward you could remember nothing. But lately . . ." She looked down. "Lately he's trusted me. He brought me here and showed me where the book was hidden."

Atrus watched her go across and, standing on tiptoe, reach into one of the holes that peppered the rock face to the left of the low-ceilinged cave, searching a moment before she withdrew her hand, clutching the slender box that held Gehn's Linking Book.

He walked over, looking down at the floor, then

back up again, fixing the position in his mind the way
Anna had taught him. Then, nodding, he gestured for
her to put it back.

"Come," he said, taking her hand. "Let's go to your
hut and get any remaining books."

She pulled on his hand, slowing him, making him
face her. "Atrus?"

"Yes?"

She leaned close and kissed his cheek—just a single, gentle peck—then, tugging on his hand, moved on,
hurrying now, knowing that there was barely time to
do all they had to do before the ceremony.

Atrus blinked, the bright sunlight hurting his eyes
after the dullness of his prison, and pulled his glasses
down over his face.

He was standing on a wooden jetty, the knapsack
holding the books heavy on his back. Water lapped
against the rocks beneath, while somewhere out in the
distant haze seagulls called forlornly. To his right the
sea was calm and green, stippled by the light breeze
that blew across the island from the northwest. Facing
him, directly east from where he stood, a barren rock,
twenty feet in height and thirty or forty in width rose
from the sea like a sawn tree trunk. To its left, the land
rose to a sharp peak, over a hundred feet in height,

while behind him and to his left, beyond a narrow shelf of rock, tall pines filled the west end of the island.

Atrus smiled. The air was clean and clear, the smell of pine strong. Overhead the sky was a pale blue, wisps of thin cirrus high up in the atmosphere.

He turned back, waiting, then saw Catherine step out of the air onto the wooden planks beside him, the heavily laden knapsack on her back.

"This is beautiful . . ."

"You wrote it so," he said. "Considering how much time you had, I think you did a marvelous job."

Atrus looked about him, breathing in the rich, clean air. "That smell. It's so wonderful."

He stopped suddenly, realizing that it was the same smell as on the Thirty-seventh Age. Before Gehn had destroyed it.

"What is it?" she asked, noting how his face had changed.

"It's nothing," he said, shrugging off the mood.

"Then come. Let me show you the cabin."

"A cabin! You've built a cabin here already?"

She took his hand and led him up a narrow track that climbed the rock slope. At the top, the ground opened out. There was grass beneath their feet now. The sound of the wind was stronger here—a strangely desolate sound, punctuated by the more peaceful sound of birdsong.

"Yes," he said, after a moment. "I could live here."

—MYST—

Catherine smiled and squeezed his hand, then pointed down the broad grass path between the trees. "It's down there," she said. "Just over on the left."

They walked on along the sloping path until they stood before the cabin.

Atrus stared a while, noting how neatly the logs were fixed, how cleverly she had trimmed the planks that framed the doorway, and shook his head, astonished. There were clearly aspects of Catherine he had never suspected.

"It's a good beginning," he said quietly.

"I'm glad you think so."

He turned, looking back up the slope toward the peak. "We could build things here. Perhaps finally a library of my own."

"Shhh . . ." she said, amused by his eagerness. "There'll be time. After we've dealt with Gehn."

"Yes . . ." The reminder sobered him. "I'll see you settled in, then I'd best get back. Two more journeys should see me finished."

"Atrus?"

"Yes?"

"Are you sure I can't help?"

He hesitated, then drew her close and kissed her gently, a proper kiss this time—their first.

"No," he said, staring into the green depths of her eyes. "Just wait for me here. All right?"

"All right," she answered, leaning forward to kiss his nose gently.

"You promise?"

"I promise."

"Then come. I'll drop the books and go back."

But even after the last of the books were transferred and safely stacked in a corner of the cabin, Atrus lingered on Myst island.

Catherine had brought blankets with her from Riven and had made up a rough pallet bed in the corner facing the books, using her knapsack for a pillow. Seeing it, he imagined her here after he had gone and realized, for the first time, how lonely she would be if he did not return.

"Well?" she asked, from the doorway, making him turn, startled by the suddenness of her appearance.

He laughed. "You frightened me."

"Frightened you?" She came across. "Are you afraid of me, then, Atrus?"

He smiled as her fingers brushed his face. "No. I could never be frightened of you. Surprised, I meant."

"Then I shall keep surprising you."

She moved past him, placing the stalk of a small white flower she had picked in the gap between two of the logs so that it hung just above the space where she would sleep.

He stared at it, then met her eyes. "What's that?"

"It's to remind me of you, while you're gone." She

stood, then offered him her hand. "Shall we have a walk, Atrus? Along the shore?"

He realized suddenly that he had outstayed his time, but the idea of walking with her seemed suddenly more important than anything else he had to do.

He took her hand then stepped out into the late afternoon sunlight.

The wind had dropped and it was much warmer now, the sky above them clear. Looking up, he realized it would be a good night to watch the stars and wondered suddenly what the stars were like here on Myst island.

If only I could stay . . .

But he could not stay. It was not fated. He had to stop Gehn, whatever the outcome.

Catherine looked to him. "Why did you sigh just then?"

"Because this is all so perfect."

They walked slowly along the path, then cut through the trees and out onto the grassy slope. Below them was the sea, stretching away into the misted distance. Close by, just over to their left, was a tiny island, separated from the shore by a narrow stretch of water.

"Come," she said, leading him down until they stood just yards from the lapping surface of that sea. "Let's sit and talk."

"Talk?" Atrus hesitated, then sat beside her. "About what?"

"About the future."

"About whether you'll make it back from Riven, you mean?"

Atrus looked to her, surprised.

"You think I didn't know what you had planned?"

He laughed. "Am I that predictable?"

She laid her fingers gently on his cheeck. "No. But I know you feel you have to do what is right, even if it means sacrificing yourself."

He laid his hand on hers. "I *will* be back."

"Yet there's a risk?"

He nodded.

"And you want me to stay here, no matter what?"

Again he nodded.

"And the Linking Book, back to D'ni?"

"Destroy it, the moment I'm gone."

"Then if Gehn links here he will be trapped with me, and with a supply of blank books."

Atrus looked down. It was the one flaw in his plan. To be certain of trapping Gehn he ought to destroy his own Linking Book from Riven to D'ni the instant he returned to Age Five, but that would also trap him there, and he wanted to get back. No, not wanted, *needed*. To be with her.

"I'll be careful," he said. "I know where he links to. I'll take his Linking Book from its hiding place then watch for him to arrive. The moment he's on Riven, I'll burn his Linking Book. Then I only have to destroy my own."

Her eyes were smiling now. Leaning forward she kissed the tip of his nose. "Okay. No more about your plans. What about you?"

"I know almost nothing about you. Your grandmother, Anna, for instance. Do you remember what she was like?"

She was like you, he wanted to say, but the reminder of Anna made him look down.

Taking the almost empty knapsack from his back he removed his journal and handed it to her.

She held the small, gray book delicately, almost as if it were a living thing.

"It's my journal. I . . . I want you to read it. While I'm gone. It might . . . well, it might help you to understand me."

"In case you don't come back?"

He hesitated, then nodded.

And suddenly, he understood what it was he had wanted from Catherine. Companionship. Someone to understand him. Someone with whom to share all his adventures and experiments. Someone to be there by his side, as Anna had once been, only not as teacher or substitute mother, but as a full partner.

He reached out, laying his fingers gently on her cheek.

For one tiny moment that was all: the two of them, sitting there in the sunlight beside the water, Catherine with her eyes closed, Atrus's journal in her lap, her face tilted slightly to meet the gentle touch of his fingers while Atrus stared at her in wonder, as if at an Age he would never visit, only glimpse through the descriptive image on the page.

And then she turned, looking to him again, her green eyes searching his. "You'd better go now, Atrus."

The idea of leaving was suddenly like contemplating death itself. All he wanted in life was right here on Myst island.

"Catherine . . ."

"I'll be all right. Now go."

As he sat in his chair back on D'ni, Atrus stared sightlessly at the cover of the Age Five book, his heart heavy, resigned now to his fate.

There was only one way—one way alone—that he could be certain of seeing Catherine again, and that was to kill his father. To link to Gehn's study and destroy the man. But that was not possible, for it was not in his nature to harm another, even for the best of reasons.

No good can come of such ill, he thought, knowing that Anna, had she been there, would have agreed with him. *If I killed my father, the shadow of my guilt would blight my days with Catherine.*

He knew it for a certainty. And so his fate was set. He had to take the risk of losing her forever.

If I cannot have her, I shall at least have something that keeps her memory alive...

He sighed, wishing now that he had asked Anna about his mother. It was only now that he realized that he didn't even know what she looked like.

She looked like you, Atrus, a voice answered in his head, so clear that he looked up, surprised.

"Yes," he said, smiling suddenly.

Atrus drew the Age Five book toward him and opened it to the final page. Then, reaching across, he took the pen from the stand and began to copy the phrases into the Age Five book.

Atrus linked. In an instant he was gone, the air where he'd been sitting strangely translucent, like the surface of a clear slow-moving stream. Then, abruptly, another figure appeared from the nothingness.

It was Catherine.

Setting the Linking Book down on the desk beside her, she closed the Myst book and slipped it into her knapsack. As she did so, a second figure shimmered out of the air, taking on a solid form. Stepping forward, it stood behind her, watching as Catherine pulled the Age Five book toward her and flipped through until she was on the final page. Then, as Catherine took Atrus's pen from its stand, the figure pointed and encouraged Catherine as she dipped the pen into the ink pot and began to write.

The cave behind the temple was dark, the smell of incense strong, wafting down from the great censors hanging from the temple ceiling. Atrus paused a moment, squinting into the deep shadow, listening, then hurried across.

Crouching, he took his grandfather's tinderbox from his pocket and lit it, moving it slowly along the bottom edge of the cave wall until he found the mark stone. Tracing up from there he found the hole where Gehn stored his Linking Book.

Standing on tiptoe, he reached into the narrow orifice, his fingers searching the cold rock. For a moment he thought he had it wrong, but then his fingers brushed the edge of the slender box. He pulled it out and, in the light from the tinderbox, opened it. The Linking Book was there.

Removing it, he returned the box into the hole and slipped the book into his backpack, then, clicking off the tinderbox, he turned and headed back through the temple.

He ducked under the low lintel and out, climbing

the steps quickly. Yet as he went to step around the screen, he heard voices from the front of the chamber and stopped, crouching low, keeping himself hidden behind the shadowed shape of the great chair that was thrown onto the golden screen.

"He will be here soon," one of them said, his voice that of an old man. "You will bring the villagers out onto the slope below the temple. They can make their offerings there, after the ceremony."

"It will be done," another, a little younger, answered. Then, in a slightly lower, more conspiratorial tone. "Did you see how she smiled at the Lord Gehn at the rehearsal? There's no faking that, is there? Now there's a match that will be consummated in heaven!"

Atrus felt himself go cold. Rehearsal? Catherine had said nothing of rehearsals. The words troubled him.

No, he told himself. But then why would they say it if it wasn't true? After all, they did not know he was there behind the screen.

He swallowed, suddenly uncertain, then slowly crept around the screen, peeping over the arm of the chair.

The two men were standing with their backs to him, their cloaks, copies of D'ni Guild cloaks, covered in the Guild's secret symbols. They were graybeards, and as he watched, they bowed to each other and made their way out again.

He hurried across, seeing what they had been here

to deliver. On a marble stand in the very center of the chamber was placed a shallow bowl made of special D'ni stone, and on that bowl were two beautiful golden bracelets, one markedly thicker than the other.

The mere sight of them made his stomach turn.

Did you see how she smiled at the Lord Gehn? Did you see how she smiled?

He felt like picking up the bowl and throwing it across the room, but knew he must deny the urge. Gehn must suspect nothing. He must think his bride was coming. He must believe . . .

Atrus shook his head, pushing aside the doubts, the endless flood of questions, that threatened to drown him.

Catherine is on Myst island. I took her there myself. She's safe. Or will be once I've trapped Gehn here on Riven.

He turned and hurried to the front of the chamber, peering around one of the pillars. The two Guild members were nowhere to be seen. Slowly, cautiously, he made his way down the steps and out across the open space in front of the temple, slipping in among the trees, then making his way along the path toward the beach.

Before he came to the cliff he stopped, searching quickly among the trees, gathering up any loose twigs and branches he could find. Satisfied he had enough for his purpose, he hurried on, making his way down the steep cliffside path.

As he came out beneath the overhang of rock, he paused, staring out across the rocky beach. Two of the strange, toothlike rocks had been broken—sheared off, it seemed. For a moment he watched the tide come in, seeing how the incoming waves seemed to undulate like a windblown sheet, tiny globules of water, heated by the late afternoon sun, tumbling across the beach, hundreds of tiny bubbles drifting above the slow, incoming tide before they merged with it again.

He would be sad to leave this world. Sad not to have come to know it better than he did.

Turning back, he went over to the cliff face. Putting down the stack of wood, he busied himself collecting a number of large rocks, placing them in a tight circle, then, gathering up the wood again, he laid out twigs and branches inside the circle of rocks to form a rudimentary fire pit.

He took his grandfather's tinderbox from his pocket and placed it on a big, flat-topped rock, then, removing the knapsack from his back, he set it down by the fire and knelt beside it, taking Gehn's Linking Book from within and placing it next to the fire pit.

Kneeling, Atrus cupped the tinder between his hands and struck it, then lit the kindling wood beneath the main stack, watching it catch, then blowing on it to encourage the flames, seeing them begin to lick at the Linking Book.

Atrus leaned back. There! Now for *his* Linking

Book! All he would have to do would be to hold his Linking Book over the fire as he linked—letting the book fall into the flames and be destroyed, trapping Gehn here forever.

Going across, he hauled himself up the pocked face of the cliff until he was facing the recess where his book was hidden. It was some way back, so he had to haul himself up over the lip and squeeze inside, wriggling in until he could reach it.

23

When Atrus came to he was standing in the open air near the temple, his arms pulled up tightly behind his back, his wrists bound, his body secured at neck and waist and ankles to a thick pole that had been embedded in the earth. The blood pounded in his head, and when he tried to open his eyes the pain was intense.

Slowly he let his eyes grow accustomed to the failing light, then, moving his head as much as the binding allowed, he looked about him.

Close by, on a small table—so close that, had his hands been unbound, he could have reached them—were the two Linking Books.

He groaned, remembering, then felt a touch on his shoulder, felt his father's breath upon his cheek.

"So you are back with us, Atrus," Gehn said quietly, speaking to him alone. "I thought for a while that I had lost you. It seems I do not know my own strength sometimes."

Atrus hung his head, grimacing at the thought of Catherine. She was there, on Myst, waiting. And now he had failed her

"Catherine, ah clever Catherine," Gehn spoke as if

he heard Atrus's thoughts. "You really didn't think she'd miss her own wedding?"

With that, Gehn turned to face a figure who stood just beyond him in the shadows of the surrounding trees. Atrus went limp as the figure stepped foward into the sunlight.

It was her!

Atrus closed his eyes and groaned, remembering the old men's words, recalling the sight of the two golden bracelets laying there in the shallow red-black bowl.

She is marrying my father . . .

The thought was unbearable. He could almost hear their laughter. Yet when he opened his eyes again, it was to see Gehn, alone, standing before the Age Five islanders, his hands raised, his appearance that of a great king come among his subjects.

"People of the Fifth Age," Gehn began, his voice powerful, commanding. "It had come to my notice that some of you . . ." Gehn pointed to a little group Atrus had not noticed, or who had possibly not been there until that moment; who knelt there abjectly, just below Gehn, their hands bound: the two brothers, Carel and Erlar among them. "Some of you, as I say, have taken it upon yourselves to help my enemies. To nurse this imposter"—he turned, this time indicating Atrus,— "who dares to call himself my son!"

Gehn turned back, raising his hands again. "Such

behavior cannot be tolerated. Such defiance must be *punished.*"

There was a great murmur of fear from the watching islanders.

"Yes," Gehn went on. "You were warned, but you did not listen. And so, in punishment, there will be great tides . . ."

"No . . ." Atrus said, finding his voice.

"And the sun will turn black . . ."

"No . . ."

"And the ground . . . the very earth will shake and the great tree fall!"

"No!" Atrus cried out a third time, this time loud enough for some among the crowd to hear him. "No! He's wrong! I've fixed it. All of those things . . . all of the weaknesses in the book. I've put them right, I've . . ."

Atrus stopped, seeing the hideous grin of triumph on his father's face as he stepped up to him.

"*Well done*, Atrus . . . I *knew* I could count on you." Gehn's smile was suddenly hard and sneering. "I shall be most interested to read the changes you have so graciously crafted for me." Then, stepping away, he clicked his fingers, calling to the nearest of the Guild Members. "Untie him!"

Turning to face the crowd again, Gehn raised his hands. "People of the Fifth Age. You are most fortunate. I have asked my servant here to do my bidding and he has done so. Your world is safe now. Yet if you transgress again, if I find that any among you have sought to help my enemies, then the full weight of my wrath shall fall on you. I shall destroy your world, just as I created it!" He sniffed deeply. "But let us not dwell upon that now. Now is a time to look forward, and to celebrate, for tonight, at sunset, I shall take a daughter of this Age to be my bride and rule the thousand worlds with me!"

There was a great cheer at that. Gehn turned, looking to Atrus, his whole demeanor triumphant.

Atrus, seeing that look, turned his head, stung by it, all fight gone from him now. He had been duped. Used by the two of them. *Betrayed*.

He pressed his hands together, the pain suddenly unbearable, then gently rubbed at his wrists where the binding rope had chafed them. He was beaten. There was nothing more he could do.

But Gehn was not done. Stepping up to Atrus, he pressed his face close to Atrus's, speaking so only he could hear.

"Don't think that I have finished with you, boy. You have caused me an inordinate amount of trouble, and I shall not forget that. As far as I am concerned, you are no longer my son. Do you understand me? I do not need you anymore, Atrus. You have served your purpose." Gehn looked to Catherine and smiled; a hideous, gloating smile. "Yes . . . you see it, don't you? Catherine and I . . ." He laughed. "She's a strong young woman. Perhaps my next son will not fail me!"

Atrus groaned. It was a nightmare. Had he still been bound to the post he could not have felt more impotent.

Catherine . . . my beloved Catherine . . .

He looked up, surprised. The ground was trembling.

No . . . he was imagining it.

And then the ground shook violently, as if a great rock had been dislodged beneath them. From within the temple came the sound of the marble stand toppling, the tray with the two bracelets on it clattering across the marble floor.

"No . . ." Gehn said, looking about him wild-eyed. "No!"

But even as he said it, a great crack opened in the ground before the temple steps.

The sky was slowly turning black. The sun, which only moments before had blazed down from the late afternoon sky, was being eaten, a curved blade of blackness devouring its pallid face inch by inch.

One by one the stars winked into place in the sudden night.

With a great low, groaning shudder, like some gargantuan animal waking from long hibernation, the ground shook once more, the quake much stronger this time, rumbling on and on, causing the temple roof to fall, throwing many of the Guild from their feet and knocking over the table on which the Linking Books had been placed.

Atrus stared about him in disbelief, seeing the jagged pattern of thick black cracks that now covered the meadow. Then, seeing the fallen books, he rushed to pick them up, yet as he did, Gehn stepped out in front of him, wielding a massive ceremonial spear he had grabbed from one of the Guild, the gold and red pennant still fluttering from its shaft.

"Leave them!" Gehn growled.

"Get out of the way!" Atrus yelled back, crouching, knowing that there was no other way now except to fight his father. Riven was doomed, and even if he'd lost Catherine, he had to stop Gehn.

But Gehn had other ideas. He laughed mockingly. "If you want the books, you will have to come through *me* to get them!"

"If that's what it takes!" Atrus said and threw himself at Gehn, hoping to overwhelm him. His first rush almost succeeded, his charge knocking Gehn back. For a moment they struggled, Atrus's hands gripping the spear's shaft, trying to keep Gehn from using it against him. Then, suddenly, Gehn released his grip, and Atrus found himself tumbling over, the spear falling from his grasp. All about them now, the earth was breaking up, huge cracks appearing everywhere one looked. The air was growing hot and everything was underlit now by the red and orange glow emanating from the fissures.

Atrus got up and, turning, went to throw himself at his father again, but he was too slow. As he charged, Gehn stepped aside and, putting out his boot, tripped him, then stood over him, the spear point pressed hard into his chest.

"You're useless. I should have killed you long ago!"

Atrus answered, his voice defiant. "Then kill me."

Gehn lifted the spear, his muscles tensing, but as he did a shout rang out behind him. "Gehn!"

Gehn turned, to see Catherine, her dark hair streaming out behind her in the wind that had blown up, one of the Linking Books in each hand, standing over a large crack that had opened in the ground, its dark, jagged shape lit redly from below.

"Harm him and I'll throw the books into the crack!"

Gehn laughed disbelievingly. "But Catherine, my love . . ."

"Let him go," she ordered, her voice unyielding now. "Let him go or I'll drop the books into the fissure."

Again he laughed, then looked to Atrus. "No . . . No, I . . ."

To his astonishment, she let the Linking Book fall from her right hand. With a gust of flame it vanished into the crack. Gone.

Both Gehn and Atrus gasped.

"No!" Gehn screamed, then, in a softer, more cajoling voice. "Come now, Catherine . . . let us discuss this. Let us talk about this *reasonably*."

He lifted the spear from Atrus's chest, then, throwing it aside, took a step toward her, his hand out, palms open. "Remember our plans, Catherine. Remember what we were going to do. A thousand worlds we were going to rule. Think of it. Whatever you wanted . . . I could write it for you. You could have your own Age. You could live there if you wanted, but . . . if you destroy that second book we shall be trapped here. Trapped on a dying world!"

Gehn took a second step.

"You *want* the Linking Book?" Catherine asked, a faint smile lighting her features for the first time.

Gehn nodded, then slowly put out his hand, a smile appearing at the corners of his mouth.

"Then have it!" she said and tossed the Linking Book high into the air, its arc carrying it out over the smoldering crevice.

With a gasp of horror, Gehn dived for the book, straining to get to it, one hand grasping in the air to catch it, but he was too late. With a burst of flame it vanished into the red glow.

Gehn stared disbelievingly, then, getting up onto his elbows he turned, furious now, looking for them. But Atrus and Catherine had gone. The wind was howling now, like a gale, bending the nearby trees and making the loosened earth tumble up the slope, as if defying gravity.

As he watched, the temple heaved a sigh and fell inward, the sound of stone grating against stone like the groan of a dying giant, For a brief instant he thought he could see the shape of a giant dagger jutting from the ruins. Then, with a great crack of sound and a fierce, almost blinding flash of light, a lightning bolt hit the summit of the great tree, two hundred yards from where he knelt. At once the upper branches exploded into flame, a huge fireball climbing into the sky above its crest.

In that sudden, blazing light Gehn saw the two of them on the far side of the copse, beneath the trees, their backs to him as they ran. As the light slowly died, their figures merged again with the darkness of the trees. But he knew now where they were headed. Getting up onto his feet he began to run, the howling wind at his back.

"Wait! *Wait!*" Atrus shouted, pulling Catherine back, barely able to hear himself over the noise of the storm. "You've got to tell me what's happening!"

"Don't worry!" she yelled back at him, pulling her hair back from her face. "Everything's going just as we planned!"

He stared at her. "As *who* planned?"

"Anna and I."

His mouth fell open. "*Anna?*"

Overhead the branches of the trees were thrashing wildly in the wind. As she made to answer him, the crash of a falling tree made them both jump.

It isn't possible . . .

Atrus stared at Catherine a moment longer, then numbly let her lead him on through the trees.

They were following a narrow crack. At first he'd thought it was just like all the others that had opened up, but there was something very strange about this one. It *glowed* . . . not red, but blue . . . a vivid, ice cold blue.

To either side, dirt and leaves, broken branches and small stones jumped and tumbled, dragged along by the wind that seemed not so much to blow from behind as to draw them on. And where those tiny particles brushed against the crack, they vanished, sucked into that ice-cold fissure.

They ran on between the trees, the crack slowly widening beside them. And then suddenly, there where the trees ended, the fissure opened out to form a kind of cleft, the edge of it outlined by that cold blue light. Inside, however, it was dark—an intense, vertiginous darkness filled with stars.

Atrus stopped, astonished. The wind still tugged at his legs, but its noise was not as strong here as it was among the trees. Even so, he had to struggle to keep his footing. His right hand gripped Catherine's tightly, afraid to let go in case she, too, was sucked into that strange, star-filled hole.

He looked to her, wondering if she was as afraid as he was, only to find her strangely calm, a beatific smile on her lips and in her beautiful green eyes.

"What is it?" he asked, his eyes drawn back to the fissure, seeing how everything seemed to be sucked into it; how leaves and earth and lumps of rock tumbled over the edge and seemed to wink into nonexistence.

And other things . . .

Atrus blinked, noticing some of Catherine's fireflies, melting and merging, pulsing with brilliant color as they flickered across that dreamlike landscape.

Turning to Atrus, Catherine freed her hand, then took the knapsack from her back and opened it.

"Here," she said, handing him a book.

Atrus stared, dumbfounded. It was the Myst book. "But what . . .?"

She put a finger to his lips, silencing him.

"Did you ever wonder what it would be like to go swimming out among the stars?"

Catherine smiled then; opening the Linking Book, she placed her hand against it. "We could fall into the night and be cradled by stars and still return to the place where we began . . ."

The last word was an echo as she vanished.

"But what do I do?" he called after her, holding up the book.

The answer came from behind him. "That's easy, Atrus. You give the book to me."

Atrus turned, facing his father. Gehn stood there, a large chunk of jagged rock in his hand. His glasses were gone and his ash-white hair was disheveled, but there was still something powerful, something undeniably regal about him.

He looked down at the Myst book in his hands. His first impulse had been to use the book to return to the island, but there was an obvious flaw with that. If he used the book, the book would remain here in his father's possession. And Gehn would surely follow him. His second impulse had been to throw the book into the fissure, but something stopped him—something in what Catherine had said . . .

He smiled.

Raising the book in one hand, he held it out, then took a step back, onto the lip of the fissure, the wind tugging at his boots, a strange coldness at his back suddenly.

A muscle beneath Gehn's left eye jumped. "If you throw the book into that chasm, I'll throw you with it!" he snarled. "Give it to me. Give it to me *now!*"

Atrus shook his head disdainfully.

Gehn took a step back, letting the rock fall from his open hand. "Unless . . ."

"Unless what?"

Atrus stared at Gehn suspiciously. Holding the book up was a strain, but it didn't matter. Nothing mattered now, not even the dull, throbbing ache at the base of his skull.

"Unless *what*? Give me a single reason why I should trust you?"

Gehn shrugged. "Because you are my *son*."

Atrus laughed bitterly. "I thought you'd already disowned me. Or did I hear *that* wrong, too?"

"Forgive me Atrus. I was angry. I thought . . ."

"What? That I'd see your point of view? That I'd realize that you were right? That I would come to see myself as a god?"

Gehn blinked. "But you *need* me, Atrus. I know so much. Things you will never know. Think of the experience I have, the knowledge. It would be a waste not to call upon it, no?" Gehn shook his head, as if regretful. "You were such a good student, Atrus. So quick. So nimble of mind. It would be such a shame if your studies were curtailed . . ."

Atrus stared back at him, expressionless.

"What is it?" Gehn said, puzzled now. His hand, which had extended toward Atrus, drew back slightly.

"It's *you*," Atrus said, lifting the book higher. "All those things you taught me . . . they were just words, weren't they? Empty, meaningless words. As empty as your promises." There was a momentary hurt in the young man's eyes, then, "I wanted so much from you. So much. But you failed me."

"But I taught you, Atrus. Without me . . ."

Atrus shook his head. "No, Father. Anything I ever

learned that was of any value to me, anything *important*, I got from Anna, long before I met you. You . . . *you* taught me nothing."

Gehn glared at him.

The sky was growing lighter, the wind slowly dying.

"I should never have left you with her," Gehn said, after a moment. "She spoiled you. You were a blank book, waiting to be written . . ."

"You would have ruined me, just as you've ruined everything you've touched. Yes, and then discarded me."

"*No!* I *loved* you, Atrus."

"Love? What kind of love is it that binds with ropes and locks its loved ones in a cell?"

"That was never intended to be a prison, Atrus." Gehn swallowed. "It was only a test. All of it."

Atrus stared back at him, silent now, the fissure behind him dark and cold, glistening with stars, the Myst book edged by that strange blue light.

Gehn studied his son a moment, taking in the situation, then took a step toward him, putting out a hand. "Please, Atrus. There is still a chance for us."

"No, Father. Whatever linked us once has been destroyed. You burned it with those books you burned. You erased it along with those phrases in my book. Little by little you destroyed it. Don't you see that? Well, now you've got the justice you deserve. You can stay here in the little haven you've created for yourself, in your tiny island universe, and play god with your 'creations.'"

The word was firm and final, and as he spoke it Atrus stepped back, out over the lip of the fissure, falling, tumbling down into that great expanse of stars, his hands gripping the book, opening the cover as he fell into the darkness.

What do you see, Atrus?

I see stars Grandmother. A great ocean of stars . . .

Epilogue

SUNLIGHT WINKED THROUGH THE TALL
pines, casting long shadows on the lawn in front of the
library. It was late now, but the boys were still out,
playing in the woods that covered the south end of the
island. Catherine, standing on the porch, listened a
moment, hearing their distant shouts, then shaded her
eyes.

"Can you see them?" Atrus asked, stepping out
from the library, his pale eyes squinting in the sunlight.

She turned, the hem of her dark green dress flowing over the polished boards.

"Don't worry so," she said, her green eyes smiling
back at him. "Anna's with them. They'll be in before
it's dark."

He smiled, then came across and placed his arms
about her.

"Have you finished yet?" she asked softly, wrapping her own arms about him and pulling him closer.

"No . . ." Atrus sighed wearily. "I'm close though."

"Good."

He kissed her gently, then, releasing her, went back
inside, taking his seat at the desk that he'd made for
himself. For a moment or two he looked out through
the brightly-lit rectangle of the doorway at Catherine,

drinking in the simple sight of her, then, taking his pen, he looked back at his journal and began to write:

> It is strange now to conceive that I could have doubted her, even for a second, and yet in that moment when my father surprised me in the cave, I was certain beyond all doubt that she had betrayed me. Certain, yes, and at the same time heartbroken, for I had transferred to her person all of that love, all of that natural affection that my father had so unnaturally rejected. Love given freely and without hope of repayment. Yet how was I to know how kind, yes, and how cunning, too, my Catherine could be. My savior, my partner, yes, and now my wife.

Atrus paused, recalling the shock he'd felt, that moment when Catherine had revealed to him that Anna was behind it all; the feeling, the overwhelming feeling he'd had, of having stepped into one of Catherine's dream worlds. But it had been true. Without Anna's forethought he would have been trapped on Riven still. That was, if Gehn had let him live, after what he'd done. He dipped the pen and wrote again:

> Only a remarkable woman would have done what Anna did, following us down through that labyrinth of tunnels and broken ways, into D'ni. She had known, of course, that Gehn would not keep his word. Had known what I, in my innocence, could not have

guessed—that my father was not merely untrustworthy,
but mad. All those years I spent on K'veer she had kept a
distant eye on me, making sure I came to no harm at
my father's hands, while she awaited the moment of
my realization.

Atrus looked up, remembering that moment; feeling once more the weight of his disillusion with his
father. Such things, he knew now, could not be passed
on like other things, they had to be experienced. A parent—a good parent, that is—had to let go at some
point, to let their children make choices, for choices
were part of the Maker's scheme, as surely as all the
rest. He dipped the pen then wrote again, faster now,
the words spilling from him:

Anna saw me flee K'veer and sought to find me in
the tunnels once again, but Gehn had got there
first. Even then she would have intervened, but
for the mute. Seeing them carry me back, unconscious,
to K'veer, she had known she had to act. That
evening she had gone to K'veer and, risking all,
had entered my father's study, meaning to confront
him. But Gehn was not there. It was Catherine
she met. Catherine who, after that first moment
of shock and surprise, had chosen to trust and help her.

So it was that Catherine had known me even before
she met me in the hut on Riven; like an Age one has

first read in a descriptive book and then subsequently
linked to.

I should have known at once that Myst was not Catherine's.
But how was I to know otherwise? I had thought Anna lost.
Lost forever.

And how was I to know that, just as I made my preparations,
so the two of them made theirs, pooling their talents—
Anna's experience and Catherine's intuitive genius—to
craft those seemingly cataclysmic events on Age Five,
in such a way that after a time they would reverse
themselves, making Catherine's former home, now
Gehn's prison, stable once more.

. . . And the Myst book?

Briefly he looked about him at the room he'd
made, pleased by his efforts, then, picking up his pen
again, he began to write, setting down the final words.
The ending that was not a final ending:

I realized the moment I fell into the fissure that
the book would not be destroyed as I had planned.
It continued falling into that starry expanse, of
which I had only a fleeting glimpse. I have tried
to speculate where it might have landed, but I
must admit that such conjecture is futile. Still,

questions about whose hands might one day hold my Myst book are unsettling to me. I know my apprehensions might never be allayed, and so I close, realizing that perhaps the ending has not yet been written.

NOW AVAILABLE IN HARDCOVER,

MYST: THE BOOK OF TI'ANA

THE NOVEL THAT TAKES YOU EVEN FURTHER
INTO THE SPECTACULAR WORLD OF MYST.

PART ONE:
ECHOES IN THE ROCK

THE SOUNDING CAPSULE WAS EMBEDDED in the rock face like a giant crystal, its occupants sealed within the translucent, soundproofed cone.

The Guild Master sat facing the outstretched tip of the cone, his right hand resting delicately on the long metal shaft of the sounder, his blind eyes staring at the solid rock, listening.

Behind him, his two young assistants leaned forward in their narrow, metal and mesh seats, concentrating, their eyes shut tight as they attempted to discern the tiny variations in the returning signal.

"Na'grenis," the old man said, the D'ni word almost growled as his left hand moved across the top sheet of the many-layered map that rested on the map table between his knees. *Brittle.*

It was the tenth time they had sent the signal out on this line, each time a little stronger, the echoes in the rock changing subtly as it penetrated deeper into the mass.

"Kenen voohee shuhteejoo," the younger of his two assistants said tentatively. *It could be rock salt.*

"Or chalk," the other added uncertainly.

"Not this deep," the old man said authoritatively, flicking back the transparent sheets until he came to one deep in the pile. Holding it open, he reached beside him and took a bright red marker from the metal rack.

"Ah," the two assistants said as one, the carmine mark as clear an explanation as if he'd spoken.

"We'll sound either side," the old man said after a moment. "It might only be a pocket. . . . "

He slipped the marker back into the rack, then reached out and took the ornately decorated shaft of the sounder, delicately moving it a fraction to the right, long experience shaping his every movement.

"Same strength," he said. "One pulse, fifty beats, and then a second pulse."

At once his First Assistant leaned forward, adjusting the setting on the dial in front of him.

There was a moment's silence and then a vibration rippled along the shaft toward the tapered tip of the cone.

A single, pure, clear note sounded in the tiny chamber, like an invisible spike reaching out into the rock.

"WHAT IS HE DOING?"

Guild Master Telanis turned from the observation window to look at his guest. Master Kedri was a big, ungainly man. A member of the Guild of Legislators, he was here to observe the progress of the excavation.

"Guild Master Geran is surveying the rock. Before we drill we need to know what lies ahead of us."

"I understand that," Kedri said impatiently. "But what is the problem?"

Telanis stifled the irritation he felt at the man's bad manners. After all, Kedri was technically his superior, even if, within his own craft, Telanis's word was as law.

"I'm not sure exactly, but from the mark he made I'd say he's located a patch of igneous material. Magma-based basaltic rocks from a fault line, perhaps, or a minor intrusion."

"And that's a problem?"

Telanis smiled politely. "It could be. If it's minor we could drill straight through it, of course, and support the tunnel, but we're still quite deep and there's a lot of weight above us. The pressures here are immense, and while they might not crush us, they could inconvenience us and set us back weeks, if not months. We'd prefer, therefore, to be certain of what lies ahead."

Kedri huffed. "It all seems rather a waste of time to me. The lining rock's strong, isn't it?"

"Oh, very strong, but that's not the point. If the aim were merely to break through to the surface we could do that in a matter of weeks. But that's not our brief. These tunnels are meant to be permanent—or, at least, as permanent as we can make them, rock movement willing!"

Still, Kedri seemed unsatisfied. "All this stopping and starting! A man could go mad with waiting!"

One could; and some, unsuited to the task, did. But of all the guilds of D'ni, this, Telanis knew, was the one best suited to their nature.

"We are a patient race, Master Kedri," he said, risking the anger of the other man. "Patient and thorough. Would you have us abandon the habits of a thousand generations?"

Kedri made to answer curtly, then saw the look of challenge in Telanis's eyes and nodded. "No. You are right, Guild Master. Forgive me. Perhaps they chose the wrong man to represent our guild."

Perhaps, Telanis thought, but aloud he said, "Not at all, Master Kedri. You will get used to it, I promise. And we shall do our best to keep you busy while you are here. I shall have my assistant, Aitrus, assigned to you."

And now Kedri smiled, as if this was what he had

been angling for all along. "That is most kind, Master Telanis. Most kind, indeed."

THE EXCAVATOR WAS QUIET, THE LIGHTING subdued. Normally the idle chatter of young crewmen would have filled the narrow corridor, but since the observers had come there was a strange silence to the craft that made it seem abandoned.

As the young guildsman walked along its length, he glanced about warily. Normally he took such sights for granted, but today he seemed to see it all anew. Here in the front section, just behind the great drill, was the Guild Master's cabin and, next to it, through a bulkhead that would seal automatically in times of emergency, the chart room. Beyond that, opening out to both right and left of the corridor, was the equipment room.

The excavator was as self-contained as any ship at sea, everything stored, each cupboard and drawer secured against sudden jolts, but here the purpose of the craft was nakedly displayed, the massive rock drills lain neatly in their racks; blast-marble cylinders, protective helmets, and analysis tubes racked like weaponry.

The young guildsman stopped, looking back along the length of the craft. He was a tall, athletic-looking young man with an air of earnestness about him. His dark red jumpsuit fit him comfortably rather than tightly; the broad, black leather tool belt at his waist and his long black leather boots part of the common uniform worn by all the members of the expedition.

His fine black hair was cut short and neat, accentuating his fine-boned features, while his eyes were pale but keen. Intelligent, observant eyes.

He passed on, through the crew quarters—the empty bunks stacked three to a side into the curve of the ship's walls, eighteen bunks in all—and, passing through yet another bulkhead, into the refectory.

Master Jerahl, the ship's cook, looked up from where he was preparing the evening meal and smiled.

"Ah, Aitrus. Working late again?"

"Yes, Guild Master."

Jerahl grinned paternally. "Knowing you, you'll be so engrossed in some experiment, you'll miss your supper. You want me to bring you something through?"

"Thank you, Guild Master. That would be most welcome."

"Not at all, Aitrus. It's good to see such keenness in a young guildsman. I won't say it to their faces, but some of your fellows think it's enough to carry out the letter of their instructions and no more. But people notice such things."

Aitrus smiled.

"Oh, some find me foolish, Aitrus, I know. It's hard not to overhear things on a tiny ship like this. But I was not always a cook. Or, should I say, *only* a cook. I trained much as you train now, to be a Surveyor—to know the ways of the rock. And much of what I learned remains embedded here in my head. But I wasn't suited. Or, should I say, I found myself better suited to *this* occupation."

"You *trained*, Master Jerahl?"

"Of course, Aitrus. You think they would allow me on an expedition like this if I were not a skilled geologist?" Jerahl grinned. "Why, I spent close on twenty years specializing in stress mechanics."

Aitrus stared at Jerahl a moment, then shook his head. "I did not know."

"Nor were you expected to. As long as you enjoy the meals I cook, I am content."

"Of that I've no complaints."

"Then good. Go on through. I shall bring you something in a while."

Aitrus walked on, past the bathing quarters and the sample store, and on into the tail of the craft. Here the corridor ended with a solid metal door that was always kept closed. Aitrus reached up and pulled down the release handle. At once the door hissed open. He stepped through, then heard it hiss shut behind him.

A single light burned on the wall facing him. In its

half-light he could see the work surface that ran flush with the curved walls at waist height, forming an arrowhead. Above and below it, countless tiny cupboards held the equipment and chemicals they used for analysis.

Aitrus went across and, putting his notebook down on the worktop, quickly selected what he would need from various cupboards.

This was his favorite place in the ship. Here he could forget all else and immerse himself in the pure, unalloyed joy of discovery.

Aitrus reached up, flicking his fingernail against the fire-marble in the bowl of the lamp, then, in the burgeoning glow, opened his notebook to the page he had been working on.

"AITRUS?"

Aitrus took his eye from the lens and turned, surprised he had not heard the hiss of the door. Jerahl was standing there, holding out a plate to him. The smell of freshly baked *chor bahkh* and *ikhah nijuhets* wafted across, making his mouth water.

Jerahl smiled. "Something interesting?"

Aitrus took the plate and nodded. "You want to see?"

"May I?" Jerahl stepped across and, putting his eye to the lens, studied the sample a moment. When he looked up again there was a query in his eyes.

"Tachyltye, eh? Now why would a young fellow like you be interested in basaltic glass?"

"I'm interested in anything to do with lava flows," Aitrus answered, his eyes aglow. "It's what I want to specialize in, ultimately. Volcanism."

Jerahl smiled as if he understood. "All that heat and pressure, eh? I didn't realize you were so romantic, Aitrus!"

Aitrus, who had begun to eat the meat-filled roll, paused and looked at Jerahl in surprise. He had heard his fascination called many things by his colleagues, but never "romantic."

"Oh, yes," Jerahl went on, "once you have seen how this is formed, nothing will ever again impress half so much! The meeting of superheated rock and ice-chill water—it is a powerful combination. And *this*—this strange translucent matter—is the result."

Again Jerahl smiled. "Learning to control such power, that is where we D'ni began as a species. That is where our spirit of inquiry was first awoken. So take heart, Aitrus. In this you are a true son of D'ni."

Aitrus smiled back at the older man. "I am sorry we have not spoken before now, Guild Master. I did not know you knew so much."

"Oh, I claim to know very little, Aitrus. At least, by comparison with Master Telanis. And while we are talking of the good Guild Master, he was asking for you not long back. I promised him I would feed you, then send you to his cabin."

Aitrus, who had just lifted the roll to his mouth again, paused. "Master Telanis wants me?"

Jerahl gestured toward the roll. "Once you've been fed. Now finish that or I shall feel insulted."

"Whatever you say, Master!" And, grinning, Aitrus bit deep into the roll.

AITRUS STOPPED BEFORE THE GUILD MASTER'S cabin and, taking a moment to prepare himself, reached out and rapped upon the door.

The voice from inside was calm and assured. "Come in!"

He slid back the heavy bolt and stepped inside, closing the door behind him. That much was habit. Every door in the craft was a barrier against fire or unwelcome gases. Turning, he saw that Master Telanis was at his desk looking at the latest survey chart. Facing him across the table was Master Geran. Also there were the four Observers who had joined them three days back. Aitrus took a step toward them and bowed.

"You sent for me, Guild Master?"

"I did. But if you would wait a moment, Aitrus, I must first deal with the news Master Geran has brought us."

Aitrus lowered his head, conscious that the Legislator—the big man, Kedri—was watching him closely.

"So, Geran," Telanis went on, indicating the bright red line that ran across the chart in front of him, "you recommend that we circumvent this area?"

The blind man nodded. "The fault itself is narrow, admittedly, but the surrounding rock is of low density and likely to collapse. We could cut through it, of course, and shore up on either side, but I'd say there is more to come the other side of that."

"You know that?" Kedri asked, interrupting the two.

Geran turned his blank, unseeing eyes upon the Legislator and smiled. "I do not *know* it, Master Kedri, but my instinct is that this is the mere root of a much larger igneous intrusion. Part of a volcanic system. Imagine the roots of a tree. So such things are. As excavators, we try hard to avoid such instabilities. We look for hard, intact rock. Rock we have no need to support."

Kedri looked puzzled at that. "But I thought it was your practice to support everything?"

Telanis answered him. "We do, Guild Master. As

I said, we are very thorough. But if it is as Master Geran says—and long experience would tend to bear him out—we would do well to drill sideways a way before continuing our ascent. After all, why go courting trouble?"

"So how long will this . . . *detour* take?"

Telanis smiled pleasantly. "A week. Maybe two."

Kedri looked far from pleased, yet he said nothing. Relieved, Telanis looked to Geran once more.

"In the circumstances I approve your recommendation, Master Geran. We shall move back and across. Arrange the survey at once."

Geran smiled. "I shall do it myself, Guild Master."

When Geran was gone, Telanis looked across at Aitrus.

"Aitrus, step forward."

Aitrus crossed the narrow cabin, taking the place Geran had just vacated. "Yes, Guild Master?"

"I want you to place yourself at Guild Master Kedri's disposal for the next eleven days. I want you to show him how things work and explain to him just what we are doing. And if there's anything you yourself are uncertain of, you will ask someone who *does* know. Understand me?"

Surprised, Aitrus nodded. "Yes, Guild Master." Then, hesitantly, "And my experiments, Guild Master?"

Telanis looked to Kedri. "That depends upon Master Kedri. If he permits, I see no reason why you should not continue with them."

Kedri turned to Aitrus. "Experiments, Guildsman?"

Aitrus looked down, knowing suddenly that he ought not to have mentioned them. "It does not matter, Master."

"No, Aitrus. I am interested. What experiments are these?"

Aitrus looked up shyly. "I am studying volcanic rocks, Master. I wish to understand all I can about their nature and formation."

Kedri seemed impressed. "A most worthy task, young Aitrus. Perhaps you would be kind enough to show me these experiments?"

Aitrus looked to Telanis, hoping his Master would somehow get him off the hook, but Telanis was staring at the multilayered chart Geran had given him, flipping from page to page and frowning.

Aitrus met Kedri's eyes again, noting how keenly the other watched him. "As you wish, Guild Master."

THE CAVERN IN WHICH THEY RESTED WAS A perfect sphere, or would have been but for the platform on which the two excavators lay. The craft were long and sinuous, like huge, segmented worms; their tough exteriors kept buffed and polished when they were not burrowing in the rock.

Metal ladders went down beneath the gridwork platform to a second, smaller platform to which the junior members of the expedition had had their quarters temporarily removed to make way for their guests. It was to here, after a long, exhausting day of explanations, that Aitrus returned, long after most of his colleagues had retired.

There were thirty-six of them in all, none older than thirty—all of them graduates of the Academy; young guildsmen who had volunteered for this expedition. Some had given up and been replaced along the way, but more than two-thirds of the original crews remained.

Two years, four months, Aitrus thought as he sat on the edge of his bedroll and began to pull off his boots. It was a long time to be away from home. He could have gone home, of course—Master Telanis would have given him leave if he had asked—but that would have seemed like cheating, somehow. No, an expedition was not really an expedition if one could go home whenever one wished.

Even as he kicked his other boot off, he felt the sudden telltale vibration in the platform, followed an instant or two later by a low, almost inaudible rumble. A Messenger was coming!

The expedition had cut its way through several miles of rock, up from one of the smaller, outermost caverns of D'ni. They could, of course, have gone up vertically, like a mine shaft, but so direct a route into D'ni was thought not merely inadvisable but dangerous. The preferred scheme—the scheme the Council had eventually agreed upon—was a far more indirect route, cut at a maximum of 3825 *torans*—22.032 degrees—from the horizontal. One that could be walked.

One that could also be sealed off with gates and defended.

The rumbling grew, slowly but steadily. You could hear the sound of the turbine engines now.

Slowly but surely they had burrowed through the rock, surveying each one-hundred-span section carefully before they drilled, coating the surfaces with a half-span thickness of special D'ni rock, more durable than marble. Last, but not least, they fitted heavy stone brackets into the ceiling of each section—brackets that carried air from the pumping stations back in D'ni.

Between each straight-line section was one of these spherical "nodes"—these resting places where they could carry on experiments while Master Geran and his assistants charted the next stage of their journey through the earth—each node fitted with an air-tight gate that could be sealed in an instant.

The rumbling grew to a roar. For a moment the sound of it filled the node, then the engines cut out and there was the downward whine of the turbines as the Messenger slowed.

Aitrus turned and stood, watching as the metal snout of the machine emerged from the entry tunnel, passing through the thick collar of the node-gate, its pilot clearly visible through the transparent front debris shield.

It was a large, tracked vehicle, its three long segments making it seem clumsy in comparison to the sleek excavators, but as ever Aitrus was glad to see it, for besides bringing them much-needed supplies—it being impossible to 'link' supplies direct from D'ni into the tunnels—it also brought letters from home.

"Aitrus? What time is it?"

Aitrus turned. His friend Jenir had woken and was sitting up.

"Ninth bell," he answered, bending down to retrieve his boots and pull them on again.

Others had also been woken by the Messenger's arrival, and were sitting up or climbing from their beds, knowing there was unloading to be done.

He himself had been temporarily excused from such duties; even so, as the others drifted across to the ladders and began to ascend, he followed, curious to see if anything had come for him.

When the last Messenger had come, three days back, it had brought nothing but the Observers—those unexpected "guests" billeted upon them by the Council. Before that it had been almost three weeks since they had had contact with D'ni. Three solid weeks without news.

The Messenger had come to rest between the two excavators. Already its four-man crew were busy, running pipelines between the middle segment of their craft and the two much larger vehicles, ready to transfer its load of mechanical parts, equipment, drill bits, fuel, and cooling fluid to the excavators.

Aitrus yawned, then walked across. The young men of the Messengers Guild were of nature outward, friendly types, and seeing him, one of them hailed him.

"Ho! Aitrus! There's a parcel for you!"

"A parcel?"

The Messenger gestured toward where one of his colleagues was carrying a large mesh basket into the forward cabin of the left-hand excavator.

Aitrus turned and looked, then hurried after, almost running into Master Telanis coming out.

"Aitrus! Why such a hurry?"

"Forgive me, Guild Master. I was told there was a parcel for me."

"Ah," Telanis made to walk on, then stopped, lowering his voice. "By the way, how was our guest?"

Tiring, he wanted to answer. "Curious," he said after a moment, keeping his own voice low. "Oh, and imaginative."

Telanis frowned. "How so?"

"It would seem we are too cautious for him, Guild Master. Our methods are, well . . . *inefficient*."

Telanis considered that, then nodded. "We must talk, Aitrus. Tomorrow. Early, perhaps, before Master Kedri has need of you. There are things you need to know."

Aitrus bowed. "I shall call on you at third bell, Master."

"Good. Now go and see what the Messengers have brought."

Master Tejara of the Messengers had commandeered the table in the chart room to sort out the post. Surrounded by shelves of bound surveys, he looked up from his work as Aitrus entered.

"Ah, Aitrus. And how are you today?"

"I am well, Guild Master."

Tejara flashed a smile at him. "You've heard, then?"

"Master?" But Aitrus's eyes had already gone to the large, square parcel—bound in cloth and stitched—that rested to one side of the table.

"Here," Master Tejara said, handing it to him.

Aitrus took it, surprised by how heavy it seemed. Unable to help himself, he held it to his ear and shook it gently.

There was a gentle chime.

"Well?" Tejara said, grinning at him now. "Are you going to open it or not?"

Aitrus hesitated a moment, then set the parcel down on the table and, taking a slender chisel from his tool belt, slit open the stitching. The cloth fell back.

Inside was a tiny wooden case, the top surface of which was a sliding panel. He slid it back and looked inside.

"By the Maker!"

Aitrus reached in and drew out the delicate, golden pair of portable scales. They were perfect, the spring mechanism of the finest make, the soft metal inlaid with tiny silver D'ni numerals. Nor were they the only thing. Setting the scales down carefully, he reached in once more and took out a flat, square rosewood box the size of his palm. Opening it, Aitrus stared open-mouthed at the exposed pair of D'ni geological compasses, his fingertips gently brushing the tiny crystal magnifier that enabled one to read the tiny calibrations. For a moment he simply looked, studying the minute transparent dials and delicate adjustable attachments that overlay the simple circle of its working face, then shook his head in wonder.

"Is it your Naming Day, Aitrus?" Tejara asked.

"No," Aitrus said distractedly as he reached in a third time to lift out an envelope marked simply "Guildsman Aitrus" in an unfamiliar hand.

He frowned, then looked to Tejara, who simply shrugged. Slitting the envelope open, he took out the single sheet and unfolded it.

Aitrus, it began, you might remember me from school days. I realize we were not the best of friends, but we were both young then and such misunderstandings happen. Recently, however, I chanced upon a report you wrote among my father's papers and was reminded of those unfortunate days, and it occurred to me that I might do something to attempt to reverse your poor opinion of me. If the enclosed gifts are unwelcome, please forgive me. But I hope you will accept them in the same spirit with which they are given. Good luck with your explorations! Yours in friendship, Veovis.

Aitrus looked up, astonished to see that signature at the foot of the note.

"It is from Veovis," he said quietly. "Lord Rakeri's son."

Tejara looked surprised. "Veovis is your friend, Aitrus?"

Aitrus shook his head. "No. At least, he was no friend to me at school."

"Then these gifts are a surprise?"

"More a shock, to be honest, Guild Master. Yet people change, I suppose."

Tejara nodded emphatically. "You can be certain of it, Aitrus. Time teaches many things. It is the rock in which we bore."

Aitrus smiled at the old saying.

"Oh, and before I forget," Tejara added, handing him his mail, "there are three letters for you this time."

AITRUS LAY THERE A LONG TIME, UNABLE TO sleep, staring at the pattern of shadows on the smooth, curved wall of the node, wondering what the gifts meant.

His letters had contained the usual, cheerful news from home—chatter about old friends from his mother, word of Council matters from his father. But his mind kept going back to the note.

That Veovis had written at all was amazing, that he had sent gifts was . . . well, astonishing!

And not just any gifts, but just those things that he most needed in his work.

Oh, there were plenty of scales and compasses he could use—property of the guild—but not his own. Nor were the Guild's instruments anything as fine as those Veovis had given him. Why, they were as good as those that hung from Master Telanis's own tool belt!

When finally he did manage to sleep, it was to

find himself dreaming of his school days, his mind, for some strange yet obvious reason, going back to a day in his thirteenth year when, tired of turning his back on Veovis's constant taunts, he had turned and fought him.

He woke to find Master Telanis shaking him.

"Come, Aitrus. Third bell has sounded. We need to talk."

ABOUT THE AUTHORS

RAND MILLER AND ROBYN MILLER are just a couple of creative brothers who managed to dream up a wildly successful CD-ROM phenomenon. In 1991, when the *Myst* project was started, no one involved imagined it would be so successful. But still, *Myst* was conceived with a complex history that might never have been made public were it not for the success of the game itself. The team of people Rand and Robyn have brought together takes great pride in attention to detail, which the brothers believe is one of the reasons behind *Myst*'s success.

Both Rand and Robyn live relatively quiet lives with their families in the Pacific Northwest. Rand lives with his wife, Debbie, and three daughters, in the foothills of Mount Spokane. Robyn lives with his wife, Beth, and son, Alex, a few miles off of Peone Prairie.